DANGEROUS TO KNOW
JANE AUSTEN'S RAKES & GENTLEMEN ROGUES

JOANA STARNES KATIE OLIVER BEAU NORTH
LONA MANNING BROOKE WEST KAREN M COX
CHRISTINA MORLAND JENETTA JAMES
SOPHIA ROSE J. MARIE CROFT AMY D'ORAZIO

Edited by
CHRISTINA BOYD

quill ink

This is a work of fiction. Names, characters, places, and incidents are products from the author's imagination or are used fictitiously. Any resemblances to actual events or persons, living or dead, is entirely coincidental.

THE DARCY MONOLOGUES

Copyright © 2017 by The Quill Ink

Cover and internal design © 2017 The Quill Ink, L.L.C.

All rights reserved, including the right to reproduce this book, or portions thereof, in any format whatsoever.

For more information: The Quill Ink, P.O. Box 11, Custer WA 98240

Library of Congress Control Number: 2017956681

ISBN: 978-0-9986540-1-0

Cover design and Layout by Shari Ryan of MadHat Books

PRAISE FOR THE AUTHORS

CHRISTINA BOYD

The Darcy Monologues, "…the best thing about this book, it doesn't ruin the characters. It doesn't make Darcy into someone else."

— SILVER PETTICOAT REVIEW

KAREN M COX

1932, "A sexy and exciting story, *1932* is a truly fresh take on this timeless tale."

— BUSTLE

Find Wonder in All Things, "…no wonder at all why it was awarded the Gold Medal in the Romance category at the 2012 Independent Publisher Book Awards."

— AUSTENPROSE

At the Edge of the Sea, "…intoxicating and heartfelt romance … Readers will be entertained and inspired by this winning tale."

— PUBLISHERS WEEKLY

Undeceived, "Love it when an author can surprise me."

— DELIGHTED READER

The Journey Home, "…a beautifully written story about second chances."

— JUST JANE 1813

I Could Write a Book, "...with eloquent style, grace, and insight Karen Cox has proven, one again, she can indeed 'write a book!'"

— AUSTENESQUE REVIEWS

J. MARIE CROFT

Love at First Slight, "There was not a single thing I did not like about this novel. ... The author's sharp wit could rival that of Jane Austen ... a pure delight to read."

— ADDICTED TO AUSTEN

Mr. Darcy Takes the Plunge, "Hilarious, enjoyable, witty, laugh-out-loud book!"

— LEATHERBOUND REVIEWS

A Little Whimsical in His Civilities, "If there's an Austen hero that deserves a good chuckle at himself, I can think of none other more deserving than the proud and staid Mr. Darcy. Ms. Croft helps him loosen up his cravat in a manner that is playful, poetic and utterly romantic."

— JUST JANE 1813

AMY D'ORAZIO

The Best Part of Love, "...reels with intense drama and is so emotionally charged."

— READERS' FAVORITE

JENETTA JAMES

Suddenly Mrs. Darcy "...a touching, sometimes dark, often playfully sexy interpretation of what might have been..."

— JANE AUSTEN'S REGENCY WORLD MAGAZINE

The Elizabeth Papers, "…a novel that will appeal to fans of Jane Austen and romantic mysteries."

— PUBLISHERS WEEKLY

LONA MANNING

A Contrary Wind: A Variation on Mansfield Park, "Many try to emulate Austen; not all succeed. Here, Manning triumphs."

— BLUEINK REVIEW STARRED REVIEW

CHRISTINA MORLAND

This Disconcerting Happiness: A Pride and Prejudice Variation, "Their love affair is a thing of beauty, I sometimes felt I was intruding—but I would have loved to intrude for another 500 pages!"

— TOP 1000 AMAZON REVIEWER

A Remedy Against Sin: A Pride and Prejudice Variation, "One of my favorite novels!"

— OF PENS AND PAGES

BEAU NORTH

Longbourn's Songbird, "North gives a voice to a whole new demographic of characters and expertly navigates the social confines of conservative Southern expectations of the times."

— SAN FRANCISCO BOOK REVIEW

The Many Lives of Fitzwilliam Darcy, "I absolutely adored this novel from the first page…one of the best books I've read this year, possibly one of my all-time favorites…"

— DIARY OF AN ECCENTRIC

Modern Love, "...a love story that cuts through to the heart of what we're looking for as we futilely swipe right—someone who knows us, all the parts of us, and loves us all the more for it."

— MAUREEN LEE LENKER OF ENTERTAINMENT WEEKLY

KATIE OLIVER

Prada and Prejudice, "...light, frothy, sexy, funny as hell"

— SUSAN BUCHANAN, AUTHOR OF THE CHRISTMAS SPIRIT

Love and Liability, "...the characters [are] BRILLIANTLY written and complex, the plot engaging and interesting."

— I HEART CHICK LIT

The Trouble with Emma, "A wonderfully witty take on an Austen classic"

— THE LIT BUZZ

Who Needs Mr. Willoughby? "...another entertaining, well-written modern retelling of an Austen classic"

— A SPOONFUL OF HAPPY ENDINGS

What Would Lizzy Bennet Do? "Katie Oliver's delivered a fun, romantic and definitely sparkly book."

— SPARKLY WORD

SOPHIA ROSE

Sun-kissed: Effusions of Summer (Second Chances), "A truly beautiful and compelling romance!"

— AUSTENESQUE REVIEWS

JOANA STARNES

From This Day Forward, "A beautiful love story…that any Janeite purist should enjoy."

— MORE AGREEABLY ENGAGED

The Second Chance, "I was completely swept up by this evocative and gripping variation!"

— AUSTENESQUE REVIEWS

The Subsequent Proposal, "I love it when Austen-inspired fiction shakes things up a bit, and Starnes certainly does that!"

— DIARY OF AN ECCENTRIC

The Falmouth Connection, "Joana Starnes writes with great verve and affection about the familiar characters — and an intriguing cast of unfamiliar ones."

— JANE AUSTEN'S REGENCY WORLD MAGAZINE

The Unthinkable Triangle, "…full of feeling…a book full of soul."

— FROM PEMBERLEY TO MILTON

Miss Darcy's Companion, "Beautiful, rather clever and shocking…"

— OBSESSED WITH MR. DARCY

Mr. Bennet's Dutiful Daughter, "'She did it again,' I told myself as I savored the feelings whirling around inside of me."

— JUST JANE 1813

BROOKE WEST

The Many Lives of Fitzwilliam Darcy, "...well-written prose with perfect balance between heart-breaking intense scenes and humorous passages..."

— FROM PEMBERLEY TO MILTON

CONTENTS

Foreword by Claudine diMuzio Pepe	10
Willoughby's Crossroads (moderate) Joana Starnes	16
A Wicked Game (mature) Katie Oliver	42
Fitzwilliam's Folly (mild) Beau North	80
The Address of a Frenchwoman (mild) Lona Manning	117
Last Letter from Mansfield (mature) Brooke West	146
An Honest Man (moderate) Karen M Cox	172
One Fair Claim (none) Christina Morland	200
The Lost Chapter in the Life of William Elliot (moderate) Jenetta James	238
As Much as He Can (none) Sophia Rose	260
The Art of Sinking (none) J. Marie Croft	292
For Mischief's Sake (none) Amy D'Orazio	326
Acknowledgements by Christina Boyd	354

MATURE CONTENT GUIDELINES AS PER EDITOR

1. None: possible kissing and affection
2. Mild: Kissing
3. Moderate: some sexual references but not explicit
4. Mature: some nudity and some provocative sex
5. Erotic Romance: explicit, abundance of sex

FOREWORD BY CLAUDINE DIMUZIO PEPE

—Claudine DiMuzio Pepe
Just Jane 1813
JASNA NY Metro, Regional Coordinator

"I am proud to say that I have a very good eye at an Adultress,"

— JANE AUSTEN IN A LETTER TO HER SISTER, CASSANDRA, 12 MAY 1801.

Jane Austen knew not only how to spot an adulteress, she adeptly—and cleverly—wrote about them too. Her books are filled with rakes, rattles, and rogues who made sport of toying with ladies' hearts all over Regency England.

As ONE WHO proudly admits harboring her own soft spot for John Willoughby, I have often imagined that was part of Austen's design in creating his character. While she herself did not condone adultery or the scandalous behaviors that many of her contemporaries engaged in, she undoubtedly knew there must be at least two sides to every story as she wrote complex characters comprised of a multitude of traits, adding color and depth to her narratives. Her protagonists undoubtedly benefitted from her skilled hand, even allowing readers to empathize on some level with even her less-than-noble gentlemen. And yet, she does not fully sketch out her secondary or tertiary characters, leaving much to the reader's imagination in regard to how each became the rake or gentleman rogue in her novels.

THE ELIZABETHAN PERIOD witnessed the emergence of the English rogue in fiction, when rogues were considered different from the outlaws of the Medieval Period. Unlike the outlaw, the rogue was not part of any criminal underworld, but instead, symbolized a figure that remained a part of normal society, while simultaneously believing that there was no issue with breaking the law. Perhaps we might acquit ourselves of harboring any affections for Austen's bad boys after all.

JANE AUSTEN even encountered gentlemen rogues in publishing. I was astounded to learn that she self-published three of four books during her lifetime. She received her first contract with a publisher for *Susan*, much later posthumously published as *Northanger Abbey*. However, that publisher did nothing with the book but allow dust to collect, and when she applied to have the rights revert to her, she was told that she must return the original ten-pound payment. At that time, she did not undertake the loss. How remarkable that two hundred years after her death, her likeness would appear on the ten-pound note!

> "Mr. Murray's letter is come. He is a rogue, of course, but a civil one. He offers £450 but wants to have the copyright of 'Mansfield Park' and 'Sense and Sensibility' included. It will end in my publishing for myself, I daresay. He sends more praise, however, than I expected."
>
> —LETTER FROM JANE AUSTEN, TO HER SISTER, CASSANDRA, DURING HER NEGOTIATIONS TO HAVE MURRAY PUBLISH *EMMA*.

JANE AUSTEN certainly must have known of a few rakes as her stories demonstrated her tremendous talent for crafting some of the most intriguing in English literature. From her first to her last published work, her canon contains several unsuitable gentlemen—Henry Crawford, George Wickham, Captain Tilney, et al. Like Miss Marianne's attentions to Willoughby, Austen's genius quickly draws us in with but a line:

> *"Her imagination was busy, her reflections were pleasant, and the pain of a sprained ankle was disregarded."*
>
> —*SENSE AND SENSIBILITY*, CHAPTER IX.

BUT WHAT OF John Willoughby's story before he met Marianne Dashwood? How did he become "involved" with Eliza Williams, Colonel Brandon's ward? What were his intentions towards Marianne from the very beginnings of their tempestuous relationship? My questions did not stop there either as I then began to think about Austen's other rakes' and rogues' histories.

CHRISTINA BOYD, one of my very favorite editors, has rallied a diverse and gifted group of Austenesque authors to take up their quills and reveal the secrets of Austen's most scandalous men. *Dangerous to Know: Jane Austen's Rakes & Gentlemen Rogues*, a singular collection of short stories, is aimed to grant Austen's "other" men an opportunity to have their stories told by a reliable narrator: the rakes and rogues themselves! And though we may not allow an absolute reprieve, shall we say,

> *"... that, from knowing him better, his disposition was better understood."*
>
> —*PRIDE AND PREJUDICE*, CHAPTER XVIII.

AKIN TO MISS AUSTEN, these writers know the delicious appeal of a dangerous and charming man, whether he be a rake, a rogue, or a gentleman. With good reason we still read Austen after two hundred years; this collection shines a new light on why all her characters deserve to tell their own account. Be prepared to swoon, sigh, and laugh aloud. Smelling salts not included!

N.B. In the spirit of the collective and to be consistent throughout, this anthology adheres to US style and punctuation, though some of the authors prefer to use British spellings. Additionally, as a work inspired by Jane Austen's great works, her own words and phrases may be found herein.

FURTHER, the stories have been noted by the editor regarding Mature Content Guidelines in the Table of Contents:
    1) None: possible kissing and affection
    2) Mild: kissing
    3) Moderate: some sexual references but not explicit
    4) Mature: some nudity and some provocative sex
    5) Erotic romance: explicit, abundance of sex

*For the creator
of such characters who
simper, and smirk, and make love to us all.*

JOHN WILLOUGHBY

Compelled to satisfy his own comfort with careless diversions and even marrying to support his preferred style of living, John Willoughby flattered and deceived to achieve his goals, exhibiting little regret. *His manly beauty and more than common gracefulness were instantly the theme of general admiration, and the laugh which his gallantry raised against Marianne received particular spirit from his exterior attractions...His person and air were equal to what her fancy had ever drawn for the hero of a favourite story. —Sense and Sensibility,* **Chapter IX.** In the end, he admitted he loved Marianne Dashwood after all.

But that he was forever inconsolable, that he fled from society, or contracted an habitual gloom of temper, or died of a broken heart, must not be depended on; for he did neither. —Sense and Sensibility, Chapter L.

WILLOUGHBY'S CROSSROADS
Joana Starnes

The knocker, a pretentious urn, falls repeatedly and loudly into place as I employ it with uncommon force but to no avail. There is *still* no answer. I knock again. No gentlemanly tap-tap-tap, but the sustained pounding of the bailiff come to collect his dues. And, just like the aforementioned bailiff, I am not above bringing the door down, if it comes to that.

It does not, which is just as well. I might have needed more than my roiling anger to prevail over the solid oak and should have brought the bailiff's men as well. The door swings on its hinges revealing Tom, the second footman, and behind him the butler, fixing me with a censorious stare.

"Mr. Willoughby, sir," the butler drawls. "Begging your pardon, but her ladyship is not receiving at such an early hour."

On a different day, I might have laughed at his shameless hypocrisy, to stand there and deliver such words with a blank face. As though he had not admitted me to her presence at far less sociable hours. I do not laugh. Instead, I grind a warning through my teeth:

"Stand aside, Higgins," I growl. "I will not be trifled with today. Where is she?"

Neither man answers, but Tom—younger and less versed in the base arts—flashes a glance towards the marble staircase. I neither request nor need further clarification and I push past the servants, disdaining to acknowledge the butler's cries of protest as I take to the stairs at a run.

I know my way of course, and all too well at that. Her townhouse and country residence are as familiar to me as my own home. Or rather as the seat of my ancestors, for no one in their right mind would regard that sad and mouldering old pile, Coombe Magna, as a home.

It had been very far from welcoming, even when my mother was alive. My "saintly mother" as my sire would invariably refer to her, and with the same inflection, both before and after her passing. I never asked him why. Speaking to him was something I have always been as eager to avoid as spending too many nights under his roof. Just about anybody's company was preferable. But this is neither here nor there. As a rule, I never ponder on Coombe Magna, my boyhood, my departed mother, or the late John Oglivie Willoughby. At this point in time, I could not give a damn for any and all, and likewise for philosophising. What I seek—nay, demand —is a direct answer to a simple question: Is it true, the report?

My opportunity to demand the answer comes sooner than expected. I imagined I would find her in the morning room or still at breakfast. Finding her reclining on a chaise longue, in her bedchamber, has me speechless. This vexes me quite as much as her languorous pose, doubtlessly assumed for the occasion, for she could not claim that my tempestuous entrance had surprised her from her rest; the din I caused to gain admittance could have roused the dead.

She rearranges the lace of her dressing gown with slow deliberation, which cannot fail to provoke me all the more, as does the casual greeting, delivered without looking up.

"John. This is a surprise."

"Is it? Did you not imagine I would come as soon as Lady Susan told me of your engagement?"

"Ah," she says. Just that and nothing more.

And then, she does raise her head and looks at me. I blink, staggered to discover my anger mellowing and melting. Struth! Is that all it takes? A mere glance to tame me? Love's fool, Captain Tilney called me not long ago, and I grinned and shrugged, dismissing it as envy. Perhaps the man had the right of it after all. Love's fool. Perhaps I am.

Still tongue-tied, I simply stand there, watching her, and she holds my gaze without blinking. And also without guile. There is none, and no shifty dissimulation either, in those hazel eyes. No change. No artifice. The report is false. It must be.

I find myself on one knee beside her. How did I get there? I could not care less. The question I stormed in here to demand an answer to comes out in a whisper:

"It is a falsehood, Isobel, is it not?"

She runs her fingers through my hair and smiles like a cat.

"Oh, John! My tempestuous, dear boy."

The caress irritates me—I never was one for having my hair stroked— and the tone and appellation vexes me even more. Her dear boy! There was I thinking I was nobody's "boy" but my own man, even before the late Willoughby's passing. And she can drop the matronly act, too. She is not that much older. Six years, seven maybe. I never asked, of course. What gentleman would, and what did it matter?

What mattered now was her reply. I toss my head back, away from the caress, and press my point.

"Is it a falsehood?"

"Of course not. When has Lady Susan ever spoken an untruth?"

Her misplaced archness revives my forgotten fury. She jests. My world has just collapsed around me—and she *jests!*

I know not what I am about to say, too many words are fighting to come out at once, and before any of them do, she speaks, and her countenance sobers.

"Yes, John, I am to marry Camborne. He asked and I accepted."

"*Why?*"

She shrugs.

"Why not? His title and estate have much to recommend him. He is worth well-nigh thirty a year, I am told."

"He is a dithering, old fool in his late forties."

She laughs again.

"Oh, for the charm of youth that finds late forties old! What would you say if I told you the marquess is, in fact, nearing his sixtieth autumn?"

"Oh, plenty!" I snap back. "To begin with, I would ask you to cease speaking of my charming youth with the vexing condescension of a matron. And then I would ask if you had lost your mind. Sixty? Good Lord in Heaven! Did you not say that you loathed your first marriage of convenience? What madness would prompt you to enter into a second one?"

"I loathed Heston and my marriage to him because he was a miserly, little man, and I should have known better than to accept him simply to please my father. This time, I only seek to please myself. Frankly, I think I did rather well. Camborne is liberal, wealthy, and oh-so-easily guided. As for his age, if anything, I find it highly recommends him. The settlement is exceedingly handsome. Incomparably better than Heston's pitiful provisions. The little that Heston left is nearly gone already. Camborne's settlement is a wholly different matter. I think I shall enjoy being the dowager marchioness rather well…"

I stare aghast as she calmly speaks of a better-placed second widowhood before she has even wed her second husband. Who *is* this cold and calculated harpy? I knew she had resented her first husband and blamed her first marriage on her youthful inexperience and her parents' persuasion. But to sell herself thus for the second time to a higher bidder—and what for?

Granted, one cannot live on air. I know that all too well. My late sire left behind a dark, old pile, staggering debts, and very little else. Yet, *I* would not contemplate selling my favours like a common trollop, or else I would have offered for the waspish and insipid Miss Grey a twelvemonth ago! The very thought that Isobel is more than contemplating it—that she has already consented to sell herself to Camborne after all we shared—sends my blood boiling.

"But what about the interim?" I ask with a cold sneer. "How will you enjoy taking him to your bed, until he obliges you by dying?"

To my utter shock her bare arms wind around my neck, and she kisses me. Not one kiss but a dozen, breathless and burning. She draws me to her, lies back on the chaise longue, and I follow. I ask no further questions —who the devil would feel inclined to *talk* just now? Of anything at all, much less Camborne?

I fumble with her lacy dressing gown and the rest of her flimsy attire, and she wraps herself around me with the ardour of old. I recognise it in a flash—and then there is no room for thought. Our joining, frenzied and quick, casts everything out of focus. The sense of triumph is exhilarating. So is the giddiness. Drunk with love? Drunk with power, more like. 'Tis mine, and mine alone, the power to make her quiver at a touch—writhe in the heat of passion—cry out my name—repeat it over and over in soft moans muffled by my kisses.

The clarity returns at an unhurried pace as we lay back on the ludicrously narrow sofa, limbs still entwined. She sighs in what I believe—however smugly—is at the very least contentment, and runs her fingers through my hair again. This time, I make no move of protest but chuckle lightly.

"I take it then that whatever sins you were punishing me for are now forgiven," I drawl.

"Punishment, you call this?" she asks archly, pinching me for good measure. "If it was a punishment for you to exert yourself, you need not have taken the trouble."

I laugh.

"Pax! No more disputes, I beg you; not even feigned ones." I lean to kiss the tip of her nose, then soberly resume: "You know full well I was not speaking of my *exertions*, as it pleases you to call it, but of that nonsense you were teasing me with when I arrived. You might wish to tell me, by and bye, how I displeased you quite so much as to deserve the taunt, and indeed how you cajoled Lady Susan to play her part so well, but that is neither here nor there—"

She interrupts me.

"What taunt are you speaking of?"

"Your alleged engagement to Camborne. I must say I am flattered you chose to play your little game despite the risks. Your 'happy tidings' could have easily been all over Town already. Lady Susan is hardly the soul of discretion and—"

She cuts me off again, a strange smile at the corner of her lips.

"The world begins and ends with you, John, does it not?"

"Your meaning?" I ask, propping myself up on one elbow to see her better.

"'Tis both provoking and endearing that you should think I would go to such lengths on your account. My upcoming marriage is all over Town already, John, and as settled as can be."

"*What?*"

"I think you heard me well enough the first time," she nonchalantly answers, and that is when I wholly lose my temper.

"Isobel, you cannot! I will not allow it!"

"And how do you propose to prevent it, John? Thankfully, you are too level-headed for a crime of passion."

I am not altogether certain as to that. There is nothing I want more right now than to wipe that taunting smirk off her lips, by any means possible. The first woman I have ever loved lies beside me, gloriously beautiful in her semi-nakedness—and rotten to the core. Why else would she drive such obvious pleasure from her cruelty? That she truly contemplates selling herself in marriage to a senile, old fool has suddenly become the lesser sin. She could have revealed it with a look of shame, love, or regret. Instead, she does it with a mocking sneer. I loved her—heaven help me, as I would dearly like to strangle her just now, perhaps I love her still—and yet, she never did. A toy to alleviate her boredom. Divertissement between the sheets—and indeed wherever else it had taken her fancy.

I close my mind to flashes from the past—they do not serve me well. Love's fool, year after year. Worse still, *her* fool, while inwardly she must have been laughing all the while, as she does now.

"How could you? I thought—"

I stop short when I hear, to my horror, that my voice cracks and breaks.

"Thought what?"

Her calm collectedness is another slap in my face, so I do not finish my sentence. *I thought you loved me. I thought you genuine and pure. I thought your past was your father's fault and that there would be a future.*

She reads my mind. She always was exceedingly good at that.

"You thought I would marry you and we would happily rusticate at Coombe together? Poor John. One should never marry one's first love, you know. Too early an attachment gives one's feelings that much longer to grow stale and bitter."

"What makes you think you were my first love?" I bluster. "You flatter yourself."

She laughs—a soft and musical laugh that nevertheless scratches my ears like a cackle. She has not been taken in by my bravado.

"If you say so," she replies with a shrug, and with all the force of my will I wish I could appear as jaded as she, as calm and indifferent. But my hands are inordinately clumsy as I seek to redress my general appearance, tuck my shirt in, and button my breeches. Behind me, she sits up and perches herself on the edge of the seat.

"That is much better," she observes. "The romantic part of the jilted lover is played to better effect when one's shirt is not hanging out of one's breeches. Let me arrange your neckcloth."

Despite the last harrowing minutes, she still has the power to shock me speechless with the callousness of her remarks. I spring to my feet and cast her a withering stare. Or at least try to.

"I thank you, but I require no assistance," I say, as coldly as I can.

There is a looking-glass hanging to my left and I seek to make use of it, but the neckcloth is a mess and I only make it worse. I curse it—liberally but inwardly—as I would much rather not give Lady Isobel the satisfaction of another display of temper. A glimpse in the glass reveals her reclining in her chaise longue again, watching me. I leave the neckcloth be and turn around.

So horribly deceptive, that look of sweetly dishevelled innocence, as if she has just risen from restful sleep, and not from her final tryst with the "jilted lover." She must have read my thoughts again—I *hate* how she does that!—for what she said was:

"I trust this is not farewell."

I do not disgrace myself by gaping, but I surmise my pose is nonetheless that of a startled fool. That is, until bitter laughter begins to bubble inside me, threatening to burst out into an unseemly snort or, worse still, into maniacal glee. So, this had been her plan all along? The best of both worlds—the services of the young buck and the old codger's purse? Well, she would have to reconsider. This young buck would rather not share the trough with the old codger. Or anyone else, for that matter.

I tame the laughter—barring a chortle—and make no answer, but the attempt to cloak myself in cold mystery is a fruitless effort. The blasted woman can read me like a book.

"Resentment is a poor master, John. It teaches you to cut your nose to spite your face. If you believe your dignity was injured, then I apologise. Perhaps I ought not have made sport of you today. But you see, my dear, you do make for a perfect target. So self-assured, yet all you can boast of is your vigorous and rather charming youth. Do grow up, John, and learn the ways of the world. Learn your way around women, too. I imagine I was your first—"

"You flatter yourself," I repeat woodenly, the earlier glee vanquished by her witching powers. They say love can turn to hatred in a flash. They are not wrong.

"Your second, then. Third at the utmost," she resumes blithely, and it makes me as mad as snakes that she had so easily garnered my inexperience. "Tying yourself to the apron strings of the first woman who takes you to her bed—or let us say the second or third woman, if it pleases you—may be endearing to some but not very manly. It would be my pleasure to turn you into a man in every sense of the word. Much as you clearly resent this shift in our liaison, as well as my stark honesty, pray tell me hand on heart, do you not find it refreshing after two years of coy games?"

"Three," I say without thinking.

"I beg your pardon?"

"I have been the recipient of your favours for nigh-on three years," I drawl with feigned unconcern, presumably fooling no one.

"Indeed! Very well. You may be the recipient of my continued interest and advice for a fair while longer, as well as Cambourne's goodwill," she replies matter-of-factly, and this time I raise a brow at the astounding confidence with which she vouches for the cuckolded Cambourne's goodwill. The staggering arrogance of her! Or perhaps not. Perhaps it is a mere statement of truth, and she has every confidence that she can make any man dance to her tune, if she wishes.

Not me. Not any more!

"Are you quite certain?" she asks, and that is when I realise I spoke my thoughts aloud.

I force my stubborn back into a bow.

"I thank you," I say as crisply as I can, "but I would rather not avail myself of your offer. I fear it would savour of payment for services rendered," I add resentfully, only to feel rather ashamed of my coarseness. But not for long.

She tosses back her mane of copper-red hair and scoffs:

"How convenient, a recently-developed set of morals! A conscience too, perchance? Too tedious for words. A pity. I was holding hopes of a better understanding. By all means, curl up with your newfound morality, dear boy. Just do not imagine the offer will still be there for the taking when you change your stance and return to my door."

Never! I would rather die before I beg or cower before her or anybody else. I am my own master, and 'tis high time I showed it. I rake my mind for something to say, a fitting Parthian shot, pithy, cold, and hurtful, but nothing comes to me, and the silence has lasted long enough. The dreary platitude of "farewell" is my sole recourse. I deliver it with a rigid bow and leave Lady Isobel's bedchamber without another word. I do not glance back either.

To the end of my days I will not know what I did with myself over the following couple of hours. I know I rode heedlessly away, cursing myself for blindness and folly, and her, for her deceitful ways.

I was not half-done when two pint-sized creatures spring into my path with shrieks and giggles, unsettling my horse. I very nearly lose my seat in my distraction. That would be a fine to-do, to take a tumble in— Where the devil am I? Hyde Park, it seems. I had wandered off from the Rotten Row without notice and almost literally stumbled over someone's offspring. The pair of them, girl and boy, are now watching me, hands behind their backs, the picture of childish innocence, as though they had not been careering through the trees like savage, little things.

Too sensitive by far, my horse snorts and bridles, still unnerved.

"Settle down, you rotter," I mutter, tightening the reins.

"Begging your pardon for frightening him, sir," the girl pipes up. "Would he like an apple?"

I am in no humour to converse with children. Nevertheless, I dismount, not averse to stretching my legs. I pat the horse's neck and answer the girl's question.

"He might, if you have one to offer."

She quickly produces an apple from the pocket of her pinafore and boldly steps closer.

"What is his name?"

"Peg."

"If you do not mind my saying, sir, that is a very silly name for a horse."

I do not trouble myself to tell her 'tis short for Pegasus—as pompous and pretentious as all the names my sire had chosen for his horses. I do believe that, of the whole estate, the only part that had ever held his interest were his stables and his thoroughbreds. And the races he had bred them for. They lost badly and often. But that had never stopped him from betting heavily on them. I choose my bets more sensibly; at least on the racecourse and at the gaming tables.

"Emily, that is uncivil," the boy admonishes her.

"Is it?" She sounds surprised. "I was merely being honest."

"Do not concern yourself," I say. "Peg took no offence."

And neither did I. I would choose honesty, however stark and blunt, over deception any day. Damn Isobel! I hope Camborne lives to be a hundred.

I grin wickedly at the thought, then grow rather ashamed when the young girl casts me a bright and genuine smile in return. The candour of children, happy souls. She hands me the apple, and I do my best to set thoughts of revenge aside, at least for the moment.

"Will your mother not be cross that you gave your luncheon to my horse?"

"Oh, no," she assures me, shaking her head. "Besides, we have already had our luncheon. We had a picnic."

"Did you?"

I offer Peg the apple and he takes it eagerly, snorting his satisfaction. The girl claps. "He liked it!"

"He certainly did. But where is your mother, by the bye? Or... governess? Hmm... minder?" I flounder as I seek to ascertain her condition in life from her attire.

"They came to walk with us—Mamma, Papa and our cousins, but we ran ahead," the girl informs me sagely while the boy, far less disposed for conversation, crouches down to study an earthworm in the grass.

"I see. You have not lost your way, I trust."

The girl grins. "Like the babes in the woods? No, sir. We can find our way back, can we not, Edward?"

"Of course," the boy replies, his eyes on the wriggling creature he had picked up for closer inspection. "But we need not try to," he adds, still without looking up. "They are coming this way. Our cousins are almost here."

I look around and wonder how the boy can tell, for I see no one, but a few moments later I hear footsteps, rustling, and a murmur of voices from beyond the greenery the children had sprung from. There must be a path behind the bushes, which he can see and I cannot.

'Tis a relief that I can be on my way without the encumbrance of returning lost offspring to their parents. I pat Peg's neck again and turn to bid my adieus, but the girl saunters away to greet the couple emerging into the clearing. A smartly dressed gentleman and a young woman. They are both young, my age or thereabouts. She is— My cursory glance turns into a long, appraising look. She is a strikingly handsome woman. I snort, sounding like Peg. I pity the fool who walks beside her grinning like a love-struck mooncalf. Yet another one fallen prey to the wiles of a good-looking woman. I want to pat him on the shoulder and tell him to save himself while he can, before the oh-so-attractive veil falls off to reveal the ugly truth beneath. I do pity the fool. And then I realise I know him. From Town? Cambridge? Or even earlier perhaps…at Eton?

That cheerful grin is ever so familiar, the countenance too, but the man's name not so much. B… B… B… Bradford? No. Burnley? No, that does not sound right either. Some other northern name with a whiff of trade. Ah! Bingley! That's the one. Thankfully I have it, just as I see the same flash of recognition in the man's eyes. It would have been devilishly mortifying if he knew my name and I was still struggling to remember his.

As the young girl proceeds to commandeer his companion's attention, he excuses himself and strides forth to greet me brightly.

"What a remarkable surprise! It *is* you, Weatherby, is it not?"

"Willoughby," I correct him.

"Of course. I beg your pardon," he cheerfully retorts, nothing as mortified as I would have been had I called him Burnley. I daresay it takes all sorts. "So, how have you been keeping?" he asks. "It has been a while. Too long. I wonder how we never met in Town. Unless you have been abroad? Have you?"

I shake my head, and before I can launch into a proper answer, Bingley starts rattling on again, chattier than a woman. He was a great deal less chatty at Cambridge, at least in the beginning. Ah, that is good... Now I remember where I know him from.

I dig deeper once I know where to look, and images come up with greater ease as Bingley goes on about some estate he has leased. I recollect that he turned up at Cambridge when I had been there a couple of years at least, and he was not well-liked, which had at first surprised me, for I found him likeable enough. But then the aforementioned whiff of trade explained it all.

To my discredit, I had shunned him too at first, and my reason for eventually befriending him was not to my credit either. To put it plainly, I sought him out and even asked him to Coombe Magna solely to spite my father, after one of his rants about how the country was going to wrack and ruin, and men brought up above their parents' shops were now rubbing shoulders with their betters in the grand salons. I doubt Bingley enjoyed his stay, seeing as my sire was at his most awful. How terribly amusing that it is always the lesser sort who make the greatest fuss about rank and status. Take the late John Oglivie, by way of example. Impecunious scion of the insignificant branch of the family: he profited from the terms of the entail in favour of heirs male, changed his name to Willoughby, and reigned at Magna as though born to riches and swaddled in ermine and purple. But never mind him now.

Bingley never came to stay again. I gathered he received a better welcome up North, in Derbyshire, once this other Cambridge man took him under his wing. A quiet sort, the very opposite of Bingley but fierce as the devil when crossed.

I never saw what those two had in common, but I had left them to it, whatever it was. Bingley's bosom friend had not been my notion of good company at all. Too solemn and reserved a fellow was Darcy, too quiet in his pleasures and too intent upon his studies, as though he were preparing to become some dusty and obscure scholar, and not the master of one of the largest estates in Derbyshire.

"...and some pretty decent spots for coarse fishing," Bingley concludes what I can only assume was an enumeration of his estate's virtues. "I hope you will afford us the pleasure of hosting you sometime," he kindly offers, before exclaiming, horror-struck. "Here I am rattling on and missing the essentials. It has just come to me that of course you are not acquainted with my wife, are you? Pray forgive me, dearest," he contritely addresses the flaxen-haired beauty.

She straightens up from her conversation with the children and comes to join us. So much for my wish to urge him to escape womanly wiles while he can. Too late. The poor fool is already wed and so early in life too. Marry in haste, repent at leisure.

Bingley performs the belated introductions, his lady curtsies, and I bow. Yet again, I barely begin to utter the blandest of civilities, when natter-jack Bingley is on again:

"I might be forgiven for singing Netherfield's praises given that my greatest blessings have sprung from leasing the place. Had I not, we might have never met, and that does not bear thinking," he says to his wife with the widest smile, then turns to me again. "The same goes for Darcy. He married my new sister. Or I should say one of my four new sisters. You do remember Darcy, do you not?"

I confirm with a nod, and Bingley motions me along.

"Come, then. I daresay there are a couple of bottles of Burgundy left in the picnic baskets, to drink to the old times. I would be honoured to introduce my wife's uncle and aunt to your acquaintance, and Darcy will be as pleased as Punch to see you."

I doubt that the solemn-looking fellow I remember would be as pleased as Punch about anything. As for myself, I have no taste for Burgundy nor for new and old acquaintances, and least of all, for waxing sentimental over our alma mater.

"I must beg to be excused on this occasion. I am expected at White's within the hour."

The lie rolls unnecessarily off my lips—I could have simply said I was otherwise engaged—and Bingley swallows it but with obvious disappointment. He presses me to call upon them whenever I can, and I escape with an ambiguous answer and a collection of tedious civilities.

But by the time I am back in the saddle urging Peg on, I begin to see some merit in going to White's. It would be far preferable to returning to my lodgings or roaming through the parks like a man possessed. A game of cards, a stiff drink, and exclusively male company would serve me a great deal better.

I nudge Peg along and, sensing my impatience, he, faithful soul, crosses the green apace. And then I spot them—the pair on the rug, lost to the world among a melange of picnic baskets. The woman sits propped up against a tree trunk; the man is lounging at leisure, his head in her lap. She is stroking his hair and they pay me no heed. Perhaps they have not heard Peg's hoofbeats over the tall grass, or perhaps it pleases them to remain just as they are, without a care for a passing stranger. I cannot see the woman's face. A host of spiralling dark locks conceal her features as she bends down to speak to him. But the man clearly looks best-pleased to remain precisely where he is. And he is no stranger; even with the years' passing, I easily recognise him as Darcy but on account of his features alone. Gone is the aloof mien I knew so well, and that is what shocks me. If *he*, the epitome of cold detachment, and I daresay level-headedness, had lost his wits as well, to the point of lying there—the lion reduced to a mere lapdog—and staring at this slip of a girl with nothing short of adoration, then for goodness' sake, what hope is there for the rest of us? Bingley, I could pity him for his infatuatio but *Darcy?* Darcy's capitulation stuns me. The Derbyshire Monk lost in the fray as well!

When he sits up and draws her to him to kiss her with sickening passion, I dig my heels into Peg's side and ride off as if chased by Beelzebub himself. Not for the sake of decency and discretion. If they have no qualms about such displays in a public place, then I see no reason why I should fret over sparing their blushes. No, I leave my erstwhile schoolfellows to their insanity simply because I cannot stand witnessing it any longer. Picnic with them and their respective Circes? Heaven forbid! Let them call upon me three years hence, when they awake from their delirium. For now, I cannot lay my hands soon enough on that stiff brandy awaiting at White's. Or better still, maybe I should opt for a flagon or two at Molly's Tavern.

I DID NOT OPT for Molly's Tavern, more's the pity, and not for White's either. I went to Brooks's instead and, sadly for my purse, I ran into Captain Tilney and an acquaintance of his, a Mr. William Elliot, who plays cards far too well to be a gentleman. Long story short, between too much brandy and Elliot's uncanny skill, on the following morning, I had found I lost one devil of a larger sum than I can afford.

Unmitigated folly it was, with dire consequences. No, I am not merely speaking of the loss itself, but of the fact that as a result here I am, bored senseless deep in the wilds of Devonshire, visiting Mrs. Smith, my mother's distant cousin and the future provider of most, if not all, my earthly joys. I am to inherit her vast fortune, which will finally set me free from my sire's debts and mine. And there is also Allenham, her home, which is due to come to me as well. A handsome place, airier than the gloomy Coombe, but cast upon this distant shore and dreary as the devil. In all the time I have been here, a month to the day, there were just two dances at Barton Park, and the Middletons also asked me once for dinner. No shooting parties, 'tis too early in the season. No roistering companions to alleviate the tedium. No plays, no assemblies, and no card parties to see if my luck has turned. Nothing to do but either ride along the coast through mist and rain, or sit all day conversing and playing piquet with Mrs. Smith in her parlour.

I generally choose the rain and I return soaked to the skin and in foul humour for bitter thoughts keep intruding as I ride. The heartache is mostly gone, but the anger is not. Anger at Isobel of course—my Lady Cambourne now—and even more at myself, for bending to her will and failing to see for such a length of time that I was merely her plaything.

When I inherit Allenham, I will rise and make her pay for every humiliation. I know not how, I know not when, but my turn will come.

As for safeguarding my inheritance, I cannot abscond every day. I do penance in the parlour too. I cannot risk offending the dear, old bat when so much is at stake. I would scarce have a penny to my name were it not for her allowance, and somehow, I must persuade her to increase it to compensate for the debts of honour I had to pay. So, I sit drinking tea or reading to her from some dull tome or playing her at piquet and chess, simpering and smiling till even I grow sickened by my guile. "Needs must when the devil drives," they say. All *I* can say is that Lucifer has assigned me a very crafty devil. No greater punishment than boredom for my sins!

Lucifer has granted me a respite and boredom was alleviated in a rather pleasing manner. But I would do well to start from the beginning.

Mrs. Smith asked me to escort her to Bath, and little as I wished to spend my mornings squiring her to the Pump Room and my evenings escorting her on her outings to drink tea and gossip with an assortment of dowagers, I told myself that at least it would be an improvement on the Devonshire tedium. And so, it is. There are assemblies and card parties, and the dowagers invariably have some some daughters, or a niece or two, in attendance.

I have not been in Bath a se'nnight when my morning stroll has some interesting consequences. I am enjoying the first spell of dry weather I have seen in weeks, and also the satisfaction that I cut a rather dashing figure in my new coat, if I say so myself, when, all of a sudden, I hear a cry and something flies right at me, misses my face, and lands on my lapel. Fortunately for my new coat 'tis nothing worse than a sheet of paper. Instinctively, I raise my hand and catch it, and I barely have the time to discern what it is, when it turns out 'tis more than one sheet. I have one clasped in my hand, but the other flies over my shoulder. That is when I notice that the girl, whose trim figure I had equably admired as she stood some ten yards away with her elderly companion, is now facing this way in dismay, a sheet of paper fluttering in her gloved hand. A second is all I need to put two and two together: the wind has blown away most of her letter. My chivalrous instincts come alive and spur me on. One page still in hand I dash in pursuit of the other, and presumably make a spectacle of myself as I clutch repeatedly at nothing but thin air, until the wayward page is finally in my grasp. Regrettably, I collide into another person. Not full-on, thankfully, otherwise I would have sent her flying, for she is a waify sort of girl. I crash into her shoulder, which is bad enough, but at least her companion has enough time to grab onto her other arm and steady her.

"Goodness!" she cries out—the companion, that is. "Have a care, sir! Martha, are you injured?"

"No. I am well. Still in one piece and on my feet, so no harm done. Pray, Eliza, do not fret so."

I apologise profusely, of course. There is nothing to be done about it: I declare myself a clumsy fool and offer to rush for a coach or a sedan chair to convey the injured lady to her destination for, despite her protestations, I notice she is limping. I must have trodden on her foot—the clod!

"I can assist with transport. I feel it is my duty," a voice says behind me, and I spin around. It is the owner of the flying letter, and I return the stray pages to her with a bow.

"I thank you, sir," she says, blushing prettily, her eyes cast down, then she looks up again with some determination. Lovely eyes. The brightest blue with a scattering of aquamarine specks.

I bow again, declaring it my pleasure. And so, it is. The lady is uncommonly handsome, and I have no regrets about being of service—the waify, young woman momentarily forgotten. But the owner of the letter is quick to bring the victim of my gallantry back to my attention and quietly addresses her.

"I fear I am to blame for the mishap. I should have waited and opened my letter in my carriage but I was too impatient for the contents. My carriage is ready and waiting, and you would oblige me greatly if you permit my coachman to escort you home."

The injured lady is quick to consent, and all I can do is offer her my arm to help her hobble to the carriage. I hand her in, and likewise her companion, who glances askance at me and seems rather cross, presumably because I hurt her friend. I assure her of my deepest remorse, and she flashes me another glare, but says nothing, as the attending footman fusses around the other passenger.

The owner of the carriage expresses wishes for a swift recovery, the elderly companion joins us and clucks in sympathy, I struggle for something more cogent to say other than more apologies, and before I know it, the door is closed, Miss Blue-Eyes orders the coachman off, drops me a curtsy, her companion nods, and they wander off towards the entrance of what must be their lodgings. I take note of the address. No._ Royal Crescent, although at present it serves me not. I cannot call. Vexingly, we have not been introduced. But they do not seem intent upon quitting Bath. Hopefully our paths will cross again under more auspicious circumstances.

With a smile and a spring in my step, I twiddle my cane and amble towards the Pump Room. When I pass Miss Blue-Eyes' carriage still struggling to negotiate the throng in the Circus, the two occupants, Miss Eliza and Miss Martha, seem to have forgiven my clumsiness already, for they flash me a matching set of smiles.

I DID ENCOUNTER Miss Blue-Eyes in more auspicious circumstances, and courtesy of the Master of Ceremonies, Mrs. Smith and I were favoured with an introduction. Miss Blue-Eyes is in effect Miss Malcolm, visiting Bath with her companion, Mrs. Wise. I have also become properly acquainted with the other two young ladies. Miss Martha, I can now address as Miss Matthews. She is staying in Bath with her father, who came to take the waters for his gout, and with her friend Miss Eliza Williams.

Miss Matthews' foot mended swiftly, so my guilt is appeased. I have come across them often in the Pump Room, the circulating library, and in Sydney Gardens. Mr. Matthews is rarely with them—almost never, in fact, on account of his severe attack of gout, which pains him exceedingly. His daughter informed me that apart from the Baths, he only left his lodgings to take tea in the Royal Crescent, at Miss Malcolm's gracious invitation.

Sadly, I was not favoured with the same, but I had the honour of standing up with Miss Malcolm at several private balls. She graced the public assemblies with her presence only once, and on that occasion, Mrs. Wise also chaperoned Miss Matthews and Miss Williams, presumably at the invalid Mr. Matthews' behest. Ever since the unorthodox encounter, the three young ladies seem to have formed a close acquaintance, although bar their age, they have little in common. Miss Malcolm has a distinct air of affluence about her. Miss Williams and Miss Matthews do not. All manner of details lend weight to my first impressions. Their respective lodgings. Their attire and jewellery. Miss Malcolm's elegant carriage. And the very fact that she has no difficulty in receiving a three-page letter, no part of which was crossed. Moreover, she is well-spoken and her conversation suggests an extensive and expensive education. The best the other two can boast of must be a middling seminary for girls. They are pleasant enough, but Miss Malcolm is thoroughly charming. It would do no harm to learn more about her.

Miss Malcolm's companion, the elderly Mrs. Wise, is far from aptly named. In response to my cleverly steered conversation, she has most unwisely disclosed some intriguing details about her charge. It seems that Miss Malcolm's parents are long gone but, much like myself, she has been blessed with a wealthy relation who has been guarding her interests for years. Perhaps Mrs. Wise had sought to ward me off, but the effect was the very opposite. I was already taken with Miss Malcolm's charming countenance and manner. The fact that she is a confirmed heiress gives her an irresistible allure.

Maybe Mrs. Smith has guessed my intentions or maybe not. It does not concern me either way. There is nothing about Miss Malcolm she could possibly object to. The sole difficulty was that, until three days ago, Mrs. Smith had commandeered too much of my time which could be better spent a-courting. But, blessedly, she has now returned to Allenham and allowed me to excuse myself from the "pleasurable duty" of attending her. Thus, my time can be wholly devoted now to sweeter pursuits.

Come to think of it, if anyone should seem to object to my attentions to Miss Malcolm 'tis Miss Williams. For quite some time now, she has given me to think she would rather have them for herself. I have more than a little sympathy for her, but such is the way of the world. The girl, however fetching in appearance, must see that she cannot prevail over the combined advantages of wealth, charm, style, and beauty. Unless rendered senseless by partiality and blind desire, any man would wish his partner in life to possess all of the above. And if they should compromise, not many would choose looks and charm over a portion. To my good fortune, Miss Malcolm is in every way agreeable and 'tis no hardship to seek to attach her. To give her her due, Miss Williams is more womanly in her appearance, with better curves in all the right places, and has no compunction about occasionally pressing them against me in a dance. I must be cut for sainthood, for despite all this enticing provocation, I do not veer from my course.

My steadfastness is so richly rewarded that I can scarce believe my luck. That dear angel, Emmeline, as I now have leave to call her, has allowed me to declare myself, and once I have done so, with as much tender eloquence as I possess, she has confessed with adorable shyness to have taken me into her heart within days of our acquaintance. I have every reason to believe we will be very happy. She is all charm and goodness, and I do believe she might have the power to attach me all the more as time goes by.

I have resolved to quit Bath the day after tomorrow to apply for her guardian's consent and asked my betrothed for his name and directions. And was beset with all imaginable sentiments when she supplied the information I requested. For her guardian is none other than Lord Camborne!

"Dearest? Whatever is the matter?" Emmeline exclaims and takes my hand. We are still secluded in the garden—most unwise in this as well, Mrs. Wise allows us to walk out, not once intruding on our privacy.

I clasp Emmeline's fingers and bring them to my lips.

"You guessed aright," I decide to tell her. "I *am* perturbed because trying times await us. Lord Cambourne will never grant his consent."

"Goodness! Are you certain?"

"Quite," I reply laconically, and she eyes me with concern mingled with doubt.

"He disapproves of you?"

Yet again, I decide honesty is in order, at least as far as such facts that a gentleman could decorously share with his future bride.

"Lord Cambourne has never met me. It is his lady who will cast every imaginable obstacle in our path. She will prevail upon him to refuse his consent. We were acquainted once, but we parted on the worst of terms."

I know not what I was expecting, but when I mention Lady Cambourne, a steely glint appears in Emmeline's eyes.

"I see," she says crisply, and I begin to wonder how much a gently-bred young lady could garner from my stilted disclosures. And then she speaks again and confounds me all the more:

"Her Ladyship might command my guardian and melt his will to nothing, but she has no power over me. She contrived and schemed to send me away and I have lost my place in Lord Cambourne's house on her account, but I will not lose more. I come into my inheritance when I am of age or when I marry—and if I must marry without my uncle's consent, then so be it!" she declares, and I stare, not quite able to believe she is in earnest.

She is. She leaves me in no misapprehension on the matter, and we lay our plans. At the end of the week, we will set off to Gretna.

I SAUNTER through Bath to make arrangements, and I feel as though I am walking on air. The sweet girl loves me and will marry me. Not only does she not shun the prospect of an elopement, but she has suggested it herself as the only solution to our predicament. We will wed, Coombe will be safe, thanks to her portion—which, by the bye, is even more considerable than Mrs. Wise has led me to suspect—and I will no longer have to bow and scrape to Mrs. Smith. And last but by no means least, I indulge the unholy but oh-so-delicious satisfaction of picturing Isobel's face when I return from Gretna a married man, bow over her hand, and call her "aunt." Ah, the joy to have her see me wedded to her niece, a lady nearly half her age and twice her beauty, and moreover, gentle and honourable too. I grin widely, pleased beyond belief with the whole world and with the sweet and ever so rewarding thing called retribution.

I DO NOT CALL upon Emmeline for two days, as agreed. We thought it best so as to avoid arousing her companion's suspicions. I knock on the door of her Royal Crescent residence on the day before the proposed elopement, also as agreed, to pull the wool over the old lady's eyes by claiming I was requested to return to Allenham, and I came to bid my adieus.

A new maid admits me into the parlour. Neither Emmeline nor Mrs. Wise are there to greet me. The one who turns around to glare at my entrance is Lady Cambourne. I gasp, or betray my shock in some other manner, for she contemptuously arches a perfectly-shaped brow.

"Surprised, are you?" she drawls.

I scowl.

"What brings *you* here?"

She shrugs.

"Your pitiful, little ruse, what else?"

I fight the sinking feeling, square my shoulders, and disdainfully glare back.

"Of what are you speaking?"

"You were never very good at games, John, so do not seek to play one now. Did you imagine I would permit the chit to elope with you?"

"What have you done with her?" I ask, incensed, remembering Emmeline's hints at Isobel's scheming to deprive her of her uncle's favour. What further harm has she in her power to inflict with such ammunition?

"Honestly, John! This is Bath, not the Castle of Otranto. Much as I might wish it, the fair maiden has not been sequestered in some ruinous tower—no tower and no dungeon are to be had in the Royal Crescent, more's the pity. I imagine you would like to see her."

"Naturally!"

"I doubt the sentiment is mutual, but there you are. You may have your wish."

She rings the bell and gives instructions with a calm that chills me. What devilry has she wrought here? And how does she know our plans? I cannot stop myself from asking the second question.

Isobel gives a dismissive wave.

"From Mrs. Wise, of course. She wrote as soon as she got wind of it. Did you flatter yourself you could hoodwink her? She is deeply devoted to Lord Cambourne and Miss Malcolm and not above spying from a window or listening at doors. She would never have permitted her charge to cast away her brilliant prospects any more than I would permit *you* to secure her and parade your conquest at my dinner table. I did not imagine you would sink so low as to extract revenge in such a manner. You have been a good scholar, then. I would be rather proud of you had you not used your skills on one belonging to my home."

I scoff.

"Heavens, Isobel! Your self-absorption knows no bounds. Not everything revolves around you."

Lady Camborne sneers.

"You will tell me next that she was the only heiress in Bath."

I shrug, exasperated.

"Believe what you will. 'Tis no concern of mine."

She stares me down in the most provoking fashion.

"You may think that, if it gives you comfort," she says as the door opens, admitting my betrothed and Mrs. Wise.

Emmeline spares me not a glance but turns to her companion.

"Pray inform the visitor he is not welcome in this house," she blandly utters, and I belatedly grasp the reason behind Isobel's glee. Despite the acrimony between her and her niece by marriage, she has turned the tide against me and I must sink or swim. I bristle. I am not the one who should sink today.

"May we speak in private?" I boldly ask, my eyes on Emmeline alone.

She wavers. Mrs. Wise shakes her head to silently advise her to refuse. Lady Isobel encompasses us in a diverted glance. Emmeline flashes her a scowl. Ah, so despite appearances they are not united against me. I derive some hope from that.

"I will not take too much of your time," I say, pressing my case, and finally Emmeline gestures towards the music room, then strides forth without a word. I lose no time in following her.

"Pray remember what you said yourself about her scheming ways," I urge as soon as I close the door. "Upon my honour, your connection with His Lordship was unknown to me until you mentioned it yourself. You must have noted my surprise. Your aunt's accusation of duplicity is a falsehood. She lies as she breathes, and she knows nothing but deception."

"I know what she is," Emmeline replies coldly. "Which is why I can scarce bear to look upon you now—"

"Em—" I plead, reaching for her hand, but she shrinks back.

"Can you aver that all her claims are nothing but scheming and deception? No, you cannot, I can see it in your face. Three years! Three whole years! How *could* you? Of all the vile creatures in the world, how could you?"

The intelligence stuns me for a moment. I had never imagined Isobel would go as far as disclosing the full truth about our past. More fool me, it seems. I should have known that she would stop at nothing. I make to speak, ill-judged as the attempt might be, for I know not what to say, but she forestalls me.

"Were you aiming to sit at my uncle's table, play the part of the dutiful addition to the family, and ask for that dear man's trust, just as *she* does, while he remained ignorant of your past connection?"

Righteous indignation flashes in her eyes. I imagine my case would not be served by the revelation that I would have been assured of her aunt's continued favour and her uncle's goodwill if I *had not* severed the connection. Before me, Emmeline balls her small fists at her side.

"Worse still, were you aiming to play the part of the dutiful husband, while she and you shared this disgusting secret? And keep me in the dark forevermore?"

"Not so! I told you—"

"That you were friends once, but you parted ill. But *intimacy?*"

My temper flares. What do they expect, these romantically-minded misses? That our lives should begin and end with them? That we should live like monks before chance brings us to their door?

"Mere days ago, you said you would not permit Lady Cambourne to take anything else from you," I tactlessly remind her, and she turns upon me like a fragile fury.

"She already has! My hopes of a happy union—ruined! I cannot even face you—"

"Em—" I plead again and clasp her hand, but she wrenches it away.

"No! Do not touch me! How do you imagine I can bear it when I know she was in your arms first?"

I sigh.

"What can I say, Emmeline? That I was callow? That I was taken in? Does it not suffice to say I deeply regret it?"

"Can you honestly tell me that you will not entertain recollections of her? Her kisses? Her doubtlessly expert caresses? And moreover, can you avow you love *me* above all?"

"I have no intention of breaking my marriage vows or my faith with you!" I retort, stung. What sort of a rogue does she take me for? And indeed, what sort of a fool, to imagine I would be caught in Isobel's web again? "You may be assured of my fidelity," I enunciate. "*Especially* where Lady Cambourne is concerned."

But Emmeline scoffs.

"Your fidelity? But what of your heart, Willoughby? What of your heart? Can you assure me that your heart is mine, and that you could not bear a life without me?"

My temper flares again. So, this is not enough, then—affection, fidelity, marriage vows unbroken. Insatiable creatures! How much more do they want? A man's future would not satisfy them. They must have his past, his every thought, and perchance a pound of flesh besides!

No, I cannot assure her that I would be heartbroken if she rejects me and spend the remainder of my days penning mournful verse like all those pasty poets who are industriously putting all this romantic nonsense in their heads. If I were a practised fortune hunter and seducer, I might have the simpering, glib patter at the ready, waiting to be delivered as and when required without hesitation. But, I am not practised in any of the above. Not even in concealing my exasperation with the demand to own me, body and soul. Emmeline must have detected it with ease, for the plea in her eyes turns into a glare and her countenance grows pinched. Should I fall on one knee and bang my chest about the violence of my affections, or should I keep onto the honest path?

I choose the latter. It does not serve me well. The candid recitation of my sentiments is not deemed sufficiently ardent and has me dismissed from her house and her sight.

"Begone, sir, and practise your tepid seduction on another. Your slyness disgusts me. I do not wish to see you nor hear your name again."

I HAVE NO DISCERNMENT, have I? Firstly, I devote three years of my life to a scheming shrew, then very nearly sign away my future to an overindulged miss who demands the moon and prefers smooth lies while honesty disgusts her. I sought to speak sense into Emmeline, but in the face of her unbending prejudice, I lost the will to fight a losing battle. Perhaps this was my greatest sin after all: I drift and easily concede defeat. Or perhaps I have not found something worth fighting for.

Granted, Emmeline's portion is not to be sneered at—but would it be sufficient compensation for a lifetime of being caught between her and Lady Cambourne? I think not. They would drive me to distraction in a twelvemonth, the pair of them. The very embodiment of the old adage about the devil and the deep, blue sea! The pun inspired by my evil paramour and my former affianced, she of the clear-blue eyes, is lamentable, I know. But I still chuckle ruefully as I pour myself another brandy.

Days go by, and it comes as a great relief to conclude I was not in love with Emmeline after all. I am not heartbroken. I do not wander about dejectedly nor do I feel compelled to flee the place where we walked or talked or danced. Bath still has the power to amuse me, and I am pleasantly diverted in the company of others. And not long afterwards, when Miss Eliza Williams boldly observes that unlike Miss Malcolm, *she* would not be dissuaded from following the man she loves, I look her up and down and think to myself, "Whyever not?"

A MONTH IS ENOUGH to tire me of Eliza's charms. Of her conversation, I tired in a se'nnight. A tedious scene will doubtlessly follow when I announce my decision to return to Town. Tears and reproaches. I was treated to the same when I disabused her of the notion that we were headed to Gretna. Nevertheless, she was easily cajoled into better humour and sufficiently well-pleased to continue on our journey. I daresay she was well-pleased with our sojourn in Chippenham for the races and with our little interlude playing the happy couple in a small house in Gloucester.

She must have realised by now that I cannot marry her, yet she is unlikely to be nonchalant about a separation.

MY EXPECTATIONS WERE CONFIRMED, indeed, exceeded. Apparently, Eliza still entertained the hope that we would eventually marry and made a dreadful scene on my departure with a storm of tears meant to play on every sentiment, from guilt to former stirrings of affection. I do wish she had refrained from seeking to work upon me thus and that we had parted in a more congenial manner. Then we might have met again. I would not have been averse to setting her up in Town under my protection. As it is, I would rather avoid the shackle of a volatile companion with unreasonable expectations, ready to deluge me with further reproaches at the drop of a hat. Naturally, I will do my duty if there are consequences from our indiscretion, but I hope it will not come to that. With any luck, Eliza will not write with the unpalatable news that she is with child. Our liaison has run its course, and 'tis high time for her to cast around for a more permanent association. There must be plenty of tradesmen in Gloucester who will be sufficiently taken with a pretty face to make her an offer and not ask too many questions.

I arrive in Town with no mishap and find it entertaining. The company is cheerful enough, and the Season has already started. Lady Cambourne is not in Town. Rumour has it—and it makes me chuckle with dark glee—that Lord Cambourne has been advised to avoid high living and unwholesome excitement, and that he grows exceedingly petulant if his lady does not keep to his side.

It amuses me a great deal less to cross paths with Lady Grenville—Miss Malcolm as was. But I bear it with tolerable composure.

What disheartens me is another downturn in my luck at cards. This time I cannot even lay the blame on William Elliot's suspect skills; it was not him I lost to. So, there I am doing penance in Devonshire again. Dull country, this, and the dullest company. Even the new additions at Barton Cottage are as predictable as can be: the doting mother; the reserved eldest daughter; the tomboyish youngest, and the indulged middle daughter—an exuberant, young miss who makes melancholy poems her staple diet and looks upon my assistance with her sprained ankle on the moors with as much favour as if it were one of Sir Galahad's most gallant deeds.

This is my lot in life, it seems: to inspire damsels in distress with wildly romantic notions. So be it. The Devonshire tedium might become more bearable. On the morrow, we are to read from Mr. Wordsworth's poems. Ha! Perhaps *he* had the right of it: seclude himself in the wilderness of the Lake Country like a hermit, away from other people and their whimsical demands. No gambling debts, no wealthy relations to cajole, no pandering to imaginative misses. A life free of irksome impositions.

"Aye, but devilishly dull," I mutter with a chuckle as I nudge Peg along the bridleway to Allenham.

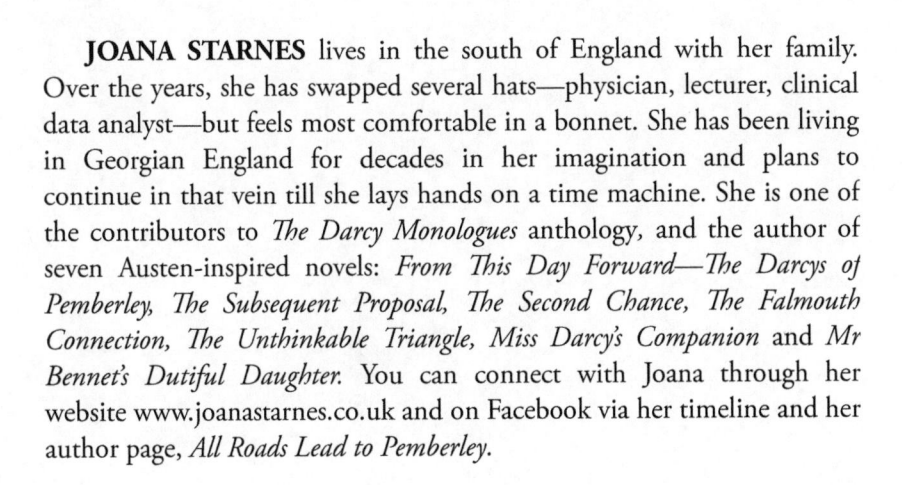

JOANA STARNES lives in the south of England with her family. Over the years, she has swapped several hats—physician, lecturer, clinical data analyst—but feels most comfortable in a bonnet. She has been living in Georgian England for decades in her imagination and plans to continue in that vein till she lays hands on a time machine. She is one of the contributors to *The Darcy Monologues* anthology, and the author of seven Austen-inspired novels: *From This Day Forward—The Darcys of Pemberley, The Subsequent Proposal, The Second Chance, The Falmouth Connection, The Unthinkable Triangle, Miss Darcy's Companion* and *Mr Bennet's Dutiful Daughter*. You can connect with Joana through her website www.joanastarnes.co.uk and on Facebook via her timeline and her author page, *All Roads Lead to Pemberley*.

GEORGE WICKHAM

Jane Austen's most infamous rake was raised alongside her most beloved hero, Fitzwilliam Darcy. Wickham's charisma and comely looks lured compassion to all he encountered including Elizabeth Bennet. *"There certainly was some great mismanagement in the education of those two men. One has got all the goodness, and the other all the appearance of it."* —*Pride and Prejudice*, **Chapter XL**. After his failed attempt to elope with Darcy's young sister for her fortune, and later, after running off with the youngest Bennet daughter, his character was exposed as a calculating adventurer and deceitful libertine.

His appearance was greatly in his favor: he had all the best parts of beauty, a fine countenance, a good figure, and a pleasing address. —*Pride and Prejudice*, Chapter XV.

A WICKED GAME
Katie Oliver

SALAMANCA, SPAIN, 22 JULY 1812

Dust swirls around me as I urge my mount forward. The clash of bayonet and sword, the explosion of muskets, and the blood roaring in my ears vie with the cries and shouts of the men around me.

Each moment is an eternity. There is nothing but the parry and thrust of my saber plunging into flesh, flashing and glinting in the sun.

Our cavalry engaged with Marmant's forces at Arapiles just south of Salamanca. Wave after wave, the enemy charged, and I fought until my arm ached and my ears reverberated with the crack of musket fire and the thunder of hooves.

Now, my regimentals are damp and heavy with sweat, and I blink perspiration from my eyes. Smoke and death and horror surround me.

But there is no time to contemplate the carnage. My horse rears as I fend off an attack from a French dragoon. Our blades clang together in a vicious struggle until I manage to dispatch him with a thrust to the heart. He slumps in his saddle and falls, dead before his body hits the ground.

BESIDE ME, one of our regiment fights off a pair of cavalrymen. He is losing the battle. I lunge forward and run one of his attackers through, then the other, without mercy or hesitation, and wonder at my own detachment. I spare no thought for their wives, or family, or the children they might leave behind; there is no time. I am conscious of only one thing. Survival.

"Thank you," the Englishman rasps, his face seamed with dirt and sweat. "I am indebted to you, sir." He gives me a brief nod before he turns his horse away.

I pause, and in that moment grapeshot rips into my chest and shoulder. My hold slackens and the sword falls from my hand. I tumble to the ground, intent only on avoiding the hooves of the horses rearing and galloping past me.

Consciousness comes and goes as the hot Salamanca sun beats down on me. All I can think of as I lie there is my wife, Lydia, whom I left behind in England. She is with child. My child.

Despite the sun's heat, a chill grips me. Poor girl. I seduced her. Ruined her. It was only through Darcy's intervention that I agreed to marry her at all... for a price. I groan. No one can deny that I have behaved despicably. How can I expect Lydia to forgive me when I cannot forgive myself?

No soul is beyond redemption.

Those were the vicar's words when I spoke to him before joining Wellington's men in Spain. I did not want to go. The thought of dying in battle in a foreign land held no appeal.

I considered deserting, fleeing to a place where I might never be found. But I could not in good conscience leave Lydia and the baby behind. I am a father now with not only a wife to think of but a child as well, and I must provide my little family with all the comforts and security they deserve.

All around me I hear the piteous cries of the dying. Like me, they lie forgotten on the battlefield, awaiting death. Begging for an end to pain. Rubbing shoulders with my own mortality has made me realize the terrible fragility of life. In the end, I did the honorable thing and decided to face the enemy, to return home either a hero or a dead man. But I would run no longer.

A laugh burbles up now in my throat. *How noble*—I close my eyes—*how fitting.* When at last I vow to mend my ways, I am struck down in battle, left to die an unlamented death in a field in Spain. What will the inscription on my headstone read, I wonder? Surely, I have done nothing to inspire respect or admiration.

Here lies George Wickham, liar, cheat, and profligate womanizer, a reprobate who failed to distinguish himself on the battlefield or in life... but who wore his uniform exceedingly well.

Not much of an epitaph, to be sure.

As the sounds of battle diminish, I wonder how long I have lain here. Ten minutes? An hour? I cough at the dust stirred up by the retreating French and attempt to lift my head but dizziness overcomes me, and I fall back against the hard ground. The enemy is vanquished. The battle is over.

I drift in and out of consciousness and add up my transgressions like an accountant totting up numbers in a ledger. Squandering my inheritance? Guilty. Refusing the offer of a respectable living as a curate? Done. I had attempted to tarnish my boyhood friend Darcy's good name out of jealousy and spite, and nearly persuaded his young sister Georgiana to elope, not for love but for want of her thirty thousand pounds. Were that not enough, I seduced Lydia Bennet into my bed, as well as countless, unremembered others, and wed her only after securing payment and promises from Darcy... among them a commission in the Regulars, which meant the risk of dangerous duty overseas but more money in my pocket.

What a persuasive, charming, thoroughly contemptible man I have been.

And now, as my life ebbs away, I carry a deep and abiding shame for my actions, and for those I have wronged. It is too late to change, to start anew, and become the man I would like to be, a man my wife and her family—even Darcy—might be proud of.

Death will see to that.

Pain wracks my body, and my vision softens and fades. Peace settles over me. The sun warms my face as it climbs higher in the sky, and I close my eyes, remembering another summer morning when I set myself so recklessly on the path that led me here...

DERBYSHIRE, 1800

A sharp tap sounded upon my bedroom door. "It's nearly time, George. Are you ready?"

It was Sunday, and Sunday meant church.

"I'll be downstairs shortly," I told Darcy and rolled out of bed with reluctance. I thrust on breeches and shrugged my arms into a shirt and waistcoat, hoping there might be time for breakfast before we departed Pemberley.

The thought of sitting on a hard pew to endure the weekly strictures against lust, greed, and other sinful vices on an empty stomach filled me with the same resigned dread a prisoner must feel as he is led to his execution.

I wanted it to be over—quickly.

I pulled on the boots I had polished the previous night and studied my reflection in the mirror as I tied my cravat. I wanted to look my best, not so much for our Lord as for the ladies. I might have no money to recommend me, nor a title or property... but am told I have a pleasing manner and an agreeable nature. And such qualities are always looked on with favor by the fairer sex.

We arrived at the parish church a short time later. My mind wandered as the vicar's voice rose and fell, the cadences swooping and diving as he shared Sunday's homily with the congregation. I heard not a word. A growing sense of ennui settled upon me and I found I had little patience for spiritual matters.

Summer stretched out before me like a vast and indifferent sea that I was impatient to cross. In autumn, I would begin my first year at Cambridge. The desire to be gone, to leave Derbyshire far behind, made me restless, and I shifted position on the Darcy family pew. My movement earned me a reproving glare from my godfather and another from Darcy himself.

I suppressed a sigh and pretended to study the stained-glass windows.

As a boy, I welcomed the summer months at Pemberley. There was much to fill the idle hours, from riding and walking to staging elaborate theatricals, and the days passed in a pleasant blur. In these things Darcy was my stalwart and constant companion.

But time, and my realization of the social chasm that divided us, changed all that.

Of course, I am grateful for the kindness and generosity of the Darcy family and owe them a debt I can never repay. I cannot imagine what my life would be had they turned me out after my father's death.

Nonetheless, I am not, will never be, on equal footing with one so far above me in social standing as Fitzwilliam Darcy. I am the son of his father's estate manager. Someone to be provided for, educated ... treated, inasmuch as possible, like one of the family. Yet, I am not one of them. I know it, and I feel the sting of my inferiority most keenly.

But I refuse to indulge in self-pity. I am lucky to have a friend like Darcy and a godfather so generous as his father has been. My options after graduating Cambridge may be limited to law or the clergy, but thanks to Mr. Darcy, I will have an excellent education. I swear I will make something worthy of myself.

When the service ended, I trailed several paces behind Mr. Darcy and his son, in no particular hurry to join them outside. I glimpsed John

Seldon, the local squire's son, and paused in the vestibule as he greeted me.

"Wickham, you devil. You're looking well, as always."

As I gripped his hand in mine it was impossible not to return his smile. "I thought you'd gone abroad for the summer."

"I depart for Italy in four weeks." He lowered his voice. "Wine, women, and… well, what else is there, eh?" He grinned and clapped me on the back. "I understand you plan to join Darcy at Cambridge in the autumn."

"King's College," I confirmed. "To study divinity."

Seldon lifted his brows. "Divinity? You?" He let out a smothered snort of laughter. "Lud, Wickham. Somehow, I cannot see it."

I felt a flicker of irritation. "My godfather has offered me a curacy upon my graduation."

"A curate? You'll make no money. And you shall go slowly mad with boredom."

"I shall have the parsonage at Kympton," I said in my defense. "And a small parcel of land."

He chuckled. "You—tilling fields, and herding sheep and lost souls? Why, the very idea is preposterous."

The sight of a new face ahead of us spared me a reply. She was slim, with a stovepipe bonnet tied beneath her chin. Unlike the other ladies, she wore a somber gown of gray crêpe, and despite its plainness and lack of trimmings, the dress did nothing to lessen her beauty. I glimpsed only a portion of her face, but what I saw of it, the curve of her cheek and a cluster of dark curls, intrigued me.

"Who is she?" I asked him and inclined my head discreetly in the direction of the young woman conversing with Mrs. Fanshaw and her daughters.

He followed my gaze. "Ah. I do not recall her name, more's the pity, but according to the latest *on-dit*, she's visiting Mrs. F for the duration of the summer." Approval registered on his face as he studied her trim figure. "She's a diamond of the first water."

"Indeed." I could not stop myself staring at her.

"George, there you are." Darcy detached himself from his father and a small group of parishioners standing inside the entrance and joined us. He did not look pleased. "Seldon," he added and delivered a curt nod. "How do you do?"

"Very well, sir, thank you."

Darcy turned to me. "Pray, do not linger too long. Father wishes to depart soon."

"Of course." I turned back to Seldon. "Will I see you before you leave for Italy?"

"You may depend upon it." He nodded politely to Darcy, gave me a roguish wink, and took his leave.

As I made to follow him outside, Darcy stayed me. "George, a moment, please."

"Yes?" I was impatient to be off.

"In the future, I suggest—no, I must insist—that you extend young Mr. Seldon nothing more than the merest civility."

"What?" I blinked. "Why? We are friends, good friends, and have been for many years."

"I understand. But you were boys then. Now you are grown, and your lives will soon take you in very different directions." He paused. "I trust you will meet more suitable companions when you join me at Cambridge."

"More suitable…?" I regarded him in disbelief. Who was more suited to keep company with Squire Seldon's eldest boy than myself, the steward's son? My face darkened and I opened my mouth to object, both to his advice and his insufferable snobbery, but an interruption spared me from uttering the angry words that remained unspoken on my lips.

"Mr. Darcy!" a voice behind us exclaimed. "How lovely to see you."

A matronly woman, clad in a gown of primrose sarsenet and matching bonnet, sailed towards us. I recognized her at once. She and her husband and daughters had let Mannering, a small but charming property several miles from Pemberley. Behind her, I glimpsed two young women. One of them I knew as her daughter; the other, whom I had admired only moments before, stood quietly behind her. My heart commenced to beat faster.

"Mrs. Fanshaw," Darcy said and inclined his head. "I hope this Sunday finds you well."

"Very well, Mr. Darcy, thank you." She turned to the girl standing beside her and drew her forward. "I believe you have not met my eldest daughter, Celia."

"A pleasure, Miss Fanshaw." He bowed.

Celia's blush deepened. "I am very pleased to meet you, sir."

"And this," Mrs. Fanshaw added as she turned to the young woman in gray, "is my sister-in-law, Lady Clémence Harlow. Lady Harlow, this is Mr. Fitzwilliam Darcy of Pemberley."

"*Bonjour, monsieur,*" she murmured and extended her gloved hand to Darcy, who bowed stiffly over it.

"Lady Harlow. A pleasure." He straightened and turned to me. "May I present a close friend of the family, Mr. George Wickham?" he said in correct but clipped tones. "He leaves for university in the autumn."

So, she was French. And married. Of course, she was. How could a creature of such style and beauty not already be attached?

I swallowed my disappointment and bowed over her hand. At least Darcy had done me the courtesy not to mention my status as the former estate manager's son. "I am honored to make your acquaintance."

She bestowed a smile on me. "It is you who do me the honor, *monsieur*. If you are a close friend of Mr. Darcy's then I hold you already in high esteem."

Her manner was subdued, but delightful...and hers was the most enchanting countenance I had ever seen. Her lips were as pink and perfectly formed as a rosebud; her eyes mirrored the tranquil blue of the early summer sky. With one look, she took my heart captive as surely as any Barbary pirate.

"You are newly arrived in Derbyshire, then?" I inquired as Darcy turned away to converse with Miss Fanshaw and her mother.

"Yes. I am staying with my husband's sister and her three young daughters. It is quite a *lively* household."

"I have no doubt they are glad of your company."

"They have welcomed me most graciously." A shadow passed over her face. "Since my husband's death last year, his sister and my nieces are all the family I have left."

"I am sorry to hear it," I said. Now I understood her somber attire and subdued manner. "Please accept my condolences."

"Thank you. How kind." She retrieved a lace-trimmed handkerchief from her reticule and touched it briefly to one eye, and as she looked at me, I imagined I saw an echo of my own attraction mirrored in their depths.

"Mrs. Fanshaw and her daughter have agreed to join us for dinner," Darcy informed me. "You will come along as well, I hope, Lady Harlow?"

"*Certainement!* I should be delighted."

"I look forward to it," I said.

She inclined her head. "I am anxious to further our acquaintance, *monsieur*. You must tell me all about your plans for the future. And thank you, *m'sieu* Darcy," she added, almost as an afterthought. "*Jusqu'à ce soir.*"

He sketched a bow.

I was too transfixed by her beauty to wonder at Darcy's marked reserve towards her and bowed as she extended her gloved fingertips once more to me. "*Au revoir, m'sieu.*"

"*Au revoir,*" I echoed.

Then she was gone.

Sunday supper at Pemberley was normally a quiet meal *en famille*. But the addition of their cousin Fiztwilliam, along with Mrs. Fanshaw, her daughter Celia, and her charming sister-in-law, made for pleasant company that evening.

I contrived to sit as far as possible from Celia Fanshaw and took a seat opposite Lady Harlow. Disappointment flickered over Miss Fanshaw's face, and I felt a moment's guilt. She was pretty enough, with her blonde curls and blushes, but I found her as vapid and silly as her mother and had no wish to converse with her.

Mrs. Fanshaw turned to Darcy's cousin. "Allow me to congratulate you on your recent promotion, Lieutenant Fitzwilliam."

"Thank you." He inclined his head and reached for his wine glass. "I must confess I grow restless. Bonaparte has crossed the Alps into Austria, and now the newspapers report that the French army has seized Milan. The man shows no sign of stopping."

"War is inevitable," the elder Mr. Darcy agreed. "I fear Napoleon will not rest until he conquers all of Europe. I have no doubt your wish to see action will be granted soon enough, Lieutenant."

"Enough talk of war, gentlemen," Mrs. Fanshaw declared. "War is tiresome. What we need is a ball! Dancing and merriment will dispel the gloom."

"Oh, yes," Celia enthused, and clasped her hands together. "That is an excellent idea. Do you not agree, Lady Harlow?"

"I am afraid it is still too soon to allow myself such frivolity." She smiled and reached out to touch the girl's hand. "But I am happy to act as your chaperone."

"We must oblige the ladies," Darcy said to his father. "We will speak no more of war, or of Napoleon." He turned to Lady Harlow: "May I ask what brings you to Derbyshire, madam? Are you visiting, or do you plan to stay?"

"I regret I am here only for the summer." She added, "My plans for the future are not quite set." She sighed. "In truth, I long for Paris. I miss the salons, and balls, and carriage rides through the Bois de Boulogne."

"I should like to see Paris one day," I said and reached for my wine glass.

"It would be my honor to show you the city, should you decide to visit."

I smiled politely but made no reply. There was no possibility of my visiting the Continent, now, or ever. I had not the means. My future was mapped out, my education and living already decided.

As if he read my thoughts, Darcy spoke. "George will attend university soon, and his studies will occupy him. I daresay he shall have no time for travel."

"Perhaps not now," Lady Harlow said, "but surely *Monsieur* Wickham will wish to marry when he leaves Cambridge. He might take his bride to Paris then, *non*?" Her steady eyes appraised me. "After all... How could any young woman resist so handsome and charming a man?"

I picked up my spoon and focused my attention on my soup. I scarce knew what to say to such an extravagant compliment, but the pleasure her words brought were undeniable. My head spun with the heady and unexpected joy of it.

"You must promise to invite us to your wedding when the time comes, Mr. Wickham," Fitzwilliam said.

"It is far too early for such talk," my godfather said sharply. "George must see to his education first."

"Indeed, you are right, sir." Lieutenant Fitzwilliam studied me. "He has all his life before him, thanks to your generosity, as well as every opportunity to succeed. I fervently hope Mr. Wickham makes good use of his time at university. He has much to accomplish before he takes on a wife."

Have I no say in my own life? Not for the first time, I felt a flicker of resentment at being discussed as if I were not there, as if my presence carried no more consequence than that of a chair at the table or the bowl of roses on the sideboard. When would I cease to be told what to do, when would I cease to be reminded of the Darcy family's generosity?

"Yes," I agreed, masking my irritation behind a bland smile. "I am in no particular hurry to be wed."

"I have no doubt you shall lead the ladies on a merry chase first." Lady Harlow studied me coolly over the rim of her glass.

"I regret there are few unattached young ladies to be found hereabouts," I replied. And not one of them, not even the bird-witted Miss Fanshaw, would consent to marry a man such as myself, without money or title to recommend him.

"You should listen to Fitzwilliam, George," my godfather said. "He has the right of it. Focus on your education first. Make something worthy of yourself, and the rest will follow."

I nodded, suitably chastened. "Yes, sir. That is exactly what I intend to do."

"Love is such a tricky thing, *non*?" Lady Harlow mused. "Before my own marriage, my *maman* took me aside. 'Clémence,' she said, 'you must marry once for a title, once for money, and once for love.'" She laughed. "Good advice, my friends, *n'est-ce pas*? You cannot have one without the others!"

Mr. Darcy, Sr. pressed his lips into a tight line. "Bring in the next course," he instructed the footman tersely. "We are all quite finished with our soup."

I looked at his son and nearly laughed aloud to see Darcy's thunderous expression. His displeasure with our guest was nearly as great as his father's and filled me with amusement. They plainly did not approve of Lady Harlow. I reached for my wine glass and managed, somehow, to suppress a smile.

HALFWAY THROUGH SUPPER, a summer storm erupted. Though the rumble of thunder and flashes of lightning were of little consequence to those of us inside, outside the roads quickly turned to mud, making them all but impassable.

As the butler entered the dining room to announce the news, another crack of lightning seared the night sky.

"Such a storm!" Mrs. Fanshaw cried and half rose from her chair. "The roads will be a soup of mud and our carriage is sure to get stuck."

"There is no cause for alarm," Mr. Darcy reassured her. "I am confident the roads will dry sufficiently by tomorrow. In the meantime, you shall stay here tonight. Chalmers," he said as he turned to the butler, "please have Reynolds ready rooms for our guests."

"I shall see to it directly, sir."

As old Chalmers departed, Lady Harlow laid a reassuring hand on Mrs. Fanshaw's arm and drew her gently back into her seat. "Thank you, Mr. Darcy. We are delighted at the prospect of staying the night at Pemberley."

"Indeed, we are," Celia agreed. "Holly jolly it shall be! Don't you agree, Mamma? Perhaps we might gather around the drawing room fire after dinner and exchange ghost stories while the storm rages outside."

"Ghost stories?" her mother echoed. "What utter, childish nonsense."

"On the contrary," I said. "I think it sounds amusing. And after we gentlemen have frightened you ladies with our tales of terror, we shall be on hand to offer our reassurances and be the heroes of the evening." My eyes met Lady Harlow's. "What do you think, my lady?"

She clasped her hands together in delight. "I adore nothing so much as a ghost story. I have not heard one since I left the nursery."

"Then let us adjourn to the drawing room," the elder Mr. Darcy said, his eyes twinkling, and stood. "A glass of brandy is just the thing to warm us."

As everyone followed him out of the dining room, I lingered behind and offered my arm to our charming French guest. "I promise not to frighten you overmuch, Lady Harlow," I assured her as she laid her hand lightly on my sleeve.

"Oh, *la*! I quite adore a good scare. I devour all of the gothic novels." She lowered her voice. "But I confess, I like to be *reassured* afterwards even more."

I met her eyes, so blue and guileless, and my pulse raced. There could be no mistaking her meaning. Could there?

As if to answer my unspoken question, she leaned forward, her breath warm against my ear. "Perhaps I will see you later," she whispered. She drew away, and the exchange happened so quickly, I wondered if I had imagined it.

Even as shock rendered me immobile, desire overcame me, and a trace of anxiety, as well. I had little experience of women, having shared only a few, stolen kisses with a housemaid. But I was eager to learn.

Oh, how I wanted to learn.

Darcy turned back to us, his expression unreadable. "Come along, George. We must not keep our guests waiting."

"Of course not."

I struggled to compose myself as we followed the others into the drawing room.

THE HOUR WAS LATE when at last we bid each other good night and headed upstairs. Our candle flames danced and flickered, casting shadows on the wallpaper, rendering Pemberley's dark corners even darker.

"Good night, *monsieurs*," Lady Harlow called out as she, along with the other ladies, turned to follow Reynolds to their rooms in the east wing.

"Good night," Darcy's father replied. "I shall see you ladies in the morning. If there is anything you or the others require, you have only to let Mrs. Reynolds know."

"Thank you." As he left, she inclined her head to Lieutenant Fitzwilliam and me. "*Bonne nuit.*"

Though I searched her candlelit face, there was no hint of the coquette who had flirted with me so boldly earlier that evening. Her expression was composed and polite. Nothing more.

Fitzwilliam bowed, and I did the same. "Sleep well, ladies."

I followed Darcy and his cousin down the hallway that led to the family wing and bid them a good night as I went, at last, into my room. I shut the door behind me and leaned back against it. At once, I regarded the four-poster bed.

Would I possibly share it tonight with Clémence Harlow? The thought left me half mad with desire … and aroused no small amount of apprehension within me at the same time.

I could not help but wonder if I would make a fool of myself. Would I know what to do, what to say? Would she laugh at me? Mock my ineptitude? Why had she behaved with such polite indifference just now? Had I only imagined her earlier interest?

Unsure of the answers, my self-doubt increased. I shrugged my frockcoat off, untied my cravat with unsteady fingers, and tossed it aside. I would wait. After all, I had little choice. I was at Lady Harlow's mercy.

I flung myself back across the bed and stared moodily at the blue silk overhead. Of course, I reminded myself, the two of us must be discreet. We could hardly allow Darcy, or his cousin, or indeed any of the others, to suspect our attraction for one other. It would not do to give the game away so easily.

Silence settled over the great house as I lay on the bed and waited, listening for the sound of the doorknob turning. But there was nothing, only the crackling of flames licking the logs in the fireplace. I yawned. I had consumed several glasses of brandy after dinner, and now heaviness tugged at my eyes. I would close them, I decided, just for a moment.

As I drifted between wakefulness and sleep, I imagined I held her in my arms, nestled close against me, with her heart beating against mine like a tiny, wild bird.

Deep in the night, I sat up with a start. Somewhere nearby I heard a door open and close. Whispers, followed by hushed, angry words. Then silence.

I waited, my heart flailing, and listened with the preternatural hearing one has in the darkness, but the sounds were not repeated, and I could only suppose I had imagined them. With a mutter and a sigh, I lay back down and slept.

I dreamt of the warmth of Lady Harlow's skin against mine. I dreamt of her mouth, so soft and sweet and yielding, as our lips clung together for the first time. She tasted of apricots. She smelled of summer and sunshine. I dreamt I touched her. Possessed her.

When I awoke, sunlight streamed into my room through a gap in the drapes, and I blinked. I found myself sprawled across the bed, still clothed, still lying atop the covers… alone.

Only in my dreams had Lady Harlow come to my room.

WHEN I ENTERED the dining room a short time later, my godfather and our guests were already seated at the table.

"Where is Darcy, sir?" I asked him.

"He is gone for his morning ride."

Although I made no remark, I was surprised that Darcy had abandoned his guests. It was most unlike him.

"Morning, Wickham," Lieutenant Fitzwilliam said with a welcoming smile and cut into his poached egg with a knife and fork, releasing a rich yellow river of yolk across his plate.

"Good morning." I seated myself beside him, as far from Lady Harlow as possible.

"Coffee, sir?" the footman asked as he appeared beside me.

I nodded. "Thank you, John."

"I trust you slept well, Mr. Wickham?" Lady Harlow inquired.

I reached for the silver pitcher of cream and splashed some into my cup. "Well enough," I said shortly. "And you?"

"I passed a restful night despite the storm. Are you not hungry this morning?"

"Not particularly. I find my appetite has abandoned me."

If she felt the intended sting of my words, she gave no sign, but turned her attention to my godfather. "Have you any word on the road conditions, *monsieur*?"

"Yes. You should be able to return home this afternoon. The roads are nearly dry."

"Such welcome news!" Mrs. Fanshaw exclaimed. "Not to say that we have not enjoyed our stay immensely," she hastened to add, "but I must admit I am anxious to return home to my younger daughters. They like to lead their governess on a merry dance whenever I am away."

"I am sure Lady Harlow shares your desire to leave," I said. My eyes locked briefly with hers before I looked away.

Unperturbed, she touched a napkin to her lips. "*Au contraire*, I would stay at Pemberley forever if I could. The house and grounds are beautiful, and the company most delightful."

Fitzwilliam finished his egg and toast, and dropping his napkin to the table, thrust back his chair and stood. "I must agree, Lady Harlow. And before I depart, may I say that we find your company equally as delightful."

"Thank you, *m'sieu*. You are too kind."

I scraped back my own chair as well. The sight of our French guest, blushing prettily in the face of Fitzwilliam's gallantries, filled me with no small amount of jealousy. "I believe Darcy has the right of it. The weather is made for a brisk morning ride." I stood and gave a curt bow. "If you will excuse me, ladies?"

As I followed Fitzwilliam from the room, I saw Lady Harlow drop her napkin onto her plate with an unhurried gesture and rise.

"Forgive me," she apologized to Darcy's father and the remaining ladies, "but I fear I must abandon you as well and return to my room to fetch my gloves."

"But you have no need of them now, Clémence," her sister-in-law protested.

"On the contrary, I do. I wish to see the gardens before we leave. They are so very beautiful, and the weather is perfectly suited for a walk. I cannot bear to stay inside on such a day."

My heart beat faster wondering what game she played, but I continued across the entrance hall. Fitzwilliam paused by the front door and eyed me expectantly. "Will you join me for a ride across the fields, Wickham?" he inquired. "I should be glad of your company."

I hesitated. "No. I will not detain you. I have a matter to take care of first."

He nodded amiably and left.

Fitzwilliam had no sooner taken his leave than Lady Harlow emerged from the dining room and approached me. Without a word, she slipped into the library across the hall and gestured for me to follow. I stood rooted to the spot. This was madness. Insanity. And it was decidedly improper.

Thrusting aside my misgivings, I strode across the empty hallway and through the double doors and regarded her in apprehension as she shut them behind us with great care.

"You take a dangerous risk," I protested in a low voice as I turned to her. "If anyone should see us…"

She leant back against the door. "No one will see us. And what I have to say to you will take but a moment."

The blood rushed, pounding, in my ears. I made no reply.

"I hope you will forgive me," she whispered and drew closer. "The brandy last night made me tired. I fell asleep before I could come to you."

When I said nothing, still nursing my pique, she leaned forward.

"Oh, dear. You are angry with me, I think." The scent of violets teased me as she pressed her lips fleetingly on mine. I groaned and reached for her.

"*Non*," she chided gently and pushed my hands away. "Not here. Not now. But soon, *mon chérie*. Soon. Leave it to me."

I bit back a sigh of frustration. I wanted her, desperately. But for now, her promise would have to be enough.

"Wait for me outside," she whispered. "I will join you in a moment. Now, you must go, and quickly."

My hand shook slightly as I opened the door, and after reassuring myself that the hall remained empty, I slipped out, and she followed a moment later. I made my way outside and waited on the steps with equal parts impatience and anxiety until, a short time later, Lady Harlow emerged and joined me.

"Ah! *Monsieur* Wickham," she exclaimed, all innocence, as she pulled on her gloves. A purple bonnet was tied in a jaunty bow beneath her chin. "What a pleasant surprise! Will you not join me for a walk? Or had you plans to go riding with Lieutenant Fitzwilliam?"

"I did. But I can hardly allow you to walk alone. And although Darcy's cousin is too polite to admit it, I have no doubt he prefers to ride alone." I shrugged. "At any rate, he is a much more accomplished rider than myself. I should never have managed to keep up."

"Then I am glad you are such a poor horseman," she replied. "It means I shall have you to myself for the duration of our walk."

All traces of my previous ill humor vanished and my pulse quickened at the thought of being alone with her, if only for a short time. "Nothing would give me greater pleasure, my lady."

She smiled demurely and took my arm, and together we made our way down the steps and across the grassy lawn, to freedom.

WE WALKED for some time without conversation and made our way towards the Pemberley woods. The ground was damp and water jeweled the grass, but the path was dry. Birds called from the branches overhead. The scent of summer flowers, newly washed by the rain, drifted on the air. A sparrow erupted from the hedgerows as we passed and elicited a cry of alarm from Lady Harlow. Her fingers tightened on my arm.

"Pardon me." She laughed. "I fear I startle very easily."

"You have nothing to apologize for. Nor anything to fear from a sparrow," I added and smiled.

"You must think me a very silly woman."

"Not at all. Clever, perhaps. But silly? Never."

"Ah. You find me clever? In what way, *m'sieu?*"

I considered her question and chose my words with care. "You know none of us well, and yet, somehow, you arranged for us to walk alone together, almost as if you knew the others would decline your invitation to join us."

She lifted one shawl-clad shoulder. "Most people are very predictable, I find."

I stopped and turned to face her. "And what of me? Am I predictable?"

"You? *Non!*" She regarded me in pink-cheeked surprise. "You are nothing like the others. Lieutenant Fitzwilliam is amiable enough, and possessed of impeccable manners and a facility for conversation, but he talks of nothing but war; while young Mr. Darcy says little and concerns himself overmuch with the proprieties. But you"—she paused to consider me—"you are singular. You care little for such trivialities."

Although I did not like to say it, I found her assessment of Darcy and his cousin both dismissive and unkind. "I think perhaps we should return." We had ventured some way into the thick, green darkness of the woods, and trees had long since blocked out the great house on the hill behind us.

She lifted her face to mine in dismay. "Have I offended you, *Monsieur* Wickham? Oh, *la*! I am most sorry. I meant no insult."

"I take no offense," I assured her. "But nor do I wish us to become the subject of idle gossip if we remain gone too long. Your reputation..."

She made a dismissive gesture. "There is no great hurry," she said in lilting tones and reached out to touch my cheek with the tip of her gloved finger. "No hurry at all."

I closed my eyes. Her touch inflamed me, and she stood so close I could smell the scent of her perfume. Still, I hesitated. Flirting with a housemaid or exchanging pleasantries with a shop girl was one thing, but this was quite another. "We... I think we should go back."

"Do you not want to kiss me, *m'sieu*?"

I caught her gloved hand in mine and raised it fervently to my cheek. "You know I do! I have been able to think of nothing else since last night," I admitted. "I scarcely slept for thoughts of you. But... What if someone should see us?"

"No one will see us here. Pemberley is quite lost to view, and so there is no one to object if I allow you to steal a kiss or two."

Thus, she persuaded me, and I pulled her into my arms. My mouth found hers, and she sighed softly against my lips, and thus emboldened, I tightened my embrace.

The heat of her mouth and body made me dizzy and hungry for more. She deepened the kiss, her tongue dallying with mine, and I groaned.

"Dearest Clémence," I whispered hoarsely. My hands rose up her back, and her nearness, along with the scent of her skin, overwhelmed me. "I want more of you. I want all of you."

She laughed and pushed me playfully away. "*La, Monsieur* Wickham, you flatter me, even as your... enthusiasm overwhelms me. Please, I must beg you to stop. I need to catch my breath and compose myself before we return."

I flushed and dropped my arms to my sides as embarrassment swept over me. Had I misread her intentions so completely? "Forgive me if I cause offense. Such was never my intention."

She waved my words away with a gesture of impatience. "Please do not trouble me with apologies. I allow only those liberties I wish to allow."

"I do not understand." And truly, I did not. I was far out of my depth.

"My husband, Lord Harlow, was much older than you. I had forgotten how... passionate a young man can be." She lowered her eyes and smoothed her gown. "But you are right. We should return. The others will notice if we linger too long."

"I do not care if they notice, or indeed, what they think."

"You cared a moment ago. As well you should." Her face shuttered. "You are under your godfather's guardianship. Your behavior—indeed, even mine—must be above reproach, lest your actions reflect poorly on him."

"None of that signifies if we cannot be together." I caught her hands up in mine. "When can I be alone with you again? Tell me."

"I do not know, *m'sieu*. Perhaps never."

"No. Promise me I might see you again. Please. There must be some way."

"You must be patient, and perhaps an opportunity will present itself." She let go of my hands and retrieved something from her pocket then pressed it gently into my hand.

"Your handkerchief." I recognized the lace-trimmed square of cloth from that morning in the churchyard when I first met her. It was small, and soft, and snowy white.

"Keep it. It will remind you of me when we are parted."

I lifted my eyes to hers. "Thank you. I will treasure it always."

"What a silly, romantic boy you are," she said, even as her teasing smile removed any sting her words might have caused.

I tucked the lace-trimmed square away in my pocket and held out my arm with a sigh. "Let us return, then, if we must."

She cocked her head to one side. "You are young and eager to seize all that life has to offer. But you must have patience. It makes attaining whatever it is you seek all the more satisfying when at last you succeed in acquiring it."

"And will I?" I asked, my attention momentarily distracted by the temptation of her lips. "Acquire it?"

"That, *mon chérie*, remains to be seen." She laid her hand lightly on my outstretched arm and smiled up at me, her eyes full of promise, and together we returned to Pemberley.

"THERE IS to be a ball at Matlock House," my godfather informed me two days later as I entered his study. "We are all invited."

Immediately, my pulse quickened and my thoughts turned to Lady Harlow. I could only hope that she and the Fanshaws would be included in the invitation. "Lieutenant Fitzwilliam's family home? When is this ball to take place?"

"In three weeks' time." He beetled his brows together and studied the card in his hand. "It seems the earl's eldest son has got himself engaged."

"But that's excellent news," I said. "Tell me, sir, why so Friday-faced? Why are you not as excited as I to go to the ball?"

He sighed. "You young people, always so excited at the possibility of dancing! I once shared your enthusiasm, but I fear my dancing days are behind me." He paused. "I need to travel to London on a matter of business soon. I am not sure when I will return, or if I will be back in time for the ball."

"I am sorry to hear it."

"It cannot be helped." He laid the invitation aside and looked up from his desk as the nanny arrived with little Georgiana in tow, and a smile lit his face. "My darling girl," he said and held out his arms to his daughter. She ran forward and clambered onto his lap.

"She wanted you to read her a story before her bedtime, sir," the nanny said in apology. "She was *that* insistent. I hope you don't mind."

"Not at all, no indeed." He took the picture book she offered and settled the child in the crook of his arm. "Let us begin, then, shall we?"

"If I may speak first, sir," I said as he opened the book, "Darcy and I can go to the ball...though he dislikes amusement in general, surely, he can have no objection." At his hesitation, I paused. "Unless you prefer I remain at Pemberley."

"Of course, I have no objection. Kindly do not tell me what I mean to say." Mr. Darcy scowled. "At any rate," he muttered, "it is not *your* integrity I question."

"Whose then?" I asked, bewildered. "I do not understand."

"Let me read to Georgiana," he replied, "and then we shall talk."

I nodded and withdrew. Like the nanny, who stood quietly by the door, I waited, but I was not nearly so patient as she. I sat down by the fire and picked up a book, riffled restlessly through the pages, and attempted to concentrate on the words. What could Darcy's father mean?

Certainly, there could be no question of his son's integrity; the very idea was laughable.

Whose, then? If not myself, or Darcy, to whom did he refer?

At last he closed the book and caught the nanny's eye. "Off you go, my lamb," he said to Georgiana as he set her gently down and kissed the top of her head. "Sleep well."

"Good night, Papa," she said as the nursemaid took her hand.

"Good night, Georgiana," I called after her as I rose from my chair.

Their footsteps had scarcely faded when I turned to him. "What troubles you, sir? Ever since our guests left you have been distant and preoccupied."

"Running the estate requires much of my time," he said. "It is nothing to concern you."

"If there is anything I can do to help—"

"There is not."

"But what of the ball, sir?" I persisted. "I am sorry to press you, but what misgivings can you have? Whose integrity do you hold in such low regard, if not my own?"

"Leave it, George." His words were unaccountably sharp. After a moment, he sighed.

"Forgive me. I promised you an answer, and an answer you shall have." His words were measured and carefully chosen. "There is much of the world you do not understand. You have lived a sheltered life here at Pemberley, as your father wished. And it has been a good life, I hope."

"Yes. It has. And that is due in no small measure to your kindness and generosity."

"Nonsense. There is no need for gratitude. You are like a son to me, George. There is nothing I would not do for you. But you are young, and although you consider yourself a man fully grown, you are not. Not yet."

"I am young, yes," I conceded. "But I am no child."

"No." His voice tightened. "Yet at times you behave like a wild, unprincipled boy, casting caution to the wind, along with your good sense. I see it happening even now, and it fills me with disquiet."

"You speak of my attraction to Lady Harlow, I presume?"

"Your *attraction*, as you call it," he said testily, "is nothing but calf-love, a passing infatuation that all young men experience at one time or another."

"You are wrong, sir. My feelings for her are deep, and strong, and true."

"You barely know the woman."

"Nor do you!" Anger boiled over in me. "You have no right to cast aspersions on her."

Mr. Darcy pressed his lips together, and I knew at once that I had gone too far.

"Forgive me," I said and let out a short breath. "It is I who have no right to speak to you in such a manner. You, who have done so much for me. You have been my champion in all things. I apologize, sir. But you must understand that I care for her a great deal—"

"I will not argue the matter further, George. I can see you have already made up your mind about Lady Harlow and will listen to nothing I say. But I strongly suggest you think carefully before you make choices that you cannot take back."

He went to stand before the fire and clasped his hands behind his back. "Soon you'll embark on a new life in Cambridge, a life of your own. You shall meet new people and make your own decisions. I trust that the lessons you have learned, the examples your father and I have tried to set, will guide you through life's challenges, for I will be unable to do so for much longer."

My throat thickened. I had lost one father; I could not bear the thought of losing another. Nor did I wish to disappoint him. "I know you want only the best for me and for Darcy, sir, and I thank you for it. I will not let you down, I promise." I lifted a determined chin to his. "I am sorry for challenging you and questioning your guidance. I pray you will overlook it, just this once, and forgive me."

He reached out and clapped a hand upon my shoulder. "You are a good lad, George. Just endeavor not to let your passions overtake your good sense."

"Thank you, sir. I mean to do my best to make you proud."

"I have no doubt you will. Go, now. I will see you in the morning."

Warmed by his words, I left the study and crossed the entrance hall to the stairs.

"Have you a moment, George?"

I looked back as Darcy, dressed in riding attire, came in the front door and closed it behind him. "Of course."

He removed his hat and set it along with his riding crop on the hallway table and turned to me. His expression was forbidding. "Join me in the library, please."

I turned away from the stairs and followed him down the hall. I was in Darcy's black books, that was plain enough. Very well. I would face him and deal with whatever charges he brought and be done with it.

As I entered the library, he shut the doors behind us and turned to face me. "What are your intentions towards Lady Harlow? The truth."

Astonished, I stared at him. "Why do you ask me such a thing? What has Lady Harlow to do with me?"

"Nothing, I hope." Darcy's face was set in hard lines. "But I have heard things. Rumors."

"What rumors?" I demanded. "What *exactly* are people saying about her? Tell me!"

"I will not repeat idle gossip. Suffice it to say that she is older than you and far more adept in the ways of the world. I only warn you to have a care in your dealings with her."

"You misjudge her. She has done nothing to deserve your disfavor. Nothing! You have taken an irrational and prejudicial dislike to her because... because she is French," I said wildly.

"Do not be absurd." His words were dismissive.

"And there it is," I snapped. I stood and began to pace the confines of the room. "Your disdain for me, your dismissal of my opinions and feelings. You dictate every aspect of my life, Darcy, from what I wear, to whom I see, and I have borne it for all these years without a single complaint. Indeed, I am indebted to you and your father for all you have done for me and will never cease to be grateful. Eternally grateful. Resoundingly grateful."

"George—"

"But I will *not* be told who I may or may not associate with. First, you warn me away from my good friend John, and now, Lady Harlow. I refuse to be treated like a boy. Soon I will be at Cambridge, and my choices—my friends, my amusements, even the very books I read—will be my own. Not yours any longer. Mine."

Instead of the anger I expected following my outburst, Darcy said not a word. He rested one hand on the mantel and stared into the fire, much as his father had done moments earlier in his study. For the first time, I saw defeat etched on his face, and despite my small victory in our verbal skirmish, I felt shame at my behavior.

"Forgive me," I muttered after a moment and shifted on my feet. "I spoke out of turn."

"No. You have the right of it." He lifted his head. "You must learn to make your own decisions and your own mistakes once you are gone from

Pemberley. Until that time, however, I feel it my duty to caution you regarding Lady Harlow. That is my only intent. I know I do not often show it, George, but you… you are like a brother to me. And I do not"—he cleared his throat—"I do not wish to see you injured."

As quickly as my anger flared, it departed. Darcy meant no insult, nor did he mistrust me; he wished only to protect me.

I went to him and clasped his hand firmly in mine. "I thank you for your concern. I will exercise caution, I promise." I met his eyes and managed a small smile. "And I will guard my heart most assiduously."

But even as I said the words, my thoughts strayed to the upcoming ball at Matlock, and already I longed for the moment when I would be alone with Lady Harlow once again.

TORCHES LINED the drive as the Darcy carriage approached Matlock House. I leaned forward in anticipation. Every window in the house blazed with candlelight, and carriages crowded our approach.

I spied Mr. and Mrs. Fanshaw and their daughter, Miss Celia, alighting from their landau some way ahead of us, and watched as the postilion handed down a fourth occupant, a vision gowned in shimmering gold-threaded silk. She held a cashmere shawl draped low around her shoulders.

Lady Harlow.

Despite my best efforts, I had no success in speaking with her. The ballroom was crowded and the refreshment room as well, and Darcy kept a watchful eye on me. I waited and watched in a fever of impatience as she danced every dance. Evidently, her half-mourning had ended tonight. At last, halfway through the evening, I managed to slip away and sought her out to request a dance with her, and she accepted. As we took our places in the quadrille, I could scarcely keep the smile from my face.

Her Ladyship would partner me for two sets. Surely, I could manage a word or two with her during that time.

"I would speak with you in private," I said at the first opportunity.

She did not answer but smiled at me enigmatically. We parted and moved in step with the Lancers' Quadrille, a dance that required all of my attention and left little time for talk.

"After the dance," she promised when next we crossed paths.

When the second set ended, I sought Lady Harlow out before Darcy came to find me.

"May I fetch you a cup of negus?" I inquired and held out my arm.

"I would be most grateful." She unfurled her fan and waved it languidly before her face. "*Tiens!* This room is warm. Let us go outside to the terrace."

Once outside, glasses in hand, Lady Harlow turned to me. "We have not much time," she said in a low voice. "I leave for Paris in two days."

"Paris?" Shock froze my features. "But… I thought you meant to stay with the Fanshaws for the summer."

"My plans have changed." She paused. "*Mon cher,*" she added as she saw my dismay, "please listen. There is an inn at Beckford, a half days' journey from here. Do you know it?"

I nodded. "I think so. Yes."

"I will take a room there. Follow me in three days' time, and when you arrive, tell the innkeeper you wish to join your wife."

My head spun. "But Darcy will never allow me to go. Not to mention, we are not married, not in truth, and your husband—"

"Is dead. Do not be a child!" she snapped. More gently she added, "Do you trust me?"

"Yes. I do. Of course, I do!"

"Then you must trust me now, and do as I ask. No one at the inn will know, or care, that my husband is dead. And nor should you."

Her indifference towards the departed Lord Harlow shocked me, and I wondered for the first time if Darcy's father had the right of it. What did I truly know of this woman? "Perhaps not. But to deliberately lie…"

"If you have not the courage to risk it"—she pressed her lips together—"then you may remain under your guardian's watchful eye for the rest of the summer and languish in Derbyshire. Or you may join me in Beckford. The choice is yours."

Uncertainty warred with desire inside me. What Lady Harlow asked of me was wrong. To defy my godfather, to lie to him, to pretend to be someone I was not in order to bed her… such actions were beyond anything I had ever done.

The elder Mr. Darcy's words echoed in my head.

"*I strongly suggest you think carefully before you make choices that you cannot take back.*"

I convinced myself that I did not care. I wanted her. Oh, how I wanted her! Lord Harlow was dead, their marriage over. Nothing stopped the two of us from being together… only my foolish hesitation. Here was an opportunity I would never have again, and if I did not seize what Lady

Harlow offered, Darcy would have the right of it. I would prove myself to be, not a man, but merely a boy.

The thought of sharing Clémence Harlow's bed, even if only for one stolen night, decided me.

"Very well," I told her and set my glass down. "It will not be an easy undertaking, for my godfather will not allow me to travel on my own, unless…"

She drew closer. "Unless?"

"I had forgotten until this moment"—I could scarce keep the excitement from my voice—"my friend John Seldon leaves for Italy next week. I cannot imagine that even Mr. Darcy will object if I offer to accompany him as far as Beckford."

"Ah! There, you see?" she said and masked her pleasure behind a dainty sip of negus. "You are not only a handsome young man, but a clever one as well."

I longed to pull her into my arms and rain kisses upon her and profess my love for her publicly, the other guests be damned, but managed to resist the impulse. "I will count the minutes until we can be together."

"Ah… here comes your jailer now," she observed, and her lips curved upwards in amusement. "He is not happy with us, I think."

I turned to see Darcy, grim faced, approaching us. Where once I would have quailed before his evident displeasure, now I squared my shoulders. "I grow weary of his disapproval. I cannot seem to please him."

"He has high expectations because he cares for you." Her smile faded and a thoughtful expression settled upon her face. She touched my hand. "Pray, do not be angry with him. His intentions are well meant."

"Perhaps." I thrust my irritation aside and forced a smile. "Then let us be on our best behavior for the rest of the evening and give him no reason to find fault with either of us."

She nodded, and I held out my arm to her. With a smile of composure, she laid her hand upon my sleeve, and we met Darcy halfway across the terrace, where I proceeded to exert every ounce of my charm until I succeeded in smoothing his ruffled feathers.

My plan to deceive my godfather fell into place with greater ease than I dared to hope.

When I told him the squire's son had invited me to accompany him and see him off on his journey to Italy, he gave me his blessing, as well as a generous sum for my travels. Seldon was only too glad to share his hired coach with me and threw back his head and laughed when he learned of my scheme.

"I did not think you capable of such chicanery, Wickham," he declared as my case was lashed to the roof and we set off in the coach. "Escaping old Darcy's watchful eye for an assignation with a French ladybird … lud! I am all amazement."

"She is no ladybird," I said sharply as I settled myself across from him.

"She is hardly an angel," he pointed out his words mild but firm. "While her beauty cannot be disputed, your rendezvous with Lady Harlow is reckless at best and improper at worst. If your godfather should find out he will be furious with her. And even more so with you."

"He won't find out, unless you tell him. And I fear you misunderstand her, Seldon. She is lonely, nothing more, and in need of comfort."

"Comfort?" He snorted. "Fustian nonsense. Please don't tell me you've gone and fallen in love with her."

"I do love her." I crossed one Hessian boot over the other and regarded him steadily. "And I mean to marry her."

Seldon shook his head. "You cannot be serious. This is madness, Wickham. You barely know the woman!"

"I know enough. She is beautiful, and clever, and as enamored of me as I am of her." I thought of her handkerchief, tucked away even now in my pocket. "Rumors are flying that she seeks a husband. Why should it not be me?"

"Why? I can give you several reasons. Your pockets are to let, for one thing. You haven't a sixpence to scratch with. How will you support a wife?"

I did not have a ready answer. "I have expectation of an inheritance," I muttered after a moment. "Three thousand pounds."

"Three thousand pounds is but a trifle when it comes to supporting a wife and managing a household." He leaned forward. "George, listen to me. Please do not mistake my meaning. No one can deny your charm or your appeal to the young ladies…"

"But?"

"But Lady Harlow has been married and widowed once already. If and when she remarries, you can be sure it will be to someone older, a man of wealth and title."

Deep within me, although I was loath to admit it, I knew he was right. But my stubborn pride held sway and only hardened my resolve.

"Once I finish at Cambridge, if she will wait for me, I will have the curacy at Pemberley and a living to offer her. It will be a quiet life, I grant you. But we can live at the rectory quite comfortably."

"Do you honestly think life as a vicar's wife will appeal to a woman as worldly as Lady Harlow?" Seldon regarded me in mingled disbelief and pity. "Then you are deluded and even more far gone than I had previously supposed."

DARKNESS SETTLED itself like a cloak over the countryside as our coach arrived at the Beckford Inn that evening and rolled to a halt in the yard. As the ostlers hurried out to see to the horses, I climbed down the steps and onto the dirt-packed yard. My body was stiff from several hours of sitting.

"Welcome, young gents," the innkeeper called out from the doorway. "Who have we 'ere?"

"John Seldon," my traveling companion said and waited as his trunks were deposited alongside him. "I require a room for the night."

"And you?" he asked, peering into the murky light his lantern provided.

I took a deep breath. I felt like a charlatan, a trickster of the first order, and was sure he would see through my ruse straightaway. "I am Lord Harlow. I believe my wife has taken a room here already."

"So she has. Yes, indeed." If he thought it odd that an earl had travelled by hired coach and not a private carriage, he gave no sign. "A most gracious welcome to ye, m'lord." He bowed.

Beside me, John suppressed a snort of laughter.

"Come along, then," the innkeeper said. "Leave the lads to deal with your trunks and come inside. It's late, and I've naught but a cold collation to offer the pair of you. I hope you've no objection to taking your bread and cheese and ale in the public room. The private dining room's already taken."

We nodded our assent and followed him inside and made our way to the public room. It was rude but comfortable, with wooden beams overhead and whitewashed walls, and a fire burned in the hearth. At such a late hour, the place was all but deserted.

I settled myself at a table near the fire and, despite my weariness, felt my spirits lift. My adventure, so rashly undertaken, would soon lead to the fruition of all my hopes and dreams—not only to spend a night alone with Lady Harlow but to stand up to Darcy for the first time in my young and sheltered life.

He regarded me now as little more than a boy. But after tonight, I would prove myself to be a boy no longer but a man.

AFTER DINNER, I bid Seldon a good night and made my way up the stairs to Lady Harlow's room. I found it at the end of the hall. The hour was late, and I hesitated. What if she slept or had changed her mind? What if she refused to admit me? The thought of passing the night on Seldon's floor, or worse, on a bench in the public room, held no appeal.

I gripped my candlestick tighter and rapped twice upon the rough, wooden door. It opened after a moment, and she ushered me inside, shutting the door quickly behind me. "You came," she whispered. "I was not sure you would."

"Of course I did. How could I not?" She had loosened her hair, and beneath her thin, muslin nightgown, I glimpsed a tantalizing hint of her nakedness. "I have lied to be with you, my lady," I said as I pulled her into my arms with a rakish grin, "and risked my godfather's wrath to be with you. Convince me now that I have not made an error in judgment."

"I need no words to persuade you." She smiled as she reached for my jacket and pushed it from my shoulders. "I can show you far more easily."

In a matter of moments, she helped me out of my clothes and I divested her of the nightgown, and we fell naked onto the bed, its ropes creaking beneath us as I reached for her.

"There is no hurry," she chided and stayed my eager, roving hands. "We have all night."

The determination not to make a fool of myself proved stronger than my desire and embarrassment heated my face as I drew away. "Forgive me."

Her laugh was low and indulgent. "This is your first time, *non?*"

When I nodded, she leaned over and kissed me. "There is nothing to forgive. I can teach you all you need to know," she said. "But first, you must learn patience." Firelight shadowed her face.

I wasted no further time on talk but leaned over to kiss her and cupped her breasts reverently in my hands. They were small but perfect. I lowered my mouth to one pink, puckered tip and drew on it as she melted back against the pillows with a sigh, her fingers threaded through my hair.

"Do I please you?" I whispered, as I kissed her neck and the slope of her shoulder.

In answer, she sat up and pushed me back, running her fingers lightly over my chest and stomach. "*Oui*. Now, lie back," she whispered as she met my eyes. "You will like what I do, I promise."

I watched, spellbound, as she kissed her way slowly, delicately, down my body, and I groaned in shock and delight as her mouth, soft and sweet, wrapped around me. Her lips were warm and pliant.

"You… are a witch," I gasped, even as I tangled my fingers in her hair and spent into her mouth. I shuddered with spasms of pleasure for what felt like eternity but was surely only a few moments.

She said nothing, only smiled and crawled back up my body. We kissed again, and I tasted myself on her lips and felt her breasts pressing into my chest. She opened her mouth to me and I plunged my tongue inside.

"And now I wish to return the favor," I said when at last I dragged my mouth from hers.

I had no notion of what to do, but she offered no objection as I kissed my way down her body. I was determined, not only to learn, but to master the lesson. Instinct and desire took over as my mouth found the place between her legs and settled upon her. She let out a low, throaty moan. As my tongue explored, tentatively at first and then with greater boldness and abandon, she gasped and opened herself to me and shuddered a moment later in release. When her cries of abandon subsided, she wrapped her legs around me and urged me inside her. I needed no encouragement. I thrust into her with a ragged exhalation and closed my eyes. Such was my ecstasy that everything else fell away—the dying flames in the fire, the creak of the bed, Lady Harlow's cries, our shadows writhing together on the wall—and I felt only sensation, and heat, and the greatest pleasure a man can know.

"The student has surpassed the teacher," she said as I rolled away, and with a catlike smile, she nestled herself against me.

"You are satisfied, I hope?" I asked and stroked her hair, damp now from our exertions, away from her face.

"Never more so." Her lips brushed mine, and she sat up. "A glass of wine to celebrate?" She reached for a bottle and two tumblers on the bedside table.

I nodded and closed my eyes as I relished the moment. I was a boy no longer. The thought filled me with pride but also a brief and unaccountable twinge of regret. There was no possibility of turning back; I had well and truly left my boyish self behind.

She pressed a glass into my hand. "Drink. You acquitted yourself well."

"Well enough to go with you to Paris?" I asked as I took a sip of wine.

She paused. "Paris?"

"Yes. I want to go with you." I sat up, enthusiasm lending fervor to my words as I added, "I won't be dissuaded. I want to spend every day, every minute, with you."

"And every night, too?" She smiled indulgently and set her glass aside. "*La*! You will soon wear me out with your passion."

"But you shall sleep like an angel every night. I will see to it."

"You talk nonsense. Finish your wine, and we will talk more of this notion of yours later."

I did as she asked and tipped another swallow of wine down my throat. I made a face. "What swill is this? It tastes odd. Bitter."

"You can hardly expect to find a fine vintage in a place like this." Her words were sharp. She took the glass from my hand and said more gently, "It is late. Go to sleep."

"Only if you promise to lay beside me." I patted the mattress next to me. I felt suddenly tired, my eyes so heavy I could scarce keep them open as she slid in beside me and rested her head on my chest.

"Sleep," she whispered.

I smiled drowsily as she caressed my chest. "I love you, Clémence."

Her fingers stilled as I closed my eyes in pleasurable exhaustion and drifted towards sleep.

She did not reply.

A LOUD KNOCKING on the door thrust me awake. I sat up in confused alarm. It was barely light outside.

I groped for my breeches and pulled them on, my head muzzy and thick as I stumbled to the door and flung it open. "What the devil do you mean, waking us at this hour—"

I stopped and stared at the man standing before me. "Darcy," I croaked.

He brushed past me and strode inside the room. "Shut the door."

I did as he ordered and turned around to face him. "Why are you here? If you think to stop me from being with Clémence, you are already too late." I looked at the bed, and I saw to my shock that it was empty. I could not make sense of it. "Where...where is she? Where is Lady Harlow?"

"Well on her way to Calais by now, I should imagine."

"What?" My eyes widened and I ran to the window, pushing roughly past him. Ostlers scurried to and fro in the yard below and passengers waited to board a newly arrived post-chaise, but of my lover, there was no sign. "You are mistaken. She must have gone downstairs. I have to find her—"

"She is not here."

Darcy met my agitation with composure as I turned back to face him. "What do you mean? She cannot be gone! We were to leave together this morning to go to Paris. We had plans."

"It seems her plans have changed, and she has gone without you." He reached into his breast pocket and withdrew a letter. "She left you this."

He held out a note sealed with red wax and I snatched it from his hand. My mind reeled. "When? How do you come to have it? And how did you know to find me here?" I demanded.

"Lady Harlow sent word to me late yesterday afternoon. She wrote to inform me"—he stopped and added with impatience—"read the letter."

With trembling fingers, I broke the seal and opened the missive. I did my best to make sense of her elegant scrawl. *"I cannot allow you to make such a grave mistake... there is no future for us... I wish you well and will treasure your memory even as I grieve your loss..."*

I looked up from the note in deepening confusion. "I do not understand. Why would she do this? She has abandoned me! If what you say is true—that she sent word to you yesterday—then she must have known all along that we... that I..." I rounded on him. "It was your doing, wasn't it? You asked her to write this letter. You demanded she leave me behind."

"I did no such thing. I suspected you might wish to run off with her, which is why I spoke with her in private at the Fitzwilliam ball and convinced her to put her own selfishness aside in order to stop you from ruining your life. And for that I offer no apologies." He turned, his face set, towards the door. "Get dressed. I am taking you back to Pemberley."

"No," I erupted. "I cannot go back there. I will not!"

"I am not asking, George. We are leaving straightaway. Gather your belongings so we may put this unfortunate episode behind us and return home."

"Home? Pemberley is not my home." I flung the letter aside. "This changes nothing. I am going to Paris, where I can be with Clémence and live out my life, and you and Pemberley be damned." I reached for my shirt and yanked it on.

"And how do you propose to fund your travel?" Darcy regarded me coldly. "You have no money, nor any concept of the cost of your freedom. You think yourself a man now, because of… this." He swept his hand out to encompass the rumpled bed in a gesture of contempt. "You delude yourself. You are but a reckless, selfish boy who allowed a scheming French baggage to seduce him—"

Rage overcame me, and I hurled myself at Darcy and drew back my fist to strike him. Whether due to the after-effects of the questionable wine or my lack of sleep, I managed only a glancing blow to his jaw before he drove his fist into my face, and I staggered back as blood spurted from my nose.

Stunned, I sank onto the room's only chair and groped in my pockets for a handkerchief, the same handkerchief Clémence had given me, and pressed it to my injury. Blood soon soaked the white folds.

He moved to brush past me to the door. "Get your things. We are leaving."

"Why would she do this? Why did she betray me and throw our plans away?" I dropped the handkerchief and plowed my hands through my hair in bewildered agitation. "And why did she not at least wake me to say goodbye?"

Darcy made no reply but regarded the bottle and glasses on the bedside table without expression.

I went to the table and picked up the bottle, and as I studied it, I remembered the bitter taste on my tongue. "The wine. Of course. She dosed me with something, a tincture of laudanum, perhaps." I shook my head in disbelief. "She never meant for me to go to Paris with her."

"No. She lied to you from beginning to end. I know you cannot see it now, but she has done you a great favor by leaving you behind."

"And how much did this favor cost you?"

He paused. "Five hundred pounds."

I remembered her remark the night of the ball when Darcy came to fetch me away from her. *He has high expectations because he cares for you.* She knew even then that he would go to any lengths to spare my name and, more importantly, the Darcy name, from scandal.

I groaned and dropped my head into my hands. Was that all I was to her… a means to an end, a way to extract payment from Darcy? I could not bear the thought. Worse still, I could not bear the pity I saw in his eyes.

"I will pay you back," I said dully as I lifted my head. "Every penny."

"You owe me nothing. You may pay me back by returning home with me."

I offered no further argument but stood to gather my things—my boots, jacket, and cravat—and reached for my case. "Tell me one thing before we go. Why did Lady Harlow leave Pemberley so abruptly? Did you send her away?"

"Yes."

"Why?"

"It does not matter. My reasons were sound, and that is all you need to know."

"I know you, Darcy, better than anyone. You would never send her away unless she did something grievous, something so beyond the pale..." All at once I remembered waking in the middle of the night to the sound of angry, hushed voices down the hall. I stared at him. "She went to your room?"

He did not answer. He did not need to.

"She promised to come to me that night." I began to pace the room like a caged animal. "But she claimed the brandy made her tired and said she fell asleep instead. And all the while she was with you."

"No." He spoke with unaccustomed anger. "I sent her away from my door and told her to be gone by the time I returned later the next morning."

"And you expect me to believe you?" But I did believe him. Darcy, with his unassailable morals and high regard for propriety, would never have taken Clémence to his bed as I had done.

"Believe me or not, as you wish. It is the truth." He reached out and caught me by the arm. "Listen to me, George. She meant to seduce me, and when that failed, she hoped to compromise me into marriage. And had anyone seen her outside my room, her plan might have succeeded."

"I woke in the middle of the night and heard voices, and I thought I was dreaming. I never imagined..."

All along, her object had been Darcy.

"She is in urgent need of funds." He regarded me with a frown. "Lord Harlow left Clémence a jointure upon his death. Evidently, it was not generous enough to keep her in the style she felt she deserved."

"So, she sought to snare you." I sank down upon the bed. "And when that failed, she turned her wiles on me. But why? She knew I could offer her little. No money, no title. Was I only an amusement to her? A passing entertainment?" I cradled my head in my hands. "My god! I cannot believe how stupid I have been." My throat thickened and closed but I would not show my vulnerability to Darcy.

He reached out to lay his hand on my shoulder. Angrily, I shook it off.

"I take no pleasure in any of this, George. I regret you had to learn such a lesson and in such a fashion. I assure you, in time your pain will ease, and you will forget her."

"Let us quit this place," I said shortly as I pushed myself to my feet. "I have no wish to speak of this—or of her—ever again."

Darcy nodded his understanding and opened the door, and I preceded him out of the room without once looking back. I was done with this room. I was done with Lady Harlow.

And I left her bloodied handkerchief lying on the floor.

SALAMANCA, SPAIN, 22 JULY 1812

"Over here!"

The shout rings out over the battlefield. Bodies lie strewn all around me, and musket smoke lingers in the air, along with the stench of death. I am barely conscious as someone kneels beside me. The sun is behind him and so his face is in shadow, but something about his voice is familiar. I struggle to sit up.

"Rest easy." The man stays me with a gentle hand. "You're lucky to be alive."

I make no reply. I cannot. My mouth is dry, my lips cracked. But I know, from the sight of the dead and dying men littering the field around me, that he speaks the truth. I *am* lucky to be among the living. Even now I hear the cries for water, the calls to God, the moans of the dying.

Two men lift me onto a stretcher, and I break into a sweat. The pain is excruciating.

"Take him to the nearest hospital wagon," the man who found me tells them. "He needs a surgeon."

"We thought 'e was dead," one of the soldiers holding my litter says and shrugs. "Hard to tell, sometimes."

"Never mind your excuses," the first man says sharply. "Move."

"Wait," I croak. I reach out to grasp his sleeve before I am carried away. "Who… who are you?"

"Sergeant Major James Beresford." He pauses. "Do you not remember? You saved my life when you ran that pair of Frenchmen through with your saber. Your act of bravery has not gone unnoticed. Wellington himself is impressed with your courage and fearlessness on the battlefield. Now I mean to return the favor."

Before I can find words to thank him, the soldiers carry me forward, and Beresford turns away.

AND SO, I find myself now, recovering comfortably in a hospital bed. My shoulder is bandaged and my chest wound is healing, and while I will never have full use of my arm, it does not matter. I am alive, and that is enough. By the grace of Providence, I have been given a second chance.

I reach for my writing desk and set it upon my lap as I recall the events of my night with Lady Harlow. The pain of her memory has lessened, but despite Darcy's assurances that I would forget her in time, I have not.

Still, he was right in one thing. She did me a great favor by leaving me behind.

Sharing a bed with Lady Clémence Harlow did not make a man of me. It served only to underscore the depth of my stupidity and inexperience and displayed my vanity in believing the lies Clémence showered upon me. It took the horrors of the battlefield, the prospect of dying, and news of the birth of our child to make me realize the tenuousness of life, and the waste I have made of my own.

With little to do while in hospital but reflect on my past, I feel a renewed sense of shame. I have not acquitted myself well in any measure.

After Lady Harlow's betrayal, Darcy and I returned to Pemberley and maintained a wary truce for the remainder of the summer. In the autumn, I began my studies at Cambridge, and it was there my bitterness and anger—with Lady Harlow, with Darcy, and most of all, with myself—turned me into a charming rogue, a scoundrel with no more concern for the young women I seduced and bedded than that which Clémence had shown for me.

But I kept my promise, and while I did not excel in my studies, I finished at King's College as I had told Darcy I would. My godfather died that same year, and I requested my inheritance of three thousand pounds the moment I returned, ostensibly to study law, and he gave it over to me without argument. I am sure he knew I was lying; I suspect also that he was as anxious to see me leave as I was to be gone.

All too soon the money was spent—squandered on women, drink, and cards. I then attempted and failed to lure young Georgiana Darcy into eloping as I had need of her dowry of thirty thousand pounds. After joining the militia as an officer with Colonel Forster's regiment, I set my sights on Lydia Bennet. I seduced her easily enough, and when Darcy found us, I agreed to wed her in exchange for his promise to settle my bills and purchase me a commission in the Regulars.

As I prepare to write the first of several letters, I sigh. I have numerous wrongs to redress. Some will forgive me; some will not. I can expect nothing more. Nevertheless, I will express my most sincere and heartfelt apologies to everyone I have wronged... Darcy, most of all.

But a mere letter will not serve to say the things I need to tell him. My apology to Darcy must be done in person. After I am discharged, I will go at once to Pemberley and make my peace with him, and only then I will return home to Lydia and our child.

Soon, I will hold my daughter. I am a father. My throat thickens and emotion overcomes me, and as I withdraw a sheet of paper, I remember the epitaph I imagined while I lay delirious on the battlefield.

Here lies George Wickham, liar, cheat, and profligate womanizer, a reprobate who failed to distinguish himself on the battlefield or in life... but who wore his uniform exceedingly well.

That George Wickham is well and truly dead. And no one, myself least of all, will lament his passing.

It remains only to prove myself a better man to the friends and family I have left behind, and I know it will not be an easy task. But I am bound to try.

I dip my pen into the inkwell and hold it poised over the page.

"My dearest Lydia," I begin, "I hope this letter finds you and the baby well. I am the happiest of men to learn that I am now become a father and wait with the utmost impatience until I may return home once again to you both..."

KATIE OLIVER is the author of nine novels, including the Amazon bestseller *Prada and Prejudice,* as well as the Dating Mr. Darcy, Marrying Mr. Darcy, and Jane Austen Factor series. She resides in South Florida with her husband (where she goes to the beach far less often than she'd like) and is working on a new series. Katie began writing as a child and has a box crammed with half-finished stories to prove it. After raising two sons, she decided to get serious and get published.

SHE IS CONVINCED that there is no greater pleasure than reading a Jane Austen novel.

COLONEL FITZWILLIAM

Little was sketched about Mr. Darcy's gallant and blithe cousin in *Pride and Prejudice* (not even his forename) excepting that he was the younger son of an earl and he shared the guardianship of his cousin, Georgiana, with her brother, Darcy. Colonel Fitzwilliam seemed to fancy Miss Elizabeth Bennet but as a younger son, he reminded her he must marry for money. *"Our habits of expense make us too dependent, and there are not so many in my rank of life who can afford to marry without some attention to money." —Pride and Prejudice,* **Chapter XXXIII.**

"*...I may suffer from want of money. Younger sons cannot marry where they like.*" —Colonel Fitzwilliam to Elizabeth Bennet, *Pride & Prejudice*, Chapter XXXIII.

FITZWILLIAM'S FOLLY
Beau North

Fitzwilliam leaned into the saddle, urging his mount on faster, faster. Dust and dirt kicked up in clouds under the horse's hooves as they thundered recklessly across the field. The cold air whipped at his face and ungloved hands, but he barely felt them. The carriage was in sight. He could not afford to be careful; propriety be damned. There was no *time*.

"Hold on," he said through gritted teeth, the words lost in the sound of his pursuit. "I'm coming for you, you right bastard."

SIX MONTHS EARLIER

THE CARRIAGE JOSTLED AND bumped along the road that would finally take them back to London. Colonel Fitzwilliam could not recall a visit to Hunsford that had gone on so interminably long nor one that had given him so much fodder for thought. He stole a glance at his traveling companion who sat in silent misery across from him. The colonel had his suspicions as to the cause of his cousin Darcy's distress, but as they had only set out and were facing a long ride together, thought it best not to press the matter just yet. As the carriage drove past the Hunsford parsonage, Fitzwilliam observed Darcy's sudden attention, his eyes narrowed in concentration. They passed the trim, little house, with its path and well-tended gardens, a place where they had passed a handful of cheerful afternoons in the company of fine, good-natured ladies and Mr. Collins, the curate. Only when the house was out of sight did Darcy slump back against the squabs, closing his eyes, and shutting out the bucolic scene.

"I must say, it was fortuitous to have such lively company visiting the parsonage for this year's visit to Rosings."

Stony silence was Darcy's reply. Fitzwilliam forged ahead.

"One might call it almost providential." In response, Darcy's color rose in an angry flush, but still he did not speak.

"Darcy, are you unwell?" Fitzwilliam asked again, concerned. He had asked the question only that morning when he had seen his cousin come in from a rather early walk, his face haggard and expression pained. He had, of course, noticed his cousin's preference for Miss Elizabeth Bennet and thought the two a good match, if only Darcy could muster the courage to actually *speak* to the lady. He had felt a great surge of hope that Darcy might not be quite so far gone into *haute ton* snobbery as to see what a superior woman Miss Elizabeth Bennet was. Now all he felt was astonishment, for surely the lady had rejected Darcy's suit. He could not think of one woman in a hundred who would turn away such an eligible match as his cousin.

"I am well enough, Fitzwilliam, if only you would cease your attempts at mothering me."

Despite his surprise at such rough speech, Fitzwilliam felt a smile tug his lips. He had seen the look of love enough times to know and, not for the first time, said a silent prayer that he had never been felled by it himself.

"I apologize," Darcy grumbled a moment later, sitting up to look at his cousin. "I did not sleep last night, not even a quarter hour. My exhaustion has made me abrupt."

Fitzwilliam dismissed his apology with a careless wave. "Do not trouble yourself, Darcy. I am used to far more changeable moods than yours." He paused, searching his mind for a diplomatic phrasing. "Should you wish to talk of it—"

"I do not," Darcy said, his tone blunt.

"You need not feel embarrassed," Fitzwilliam assured him with a smile. "You are not the first man I have seen laid low by love."

"Fitzwilliam, I pray that one day you have the misfortune to know love so that I might have my turn in laughing."

The colonel *did* laugh at that. "Save your prayers for more likely outcomes, Darcy. I shall continue to adore many but love none."

Darcy made a sound of discontentment, closing his eyes once more. He muttered, "We shall see," before falling into an uneasy slumber.

FITZWILLIAM STEPPED out onto the balcony, savoring the cool air after the close ballroom. Lady Snowley's ball had never been so well-attended as it was this season. He had come in the hope that he might see Darcy there, resembling something of his old self again. The last time Fitzwilliam had been in his cousin's presence, the poor man had looked a wretch, red-eyed and unshaven, with the ghost of the previous night's brandy still clinging to him. Poor, foolish Darcy. What he needed was a discreet visit to the right sort of lady. *Come to think of it, I could do with a visit myself.*

INDEED, there were such a number of fair creatures inside he felt nearly giddy from having his head turned all evening and was convinced he was half in love with most of them already. The thought made him cheerful, and he began to whistle a happy tune as he gazed up at the twinkling stars.

"That is a very annoying habit," a voice said from behind him.

Fitzwilliam spun around to see a pair of wide, doe eyes of indistinct color with a fringe of straight, dark lashes, pale ivory skin, and a full, pink mouth.

"Madam, pray forgive me," he stammered, taking in the newcomer. She was tall, nearly as tall as himself, with a cap of dark hair that shone in the moonlight.

"I apologize for startling you," she said in a flat, strange accent.

"Madam, you are without chaperone," he said. "Allow me to escort you back to the party."

"Just a moment, if you please. I could not think of another way to approach you."

A warning sounded in his mind. This girl might mean to trap him; it had been attempted before with other, far more cunning women.

"Approach *me?* I am certain we are unacquainted. I would surely remember *you.*" He did not say so gently, censure coloring his words.

She smiled crookedly and dropped a curtsey. "I am Calliope Campbell. We have not met, but I am certain you have heard of me. As I have heard of you."

Fitzwilliam *had* heard of the Campbell sisters: daughters of a wealthy, American merchant who had been quietly buying up storehouses on the waterfront. Campbell acquired his vast fortune in shipping, though there were whispers that he had become rather cozy with some of the more infamous, shoot-and-loot travelers of the high seas. Campbell had no sons, a dead wife, and three daughters—Calliope, Clio, and Thalia—each endowed with enormous dowries. There had been a great deal of fuss and expectation in the *ton* that these American sisters would be a great scandal in society. Instead, they were proper young women whose manners, while not being especially fashionable, left nothing wanting. In an entirely too predictable twist, London society despised them anyway, disappointed by their mediocrity.

Fitzwilliam could not count how many times he had heard some of the more impoverished nobles jesting about marrying a Campbell sister to improve their fortunes, only for the so-called Quality to erupt into laughter. He thought it rather cruel, for it was commonly known that their father was a vulgar man, and as Americans, they already had enough set against them. He suspected that all three Campbell sisters would be rather wealthy spinsters in due time. He thought it a shame, for the woman so brazenly introducing herself was a rather fine specimen of a female, with her large eyes, slender neck, and exceptional figure. His eyes strayed, briefly, to the neckline of her gown, thanking the heavens that she wore no fichu. He swallowed and shook his head, attempting to quell an unexpected pang of desire.

"Miss Campbell," he said her name more formally than was his wont, "we have not been introduced. How is it you know me?"

She moved, nervously shifting her weight from one foot to another. Her white gown appeared silver in the moonlight, giving her the look of another world. Her hesitation gave him a chance to resume his study of the far-too pleasing neckline of her gown. His palms became dewy with sweat.

"You are Colonel Fitzwilliam, are you not?"

He bowed slightly out of habit, feeling foolish as he did. Had she noticed the direction of his gaze? "I am."

She sighed, a sound of relief. "Very good. I've come to you because I need your help rather desperately."

"What might *I* do? I am not agreeing to help you in any way, Miss Campbell, but I would like to know why you would risk your reputation to follow me."

"But you see, Colonel, my reputation is just what I need your help with."

A queer feeling washed through his stomach. He did not like the direction of this conversation.

"The truth is, sir...I require a rake. And only the best will do."

HE FUMED SILENTLY as the carriage made its circuitous route to Grosvenor Square. His mind spun in tight circles, thinking over the conversation that had taken place earlier that night. He needed Darcy's council. Gods above, he was actually *considering* her proposition!

I require a rake, and only the best will do. He nearly fainted at the words. What the deuce was she playing at?

"Madam, I am sure I do not know what you mean. I am certain *you* do not know what you mean either." He was deeply offended, not for her bold approach—it simply was not *done*. Ladies were not supposed to know the inner lives of men, the dark and carnal secrets they kept. It seemed, to Fitzwilliam, like the crudest sort of trespass.

"Please explain yourself," he said coldly.

"Do you know Brigadier General Harrington?"

He did and more was the pity. Harrington (known quietly by the men as Bloody Benedict) was a short, slight man who was pale of complexion and had fine, feminine features. He always had the appearance of ill health, but Fitzwilliam knew that appearances could be quite deceptive. Harrington was quick as a snake, and deadly with a blade, and had a mind that worked like lightning. Harrington was a strategist of the first order.

"What of him?"

"He has approached my father…about courting me."

Fitzwilliam held back a shudder. He would not wish to be a dog in Harrington's house, much less a wife. "My felicitations."

"I will *not* be tied to Harrington. Nor any man who would treat me as his property."

"Bold words for one so young."

"I am old enough to know my own mind," she said fiercely. He felt a warmth, a kindling of admiration for her. She seemed to have a bit of the soldier's spirit in her.

"What have I to do with it?"

"It is very simple. I wish you to seduce me."

Fitzwilliam felt a sharp stab of desire at her words and a cold shiver of something else, something far more troubling—he could not put words to it. He thought perhaps it might be shame.

"Not *truly*, you understand," she continued. "I only wish you to pay court enough to set Harrington off his course. You and I will know that you do not mean it, but he will not."

Fitzwilliam took a deliberate step closer to her. She held her ground, so he took another. Still, she remained unmoved. He reached out, tracing a line from her temple to her jaw in the lightest of touches.

"And why do you think I would ever go along with such a scheme?" he said softly, dangerously.

"Because I will make you rich."

He dropped his hand as though he had been scalded. "Will you indeed?"

"I know more about you than your propensity for visiting widows. You are a second son with no fortune of your own. If I am unmarried when I reach my majority, I shall receive some twenty thousand pounds. Help me keep my freedom, and I shall give you a piece of that...say, five thousand pounds?"

His mouth fell open in wordless surprise.

"Very well, I shall give you eight but not a shilling more. Is that acceptable?"

Fitzwilliam reeled. *Eight thousand pounds!* It was not Darcy's fortune, to be sure, but it would be enough that he might purchase a small estate, perhaps begin earning his own income. It would be...*freedom*, she said. It was fitting. He was not mercenary. There had been several opportunities for him to marry well, but he had not wished to tie himself to a woman for life for the sake of fortune alone. And here was this outrageous girl offering his freedom, without the shackles of marriage. It was too good to be true. Perhaps that was why it made him feel so unseemly. So *cheap*.

"You realize that when Harrington is chased off and I do not marry you, your reputation may not survive? For you can be certain of one thing, Miss Campbell. I will not marry you."

She shook her head. "My reputation will be enough to ensure my spinsterhood, which suits me very well."

"And what would you have me do? Ravish you in the middle of dinner?"

She recoiled as if he had struck her. He half-disbelieved it himself, that he could say something so coarse to a young woman while twenty feet away half the nobility in England danced and sipped lemonade. Her color rose, even in the moonlight he could see the pink wash across her cheeks. He thought her eyes might be green, or perhaps blue. It was difficult to tell in this light.

"I was thinking you might ask me to dance at balls. Ask to open, ask for the supper set. Escort me about Town, a drive down Rotten Row, things like that. Nothing vulgar."

"You understand that it is vulgar that you would even *ask* this of me?" he asked coldly.

She dipped her head for a moment before tilting her chin up, eyes flashing. "I had heard too that you were a man of honor."

"Which would you have me be?" He seethed. "The rake or the gentleman? A man cannot be both."

"Very well, I will have the rake. Do you accept my proposal?"

He stalked over to the doors that would lead him inside, back to the party, but not before stopping close to her, close enough that when he spoke, the force of his words made a loose curl at her neck bob and sway. He watched as gooseflesh raced across her skin, again feeling that curious mix of desire and shame. She looked up at him with her shining eyes. *Green.* He decided their color must be green.

"I do *not* accept. Farewell, Miss Campbell."

Too late, Fitzwilliam only realized his error when he was admitted into Darcy's study.

"My god, Cousin, you look terrible!"

Darcy looked up from the ledger on his desk, bleary-eyed and unshaven. Fitzwilliam knew that Darcy had *not* been studying accounts, as the ledger was currently situated upside-down.

"What do *you* want?" Darcy asked. "I am busy."

"Yes, I can see that you are," Fitzwilliam said, smirking. "Georgiana told me I could come up. Poor child nearly begged me, and now I see why. This will never do, Darcy, not for you."

"Oh, surely not," Darcy said with heavy sarcasm. He opened his desk and produced a bottle of brandy, which he drank from, offering none to his cousin. Fitzwilliam sighed and threw himself into a seat.

"Still wretched, old man?"

"As you see. Have you just come to laugh at me, then?"

Fitzwilliam shook his head. "Why do you always assume that I am laughing at you? It distresses me to see you so unhappy. You must allow me to care, Darcy."

Darcy sighed with his whole body, shoulders rising up and slumping down dramatically. "I *am* out of sorts."

While Fitzwilliam *was* amused in some small part by Darcy's antics, he did feel a great deal of pity for him, for the man was clearly in pain and suffering. Fitzwilliam's own brother was ten years his senior, as Darcy was to Georgiana. He and Darcy had always been more like brothers than cousins, and he was glad that connection had not diminished with age.

So, when he said, "I am sorry to see you thus," it was with all warmth, affection, and sincerity. Darcy looked at him, somewhat calmer and more resolute than he had been a moment ago.

"It is I who am sorry, Fitz. What might I do for you this evening?"

He found that now that he was there, he could not bring himself to speak of Miss Campbell and their exchange on the balcony at Lady Snowley's ball. He could not make himself say the words that made him sound no better than a common tart. He did have a reputation; Miss Campbell had been quite right in that regard. He had never felt ashamed of it, until this night, until this very moment, looking into the face of his cousin, who was suffering mightily over a woman. *Women!* The word had never been considered a curse by him, not even silently, until this moment.

He shook his head. "'Tis nothing. I happened to be passing this way and wanted to see if you were still in high dudgeon."

Darcy stood up and fetched two glasses from the sideboard. He brought them back to his desk where he poured them each a portion.

"I am afraid my dudgeon is rather low these days," Darcy muttered, handing Fitzwilliam his drink. "As is the rest of me."

"I have just come back from Lady Snowley's ball," he said lightly.

Darcy scoffed. "Lady Snowley's ball is the dullest affair of the season. I am not sorry to have missed it."

"Actually, I thought it rather interesting this year." He considered for a moment before forging ahead. He would not reveal more than he ought, but Darcy's opinion and judgement counted a great deal in Fitzwilliams eyes. Or, it did when Darcy was not acting a proper ass.

"That American was there. The Campbell girl." He supposed the younger two had been there as well, though he had not seen them. Calliope was the eldest; Fitzwilliam would have guessed her to be one and twenty.

"Oh lord, how dreary." Darcy grinned into his glass of brandy. "Did anyone dance with her?"

He opened his mouth to speak but Darcy's chuckle cut him off. "Of course, no one danced with her. Probably spent the whole evening with the other wallflowers. This town is going to eat those girls alive, poor dears."

Fitzwilliam felt an indignant sort of irritation on the girl's behalf. She had not seemed a shrinking wallflower to him, as she faced him down. *I wish you to seduce me.* Dangerous words to mutter to a man such as him. Even now, as furious as he still was over the scheme, he wished to rise to the challenge she laid at his feet. For the sport of it.

"Perhaps I shall marry her," he said out loud. "She has a pretty bosom and an even prettier dowry."

"If it were a pretty dowry you were after, you would have married Caroline Bingley by now. She has the added inducement of at least being English."

"No bosoms though," Fitzwilliam said with a grin. Darcy's countenance sagged.

"No, Cousin. You think I do not see it but I do. You would not marry for money, or you would have by now. You are the worst sort of romantic…you wish to marry for love." Darcy pushed his empty glass aside, to the very edge of his desk. "We have never been so very different, you and I. Not in essentials." Darcy shook his head, pointed at the glass. "This is me, or rather you. You know what you are. You have a purpose. And then comes this." Darcy wiggled a finger in the air. "This. This is love."

He brought the finger down, touching it to the rim, trailing down the curve of the vessel. "At first, love is a touch. A caress. But soon enough…" He tipped the glass with one finger until it slid off the edge. Fitzwilliam watched it fall, saw the moment it met the floor, the moment it changed from one thing to another. Scattered. Less than it had been. Broken.

Fitzwilliam cleared his throat, looking at his cousin's expectant face. "Darcy, that is a ridiculous demonstration. And now you have broken a glass."

Darcy looked crestfallen, for a moment, before both men erupted into laughter. A fresh glass was procured easily enough, and by the time one of Darcy's footmen piled him into a carriage, he had forgotten all about the ball, marriage, and Calliope Campbell.

FITZWILLIAM WOKE the following morning with a pain in his head and a curse on his lips. Without opening his eyes, he knew he had been delivered to his family's house and not returned to the barracks after drinking far too much of Darcy's excellent brandy. The shuffle of servants in the corridors and the smell of fresh flowers told him as much. He rolled over, his arm slung across his eyes as a groan escaped him. He had slept fitfully, not the leaden sleep of intoxication, but a sleep plagued with dreams. Lurid, unsettling dreams.

He roused himself and rang for a servant, his head exploding like cannon fire as he gave his instructions. Coffee, not tea, the hottest and strongest to be had. A headache powder and plenty of hot water for washing. He fancied he could smell the spirits seeping out of his skin. Once refreshed and feeling somewhat less dreadful, he made his way down to breakfast.

"Hello, darling." His mother, Lady Matlock, greeted him in her usual way, with a pat on the cheek.

"Morning, Mater," he said, taking her hand and placing a kiss on her knuckles. He looked at the breakfast spread out on the sideboard and turned away, stomach clenching.

"Will you not eat?" Fitzwilliam groaned, shook his head as much as he dared, and helped himself to a cup of coffee.

"It must have been quite an evening," she said with a knowing smile. "I am glad Darcy had the good sense to send you here in his carriage."

Fitzwilliam scoffed. "*Darcy* was laid 'cross his desk, sleeping like a babe when I left. Darcy's *butler* had the good sense to send me here."

Lady Matlock chuckled and shook her head. "You boys always did have a bit of the devil in you when you were together."

"A bit too much of a very particular devil last night, I should say." Fitzwilliam looked up from his coffee. "Where is the earl this morning?"

He was not so stupid from drink that he missed the sudden tightness around his mother's eyes, the downturn of her lips.

"Your father set out to see your brother at first light."

Fitzwilliam sighed heavily. His elder brother and heir to the earldom had always been a lazy, self-indulgent man, but since his marriage his bad habits had only grown in extravagance and frequency. He had made a splendid match in Lady Isobel Weston, daughter of the Marquess of Huntley and society darling, but her beauty and popularity was only exceeded by her love of finery and talent for entertaining. Together they made a costly pair. Fitzwilliam worried that, left to his own devices, his brother would bankrupt the earldom. And then, what of the tenants of their Matlock estate? Or the people under their employ, both in the North and in London?

"What was it this time?"

Her lips compressed together, turning white. "I believe it was the horses."

"Buying or betting?"

"Both." The countess sighed.

He cursed his brother silently. Unbidden, a voice whispered in his ear, a low, feminine voice ripe with promise. *Because I will make you rich.* The thought lingered like smoke, tempting him more than anything ever had before. He could do much with half such a sum. Would it really be mercenary of him to simply comply with the lady's request?

"Enough unpleasantness," he said, smiling at his mother. "I am at your disposal today, my lady. How shall we entertain ourselves?"

THE DRESS WAS DIFFERENT, a pale pink with an abundance of lace covering her *décolletage*. Fitzwilliam found himself longing for the daring frock she had worn to Lady Snowley's ball. Now, in the well-lit theater, he could see that her hair was somehow deep brown and shining red at the same time, like the finest mahogany. He assumed an air of nonchalance as he made his way towards her party, up until the moment he "accidentally" bumped his shoulder against hers.

"Oh, Miss Campbell! My sincerest apologies, I did not notice you there!" *What a bold lie.* As if he had been able to look at anyone, anything else all evening. She looked at him, her eyes wide with feigned innocence. *Green, the exact shade of a summer leaf.* She dropped a quick curtsey, her ducked head not quite hiding a small smile curving her lips.

"Colonel Fitzwilliam, do not apologize. It is true I do not stand out any more than the furniture. Yours was an understandable error."

Fitzwilliam wanted to laugh. Surely, she did not actually *think* that? He gave her his most winning smile. The ladies standing with her, one older and one younger, tittered, making Calliope blush.

"Would you introduce me to your friends, Miss Campbell?"

The younger woman was Calliope's sister, Miss Clio Campbell. She had a blandly, pleasant face but neither the spark or excellent figure of her elder sister. The older woman was introduced as Lady Morgan, widow of Admiral Sir Rollo Morgan. Fitzwilliam recalled the name and knew that Sir Rollo died in the Trafalgar Action. Lady Morgan had only just come out of a long period of mourning to sponsor the Campbell girls' entry into society.

"Lady Morgan is our aunt," Calliope explained, "sister to our mother."

Fitzwilliam felt a slight relief. She was *half* English, so she could not be all bad.

"My cousin Darcy has generously given me use of his box tonight, as he is unfortunately unable to attend. It would be my honor to have you join me."

Calliope looked as though she did not quite believe him. She looked to her sister and aunt.

"We should be delighted, Colonel," Lady Morgan answered. Fitzwilliam offered her his arm, which she declined. "Perhaps you might escort my niece," she said with a knowing smile.

Snared already! It has already begun before I even agreed to the scheme. He offered Calliope his arm; she paused for a moment before taking it, not meeting his eyes. Her hand was a warm weight; he fancied he could feel it through his jacket and shirt, right down to the skin. He was a man of simple pleasures, and in that moment, he wished for nothing more than the sensation of her bare hand.

"Have you reconsidered?" she asked, her voice barely above a whisper.

"I am still considering. I would like to speak to you privately on the matter," he answered, keeping his voice low.

"Tomorrow. I walk in Hyde Park most mornings before breakfast. You can meet me at the entrance nearest our house, on Pelham Row."

He knew the place. It was a stone's throw from his family's home. The thought of her slumbering so near was itself a far too intriguing thought. He was suddenly too aware of her presence—her soft, jasmine scent tickling his senses. Once they were seated in Darcy's box and the lights dimmed, Fitzwilliam wondered if this scheme had been a terrible folly on his part. There, in the dark enclosure, she seemed so unbearably close and still so untouchably distant. He felt a surge of ire. She was no more beautiful than any other girl in the *ton*; aside from having an excellent bosom and a pair of remarkable eyes, he could see nothing special in her at all.

Yet, again and again, his eyes turned to her, drinking in the pale line of her neck, the fullness of her lips as they curved into a smile, the tempting bit of bare skin between the top of her glove and the sleeve of her gown. *Calliope, queen of the muses.* Watching her in the dark, Fitzwilliam found himself remembering the cheeky verses of Donne he had gleaned in school:

> *By this these angels from an evil sprite,*
> *Those set our hairs, but these our flesh upright.*
> *License my roving hands, and let them go*
> *Before, behind, between, above, below.*

He wondered if it had been just such a woman as Miss Campbell who had inspired the randy poet—Miss Campbell, who was far too distracting, far too clever to be so unassuming. *And brave,* he silently amended. *The courage it must have taken for her to even approach me!* He turned his eyes back to the stage, feeling a scowl pull at his face. His admiration was far less reluctant that he liked.

Fitzwilliam awoke before dawn, though that was more out of habit than any particular urgency to get to his morning appointment. Or so, at least, he told himself. He dressed quickly and made his way outside, deciding he would wait for her near the park. Outside, the air was cool and foggy, and the morning chill clung damply to him. He did not mind; the early quiet was worth enduring a bit of cold.

He cut across and walked Pelham Row, wondering which home was hers, before making his way to the park entrance. He did not have to wait long. He begrudgingly admired her confident stride, the way she walked with her head up and her shoulders back, unbothered by the chilly air. She was there, walking towards him, but her eyes were somewhere else. Back in America? He stepped out to greet her. His light tread did not betray his presence, so he spoke up, startling her.

"Miss Campbell, is it?" He bowed, hiding a smile at her feminine gasp.

"Colonel Fitzwilliam! You gave me quite a fright!" She curtseyed quickly, almost as an afterthought.

He offered her his arm; she took it with a wry smile. They walked in silence for a few moments, looking at everything but each other. Fitzwilliam could not fathom why he felt so strangely nervous in her presence. He wanted to be bigger, smarter, richer than he was. As yet, the only thing that seemed to have impressed her were the rumours of his male prowess. He wanted to be *more.*

"Before I agree to do this for you, and I have not said that I would, mind you, I need to know that you are sure about this course you are taking. You could always refuse the brigadier general's suit."

"I have tried, believe me, Colonel. My father rejects my refusal. General Harrington wishes to use my dowry to climb, you see. And my father wants nothing more than for me to be *Lady* Harrington."

Her mouth turned down at the corners, as if her words tasted sour. Fitzwilliam was not so naive to think that a title could not be bought; he had seen enough wealthy tradesmen become Sir This and Lord That in his time. A bit of pressure here, a trove of gold there, and Brigadier General Harrington could easily be *Sir* Harrington, at the very least.

"You would not wish to be the wife of a peer? To make all those society snobs who shun you show deference?"

She gave him *A Look*, her eyes sharp enough to cut. "I would not gamble my future away for the sake of petty revenge."

Of course, she would not. Fitzwilliam felt like a heel for even suggesting it. She took a breath and continued.

"I should like my dowry to be put to *good* use, in the running of an estate. I wish to see it used to help families prosper and grow. Not for petty preening."

He admired her for her answer. If he were being honest with himself, he would have to admit that he admired *her*, full stop. That she was bold, he could not deny, but that boldness was tempered with good sense. It did not hurt that she was quite lovely, her cheeks pink in the morning chill.

"Miss Campbell, I will assist you," he blurted out before realizing fully what he was doing. The look of gratitude and relief that stole over her face swept away the voice of warning in the back of his mind, the one that sounded all too much like Darcy.

"Oh, sir," she said in a breathless voice that near made him swoon. *Wait. Not swoon. You feel a racing pulse. A vigorous, manly feeling.*

"You have made me so happy."

Balls. I'm swooning. An unlooked-for warmth pooled in him, catching him off guard. His steps faltered as he felt her words, like a mouthful of the finest brandy. *You have made me so happy.* He could not recall anyone ever saying those words to him, not once in his thirty-three years. Satisfied, gratified, and quenched. Those were words his actions had bestowed upon him but not happy. Never happy. He cleared his throat and tried to regain some control on the situation.

"Very good, Miss Campbell. We shall begin tomorrow. I believe you are to attend Lady Barton's fete?"

"I am."

"Then it would be my honor to secure the first set with you."

She raised her brows. "*Ahem.*"

"And the supper set."

She smiled fully, and the warmth within him became a blaze. "I should be delighted, Colonel."

FOR THE FIRST time in his life, Fitzwilliam wished Darcy away. The man was *hovering* as Fitzwilliam watched for Miss Campbell's entrance.

He had not expected his cousin's company that evening, but he sensed that Darcy had passed some critical point in his lovelorn state. He was now turned out as immaculately as was expected from his fastidious valet. His eyes were no longer rimmed in red from drink and lack of sleep. There seemed to be a newfound determination about him, for which Fitzwilliam could only be grateful, but while the thoughtful silence that seemed to envelop Darcy might be an improvement over drunken misery, it was no good at a party.

"Oh, good lord," Darcy muttered, stepping behind a nearby column.

Fitzwilliam followed his cousin's gaze, grinning when he saw Charles Bingley enter with his sister.

"I know you don't favor Miss Bingley's company, Cuz, but it is not like you to *hide* from the woman."

Darcy looked mightily embarrassed. "It is not *Miss* Bingley I am hiding from."

Fitzwilliam was about to reply when the Misses Campbell and Lady Morgan were announced. He looked past the Bingleys, now approaching him, towards the door where the trio of ladies were just stepping through.

His breath caught. She entered the room swathed in the thinnest shimmering gold crepe covered by a whisper of lace set with sparkling beads. *That gown...that neckline, by the gods!* The room seemed to brighten at her entry, as if the candles themselves snapped to attention. Her dauntless gaze skimmed the room, from the enormous sprays of flowers to ladies in their finery, until her eyes found his. Their secret burned in that look. He realized that, in a strange way, they were now bound to one another.

"Halloo, Colonel. What a pleasant surprise!"

Fitzwilliam looked at the Bingleys as if he had never seen them before. He liked Charles Bingley well enough, but when in the presence of a goddess, it did not do to hobnob with the other mere mortals before honoring the divine. Such an insult would surely be paid in blood. He bowed briefly to the Bingleys.

"Bingley, Miss Bingley, please excuse me. Darcy is just behind that column." And with that he walked away. He knew it was abominable manners on his part, but he could not resist the pull of the line that tethered him to her. To Calliope. A line of Dante flitted through his mind: "Here rise to life again, dead poetry! Let it, O holy Muses, for I am yours." As if hearing his thoughts, she offered him a welcoming smile, and Fitzwilliam felt a piece of the farce begin to crumble. Would he be pretending to woo this woman? He could not say. He only knew he wanted to make *her* feel what he was feeling. He wanted her to know the simmering pleasure he felt when she looked at him like that. He stopped and bowed.

"Lady Morgan. Miss Campbell, Miss Clio."

They curtsied in unison, their movements fluid and graceful. Indeed, they were everything proper. It seemed astonishing to Fitzwilliam that the young ladies were so scorned simply for their American origins. They made polite chatter for a few moments until a tall, elegantly dressed shadow fell across the group. Darcy was there, his face unreadable. Charles Bingley, as ever, was attached to Darcy. Caroline Bingley was nowhere to be seen, doubtless she would have objected to her brother making himself known to the Campbells.

"Fitzwilliam, would you do me the honor of introducing me to your friends?"

Fitzwilliam felt his brows rise in disbelief. Darcy knew perfectly well who the Miss Campbells were and had never had a kind word for them before. Nor an unkind one, he allowed. He had simply shown them the same cool disdain he showed for everyone when not in smaller, more familiar company.

"Certainly. This is Lady Morgan and her nieces Miss Calliope Campbell, Miss Clio Campbell. Ladies, this is my cousin Mr. Darcy, and this smiling fellow is Mr. Bingley."

The ladies answered Darcy and Bingley's bows with curtsies, giving Fitzwilliam a chance to observe all. Lady Morgan's countenance never lost its good-natured serenity, but the younger ladies had quite different and far more interesting reactions. Bingley seemed distracted, his smile slipping. Clio was clearly smitten with Darcy, the poor thing. A pink wash stole across her cheeks, making her look almost becoming. Calliope's lips curved into a polite smile that did not reach her eyes. She seemed suspicious of the imposing figure that Darcy cut. Wary, even. That look did not fade when, much to the surprise of all, Darcy asked Calliope if he might secure a set with her. Fitzwilliam thought he could not be more shocked until he heard Darcy say, "The first set, perhaps."

"Colonel Fitzwilliam has already spoken for the first set," she said, somewhat stiffly. Darcy seemed unfazed. "You may have the second set, sir."

He bowed again. "I should be honored." He turned to Clio and asked if she might like to dance. She shook her head violently, looking as though she might cast up her accounts right then and there. *Poor little wallflower.* Fitzwilliam did not know what had gotten into Darcy but he found himself as amused as he was perplexed by the change. And, perhaps a trifle jealous. He had never competed with Darcy for the attentions of a lady and damned if he was going to start then.

"And you must allow me the third, Miss Campbell," Bingley said, all affability. If Fitzwilliam had objected to Calliope dancing with Darcy, he was practically livid at the thought of her dancing with Charles Bingley, whose amiable nature could thaw even the coldest dislike. And they shared a connection—both had acquired wealth from trade. Both had known the cool reception of those deemed of less respectable origins. In that moment, Fitzwilliam could have given both men, men he respected and admired, bloody noses.

He was so intent on these cheerful thoughts, Calliope had to nudge him when the music began. "Should we not take our places?" she asked, cheeks flaming.

Fitzwilliam bowed, taking her hand in his and leading them to their dance. He could feel the scornful gazes of the Upper Ten Thousand in the room, hear their shocked gasps as he led *that American* to the ballroom. The music swelled as they approached. A waltz. It would be a waltz. He looked down at her whispered.

"Well, Miss Campbell, you *did* want a scandal."

Her mouth puckered into an insouciant smile. He wanted to kiss her silly. "Do you not know this dance, Colonel?"

His smile widened into a grin. "Oh, I know it *very* well. We shall have every tongue in the ballroom wagging."

She seemed unsure.

"Calliope, do you trust me?"

If she was shocked by his use of her Christian name, she did not show it. She nodded once and then she was in his arms. They flowed like water across the floor, their movements lighter than air. He focused on her glossy curls as they floated through the steps, trying to calm the quickening of his pulse.

"Cal," she said softly.

"I beg your pardon?" He looked down at her to see her leaf-green eyes studying him.

"If we are going to be informal, please call me Cal."

"Not Callie?"

She pulled a face, making him chuckle. He pulled her closer. Scandalously, dangerously close. Fitzwilliam fancied he could hear a chorus of snapping fans. *Soon the room will undoubtedly reek of smelling salts.*

"Very well. Have I told you how very lovely you are tonight?"

Calliope, *Cal,* looked over his shoulder, not meeting his eyes. "You need not pretend when they cannot hear you."

Fitzwilliam shook his head, twirling them around in the dance, his steps sure.

"I do not give a damn if they hear me or not. I think you know by now that I am a man who speaks his mind. When I say you look lovely, I mean it. You take my breath away, Cal."

He was rewarded by a creeping blush that spread across her face and down, down, down past the too-tempting lace trim of her *décolletage.*

"My, but you *are* good."

"You asked for the best." She smiled at that. The look of her in the candlelight, her warm, graceful body so close to his, the scent of sweet jasmine—all of these things were beginning to affect him in such a way, that when they parted for the dance, he would not be able to conceal it. To distract himself, he asked what she planned to do with her spinsterhood. *Think of her growing old and going on the shelf. A damn travesty, that.*

"I shall do what all spinsters do, I suppose. Retire to some seaside village. Give to the poor, improve my watercolors, and spend my days in solitude."

He lowered his voice to a silky caress. "And what do you *want,* Cal?"

Her chin tilted stubbornly up as she straightened her spine, her steps never faltering. They had transcended the music, become one with it. Fitzwilliam could not recall ever having a dance partner who made waltzing so effortless.

"I want to do some good in this life," she said quietly, so that only he could hear her. "I want to leave the world better than it was when I came into it. And I want adventure. I want passion. I want to dance among the stars with a divine man. Laugh at me if you like."

Mercy! He felt the word as a plea. His imagination ran wild at her words, picturing himself giving her everything she ever asked for. *Passion. Now that I could give you, my lady.*

"I would not dare laugh. A practical *and* a romantic." He tutted as their dance came to an end. They clapped politely before he took her hand to escort her off of the dance floor. "'Tis a fearsome combination, Miss Campbell."

"I believe you mean it is a *lonesome* combination, Colonel." Their dance over, they returned to formal propriety. As he led her towards the refreshments, people gawked, stepping out of their way as they approached. From the corner of his eye, Fitzwilliam saw Darcy regarding him seriously across the room. Charles and Caroline Bingley still fluttered about him like moths. On his arm, Cal's grip tightened, pulling his attention away from Darcy.

Blast.

Brigadier General Harrington, Bloody Benedict himself, stood holding two cups of lemonade. One he passed to Cal, who accepted it silently. The other he kept for himself, lifting it to his face and taking a sip, his eyes never leaving Fitzwilliam's.

"Fitzwilliam," Harrington drawled. Pale and slight, looking delicate even in his red coat. But for all this, he knew Harrington to be a dangerous man, intelligent and ambitious. Fitzwilliam's own good nature had given him a talent for liking everyone he met, with two exceptions. One was the man looking smugly at him. The other was George Wickham.

"Brigadier General." Fitzwilliam gave the most perfunctory bows, fuming that Harrington would greet him over the woman he was supposedly courting. Harrington gave him a cool, measured gaze before finally, *finally* turning his attentions back to Calliope.

"Miss Campbell. I did not think you fond of dancing."

"I enjoy it very much but am seldom asked, sir." As she said this, she took a sip of her lemonade, smiling into her cup. Harrington did not see it but Fitzwilliam did.

"Then you must grant me the next set."

Fitzwilliam's hands balled into fists. *Officious prig.*

"I am afraid Mr. Darcy has already been promised the second set, and Mr. Bingley the third."

"The supper set, then."

"Oh, dear. I am afraid that one is—"

"How odd, Miss Campbell, that after a season of being *seldom asked* that your dance card should now be suddenly full."

How odd that you have not bothered to ask her to dance until you see her dancing with others!

"Indeed, I cannot account for it at all," she said, sounding mystified.

He knew Harrington did not believe that equivocation for a moment. The awkward silence was made only slightly less by the arrival of Darcy, come to claim his dance. She handed her lemonade cup to Fitzwilliam, giving him a sly smile as she took Darcy's arm. He watched her go, admiring her graceful stride, silently thankful that this dance was a more sedate quadrille. He did not think he could bear to see her waltz with his taller, handsomer cousin.

"*Ahem.*" Fitzwilliam looked over at Harrington like the man was something stuck to his boot.

"I know your game, *Colonel.*" Fitzwilliam doubted that. "A second son cannot live on a soldier's wage forever. But I must warn you, I have already begun negotiations with the girl's father."

Inwardly, Fitzwilliam seethed. *The girl, indeed.* Outwardly, he put on his laziest, most infuriating smile.

"Is that so? She made no mention of it to me." And then, never breaking Harrington's stare, lifted Calliope's cup to his lips and drank.

"I DO BELIEVE that peacock is following us," Fitzwilliam said as they ambled through Kew Gardens, the vibrant blossoms nodding gently in a light summer breeze.

"Which one?" Calliope answered dryly. Fitzwilliam turned to see the monstrously large bird following with a proud strut, chest puffed out, tail feathers extended into an enormous, ornate fan on greens and blues. Some distance behind the fowl, a man followed in what, to Fitzwilliam's eyes, was a comical imitation of the bird. Harrington, no doubt coming to seek Calliope out in some gesture of courtship.

Damn, but the man was persistent. Fitzwilliam shot him a glare as Calliope called out to her sisters not to get too far ahead. Reluctant as he had been to have the young Miss Campbells accompany them, he could not begrudge the delight on the faces of Clio, so quiet and shy, and the vivacious Thalia, only fifteen with a bit of her eldest sister's boldness. Neither girl was as handsome as Cal, but he felt a curious fondness for the girls. He supposed because *she* doted on them so, he felt naturally inclined to like what she liked.

Disturbed by the thought, he pushed it away and spoke to Cal in a low voice. "Has he been to see your father?"

The corners of her lovely mouth turned down. "Like clockwork. Thankfully, Father is too intrigued by your presence to speed things along with Harrington. An old and venerable family such as yours may outweigh Harrington."

Fitzwilliam would say a prayer of thanks for that, at least.

"I am afraid it will take a proper scandal to dissuade him. You might have to make love to me in the middle of St. James' to scare the man off," she said with a giggle.

Hot, greedy need gripped him at her words. It had been a subject he had pondered far too often of late. Imagining such a thing with Calliope, as he did with alarming frequency, more often than not made him feel like a man dying of thirst in the desert. The fact that he did not pause, nor miss a step, or appear in any way out of sorts by this brash statement was pure heroism on his part. He thought he deserved a medal for not throwing her over his shoulder and carrying her off right then and there. Instead, he laughed roughly.

"I assure you, I would not allow *that*. Were I to make love to you, Cal, it would be an act of worship such as would shock the pagans themselves."

He was gratified to see her face pink, her throat working to swallow.

"The things you say," she teased. "You are quite shocking."

"I know better than to think I can shock *you*. But play the coquette if you like, Goddess."

She sighed, but Fitzwilliam fancied he could see it behind her eyes, the same raw yearning he felt, sensitive as new skin over an old wound.

"I have told you not to pretend when it is just you and I."

He turned, took her hand and, in full view of everyone, planted a reverent, lingering kiss on the back of her hand, clad only in light lace gloves.

"Now what," he said, still holding her hand close to his lips, "would give you the idea that I am pretending?"

Of all the bloody...

"Colonel Fitzwilliam." Brigadier General Harrington peered down his nose from atop his mount. *Only way the pup could do it without a ladder,* he thought with grim satisfaction.

"Brigadier General." Fitzwilliam saluted dutifully. However, much he disliked Harrington, the man was still a first-rate officer.

Harrington dismounted in a fluid, agile motion that surprised

Fitzwilliam. Now standing on his own two feet, the man had to look up to meet his eye.

"A word."

Fitzwilliam followed from the training yards, where his men had just been dismissed, to the cool, dark confines of the officers' mess, where the brigadier general had a small office that smelled strongly of pipe tobacco and parchment.

Harrington seated himself. He did not invite Fitzwilliam to sit but sat peering at him with cold, gray eyes over steepled fingers.

"I saw that you recently attended the summer exhibition," Harrington drawled.

"I did." He had, of course, escorted Calliope to Somerset House, where half the *ton* watched them studying paintings and statuary, giggling like the conspirators they were at well-placed fig leaves.

"And Kew Gardens before that."

"Indeed."

"Lady Snowley tells me she saw you escorting two of the Campbell girls to Vauxhall last month."

"Lady Snowley sees much and comments often," Fitzwilliam said with mild amusement.

"I will be plain," Harrington snapped. Fitzwilliam nodded, showing all due deference to his superior. Inwardly, he was inventing new curses for the man.

"I do not like your attentions to Miss Campbell. I do not like *you*. You are a spoiled, second son from a wealthy—or rather *formerly* wealthy —family. Your elder brother has made your family a laughingstock with his expensive tastes and a fondness for the card tables. However, his transgressions pale in comparison to yours: the unapologetic rake with a talent for flirting and known penchant for visiting certain widows and has never, to my knowledge nor anyone else's, paid court to a lady. Have I forgotten anything?"

"I look very well in blue," Fitzwilliam said from behind clenched teeth. If this man were not his superior officer, he would have planted him a facer or called him out. Harrington's eyes narrowed dangerously.

"Always so self-assured. I have suspected, since Lady Barton's fete, that you have designs on Miss Campbell's dowry, which you will no doubt spend as greedily as that dissolute brother of yours."

"And you are so fond of the lady?" Fitzwilliam seethed.

"Fond? No, I would not necessarily say that. She is agreeable enough, though a bit too sharp and in need of a firm hand. But all that matters little. We need not get on so long as she gives me sons, and *that* process, I believe I shall rather like. She would not be mismanaged with me, if that is your concern."

Only once before in his life had Fitzwilliam felt such a violent rage rise up in him, when he learned of George Wickham's treachery with young Georgiana Darcy, whom he shared guardianship of with her brother. Even that paled to the cold hatred now coursing through him. Harrington looked pleased with himself, knowing his words were having their desired effect. Fitzwilliam felt his fingers curl into a tight fist, knowing it was what the smug bastard wanted. Harrington *wanted* to be struck so that Fitzwilliam could be court-martialed and disgraced. He did not care. He would take a hundred court martials before he let Harrington touch one hair on Calliope's head. He began to move towards the other man, seeing the triumph in his eyes and not caring…

A sharp, urgent rap on the door saved him. He paused. The moment ticked by in heavy, palpable tension. The knock came again, more insistent this time.

"Enter!" Harrington barked. A young cadet, barely old enough to wear a red coat, stumbled into the room, terrified by the fury on the brigadier general's face.

"What is it?" Harrington snapped at the lad.

"Sir. 'Ere's a gentleman askin' to see 'im"—he pointed at Fitzwilliam. "I told 'im you was busy, sir, but 'e says it's a matter a utmost urgency. 'Is name's Darcy, sir."

Fitzwilliam said a silent prayer of thanks for his cousin. Solid, dependable, Darcy! Fitzwilliam had no idea what brought his cousin looking for him, but the timing of Darcy's arrival had prevented Fitzwilliam from making a grave error. He had almost let Harrington win. He turned back to the brigadier general.

"Will there be anything else, sir?" he asked, all politeness. Oh, it cost him, that.

Harrington flapped a hand at him as though swatting a fly. "You are dismissed. But do think on what I have said, *Colonel.*"

"Oh, I assure you, I shall think of little else, *sir.*"

THE SHUFFLING THUD of Darcy's pacing was driving him to madness. It had been an exhausting couple of days, searching through the rottenest parts of London for Wickham and his purloined lady. Fitzwilliam felt dirty for even having been in Wickham's presence, unsurprised to see the man unchanged. Showy and brash as a bantam cock, that one, absconding with Miss Elizabeth's sister, no doubt to ruin any chance of Darcy's future happiness.

He felt a strange relief as Darcy had, days prior, recounted the tale of Elizabeth Bennet's startling visit to Pemberley, glad that the lady had with time come to see Darcy's hidden worth. It lay not in his wealth (though that helped) but in the strength of his character.

"It is done now, Darcy." Fitzwilliam attempted to placate his cousin. "Wickham will wed the girl, poor silly child that she is, and you shall be free to resume your acquaintance with her sister."

"She will not wish to see me," Darcy said gravely. "I, who she confessed all to in a vulnerable moment. How she must blame me now for having listened!"

Fitzwilliam sighed wearily. There was no talking to Darcy when he was like this. He would rather be back in his quarters—or somewhere with Calliope. The thought of her unflappable presence was a balm to his fatigued mind. He stood, pouring a glass of port wine for Darcy and another for himself. Nothing too strong, not after last time. He handed the drink to his cousin, clapping him on the shoulder.

"All will be well, Darcy."

Darcy looked skeptical as he took the port from him. "What makes you so certain?"

"I just am. Now do as your older cousin says and take your medicine like a good lad."

"My apologies, Fitzwilliam."

"No need for apologies. It has been a long day."

Darcy shook his head, one dark curl falling across his brow. Fitzwilliam knew women found that irresistible. How shocked they would all be when England's most eligible bachelor married an obscure girl from the country, for Fitzwilliam had little doubt that Darcy would propose again. And they thought *he* was a scandal.

"No, I mean…I am sorry for the things I said the last time you were here."

"You shall have to refresh my memory, I was utterly foxed that night."

"I implied that love was a great catastrophe. That it broke men like you and me. I could not have been more wrong. Love, even an unrequited love, has indeed transformed me but for the better."

Fitzwilliam's thoughts flew to Cal once more. "Not to worry, Darcy," he said, brightening. "There was not much room for improvement to begin with."

"Is it that American?"

Fitzwilliam held a hand out, suddenly solemn. "I beg you, Darcy. Do not call her that. Miss Campbell is more than just *that American*. 'Tis bad enough I have to hear it in every ballroom and museum in Town, I would not hear it from my own relations."

Darcy seemed surprised by this but bowed slightly. "You are entirely correct, Fitzwilliam. Miss Campbell seems an intelligent, worthy sort of girl."

Fitzwilliam nearly choked on his port. "Darcy, you are beginning to sound like Lady Catherine."

Darcy's handsome features paled. "Good god. We had better switch to brandy after all."

"Yes, let's."

FITZWILLIAM WIPED the sweat from his brow as he led his mount to the stables. He was bone-tired and thirsty from training exercises, overheated despite the autumn chill, and now made anxious by the square of ecru which had been handed to him by a young cadet only moments ago. It bore a name in looping, elegant script:

Lady Matlock

HE UNDERSTOOD the message clearly as if his mother had spoken in his ear. It was a summons. Making his way back to his quarters, Fitzwilliam wondered if his brother had at last driven the family into penury. He thought of Calliope Campbell and her ten thousand pounds before a sharp discomfort somewhere under his breastbone forced his thoughts from that subject.

The summer had come and gone since their agreement, since that glorious waltz at Lady Barton's fete. Outside of his family obligations and military duties, Fitzwilliam spent every moment he could paying court to Calliope Campbell, escorting her to the park, to Bond Street, drinking endless cups of tea in the sitting room of the house on Pelham Row. The gossips of the *ton* had certainly taken an interest. Unfortunately, this only seemed to encourage Harrington, who at least seemed to understand that he could not merely woo the girl's father. Fitzwilliam began to worry the man might try to abscond with her and hie her off to Gretna Green. He could feel the brigadier general's dogged pursuit like a hand hovering over his neck.

His concern had little to do with the money. He truly wanted Calliope to have all the things she wanted. Adventure. Romance. That dance among the stars. While he might have begun in farce and on mercenary grounds, his feelings for the American heiress was that of heartfelt adoration, and a simmering passion that sometimes threatened to boil over. He thought she felt it too. There were meaningful looks when they were alone. Small gestures like a brush of the hand. The times when he was at his most charming, the stubborn tilt of her chin that betrayed her discomposure. If only he could be certain it was true and not part of the ruse. He still felt daily frustration that she thought his admiration of her to be insincere, part of an act.

Once he bathed and donned fresh clothes, he set out to his family's house, where his family had only returned from Matlock. Fitzwilliam expected his mother wished to rake him over the coals over the news of Darcy's betrothal to Miss Elizabeth Bennet. He had been expecting it. He was prepared to do battle for Darcy and Miss Elizabeth if need be, particularly after hearing of Lady Catherine's most abominable treatment of Miss Elizabeth and her family. Perhaps he could do his family *some* credit.

His mother was waiting for him in the sitting room, squinting at a newspaper when he entered.

"Hullo, Mater. Alone again?" He bent to kiss her cheek, only to have her slap the newspaper across the crown of his head. He drew back, startled.

"What the deuce was that for?"

Her eyes narrowed, the same blue as his own. "I know what you are doing," she said without preamble. She shook the paper at him. "We are not so destitute that you should have to court an…an…"

"Yes?" he said coolly.

"An *American*. A *tradesman's* daughter."

"Technically, she is half-English, with an excellent dowry and many other pleasing…assets."

"Do not be vulgar with me. I am your mother!"

Fitzwilliam sighed. "And...what if..."

"Yes?"

"What if I were courting Miss Campbell because I truly cared for her?"

The countess looked like she had sooner believed he could fly. "Do you?" she finally asked.

He felt his breath leave him in a rush. "I confess I do. I think I am well on my way to being in love with her."

He turned and strode to the window, jaw clenched in mute frustration. He could not, of course, tell his mother the whole of the truth. About their pact.

"And I am sure twenty thousand pounds has nothing to do with your interest," the countess said. He spun around, suddenly furious.

"Hang the money!" he spat violently.

She studied him for several long moments before putting the paper aside. "Very well. I wish I had not learned of it from these vulgar gossip pages, but if you are sincere, I would hear it now."

And so, he told her. Not about their first meeting nor their bargain. But he did tell his mother of the way he felt taking her in his arms for that first waltz, of how much he admired Calliope, her intelligence and wit, her wish to do good in the world, the way she carried herself like a queen through rooms full of people that despised her.

The countess sighed, a heavy, tired sound. At last, she reached out to pat his hand. Fitzwilliam noticed that her fingers were sporting fewer jewels than usual.

"You are a good son and loyal to your family. I had worried..."

"That I might toy with a woman's affections to save our family from ruin?" he interjected bitterly. His mother grimaced.

"You *do* have a reputation, my dear."

That he knew too well. He felt it now, a yoke around his neck. From arrogant youth to full-grown cad, he now loathed that his libertine past cast a shadow over this new tenderness he fostered in his breast. Of course, had he *not* had such a reputation, would Cal have ever approached him? Would she have gone to some other, less honorable rake, who might have taken full advantage of her situation? The thought made his stomach boil.

"I can assure you, Mother, my intentions are entirely honorable," he said, realizing it was true. There was only one solution, only one way forward. He would marry Calliope Campbell. The moment he realized it, the weight disappeared from his shoulders, the burden of lies lifting. He knew exactly how he would ask, though it might take time and some careful planning.

"Tell me, Mater, does Pater still attend those tedious meetings in Greenwich?"

THE CARRIAGE CAME to a stop around the back, where a tall figure, distinctly feminine despite the cloak that obscured her face, waited outside of the servant's entrance. Fitzwilliam leaned out of the carriage, his hand outstretched. A moment later she took it, climbing in. Her eye seemed to glitter when it caught his, a bemused smile on her full lips.

"You are very mysterious," she said, holding a square note that simply read:

Servants' entrance. Midnight— F

"YOU WANTED ADVENTURE," he said with a smile, rapping on the roof. The carriage rolled forward. "Tonight, you shall have it."

Her face colored. "Do you remember everything I say?"

He put a hand over his heart. "Like you carved it here yourself."

"You are too much. How many times must I tell you not to pretend to like me when it is just you and me?"

He chuckled, shaking his head. Instead of replying to her maddening statement, he reached into his coat and produced a dark, silken bit of cloth.

"Lean forward."

Smiling gamely, she obeyed. He reached up, winding the fabric across her eyes and tying it into a firm knot at the back of her head. Her lips opened in surprise, making him feel a hot stab of desire. Ever so lightly, he traced the tip of his ungloved finger up the long column of her neck. She startled at first, then stilled. He took his hand away for a moment, waiting to see if she would rip off the blindfold, try to escape. Instead, to his delight, she leaned forward, tilting her head slightly. Offering herself to his touch.

Once more he traced the line of her throat, up along the underside of her chin, skimming her fine cheekbones, around the bow shape of her still-parted lips. He felt a keen sort of desperation to kiss her, but did not, resuming his light touch along her face, neck, wandering bravely down, where his fingers made quick work of the ribbons that tied her cloak closed. He was gratified to see gooseflesh rise across her skin as he skimmed his fingers along her collarbone. His fingers came up to trace the shape of her mouth. She made a little sound of frustration, and it nearly undid him. He leaned forward, bringing himself close enough to her that he could feel the tickle of her breath across his face. Reaching up, he plunged his hands into her hair, feeling some of her pins come loose. Her hands came up, grasping his arms in a surprisingly tight grip. Keeping her head still, he leaned forward just enough to brush his lips against hers. It was not a kiss but a touch he felt all over his skin, down to the bone. She inhaled and pressed closer, wanting the kiss. It took all of his strength to pull back, needing to savor this sensation a moment longer.

The carriage rolled to a stop, startling them both. He peered out of the window and saw that they had reached their destination. When he looked back at Calliope, her breath was labored, her wonderful bosoms straining against her gown.

"We're here," he whispered, fingers still curled into her silken tresses. He did kiss her then, lightly, almost perfunctorily, before releasing her and setting her cloak back to rights. Her hair was coming loose, spilling across her shoulders.

"Can I take this off now?" she asked in a shaky voice, touching the blindfold.

He took her hand, kissing the tips of her fingers. "Not just yet."

"Am I expected to walk without eyes?" she asked testily.

He hopped out of the carriage, turning back to her. He reached inside the carriage and took her hand, pulling her towards the door and placed his hands around her waist. "Of course not."

She hesitated, making him sigh.

"Cal, do you trust me?"

The next second, she was in his arms. Wild joy surged through him. *A virile, manly sort of joy.* Her arms came up to circle his neck.

"Am I very heavy?" she asked in a small voice.

"When I am holding you, Goddess, I have the strength of ten men."

She laughed and, to his delight, rested her head on his shoulder. "You are impossible."

Once they were safely inside, he reluctantly put her back on her feet and at last removed her blindfold. He smiled gently as she blinked, saw him and—remembering what had just transpired in the carriage—blushed most becomingly before turning to look at their surroundings. They were in a large receiving room that was cool yet welcoming. The walls were stone, painted white. A servant greeted them with a bow and asked that they follow him, leading them through a door and to a stone staircase. At the top of the stairs, they were led through another door, out onto a flat rooftop cut in a rough hexagonal shape. Above them, the night sky glittered like jewels scattered across black velvet.

Calliope gasped, her hands flying to her mouth. Behind them, the servant that had led the way retrieved a small object and stepped inside the open door, just out of sight. A moment later, the sweet sound of a violin floated out onto the rooftop. Calliope turned back to him, eyes wide with shock.

"This is…"

"The Royal Observatory, yes." He held out his arms. She walked to him, still stunned. Her breath fogged in the cold air.

"How?"

He put one hand on her waist, the other taking her hand as he led them into a dance.

"It's all in who you know. And, as you see, I *do* remember everything you say," he said in a low voice. "You wished for adventure. For passion. To dance among the stars with a divine man."

This last seemed to break through her surprise. She looked up at him, a little laugh escaping her. "You do think highly of yourself."

He grinned. "Depends on how you interpret the word, I ken. You're Calliope, yes?"

She nodded, never breaking her steps. They waltzed. Of course, it would be a waltz, he thought happily. He decided then that they would always have waltzing.

"Calliope was the lover of Ares, yes?"

She blushed. "So the legend goes."

"Remind me, who was the Roman version of Ares again?"

"Mars."

He stopped, releasing her long enough to give her a deep bow. "Marcus Henry Fitzwilliam. At your service. *Marcus*, derived of Mars. I'm afraid you shall have to do with secondhand divinity, Cal."

A startled laugh bubbled up from her chest as they resumed their waltz. "*Marcus?* How is it that in all this time you never told me your name?"

"You never asked. And besides, there are many things I have yet to tell you," he murmured, his words for her alone.

She leaned in close. His hand pressed more insistently on the small of her back. "Such as?" she asked, the undertones of her voice making him shiver. That voice was for dark rooms, soft beds, and endless kisses.

"I never told you how much I adore you, or that Harrington's greatest crime is that he only sees you for your money, or that somewhere along the way, I forgot about our deal."

She was sharp now, her attention holding him at knife point. "What do you mean?"

He stopped the dance again. At some point the violin-playing servant had departed, and there were no sounds but their own breath and the biting winter wind slipping through the trees below.

Fitzwilliam looked down at her, so strong and lovely and brave in his arms. He took her face in his hands.

"What I am saying, Cal, is that I don't give a fig about your money. You keep it. I want *you*."

Her face turned crimson in the faint light of the lanterns that had been placed at intervals along the roof. "But you...you don't do this! You're a rake! A scoundrel!"

"Not anymore. I'm completely reformed. Well...I may still be a bit of a scoundrel, but only with you, if you will permit me."

"Oh," she said, stunned.

"I leave for Hertfordshire tomorrow, to attend Darcy's wedding. And Bingley's too I suppose!" He recalled that it would be a double wedding. "Before I leave, I plan to call on your father and ask for your hand, if you will have me."

"You are not serious."

"I am about to show you how serious I am."

"How are you—"

The words were cut off by his kiss, a *real* kiss this time. Her lips were soft and firm and tasted sweet. Her breath caught before her arms came up to circle his neck, her fingers sliding into his dark hair.

"Believe me, Cal," he spoke against her lips, his words a plea. "Believe that this is real, that I utterly adore you. Tell me you feel the same, that I have not imagined it."

"No. I mean, yes. I mean...Marcus..." His name on her lips entranced him surer than any spell.

"Say it again, Goddess."

"Marcus."

He kissed her again. They repeated this act several times. The only witness to whispered confessions of these young lovers were the stars that twinkled merrily overhead.

THE MILD WEATHER at last broke on the day of the double wedding. It was a cold morning made warm by promises of devotion and fidelity, and Fitzwilliam was surprised to feel himself filled with sweet contentment, thinking of his own betrothal. He had shown up earlier than was entirely proper the day he departed for Hertfordshire, and after a brief conversation with her father, had secured his blessing to marry Calliope. His future sisters rushed to embrace him, delighted that he would be their brother and not "that other one, the horrible one." For his part, Fitzwilliam could only agree. Having Cal's sisters under his protection would do much to dissuade the Harringtons of the world. Clio seemed particularly happy by this turn of events and even managed to put three words together. Fitzwilliam fancied she and Georgiana would get on rather well.

Most importantly, when he got a few moments alone with his future bride, she did not insist he stop pretending. She accepted his compliments with a knowing smile that promised great reward.

He longed to tell his family, to tell Darcy, to shout it from the rooftops. The only person who knew, besides himself and Cal and her family, was Mr. Bennet. Two nights before, when he had come with the others to dinner at Longbourn, the older man had taken one shrewd look at him and said, "Not another one! Have you come to ask for one of my daughters? If you have, please do so with haste, for I am growing weary of young men in love!"

Not knowing what to make of this strange speech, Fitzwilliam had stammered, red-faced like a schoolboy, that he was indeed in love, and that his remaining single daughters were safe from him. Mr. Bennet nodded and said it was just as well, he could only do with so many sensible sons, before ambling off to his library alone. He was an odd man. Fitzwilliam rather liked him.

The wedding breakfast over and the couples departed for their respective destinations of Netherfield and London, Fitzwilliam hastened back to the inn in Meryton where he had let rooms. He was eager to be gone at first light, back to London. Back to Cal.

The burly, kind-faced innkeeper ran out to meet his horse as he approached, holding out a letter.

"An express for you, sir! Only just arrived!"

Dread certainty gripped him. Fitzwilliam snatched the letter, a sinking feeling making him suddenly ill. He broke the seal. It was but two simple lines:

He has taken her north. Father follows.

A SIMPLE C by way of signature told him this was from Clio. He cursed, the paper crumpling in his hand.

He looked down at the innkeeper. "Can you pack my belongings and have them sent to Fitzwilliam House in London? I cannot stop. Urgent business calls me back."

The man agreed. Fitzwilliam dug some gold from his purse and paid him. "For your troubles." And with that he was off. Meryton was north of Town, so Harrington would have passed by that way on the Great North Road. He doubted the brigadier general had counted on Fitzwilliam having a head start.

Miraculously, he spotted the carriage thirty miles out of Meryton. He had stopped only once, where a barmaid at an inn informed him that a "high n'mighty officer" had been in with a young woman matching Cal's description who had loudly insisted on a large meal and many glasses of wine.

"Good girl," Fitzwilliam said as he climbed back onto his horse. "Brave, clever Cal."

He knew his Calliope was not cowed by Harrington. She was slowing him up.

He spotted the carriage clattering over the bridge that divided the village of Bedford, over the Great River Ouse. He wondered if Calliope had demanded yet another meal, to buy him the time. Fitzwilliam's horse crossed the bridge like a flash of lightning. He seemed to have the devil's own luck, catching them. Fitzwilliam leaned into the saddle, urging his mount faster, faster. Dust and dirt kicked up in clouds under the horse's hooves as they thundered recklessly across the field. He meant to cut them off. The cold air whipped at his face and ungloved hands, but he barely felt them. The carriage was in sight. He could not afford to be careful, propriety be damned. There was no *time*.

"Hold on, Cal," he said through gritted teeth, the words lost in the sound of his pursuit. "I am coming for you, Harrington, you right bastard."

He got far enough ahead of the carriage so that he was hidden by a bend in the road. He planted himself in the middle of the lane, his mount breathing heavily, his pistol heavy in his hand. The carriage came around the bend, the driver looking fearful and harried. Fitzwilliam fired his pistol into the air.

"Halt!" he commanded in a voice that surprised him, drawing on reserves of strength he did not know he possessed. The driver pulled the coach to a stop.

"Careful!" the driver said. "He is a bit touched, that one!"

The door to the coach swung open and, to his astonishment, Calliope emerged, looking furious, not a hair out of place. His heart lurched in his chest.

"What took you so long?" she demanded, her hands on her hips. Fitzwilliam was off his horse in an instant, and in her arms the next, kissing her face, her neck, her hair, every part of her he could reach.

"Oh, god!" she said, her voice breaking into sobs as he pulled her close to him. "You smell terrible!"

He laughed. "I've been riding hell-bent for the entire day. Are you alright?" She nodded, tears flowing.

"I was about to get the carriage to stop. You are lucky he did not run you down, you fool."

"What of Harrington?"

"He would not take no for an answer, so I had to resort to more tactical measures." She took Fitzwilliam's hand and led him back to the carriage. Harrington was slumped over, snoring noisily. His hands were tied together by what looked to be a woolen stocking. Another stocking was tied 'round his ankles, and the two ends of each tied to the other. The brigadier general was properly trussed.

"The man has no head for brandy," she said scornfully. "I have been goading him into having some every time we stopped. I told him if I was to marry him, we should at least celebrate this once." She batted her eyelashes and said in a coquettish voice, "Oh, General. How clever of you. How dreadfully romantic, absconding to Scotland." The simpering smile disappeared, replaced by a look of cold fury that settled over her like a queen's raiment. Gods, but he loved her. Who but she could have taken such an unrepentant sinner and made him yearn for nothing more than the pleasures of a devoted husband? She was glorious.

"I ordered wine for myself and brandy for him," she continued in her normal voice. "Kept talking about what a great lord he would be and continued to fill his glass. He only just fell asleep moments ago."

Fitzwilliam shut the carriage door as quietly as he could. Harrington did not rouse. After some instructions to the driver and parting with a few more coins, the carriage began moving again. It turned in the opposite direction, back towards London.

Fitzwilliam held his horse's reins with one hand, the other clasped Calliope's hand. They walked slowly back towards Bedford.

"That was very, very smart, Cal," he said at last.

"Are you surprised?"

He shook his head slowly. "Not at all. Harrington underestimated you. He always did."

They lapsed back into silence. Night was descending. She pulled her cloak around her. "I had a wicked thought," she said.

"I think I know what you may be thinking, Goddess."

"We *are* already on the road…"

He grinned. "And after a night at the inn, we could hire a coach…"

"It would be a terrific scandal," she said, smiling at him.

"I hear Scotland *is* lovely this time of year."

"Notorious Newlyweds!

Tongues are still wagging and Society still reeling from the marriage of that brooding, handsome gentleman from the North to an unknown gentleman's daughter from Hertfordshire. Not to be outdone, his cousin, a former colonel in the King's Guard—stole away to Scotland with an heiress. Yes, *that* American! It is on good authority that the new brides have been welcomed into the home of the former colonel's parents, Lord and Lady —. Both couples were last seen traveling north, no doubt for an extended stay at his cousin's vast family seat…"

THE COUNTESS PUT the paper aside with a smirk. From the next room, the loud voices of her husband and Lady Catherine could be heard. When she had learned that *both* of her nephews had wed disagreeable women, Lady Catherine made all due haste to Town to demand that the earl and his wife bar their door to the newly-minted Mrs. Fitzwilliam. The countess found that she rather liked her son's American bride. She had excellent manners and a quick mind, and the good sense to adore her younger son. There had been no doubt that the two were utterly devoted to one another.

"This is an *outrage!*" Lady Catherine's stout voice cried from the other side of the door. With a satisfied smile, the countess gathered up the gossip pages and rang for a servant.

"Do place this in Lady Catherine's room." She handed the footman the paper. "On the pillow."

She thought she saw a ghost of a smile pass over the footman's face before he bowed and left the room. Lady Matlock took up her new occupation, knitting. She was rather enjoying it. A tiny cap was taking shape under the clicking needles. She smiled, hoping it would not be long before such a gift might be welcomed.

BEAU NORTH is the author of three books and contributor to multiple anthologies. Beau hails from the kudzu-strangled wilderness of South Carolina but now hangs her hat in Portland, Oregon. In her spare time, Beau is the co-host of the podcast *Excessively Diverted: Modern Austen On-Screen.*

THOMAS BERTRAM

As the heir of a baronet and wealthy landowner, Tom Bertram was cavalier and profligate at cards, horses, drink, and lavish lifestyle. Even after his father, Sir Thomas, told him he must sell the living intended for his youngest son to pay off Tom's many debts, he continued to spend recklessly in pursuit of diversion. *...could soon with cheerful selfishness reflect, first, that he had not been half so much in debt as some of his friends; secondly, that his father had made a most tiresome piece of work of it; and thirdly, the future incumbent, whoever he might be, would in all probability, die very soon.* —*Mansfield Park,* **Chapter III.**

"If you can persuade Henry to marry, you must have the address of a Frenchwoman. All that English abilities can do has been tried already." — Mary Crawford to Mrs. Grant, Mansfield Park, Chapter IV.

THE ADDRESS OF A FRENCHWOMAN
Lona Manning

Gentlemen, allow me to propose the first toast. To our host. Thank you for your hospitality, George. Here we are, half-a-dozen of the most eligible bachelors in the country, in exile from all womankind and happy to be so. We have dinner, a fire, plenty to drink, the races to talk over, and no other company wanted. To George!

Yes, fellows, since you press me so hard, yes, I confess it: Cupid's darts have winged me severely. If you must have the story, pass me that bottle first. I can lift it with my left hand without paining my collarbone too much. Now, you may not like what you are about to hear. You think lightning will never strike *you*. But let me tell you, last year at the Basingstoke Races, I was neither looking to fall in love, nor looking for someone to fall in love with *me*, when all unawares—but stay, I must go further back....

It was in late June, I believe, when Henry Crawford and his sister arrived in Mansfield. Now, there's a charmer—some of you have met Miss Mary Crawford in London, I daresay. Some may fault her figure—or lack of it—or some may fault her colouring. Personally, I fancy a nut-brown maid, but that is by-the-bye. What distinguishes Miss Crawford from the rest of her sex is her excellent discourse and her wit.

She took a vast liking to *me*, of course, and we bantered most agreeably for the first few weeks of our acquaintance while her brother, Henry, flirted with my sisters. A pleasant way to pass the summer; in mutual admiration but with no hearts involved. That is all that I thought or wished or intended. Then, by merest chance, one evening when we were all gathered together in the drawing room, I saw that my brother, Edmund, was following Miss Crawford with his eyes, most intently. *What's this?* I said to myself. I undertook to watch him carefully and before long had discovered his little secret: he was harboring a *tendresse* for Miss Crawford. If you know Edmund, he is not one of those fellows who falls in love with every pretty face he meets; still less is he a flirt, like Crawford. But then, I imagine that Henry Crawford must labour twice as diligently to charm the ladies to compensate for his lack of height and his plain features, poor fellow. Edmund, on the other hand, is very well-looking but a most indifferent lover with no more idea of *repartee* than an infant!

So, what was I to do? Here was Edmund, making calf eyes at Miss Crawford. Here was Miss Crawford, working her eyelashes at me, and hinting, more than hinting, that she would like to be invited along to Basingstoke so she could watch my horse run! And, she added, with such an air of innocence, how much she would *love* to learn to ride, if only someone could undertake to give her some lessons, how *grateful* she would be. As long as I was in the picture, what chance did Edmund have?

Then I had an inspired thought. "Oh," said I, "you should apply to Edmund. He has a gentle little mare, who would be capital for you. While we have such excellent weather, you should remain here at Mansfield and take your lessons with Edmund; it would be his very great pleasure. And after I return from Basingstoke, we can all ride out together!"

Damned clever of me, if I do say so. I not only took myself out of the race by going to the races but gave my brother an excuse to attend on Miss Crawford every morning: to guide and advise her, to help her up on her saddle, and lift her down again.

Oh, but she gave me a look when I proposed it! She was taken aback, to be sure. No doubt her sudden enthusiasm for horseflesh and racing had little to do with horses, but more with—well, no need to puff myself, fellows. But she agreed with a good grace, while Edmund looked grave, and said something about asking Fanny—that's our little cousin—for permission. Honestly, I felt embarrassed for him. Not "I'll wager that you will make an excellent equestrienne, Miss Crawford." Not "I am yours to command, Miss Crawford" but "I must ask Fanny." If he had not the spirit or the ardour to woo the lady under such a pretext as this, well—I washed my hands of him, that's all. I had done all I could, more than many would do. The rest was up to him.

No regret on my part. Miss Crawford is charming, we all agree, but I never had a serious thought about her, and Edmund, as I said, is besotted with her. Here's to Miss Crawford, then. "Miss Crawford."

So, I set out for Basingstoke Down, well pleased with myself! I daresay, it really is gratifying to sacrifice present pleasure for the sake of someone you care about.

Now, as to what happened next. You will recall how miserably rainy it was at Basingstoke last year. Our carriage wheels half buried in mud at the race course, no decent shelter anywhere. But my horse, young Benedick, was in excellent form and my groom assured me he could make a good showing, mud or no. I had placed a few private wagers—trifling sums, on account of my promise to my father. But I came across a stall at the racecourse, one of these blacklegs, and he was offering me odds of ten to one to win, place, or show. He had the mashed-in nose and the flattened ears of a boxer, so I decided he must be a stupid fellow whose brains had been well-jangled around in his head. Well, thinks I, here is a way to gain a handsome return for a small outlay. I laid out the remainder of my ready cash and placed a bet on Benedick. So, my purse was as empty as—as this glass—do be alert, fellows!

Thank you.

The rain was beginning to fall and I was picking my way through the crowd to return to my carriage. And suddenly I heard a woman's scream nearby, high-pitched, frightened. *"Non! Non! Je vous en prie, messieurs!"* Everyone around me, as well as I, started looking for the source of this commotion, and I spied a young woman with two large brutes gripping either of her arms and shaking her like a terrier shakes a rat. I quickly drew close enough to hear and see. The first thing I noticed was that she was not a common drab but a gentlewoman. They were abusing her so that her hat fell off and some of her dark, curling hair was coming undone, and she was both frightened and angry. The second thing I noticed was that she was very beautiful.

In fact, sirs, raise your glasses, every man jack of you, and drain it dry. "To Beauty." And fill mine up again, will you?

I was not the only young man present ready to spring to her defense, I fancy. As I glanced around I saw other fellows just as riveted by the scene before us as was I—but we all hesitated for a moment, to get the lay of the land—the two men might have been constables and we might have gotten a blackjack across our heads for our gallantry. But these two scoundrels appeared to have no weapons on them except for their meaty fists. The bigger one, I shall call "Carbuncle" and the smaller one "Pox-face" so you can follow my story.

"I say you are a thief, madam!" exclaims Carbuncle. "You brushed by me just now and my purse is missing!"

"Search her, search her!" urged Pox-face. "She must have it stuffed in her skirts somewhere." Carbuncle pinioned her arms to her sides while Pox-face lifted her skirts to examine her while she begged them to desist.

"Oh, *non*! Do not do this! Do not shame me!"

Pox-face took a good look—as could we all—she had the most shapely legs you can imagine with pretty, blue garters—but no purse, no hidden pockets.

"I protest! I am no thief! I have done nothing! Please, let me go!" the young lady cried again.

"I vow that you have, madam, and it will go hard for you at the Assizes if you do not confess!" cried Carbuncle. In vain did she plead, in vain did she writhe and struggle—his large hands were like steel bands around her slender arms, and his dirty, sweaty, bleary, red face was close alongside her fair one. She began to weep.

"I swear, *messieurs*, on the Holy Virgin—"

"None of your popery, you damned Catholic." And Pox-face yelled across the crowd, which was growing ever thicker and closer around this interesting *tableaux*: "Hoy! Someone call the militia! Is there a constable here?" Then to her—and he came close enough so that his spittle flew in her face—"I will swear before the magistrate that you are a thief, and a pickpocket, and a whore, and you will be hung by the neck—but first you will return my friend's money! Where have you hidden it?"

A sharp intake of breath was heard all through the crowd when Pox-face suddenly pulled her fichu from her neck, revealing an uncommonly fine bosom, which, as you can imagine, was heaving deeply owing to her excited state.

"Oh, *non! Non!* Pray do not, *monsieur!*"

And Carbuncle thrust one hand into her hair and pulled her head back cruelly. "Be quiet, damn you!" And he gave her another vicious shake.

As I say, there were other young gentlemen present, raptly watching the spectacle as well as I, but I had the advantage of height and broader shoulders, and I pushed my way through the crowd and reached them quickly. That leering bastard Pox-face was about to insert his filthy hand down the front of her bodice when my right fist made contact with his jaw and sent him flying.

Carbuncle gaped at me, released the lady, and stepped back. Once freed, she did not run but froze in place, looking at me with astonishment.

"Madam," said I, with a quick bow, still keeping an eye on the two scoundrels and ignoring the fact that my arm hurt like the devil, "Will you place yourself under my protection?"

"Oh! *Monsieur!*" She took a little step backward, perhaps wondering if

I was an apparition, and nearly trod on Pox-face. She pulled her skirts away from him as though he was a snake, then tottered forward, swooning, into my arms.

"Now, sir," said Carbuncle, "we only meant to startle the lady a little, for we could swear upon a stack of bibles that she took my purse. We wasn't going to hand her over to the magistrate, as pretty a lady as she is. It's better that we settle this matter privately, don't you agree?"

"If you are insinuating that you want a bribe from me before you will leave this lady alone, be warned that I shall not countenance one more slur upon her honour. If she says she did not take your purse, then, by heaven, she did not take it, and she and I owe you nothing but a black eye and a kick up your fat backside."

As I spoke, I was keenly aware of the warm, breathing woman I held in my arms. She fit so neatly against me with her head resting on my chest.

"Oy! Simon!" cried Pox-face from his recumbent position. "Simon! Is *this* your purse?" And he reached out his hand and plucked from the mud, a little, brown leathern pouch. You could have easily missed it, but as he happened to be down at mud-level, he spotted it, half-trodden into the ground.

I swear, if I had not been holding the lady, I would have thrashed the two of them until I had broken every bone in their bodies. I have never felt such rage, and it astonished me. My countenance must have announced my feelings, for Pox-face jumped to his feet, holding out the lady's fichu to me while backing away.

"We beg your pardon, sir. We beg pardon, madam," and he craned his neck and looked all around nervously and started shouting to the crowd, pleading his case. "An honest mistake. She brushed against my friend, you see, and right away he felt for his purse and it was gone. He must have dropped it. But, all's well that ends well, as I always say."

"We'd be pleased to stand you to a drink, sir." Carbuncle added. "No? Well, then, we'll be off. Begging your pardon, madam, and enjoy the races."

And they disappeared into the throng—I wanted to bring a complaint against them, but just then the lady regained her senses and gave a modest cry of alarm at finding herself in the arms of a perfect stranger. My anger melted instantly, replaced by—well, replaced by feelings better imagined than described. If you could have seen her. She was ravishing, her hair half down, her large, brown eyes looking up at me, a mixture of raindrops and tears sparkling in her long, dark eyelashes, her dress in such an interesting state of disarray....

"Oh, *monsieur,* I do beg your pardon. I was overcome. Are—are they gone? Those horrible brutes! Those barbarians!"

You like the music of a Frenchwoman's accent, do you not, fellows? Well, as long as I live, I shall never forget the way she said "barbarians." It was—it was like a nightingale singing. It was liquid silver. It was—I cannot explain it, but I was very nearly done for there and then. Goodness knows what thoughts were showing on my countenance, for she looked up at me, and blushed, then she looked down and saw that her bosom was quite exposed. I blushed too, I think, and looked away and handed her fichu back to her. Once she covered herself again, the crowd started to melt away and go about its business.

"Madam, allow me to assist you," I said, reaching for her hat which dangled by its ribbon down her back. "My carriage is nearby. Will you step into it? I assure you, you will be perfectly safe." She took my arm, so gratefully, so confidingly, without a word, and in a few moments, I had her inside my carriage, with the rain softly drumming all around us, and I was rubbing her cold, little hands between mine.

"Please assure me, madam, are you unharmed? Have those ruffians hurt you? Shall I send my servant for a physician?"

"I think not, *monsieur*. I hardly know. Only—only let me sit and rest awhile."

"You are wet from the rain, I fear." Indeed, her skirts were damp enough to cling to every curve of her figure.

"No, not very." (But you must remember she said, *verree,* like this, not *very.*) "And muslin dries quickly. I thank you, sir. My name is Rose de Laval. To whom am I indebted?"

"Thomas Bertram, madam, of Northamptonshire, at your service."

At your service. How often have we tossed off "at your service" with a bow and smirk? How often have we meant it? Whenever I think back on that moment, a bit of Shakespeare comes to me. Yes, well, I only vaguely remembered it, and I had to go look it up to get it right, but it is from that play with the plaguey, little fairy—no, not *Midsummer Night's Dream,* the other one—anyway, the fellow Ferdinand says:

> Hear my soul speak. The very instant that I saw you, did my heart fly to your service—there resides, to make me slave to it...

There! Now you know my sad condition. I wanted to be at her service. I wanted to protect her. I wanted to give her anything she wanted and to have her look up at me with those big, brown eyes. And as I felt those things, I felt myself growing stronger, better, more—how shall I say? More of a man and not an overgrown boy. A man who had someone to think of besides himself. And I had always rather dreaded that notion, for do we not all love our freedom?

Yes?

Oh, very well. "To Freedom."

No, plague take it; if you are going to laugh at me, I shall leave off now and the devil fly away with you. You are none of you worthy to clean her boots. Let's play *vingt-et-un* instead, damn you, for pennies, or the buttons off my waistcoat, like good children.

Very well. First, apologize, and second, refill my glass. And Wilkinson, tell the servant to knock down that fire. It's growing hot as Hades in here.

All right then. Where was I? In the carriage with Rose—Miss Laval to you—with the crowd milling about, and I had completely forgotten about the races. She had forgotten as well, but when we heard the trumpets, she sat up and exclaimed, "Oh, *mon frère*!"

For of course, she was not there at the races alone. Her brother, it comes out, is the manager of Lord Delingpole's racing stables, if you please. And if I were not the oldest son of a baronet, I can think of nothing *I* would rather be.

Miss Laval was all for going out and finding him, but I persuaded her to stay with me, out of the rain, and I sent Phillips to find him and tell him his sister was safe.

My carriage was placed to command a good view of the track for the final stretch, and Miss Laval and I were just exchanging information about our horses—that is, Lord Delingpole's and mine—when we saw them thundering around the track. I could tell by the way she watched, barely breathing, that she was heart and soul for her brother and that she was very familiar with horses and racing. There was Delingpole's filly, Lelantos, in the lead and to my great joy, Benedick was near the front of the pack, churning through the mud. In a twinkling, they passed us and we craned our necks out of the window to watch the finish. A tremendous cheer went up and soon the word passed back to us that Lelantos had won and Benedick—my Benedick—was second.

We congratulated each other—and believe me, contemplating my winnings was only a small part of the pleasure. The real pleasure was studying that face, those dark, sparkling eyes, the play of her countenance, those lovely, pink lips, seeing her smile, hearing her laugh. I have never been at a loss around the ladies, but with Rose, it was all so easy, nothing studied, no affectation.

Rose and I seemed destined to come together to share this victory. She had quite recovered from the horrors of Carbuncle and Pox-face. By Jove, I had never spent a more pleasant afternoon.

Perhaps an hour passed by when Phillips returned with Rose's brother, René de Laval. He was a short, slender, sleek fellow with dark hair and eyes like his sister. He was a little stand-offish at first, but I allowed for him being a Frenchman, don't you know. In fact, I learned from Rose that their father was the Marquise de Laval. If it were not for Robespierre and those other bastards, they would be in some chateau back in France. Instead, her father got the chop from Madame La Guillotine.

Once Rose told him—in very excited, rapid French which I could but half follow—how I had rescued her from Carbuncle and Pox-face, I thought he might have thanked me. But that would be expecting too much of a Frenchman, wouldn't it? Instead, he looked very severe upon *her*, as though the whole affair was her fault.

"*La prochain fois, tu doit etre plus prudent, Rose,*" he said, frowning.

"The next time?" I asked. "There will be no next time, Monsieur de Laval, surely."

"I meant, *monsieur*, that the next time we go to the races, she must stay close to me. She has a lady's maid in Weymouth, but we did not bring her with us. And she walked out alone today and nearly came to grief, it seems."

The rain had stopped and the setting sun was sinking through the distant trees, and I realized that in addition to being besotted with Rose, I was also hungry. I did not think it at all out of place that I should invite the de Lavals to dine with me, no matter that de Laval worked as a horse trainer, considering their noble birth.

Except of course, I had no money.

"Oh, but you said you placed some wagers!" Rose recalled. "Where can you collect your winnings?"

Leaving my coachman and groomsman to prise the carriage out of the mud, we trod back over the field. With the crowd thinning and in the half-light of dusk, everything looked somehow different, and I could not spot the stall of my blackleg who would pay me out ten-to-one. We walked and we searched, but we could not find him. Happily, though, we came across my particular friend Sneyd—you have heard me speak of Sneyd—who paid off our gentlemen's wager, and that was more than enough to purchase a private dining room, some decent wine, and a good dinner.

And then, I had the pleasure of looking at Rose by candlelight and hearing more of her story. Rose's chief memories of France were of the convent school in which she had lived. I wonder which of us had the more Spartan childhood? Which has the more brutal regime or worse food, Eton or a French convent school? At any rate, I never had to cross the Channel at night in an open boat, disguised as a peasant, clinging to my poor mother, as these two did when very young. Their mother fell ill and died shortly after they arrived in England but Rose and her brother were sent to good boarding schools. They were both so well-informed, and of such good discourse, that believe me, I was cudgeling my brains, trying to remember more of my school room French. I suddenly wished I could quote Moliere and Montesquieu; I wished I had paid attention at Oxford. I wanted to be better than I was—for her.

We discovered we had a hundred shared pleasures and interests. We loved music—

Dash it, of course, I love music! Who said I don't love music?

And the countryside, and good food, and we laughed at the same things. I realized that I had always been one to talk *to* the fair sex, trying out my wit, or my gallantries, but with Rose, I was talking *with* her, if you understand my meaning.

As for René, while there was still something cool and reserved about him—perhaps he was ashamed of the gulf in our stations in life—by Jove, there never was a fellow who knew more about horses. It was a delight to converse with him. And there was Rose, sitting opposite me, watching us both, with a little smile which seemed to say she hoped that her brother and I should become good friends.

Well, I saw them to their hotel with a promise to call on her tomorrow, and René gave his consent that Rose could watch the races from my carriage, for the rain never let up all the next day, you know. What did I care, when I was picnicking on chicken and champagne with Rose? Of course, my servants and I tried to run down that blackleg—we never found him. But I spoke to the race committee and left a damned good description of him with his stupid boxer's face. I should have minded more, but I was otherwise preoccupied, as you can see.

So that was Basingstoke. I left lighter of pocket than I arrived but never happier, and I sent my groomsmen to walk Benedick back home because Rose and René were going on to the seaside, and I determined to follow them to Weymouth. My father's name, of course, is good for credit anywhere, so I took a respectable hotel room overlooking the water and had no other aim in view but to entertain my new friends in the most liberal manner. But he had Delingpole's horses to look after, and she had concerts to give, you know, and I was jealous of every moment she spent away from me.

You may remember, when we were young, and all the émigrés came pouring over from France, and what a to-do there was about helping them? Well, many of our society ladies organized concerts, and they discovered that Rose could sing like a little bird. They taught her to sing all the saddest arias and put her on display at these affairs, to raise money for the *émigrés*. *O Malheureuse Iphigénie*— Stay, I shall give it to you in English...

O! miserable Iphegenia
Your family has been destroyed
You, my people, have no more kings
And I have no more family.
Mingle your plaintive cries
with my endless lament.
You have no more kings;
and I have no more family.

CAN YOU PICTURE IT? The little orphan of the Revolution with her enormous dark eyes and long ringlets. *Vous n'avais plus de rois, je n'ai plus de famille.* No doubt the *ton* emptied their wallets for her.

Damn, the smoke is stinging my eyes. Trim that candle, why don't you?

René told me that the King himself used to have her sing for him at Weymouth—back when he used to go there every summer—and he was quite enchanted with her. So, she is still often engaged to perform there—privately, you understand, at private concerts, not on the public stage. She is, in every respect, a perfect gentlewoman, and I would have knocked any rascal flat on his backside who dared to say otherwise.

Thus began the happiest six weeks of my life. I claimed Rose's company every evening that she was disengaged, and every day as well. Sometimes she and her maid would go sea-bathing, and I would meet them afterwards and take them to eat ices or escort them to the shops. I never spent so much time at the library either, for, as I said, she was no feather-head and she was always reading some book or other. And some of my friends happened to come and go that summer, such as Charles Anderson and his sister—you have heard me speak of Anderson—and we would get up little parties to explore the countryside in my carriage, or hire some horses and go riding together. Of course, Rose sits a horse beautifully. I even arranged some excursions on a little sailing boat, up and down the coast.

Rose had some acquaintance there, too. She introduced me to Mr. Wilmot, a very decent old fellow. He knew my father, from when they sat in Parliament together. Rose told me that he helped raise piles of money for the French refugees, back at the time of the Terror, and he has known her since she was a child.

Wilmot's wife invited me to a concert she held for her friends, and Rose was the star performer. She was dressed all in white and silver, in the costume of a Grecian goddess or priestess or something, with a tunic of some light fabric, held together with silver clasps at the shoulders. She had silver bracelets winding like snakes around her bare arms. Her long hair was caught up in silver ribbons and the rest flowed down her back in dark ringlets. I cannot even try to tell you how beautifully she sang, with her voice throbbing with emotion, and her graceful gestures, like a Grecian statue come to life. I wanted to cuff every blockhead who spoke, or who sneezed, or yawned during her performance.

Hah! I recall, that is same the night I met Yates—John Yates, d'you know him? Lord Pencroft's youngest son. He had volunteered to recite an epic poem for the concert and I expect Mrs. Wilmot was too kind-hearted to refuse him. He gave us a portion—thank God!—a portion only—of *The Grave,* and quite a piece of work he made of it too, bellowing in a huge, hollow voice and rolling his *r*'s like a demented Scotsman and waving his arms like a tree in a gale. Like this:

What groan was that I heard? Deep groan indeed...
With anguish heavy laden! let me trace it:
From yonder bed it comes, where the strong man,
gasps for breath.... What now avail
The strong-built sinewy limbs, and well spread shoulders!
See, how he tugs for life, and lays about him
Mad with his pain!

Et cetera, et cetera. Oh, thank you, fellows. I do think I did him justice there. It was all we could do to keep our countenances. Yates was very evidently wanting some puff of praise afterwards, so I told him that "the artistry of his performance exceeded my powers of description," which pleased him very much. But, you mustn't betray me to Yates. He's an agreeable fellow, and we became friends after that.

The month of August passed away very agreeably in Weymouth, but then, I would have been happy in Timbuctoo if Rose was there, and fortunately Lord and Lady Delingpole were spending the summer at the seaside, so René continued in attendance on His Lordship, and Rose had several more engagements to perform.

I think she was proud of her independence. She would not let me buy anything for her but flowers, although I wanted to shower her with gifts, with anything her heart desired. She dressed beautifully, but not in a showy fashion—I am no expert on these matters, but I think no one can compete with a Frenchwoman when it comes to looking smart on a small income. No one made so good a figure on the promenade as Rose, nor, I fancy, could you have seen a happier couple than she and I.

René was more than complacent about my attentions to his sister. I fancy that I would be more watchful on my *own* sisters' behalf if some designing rogue was being too encroaching with them! For truthfully, I took as many liberties with Rose as she would permit. René would hide behind the newspaper while Rose and I whispered at the breakfast table or let us dawdle behind him when we walked through the park in the evening. When we went to the theatre together, he would sit at the front of the box and actually watch the play, and Rose and I sat behind so that we could give all our attention to each other. Say, however—when we were watching *The Heir at Law*—you recall that part when the fellow from the country finds his father's old lottery ticket, and you know, of course, this means he's going to be very rich by the third act. Well, Rose must have been watching the stage, for she scoffed and rolled her eyes and exclaimed, "Imbeciles! The lottery! It is a tax upon idiots!"

"Why," I asked, "do you not like to take a little flutter now and again? What about your brother's horses? Don't you wager on them?"

She turned and looked at me with the utmost seriousness. "I despise gaming. I despise gamesters. What—these so-called lords of creation"— and she gestured out across the theatre, where the cream of society was gathered—"they call it a 'debt of honour' when a man bankrupts himself, and ruins his name, and condemns his wife and children to misery?"

So, then it came out. Her own father, the marquis, had destroyed the family's fortunes because he would not leave off gambling. He lost his head during the Revolution—he had lost everything else *before*.

Well, no wonder she hated gamesters and she could not properly mourn for a father who had reduced his family to such dire straits. "All because he would not stop playing at cards! Cards! *Le diable!* My mother begged him, weeping, on her knees! The servants left us, the bailiffs came and took the furniture away; then they took me away from *Maman* and sent me to the convent.... I was five years old...." She brushed away a tear. "The idiot who places a wager on chance—'The next card will be an ace. My horse will be the fastest.'—Bah! I say they deserve to lose their money if they have such contempt for how hard it is to earn it. They, none of them, have worked a day in their lifetimes, but they spend as though they were pouring out the water!"

"There, there," I whispered as more than one head was now turning our way in the theatre. "My dear Miss Laval, you honour me with your confidence. Please, forgive me for awakening these painful memories." The heroine in the play, you remember, became destitute when her father died. "What an unfeeling fool I was to take you to see such a play! Er, although of course, it ends happily."

And then I blurted out: "If I had my dearest wish, Miss Laval, it would be to devote myself to *your* happiness for so long as you will permit me."

She trembled—I was startled myself at what I had just said. I had as good as proposed marriage to her, a thing I had never been in the least tempted to do with any other young lady of my acquaintance. I hardly knew myself at that moment—and hardly cared.

She smiled up at me, with another tear glistening in her eye, and answered, "What a woman needs to make her happy, Mr. Bertram, is a man who respects the woman he loves, who will not destroy her life and his through his vices and imprudence."

This took me aback. I had everything—my family, an estate, the promise of a baronet's title, servants, carriage, horses, the best education money could buy. And while I had been taking my ease, and doing exactly what I pleased, Rose and René had struggled for everything they had, through their own skill and pluck. My darling Rose had lost her beloved mother, her home, and her fortune, because of the vices, cruelties, and follies of men. No wonder she mistrusted Dame Fortune. Deuce take me, but I wanted to lay all I had at her feet at that moment.

As we were leaving the box, I think that René chanced to see someone in the corridor that he did not want to meet, for I saw him stiffen and change direction and then swiftly hurry on ahead of us. His affairs held no interest for me, because it meant I was suddenly alone with Rose. Unable to help myself, I pulled her back into our little balcony and whisked her behind the side-curtains, pulling her close. I caught the scent of her perfume—ah, I am certain you think I am about to describe the aroma of roses. But my Rose was not so obvious. She preferred verbena. Roses are too sweet, she told me.

"Rose, my darling Rose," I murmured. "Tell me what I may do to be worthy of you."

She tipped her head up to look at me—I could not resist—I cupped that beautiful face between my hands and drew her to me for a kiss, as I had so often dreamt of doing. She did not resist or make a sound. I gently brushed those full lips and stroked that perfect, downy cheek. Her eyes were closed and a tear glistened in her long eyelashes. She laid her head on my chest, and she felt as though she belonged there, nestled in the shelter of my arms.

"Tom—Tom Bertram, I believe you are a very kind man, a very good man. I do not think you could be selfish or thoughtless or cruel, not with anyone you loved."

"Kiss me, Rose" was all I could manage, and my beautiful girl—well, they say a gentleman does not kiss and tell....

Well then, more brandy, please.

Dammit it all. If I could relive one moment of my life, it would be that moment when she turned her face up to me, and her lips met mine, and sweetly parted and—I was in danger of losing control of myself, but Rose managed to pull away and then—she winked at me and grinned and said, "And how did you like the play, Monsieur Bertram?" That was my Rose. She could fly from tears to mirth like a child. I believe we were both laughing like naughty schoolchildren when we reappeared and found René, who rolled his eyes but otherwise said nothing. It was his duty to have a serious talk with me. But he had other things on his mind, I fancy.

Another thing, by the bye—I have not, from that moment, played a single game of chance, or placed a wager, or bought a lottery ticket. I have sat through plenty of sermons against gaming, and of course, my father has raked me over the coals many a time, but no one, I suppose, has the address of a Frenchwoman. Rose convinced me, when no one else could.

One evening soon after, Rose and I were walking together along the shore with her lady's maid trailing obligingly behind. Rose was looking out over the Channel, thinking, as I imagined, of her old home in France.

"So many of your countrymen went home after Boney was crowned," I remarked. "Why did you and your brother stay behind here?"

An elegant shrug of her shoulders. "There is nothing left for us to go back for, Tom. We have been in England longer than we lived in France. You notice René has hardly any accent. But"—and she looked up at me mischievously—"I kept *my* accent because—the gentlemen like it!"

I had to catch her and kiss her for that impudence, but she was right. I was enchanted by my Frenchwoman—*my* Frenchwoman—her accent, her voice, her smiles, her pouts, her grace, her laughter. I can close my eyes and see her as she was in the dusk that evening, as the tide washed over the shingle, the breeze making the curls about her forehead dance, and lifting and teasing her shawl and her skirts, now billowing, now pressing against her supple figure as she laughed and danced and twisted just ahead of me, out of my reach. What is it about love that turns people into children again?

I do not know when I first entertained the thought of asking her to marry me, but that night I was utterly determined—I would ask her as soon as the opportunity presented itself.

That night I escorted her to the Wilmots' home because René had gone away with Lord Delingpole to examine some horses. I asked her if I might call on her privately the next day, and she agreed.

To my own surprise, I slept soundly that night and woke up feeling fit and fresh and absolutely knowing my own mind. No, I was not nervous or hesitant. In fact, I was impatient to pose the question; I had no doubt of being accepted. She was not an early riser, so I had to wait, impatiently pacing up and down the promenade like a fool. Finally, I decided it was late enough to call upon the Wilmots and the butler escorted me into a small parlour. Rose was there, alone, sitting at the pianoforte and playing a melancholy tune. She was wearing white muslin, I recall, with yellow trimming, and she received me very quietly, without her usual mirth, then took a seat and looked at me gravely.

I had been practising my speech for hours and I believe I spoke well. I told her that I had loved her from the moment I saw her, but upon better acquaintance, I had learned her beauty was merely an adornment to her excellent character, intelligence, and sweet nature, perfections that I had never seen assembled in one woman before. I could not imagine life without her. I promised her security, comfort, and luxury. My name and fortune were hers if she would make me the happiest of men. Nothing new or original there, I suppose, but it was all new to *me* and if my words could not convey the depth of my emotions, I believe my eyes and countenance did. I knelt before her—of course—and she reached out and stroked my cheek. I had fondly imagined that at my conclusion she would embrace me, and I her, and we would share a passionate kiss. But she did not move or speak and she appeared to be deep in thought. Finally, awkwardly, I jested, "How long shall I stay on my knees before you, my love? If you tell me, 'a fortnight,' I shall do it and willingly, although you might provide me with a cushion to kneel upon."

"My dear, sweet Tom," she said softly. "Please, please come sit beside me."

I sat next to her and she rested her head on my shoulder and held my hand. I wanted to think this was a good sign, but an anxious feeling grew within me.

"Thomas Bertram," she said at last. "When I first met you, I saw that you were so free, so happy, with no cares or worries. I did not know that your father was a baronet, who would undoubtedly expect his son to marry a woman worthy of his name and title. And when I did learn, it was too late for me. I could not deny myself the pleasure of your company. Every day with you has been like a charming dream and I did not want to wake up.

"It never occurred to me that you would ask me to marry you, that you would do me this inexpressible honour. I believed"—she laughed softly—"I believed that you intended to seduce me, as so many others have tried! But you have always shown me the utmost of tenderness. How lucky will be the future Lady Bertram!"

"*You* shall be my future Lady Bertram—I mean, my *only* Lady Bertram!" I exclaimed, slipping my arm around her waist and pulling her to me. She shook her head and pushed me away.

"No, no, I cannot. Please hear me. We may be happy today, Tom. We may be happy for a time. But the difficulties, the problems, they cannot be overcome. We are from two different worlds. And I know one thing—the day would come when you would regret choosing me for your wife."

"Rose! No! Never, my darling, never!"

I tried to protest, but she laid her fingers against my mouth and continued.

"I have no dowry, which is sufficient cause for most families to disapprove of our marriage and to prevent it if they could."

"I am of age, my love. I can marry whom I please!"

"But that is the least of it. *I sing for money.* We cannot deny it. Some of the friends you might invite to Mansfield Park have seen me at some concert or another. I am a performer—you could not proudly call me your wife, if you knew what"—she paused and bit her lip anxiously. "In many people's eyes, I am not even a gentlewoman. No lady would display herself in public as I have done."

"And what of it! I defy them all!"

"Would you defy your own father? Mr. Wilmot told me he is a most upright, formal gentleman. Can *you* be indifferent to the pain you will cause your father when you present him with a daughter-in-law whom he would think is little better than a courtesan?"

"No, but once they come to know you, Rose...." I tried feebly but with a rising feeling of panic.

"And what will your father say, what will your mother say, what will your brother, who is to become a clergyman, say—when you tell them that you are going to marry a Catholic?"

I did not suppose I had given the matter much thought. Any thought, in fact. Perhaps Rose went to mass on Sunday morning, but if she did, it was while I was sleeping off Saturday night. We had never discussed religion. "My dear one, if it does not matter to me, or you, why should it matter to others?"

"But it does matter to me, my love. Our children, Tom. How will they be raised? As Protestants?"

"Why, I imagine so.... Otherwise they could not go to the right schools and so forth."

She sighed and continued. "I do not say this with the resentment. I am not blaming your family for rejecting me. *My* parents would reject *you*, if they were still alive. They would forbid this marriage absolutely. And in their place, my brother will say the same. Because you are not of the true Church."

"René does not strike me as being particularly devout! And, while I confess I have nothing to boast of in that regard, why should René care, one way or the other, about which church I *do not* attend regularly?"

"You are still a Protestant whether you go to church or not, *mon cher*. That is who and what you are. Unlike Catholics, you can stand for Parliament and follow your father's footsteps. But if you have a Catholic wife, you will always be under suspicion and so will your children. You know that, Tom."

Yes, I knew it. Still I disputed with her for at least another hour, repeating the same arguments, again and again. I said that love conquers all. She tried to tell me that a great many things can conquer our happiness and even destroy our love. She got me to calm down at last and to stop and imagine what my father would say, how distressed my mother would be. Then I could picture it. I could see myself handing Rose down from the carriage and presenting her to my parents as my wife. I could see my father's face as he endeavoured to command his emotions, the formality and coldness of his address of welcome. And, I realized with dawning horror, even if my father refrained from expressing his true sentiments, my aunt Norris would *not*! She would torment my sweet Rose and be completely miserable to her every time we came together. Everyone dear to me would regard my choice of wife as a piece of wild folly, and my love for her would compel me to reject *them* in turn.

"That is what it means, Tom. It means spending every Christmas apart from your family. Or having to choose between your wife and your family at every important event in your life. Or, it means watching as they snub me, seeing their cold looks and their lips like they were sucking at a lemon! As for me—if my children are not raised as Catholics, all of the dear old refugees who took care of me after *Maman* died, the good priests and nuns who educated me, they will say that I have shut my children out of Heaven for all eternity! *Your* friends will have contempt for me. *My* friends will condemn me—cut me out entirely!

"I have almost nothing left from my old life, Tom, and it would grieve me deeply if I had to give up what little I have. Can you not see?"

I had thought I was giving her everything she did not have. It never occurred to me what sacrifices *she* would have to make in return. Perhaps, *I* would have given up everything, if I could only have her for my own. But she would not consent to it.

"Tom, you were born to be a baronet. It is impossible that you would give up your life to have me, and not, in the end, resent me for it. On my honour, I did not mean to hurt you this way. You are so sweet, so trusting. I cannot take advantage of your good nature and condemn you to a marriage which will cause you such harm and bring you lasting regret."

She was unbending, and I am afraid I did not behave very well. I was angry—at her, at her brother, at the Pope, at everybody's bloody-mindedness. Finally, she began to hint that it was best that we part.

More brandy, please.

Yes, *more*, damn you.

What are you insinuating? That since I could not have her as my wife, I should have offered to make her my mistress? As a token of my great love, respect, and esteem for her, to ruin her absolutely? No, I did not, but thank you for your kind enquiry.

All right. I thought of it. I confess it. As long as I am confessing everything else. I was burning for her and could never have her. In my resentment, I almost forgot myself. I grabbed her by her shoulders and she gave a little cry of alarm. My mouth came down on hers and forced her lips apart. I held her tightly to me, so that she could feel the heat surging within me. My hands roamed all over her body. I left a trail of passionate kisses down her jaw, her neck, her shoulder, her bosom, and I heard a moan of pleasure escape her lips, even as she struggled feebly to push me away. In answer, my hand tangled itself in her hair and I pulled her head back to kiss her savagely. Then suddenly I had a vision of Carbuncle and Pox-face, and the way they had used her—and I released her. I was panting like a wild beast.

"Oh, Rose. Forgive me, Rose."

She waved her hand feebly and turned away from me. "I think you are not accustomed to not having what you want," she said in a low voice. "I, alas, am all too used to it." She looked up at me with a brave, little smile on the lips that were swollen from my kisses. "Please, my love, let us not part in this fashion. Let us try to remember the joyful times together, yes? Please say that you will remember me with fondness, as I will always remember you."

I do not know how I managed to collect my hat and bring a close to this interview which was so disastrous for my hopes and wishes—certainly I could not sufficiently command myself to be gracious or easy when I bid her *adieu*. My poor valet had to receive me at the hotel, hours after I had set out, so cheerfully, and I gave orders for us to depart Weymouth immediately, never to return to the cursed place.

So, summer was over, and I crawled slowly back to Mansfield.

I had lost the love of my life, and everything was ashes. Have you ever experienced anything like it? Have you ever travelled along a peaceful country lane, with the gloriously beautiful countryside unfolding in a dozen shades of green and brown before you, a breeze tickling your hair, birds singing all around—and everything is ashes?

I dreaded every sunset and every starry night, and I hated opening my eyes in the morning, and I especially hated rainy days, and I hated music, and I was in no humour to confide in anyone about my wounded heart. I hit upon the idea of inviting everyone I could think of to come and visit us at Mansfield—that way, I would never be home alone, *en famille*, where my brother or my sisters might observe that I was not quite myself. Fortunately, my new acquaintance, Yates, was at liberty, and my sister Maria's tiresome fiancé was often hanging about, in addition to the Crawfords. Edmund had been making *some* progress with Miss Crawford, by the bye, and she had transferred her affections from me to him, which was the only consolation I could take for the ruin of all my own hopes.

I know I was restless and in an ill-humour, try as I might. Luckily, Yates proposed that we put on some private theatricals and most everyone fell upon the idea with great enthusiasm. Here was the perfect diversion for my mind and my spirits. At first, we quarreled as to which play we should attempt. I wanted *The Heir at Law*—then at least I could secretly relive a private memory of Rose—but, no, we settled upon *Lover's Vows*, which is a little risqué, and I knew my father would have disapproved, for my sisters' sake. But he was overseas, so I did not care. I declined to play the role of the lover because I could not bear to draw laughter upon myself after my tragedy in Weymouth. So, I took the part of the Butler, a comic fellow who sneers at love, in keeping with the character of the Tom Bertram that everyone knew—before.

And I think I *would* have restored some of my composure by leading my little theatrical company had not everything and everyone conspired against me. There was Edmund, as solemn as a funeral, pulling his long faces at me; that rascal scene painter I engaged spent half his time flirting with our housemaids, and even my little cousin, who would not say "boo" to a dormouse, refused to oblige me by taking a trifling role! Oh, and by the bye—I had insisted that Miss Crawford must play Amelia because I had assumed Edmund would leap at the chance to take the part of Anhalt and play her lover—and if you can credit it, Edmund refused! Unbelievable. But she overcame his scruples in the end.

And then—oh, it gets worse—at the worst possible moment, my father returned from Antigua! It took all my diplomacy and dispatch to smooth matters over with him. But that all belongs to another story, I suppose.

So, I kept busy with hunting and riding until the weather turned, feeling like a man carved out of a block of wood, moving my legs and arms and opening my mouth so I could put food into it. Saying the right things and doing the right things. The evenings after dinner were the worst, when the family gathered in the sitting room. Maria or Julia would play the piano, or we would sit around in silence and say "yes, sir" and "no, sir" whenever my father made some remark. I could not endure it. I needed the solitude that could only come from being in the city, surrounded by multitudes. I did not even stay at home for Christmas but went up to London.

I expected—I thought—I desired, that I would come to regard Miss Laval as only a pleasant memory and certainly no cause for lasting bitterness or regret. But in the city, I learned what it was to be always looking and watching for a certain walk, a certain turn of the head—to be listening for a particular voice, for a silvery laugh—and sometimes thinking *there she is, just up ahead at the corner*, or, *is that she, just entering the theatre?* But it never was her. I tried to take myself in hand, the devil take me if I did not. I believe you saw me at every gathering around Town, and in tolerable good humour. Winter gave way at last, and while I was still privately longing for Rose every day, at least I was becoming accustomed to it, to a dull ache of pain, a constant absent-mindedness, and a conviction that I could never love another woman as I had loved her. By the time March turned to April, and George invited us all to Newmarket to watch the races. I was glad to be one of the party.

Yes, now at last, the incident you are *really* curious about. You want my explanation about what happened with Miss Laval and me at the racecourse. And if you refill my glass, I shall tell you.

All right, all right. After we all arrived at George's house, I washed and changed my linen and then rode over to the racetrack. I left my horse at the stables to go for a walk through the crowd, looking for any old friends I might meet. It was a pleasant scene and a beautiful day. There were the punters, looking to place their wagers; there were the townswomen with their trays hanging about their necks, crying meat pasties and baked apples and toasted chestnuts; there were the important little jockeys leading their horses to the starting line; and people from high and low—elegant ladies, fat merchants, merry widows, and pale, shabby clerks stealing a half day's holiday.

And suddenly I heard a woman's scream nearby, high-pitched, frightened.

"*Oh non, non, messieurs!* Please, I have done nothing!"

I froze.

Had I gone mad? Had my memories of last summer overpowered my reason? But it was clear from the reactions of the people around me, they heard it too. They were looking and craning and pushing to see what was causing the commotion.

"Hold still, you artful baggage! How dare you steal an honest man's purse! Return my friend's property, and do it quickly, or it will be the worse for you!"

We all moved closer to the sound, and, since I am taller by a head or more than most fellows, I could hear and see everything, even when standing at the back.

There was my Rose; with her brother holding her by one wrist, and a second man holding her by the other. She struggled and squirmed between them.

"*Non!* I swear by St. Catherine, I have not stolen anything! I am an honest woman!"

"Now, there's a blasphemous lie!" cried the other man, and I suddenly recognized him. He was my missing blackleg, the old boxer with the mashed-in nose. "Don't make matters worse for yourself, missy. Give over with my purse, or you may very well swing from a rope."

I felt as though I was one of those archery targets made from straw, and every thing they said was like an arrow shooting straight into my heart.

Do you see what this meant?

I looked around and saw what I expected to see—not far away—a crooked, little wooden stall where two men were swiftly taking down their banners: "Place Your Bets Here," "Racing Forms for Sale," and stowing everything into two portmanteaus.

"Search her! Search her! No doubt she has hidden your purse inside her pelisse!" I heard René exclaim, and I heard Rose wail in distress.

It was all play-acting. Rose and her confederates created a diversion— a very titillating diversion. While the punters watched a beautiful, frightened French woman being stripped half-naked, the blacklegs pocketed all the bets they had laid and slipped away. At Basingstoke, I had interrupted their play in the second act, so to speak, which is why they were all so surprised, including Rose. And no doubt, when I intervened, they were worried that their confederate had not made his escape in time, but he did.

The next time, you must be more careful, Rose.

And I had likened myself to a hero in a romance. Instead, I was a fool, a complete booby.

I became aware that I was running madly after the two men with the portmanteaus. I had no trouble catching up with the fatter of the two and knocking him down. It was Carbuncle. Of course, they changed roles at every racecourse. Last time, he was the tormenter of Rose; this time he played the part of the blackleg. Because a punter might have placed a wager with him at one racetrack and then recognized him at the next. I certainly should have. But only *I* had discovered the connection between the poor woman accused of being a pickpocket, and the blackleg who absconded with everyone's wagers.

I explained my theory to Carbuncle, while I had my knee in his back and while smashing his face into the ground, and he conceded that I was correct. "Sir," he added, "I'll give you—all the money—I have here—take it all—if you will let—me get away. I beg you, sir."

Exhausted, and as miserable as a man could be, I rolled off his back and collapsed in the dust beside him. "I am going to let you go but not because I want the damned money. If I were to bring a charge against you, you would turn King's evidence and testify against—against the rest of them to save your own neck."

Carbuncle had nothing to say to that because it was true.

"Would you give Miss Laval a message for me?" I said, trying to keep my voice steady and cool.

"Yes, sir. Thank you, sir!"

"Tell her—" I stopped. *Tell her what? Tell her that I thought she had broken my heart before, but I did not know what a broken heart really felt like until this moment?* No, I could not confide my feelings to Carbuncle. Rose had *permitted* him to grab her and paw at her in front of a crowd of men so that they could steal my money and everyone else's. I loathed him so much I could barely stand to look at him.

"Tell her that Mr. Tom Bertram sends his compliments and advises her that racecourses are unsafe places for an unaccompanied lady."

"Yes, sir. I will sir, thank you, sir." Carbuncle scrambled to his feet, grabbed his portmanteau and paused, looking at me apologetically. "If it makes any difference, sir, Rosie—Miss Laval that is, she didn't want to do it. She hates it. She begged her brother to leave off. He told her 'just one more time.' You see, he has lots of gaming debts he must pay off, or it will be the worse for him."

"Debts of honour. Of course." I closed my eyes and swayed a bit, for I was still reeling from horror and despair. What a pathetic figure I must have made, sitting in the dust. I suppose people took me for a drunk. When I opened my eyes again, Carbuncle was long gone.

All right. So, I stood up, picked up my hat, retrieved my horse, and left the racetrack. I thought that before I went back to George's house and re-joined our party, I would take a long gallop through the fields and clear my head. Of course, I went riding like a madman, and that's when I tried to take the hedge.

And lost my seat. And broke my collarbone.

I lay flat on my back for several hours, looking up at the sky. The pain from my collarbone was sharp and cleansing and somehow served to numb my feelings. I tried to think, coolly, what had it all meant? How much did I resent the woman I thought I loved? On the one hand, if Rose had not helped her brother, he would be flung into debtor's prison or be broken in two by some footpad who made Carbuncle look like a sweet maiden aunt. On the other hand, she had been deceiving me from the first moment of our acquaintance. How much did I hate René for getting Rose into this scrape? How angry was I with her that she could not break free of him—her only living relative? How much had she and her gang stolen from me? Ten pounds? The laws of England provided they should all be hung by the neck. Ten pounds. But stay, I was offered odds of ten-to-one on my horse. That is *one hundred* pounds they robbed from me! But of course, that was just a lie. I cannot be robbed of one hundred pounds that never existed. What is a wager, anyway? One fellow convinces another fellow that a winning hand at cards is worth a guinea, when they really have no value at all, and by the end of the night, one man walks away rich and the other fellow is a pauper. Nothing has been purchased or even exchanged. But the money is gone. I myself have managed to lose hundreds of pounds at cards and at the racetrack, money that was never mine in the first place...

Thinking of that, a memory washed over me. It was a little over two years ago. I was in my father's study. He held out a piece of paper, listing all of my debts and expenses since I had left Oxford. I knew I had been exceeding my allowance and borrowing against my father's name, but I never kept a close accounting of it, and the total figure shocked me into silence. Even *this* was not the worst of it because I had contrived to keep some of my gaming debts from my father's knowledge. I am too ashamed to tell you the figure written on that piece of paper, but believe me, had I taken that money from a stranger and not my father, I could have been sentenced to hang a thousand times over.

My father told me because of my spending—on clothes, drink, horses, my carriage, travel, cards—he was unable to keep the living at Mansfield parsonage for my brother, Edmund, and would have to sell it to another clergyman.

"I blush for you, Tom," he had said. "I blush for the expedient which I am driven on, and I trust I may pity your feelings as a brother on the occasion. You have robbed Edmund for ten, twenty, thirty years, perhaps for life, of more than half the income which ought to be his."

Robbed. Yes, that was the word he used. And I remember that at the time I felt ashamed but brushed it off tolerably quickly and, in fact, seldom thought of it afterwards. And do you think Edmund has ever once thrown it in my face? No, not once.

I had robbed my own brother, perhaps for life, of more than half his income, and here I was, lying on my back in a field, wondering how to revenge myself on the woman I loved for stealing ten pounds from *me*.

And then I realized—although Rose deceived me, I deceived her in return, for she truly thought I was a good, kind man. When in fact the evidence would suggest that I am a selfish, lazy, thoughtless, conceited, bullying, contemptible ass. But I desperately want to be—I want to be—the man that she thinks I am. And in the end, that is all I can take away from this past ten months. I want to be a better man.

What? Have none of you anything to say? George? Edward? Charles? Perhaps you take me for a fool. Perhaps you have contempt for me. I am still Tom Bertram, your old friend and comrade. Was I wrong to expect some pity from you?

I fear I may have had a little too much to drink. Never mind. I am sorry.

Ah, I am damnably thirsty! I just want some water. Some water.

Please, ring for the servant. Water, damn your eyes!

Why won't you say something?

Oh God, this cursed collarbone. It aches so badly.

All right, if no one will help me, I am getting up. I shall get some water myself, curse you.

What groan was that I heard?

Oh. It was me.

Where is everyone? Where is the bell? Will someone help me.

Help me, please.

Just some water.

Water.

"Oh, Tom! My poor Tom. Sssh, sssh. I am here, *chéri.*"
Rose?
Rose?
I was dreaming.
Or I am dying, perhaps. That's it. I'm dying. Well, if this is dying, it is not so bad. It's very peaceful.
But on the other hand, I have not apologized to Edmund yet. I need to talk to him. I need to tell him how sorry I am. I was going to be a better man, and now it is too late. I have got to get up. I have got to go home.
Why am I still on the floor? I have got to get up. I must get up.

Cool water on my lips. *Cool hand on my forehead.*
"*Mon dieu*, Tom. You are on fire! Quickly, Mr. Sawyer, please help him."
Rose. Rose.

I do not know if it was because of the fever or because I was thoroughly foxed—they found half a dozen empty bottles scattered all around me—but I was not rational for a day and a night. When I regained my senses, I was washed and bandaged and lying in bed with Rose sitting quietly at my side.

Rose explained to me that she had heard talk at the racecourse that Tom Bertram was lying ill at a nearby house, that his friends had left him behind to join another party of pleasure. Alarmed, she took a horse, found the house, knocked on the door, then went around to the window and spied me, lying on the floor in front of a cold fireplace. It seems I was insensible and had been for some time, in a dream-fever, imagining that my friends were all there, listening to my story. Rose did what she could for me, then hurried to fetch a physician.

I think Rose never left me for a week. She held the basin while the physician bled me; she sponged cool water on me and fanned me by the hour when I roasted, and wrapped me up well when I shivered, as the fever that had seized a hold of me came and went. She spooned warm broth down my throat and held my head when it came back up again.

And she sent an express to my father, describing herself simply as "a friend" and telling him how matters stood.

I seldom was able to say more than "thank you" and to bless her again and again for her goodness. I held her hand in mine and could sometimes summon the strength to lift that hand to my lips. Mostly, I slept. I was so tired and too weak to even lift my head off the pillow.

I knew I was feeling a little better a few days later when I first started to wonder—how did I look? That is, how did I appear to her with my hair soaked in sweat and my skin pale and clammy? I believe I had already lost a lot of flesh in those few days.

"Rose, I fear I must make a very poor figure," I began, and she laughed and shushed me.

"Do not be so vain, my dear Tom." She laughed again. "We must get you healthy. We *will* get you healthy again. I promise."

"I love you, Rose," I breathed.

"It is a miracle, you have forgiven me for my terrible secret. When you first rescued me at the Basingstoke Races, I could not believe it. Before, all the young gentlemen only watched me, as René and the others humiliated me and uncovered me in front of their eyes! You came and rescued me—like a knight from King Arthur's stories! And when you asked me to marry you, I thought I would die of the remorse! Ah, I was so ashamed when Simon brought me your message! Now I can be at peace. *Je t'aime, mon cher. Je ne t'oublierai jamais, pour le reste de ma vie*, do you hear?"

"And I will never forget you, Rose. Or cease to regret losing you."

Those soft lips brushed my cheek. I closed my eyes and savoured the light scent of her perfume as I drifted back to sleep.

"My dear Tom," she told me a few days later, "you have a letter from your mother. Your brother is coming to take you home. I believe he should arrive by this afternoon. I shall not be here when he comes for you."

"I understand your feelings, Rose, but I am sorry that you will not meet him. He is one of the best fellows who ever breathed."

"Your mother says he is riding up by way of London and will retrieve your carriage to take you back to Mansfield Park. *Mon chéri*, are you sure that you are well enough for the travel?"

"Apart from leaving you, Rose, I am anxious to get home again."

And as soon as we get back to Mansfield, I am going to sell the blasted carriage—and my racehorses, and I will do everything in my power to make amends to Edmund, and take lessons from him, too, on how to be a decent human being.

"God willing, we may meet again one day, my dear Tom."

"I wish you every happiness, my love. If you ever need me, if I can ever be of service to you, please call on me. You risked your life coming here to help me. For all you knew, I could have had you thrown into prison. But you came anyway."

"No, no, Tom, I trusted you. I knew you were the kindest and best of men!"

"I am not the kindest and best of men, but I am going to become a better man than I am. And it is because of you, my Rose, my darling."

TOM RETURNED to Mansfield Park to be reunited with his family. He still had to endure a lengthy convalescence with several relapses before he:

"...gradually regained his health, without regaining the thoughtlessness and selfishness of his previous habits. He was the better for ever for his illness. He had suffered, and he had learned to think, two advantages that he had never known before.... He became what he ought to be, useful to his father, steady and quiet, and not living merely for himself." —Mansfield Park, Chapter XLVIII.

LONA MANNING is the author of *A Contrary Wind*, a variation on *Mansfield Park*. She has also written numerous true crime articles, which are available at www.crimemagazine.com. She has worked as a non-profit administrator, a vocational instructor, a market researcher, and a speech-writer for politicians. She currently teaches English as a Second Language. She and her husband now divide their time between mainland China and Canada. Her second novel, *A Marriage of Attachment*, a sequel to *A Contrary Wind*, is planned for release in early 2018. You can follow Lona at www.lonamanning.ca where she blogs about China and Jane Austen.

HENRY CRAWFORD

Rich, fashionable, self-satisfied. Henry Crawford was accustomed to having his own way and motivated to find pleasure in all his pursuits. Though not depicted as good looking, his affable and pleasant manners more than offset his plain countenance. He and his sister had been raised by their uncle, Admiral Crawford, who after the death of his wife, invited his mistress to live in their home. *"My dearest Henry, the advantages to you of getting away from the admiral before your manners are hurt by the contagion of his, before you have contracted any of his foolish opinions..."* —*Mansfield Park,* **Chapter XXX.** After an indecent flirtation with the engaged Maria Bertram, he decided to seduce her timid and penniless cousin, only to discover he had indeed fallen in love with the virtuous Fanny Price.

"I am afraid I am not quite so much the man of the world as might be good for me in some points. My feelings are not quite so evanescent, nor my memory of the past under such easy dominion as one finds to be the case with men of the world." —Henry Crawford to Maria Bertram, *Mansfield Park*, Chapter X.

LAST LETTER TO MANSFIELD
Brooke West

OCTOBER 5, 1809, EVERINGHAM, NORFOLK

M*y dearest Fanny*—

He stared at his handwriting, the ink drying with his slow exhale. How to address…? Those words would fit his purpose, his desires, but not his situation. *Dearest*, she was. *Darling. Beloved. Admired.* But *Fanny* she could not be. Not anymore—not ever. He crumpled the paper with one hand and tossed it aside to join its fallen brothers on the floor, evidence of many discarded attempts.

My dearest Miss Price

Before the ink had dried this time, he set his quill aside. *Dearest* and *Miss Price* could not coexist. Even now, he could not reduce the salutation to such a common expression of friendly affection. What right had he to even that intimacy? And how could he so diminish his love?

My love, most unluckily absent forever

Sweetest girl, whom I should have liked to spend decades learning and pleasing

My lovely Fanny

The kindest and warmest woman I have known, and without whom my home will be cold and joyless

These he could not commit to paper. These he could only hold in his thoughts as he struggled to keep his resolve to not return to Northamptonshire. Immediately. To not throw himself at her feet and beg forgiveness for his lack of thoughtfulness, for his vanity, his folly. The months he had spent with Maria kept him numb. Seldom had he allowed himself a moment to dwell on his Fanny with Maria so nearby. Now that he was free of Fanny Price's more determined cousin, his love was never far from his mind.

Henry was thoroughly unused to the tortured pangs of a broken heart and ungratified desires. He was desperate to relieve this new experience of heartache and loss. *The only way out is through.* He picked up his quill, his hand less steady than he would have liked.

> *I know not how to address you in a manner that does not insult either of us—your proper understanding of what intimacies may be allowed even if not encouraged, and my sensibilities of both my affection and my error.*

Knowing he could not send the letter, regardless of address, gave him a grim resolve to continue. For months, Henry had tried to wish away the affair with Mrs. Maria Bertram Rushworth, hoping that if he could scrape it from his mind then society must as well. Hoping that word would not reach Fanny or that time would erode the effect of his actions. He knew better than continue those hopes. Little news from Mansfield Park reached his ears anymore, but what he heard, and what he knew of Fanny, told him she was lost to him.

> *There is nothing I would not do to unwind time and retreat to Everingham, as you so wisely counseled, rather than return again to London. My sister begged me to stay in London. No man can refuse our Mary's wishes, and I had ceased trying to resist. I flatter myself that I now have a firmer resolve— No. I shall not flatter myself or others. It was flattery that landed us here, was it not?*
>
> *There must only be honesty between us.*
>
> *I admit my first thought of renewing the acquaintance with your cousins piqued my interest. I could tell you I did not intend to seduce, or be seduced, but instead wanted only an easy cordiality with your family in the hopes they would soon be <u>my</u> family as well. This I told myself as a reason to stay. I will not call it a lie because it was at least part truth. In my heart, Fanny, I was yours. Would be yours once you consented to have me. But, if we are to be honest, I must also tell you that flirtation was on my mind. Truthfully, I did not intend for what happened between Maria and me. I more slipped into sin than designed it. But once I had . . .*

SEPTEMBER 1809, THE DARK HORSE, TROWBRIDGE, WILTSHIRE

HENRY WOKE TO THE SOUNDS of wardrobe doors being flung open and slammed shut. For the first time since spring, he felt a spark of hope.

Dragging himself from bed, not even bothering to smooth down his hair or find a shirt—anything to further shock or dismay that woman—he leaned in the doorway between his sleeping room and the suite's sitting room. Maria, as perfectly put together as ever, was throwing gowns and hats into chests and boxes.

He yawned loudly, stretching his bare arms high above his head. Her head snapped up to glare at him. He knew he cut a fine figure. That Maria's gaze did not stray from his face told him precisely her state of mind. Any other day, her eyes would roam over the planes of his muscles. The spark of hope grew a bit brighter.

"I am *done* with this charade!" Every word rang with anger. Her eyes burned. Her face contorted into a scowl the likes of which he had never seen.

At last. Relief flooded him as he recognized in her countenance the same hatred he had felt towards her for weeks. "I trust you've enjoyed your holiday."

Maria cried out sharply, like a startled hen, twisting the silk gown in her hands. Henry laughed out loud at her explosion of fury. She complained nearly daily about the boredom and indignity she endured being sequestered in the inn and would beg often to be taken to Everingham. The society was no better at his Norfolk estate. Indeed, there was even less at his home to keep a young, lively woman entertained. The travelers who came through the inn brought with them their own dramas and histories, and Henry's only enjoyment in recent weeks came from conversing with them at dinner or around the fire with a brandy. Maria seldom left their rooms.

Henry suspected that it was more the lack of an enviable standing in society that grated on her. Back at Mansfield Park, she held reign over all as the eldest Bertram daughter. As Mrs. Rushworth, she had an idiot husband and household to rule with thousands of pounds at her disposal to convince others of her value in society. But here, in The Dark Horse, Maria's continued residence only raised questions amongst the locals, forcing her to steep in the scandal she so clearly desired that morning in early May when she appeared on Admiral Crawford's doorstep demanding to see Henry.

She was not one to suffer consequences with grace, Henry found.

He had no intention of ever allowing Maria Bertram Rushworth to breathe the air at Everingham. Henry had chosen this esteemed, venerable inn in Wiltshire to keep her as far away as possible from his home without having to spend an unbearable amount of time in a carriage with her when they left London. With every complaint, he would point out that she could leave under her own power at any time—to which Maria would spit back that she had nowhere else to go. The satisfaction he drew from seeing her suffer was bitter indeed when coupled with his misery at being in her presence.

Anger colored her cheeks a flattering pink. Her bosom swelled prettily with each quick breath. A single curl had escaped from her loose coiffure as she had tossed her clothing about. It brushed at the gentle curve of her slender shoulder and graceful neck. He stared at that curl, remembering how his lips had been just there when his world tilted, upending his plans and destroying his happiness.

He wondered at what drew him to her so many months ago at Mansfield Park. Henry could not fail to recognize her beauty, even now, but he could no longer help but see past it to the creature beneath: the callous, selfish woman who was incapable—or unwilling—to consider anyone but herself.

Despite what Maria had promised that day at his uncle's home, there had not been a single happy moment together once they left London. Henry did not intend to be happy with her and would not allow for her happiness with him. He *intended* for them both to be quite miserable. While all the world would see Henry as the scoundrel who ruined a gently bred woman, Henry could only think of Maria as the vixen who willfully parted him from his love. Many times, he was tempted to saddle a horse and leave her at the inn to find her own way out of the muddle she created. Henry would own a great many failings of character, but he was not so callous as to leave a woman without protection. Until she grew tired of their games and decided to leave, or her family came for her at last, Henry was stuck in this Wiltshire purgatory.

Upon learning that knowledge of his and Maria's absence was widespread, his first instinct had been to ride immediately to Fanny, to bare all to her, to let her goodness and kindness absolve and cleanse him. Half his impulse, he knew, was to vex Maria and remind her that she was not wanted, not preferred, would not be his wife. He had not smiled at her since she displayed herself in that garish gown at Hill Street in May, when she took away any power he had to free himself from her. He would not take meals with her and seldom returned to the inn before she slept. When he did return to find her awake, he would silently take her to bed —or on the divan, or by the fireplace—wherever he found her. There was no tenderness or passion between them any longer, yet Maria never once turned him away. Henry marveled at her brash hopefulness in those moments when nearly every night he could hear her crying herself to sleep.

Knowing that inconsequence was worse than hatred to Maria, Henry would not let his elation at her imminent removal show. Instead, he affected boredom as he lifted a pastry from the breakfast tray. "When do you leave?"

"Immediately."

Henry was silent as he stuffed the morsel into his mouth. He watched her as he chewed. For just a moment, her chin quivered, betraying her unreasonably tenacious love for him. His chest tightened for a single heartbeat. Anger he could counter—tears were more difficult to resist. There was no joy for him in hurting another, but he could not soften or she would sense it, and then they would become locked in this cycle of never-ending misery.

He licked the sweetness off his fingers as they watched each other.

"My aunt Norris has arrived for me. She is waiting below."

Henry wondered that her father or one of her brothers had not come. *Lucky, I suppose.* He did not relish the thought of the posturing and accusations that would be involved in a meeting with her male relatives. He had never fought a duel and intended to keep that record clean. Edmund did not worry him, and Tom was not often sober enough to hold a pistol. But he was a gentleman, and Fanny would not like it.

He grabbed two more pastries from the tray. "Give her my best," he called over his shoulder as he shut the door to his bedroom.

He perched on the edge of his bed, tense, listening to the sounds of her packing. Muffled sobs reached his ears but not his heart. He felt no regret at her leaving, no emptiness at the loss of an admirer. He felt, for once, whole within himself. He was *enough* and did not yearn for another's adulation and attention. Awareness crept over him, the understanding of what it means to be a steady man, reliable, and self-possessed. To be the man a woman like Fanny needs and deserves. The irony of his situation was not lost on him.

Henry waited until all noise from the adjoining bedchamber ceased and he was certain Maria was gone, truly gone, before moving to his writing desk.

M—

> *The pigeon has, at long last, flown with the old crow. I am coming home, my sister.*
>
> *H.C.*

OCTOBER 5, 1809, EVERINGHAM

> *... but once I had, I seemed powerless to stop. The heady intoxication of secrecy, the delight in being wanted was too much to resist.*
>
> *Why could <u>you</u> not want me, Fanny?*

"The affair was a mistake, Mary." Henry traced his finger along the slightly frayed edge of the paper and his thumb along the neater edge of the bottom, where it had recently been trimmed to size. *At once soft and able to cut.* He stilled his hand and looked to his sister.

She gazed out of the window and did not stir at his words. The wind picked up outside, swirling the dry oak leaves fallen in the avenue. The sky beyond the eastern hedgerow was a deep, brilliant blue, barely visible through the far window of the sitting room. Behind Mary, the low, autumn sun burned orange and red through wisps of clouds. The oak limbs swayed, their stark lines black against the fiery sky.

"I should not have stayed at the Frasers."

"There we have it." She turned, the sunset glinting red on her curls, silhouetting her against the fire as if she were one of the oaks beyond the glazing. Placed for beauty, tended for gracefulness. Unable to do more than thrash about in the buffeting wind. "Your misfortune is my doing? What of *my* misfortune?" Her eyes were narrowed, furious.

His heart hurt for his sister's disgrace. *And not by her own doing. She suffers because of the actions of men, those of us who should have been protecting her.* "Mary. Of course not. That was not my intent. How could you have foreseen such mischief?"

"I know you, Brother. How could anyone *not* have foreseen such mischief?"

Henry colored at his sister's bite. *She has every right to remain angry. It was my scandal that drove away her Edmund. And my uncle's scandal that drove her into my inept protection.* Henry did not think he would ever live to see the end of his shame over how he had failed his beloved sister.

"Let us not quarrel. All we have now is each other."

"Nonsense. You'll be forgiven in a blink and none will consider your misstep again. Men are always forgiven—forgiven their indolence, their vanity. It is the women who suffer the ill effects, even for something so small as wanting happiness. Society will always welcome a young man with an independence."

"Society can hang."

Mary sighed. He could tell she was in no mood to spar. "You have been haunting these halls like a ghost for a month, which gives me no choice but to do the same." Her voice was weary. "I feel that we are in exile."

"Do you not have some needlework that needs doing?"

"Ha!" Her laugh was short but genuine. Even if she lived into an aged spinsterhood, he doubted Mary would ever take up a needle. He was glad to see her humor had not left her entirely since leaving London. Since losing Edmund.

"Why do you while away at that letter? Even now you cannot lay aside your vanity." Her humor was not gone, perhaps, but more short-lived than before.

"It is not vanity that keeps me at this letter, Mary."

"She'll not have you now."

"It is not hope, either."

Mary turned back to the window. The sky beyond had cooled, the darkening gray spreading from the east, pushing the last light below the trees and out of the day.

"You cannot send it to her."

"I know."

"You are selfish, Henry." He winced at her softly spoken words. "You are selfish to write her this letter. To have seduced Maria. Refused to marry Maria."

"I could not marry her and be happy."

"And what of *my* happiness? I could have been happy with Edmund!"

Henry froze at the anger in her voice.

"Perhaps you should be writing your own letter."

She nudged one of his discarded attempts with the toe of her slipper. "No. I think not." Her eyes were hard and dry, but he could see the anguish behind them. She huffed in irritation and moved past the escritoire.

"Mary." Henry caught her wrist, his word and touch gentle. She turned, her features still rigid. He pressed her hand affectionately, hoping she could read the remorse in his eyes, his yearning to be at ease again with his sister. She smiled sweetly and gave him a playful pat on the cheek.

"Of course, Brother. Selfishness always must be forgiven, you know. We Crawfords can have no hope of a cure." He released her and she left quietly.

Mary's insistence on his selfishness unsettled him. He had long thought of himself as generous and affable. Exactly the sort of young man sought after for balls, house parties, and card games. But, he could not shake the truth he heard in his sister's words. *Selfish. Vain.*

No. It was not just his happiness that mattered to him. Fanny's happiness was paramount. And he had tried to make her happy, tried to give her a full and easy life. He had only fallen in Maria's trap after Fanny continued to evade him.

We could have been happy. Could we not? If you would had but accepted me.

Why would you not have me, Fanny? Why could you not have given in at Portsmouth as I saw you wanted to? Mary, as is often the case, is quite correct once more—none of this would have befallen the lot of us if you had just put your prideful sensibilities aside and surrendered to the desires of your heart. But you are too moral to give over to vanity, to passion.

If I had been given even the smallest bit more encouragement, I would never have pursued her acquaintance again. And it might have been you here with me this evening, and Mary at the parsonage with her Edmund. Precisely where neither she nor I would have expected to land but without a doubt where we most wanted to be in the end.

Alas, I know I will only ever see your pretty frame gliding through the halls of Everingham in my dreams . . .

FIVE MONTHS EARLIER…HILL STREET, LONDON

The last thought before he fell asleep was *not* of luxuriating in the hands of a beautiful woman or the shame at having carried on an affair with a married woman—when he himself was all but engaged. No, his only thought was of the potential unpleasantness of exposure. And that would be handily avoided by removing himself from Maria's reach. Deciding on a course of action assuaged much of guilt and uneasiness.

He woke early, a light breakfast tray already set out in his room. He swung his legs over the edge of the bed, eager to be gone from London and its temptations.

His uncle had always loved London for those very temptations—the women and the gaming, the theaters and soirees. *So many opportunities for pleasure*, the admiral would say, smirking. Henry had learned his uncle's vices and, for a time they were his own weaknesses. Pretty women and flirtations, cards and billiards, races and boxing. His time with Fanny had taught him differently. Or so he had thought.

He wanted Fanny for a wife, his love for her exposing the lies in his uncle's words, the maxims that poisoned his youth. "You are a man," his uncle had told him on many occasions. "Men have their needs and must tend to them. Women know this. They accommodate with purposeful blindness or purposeful wantonness. If you find one who will give you both, consider taking her for a mistress. Once a wife, they will never accommodate."

Henry shuddered at the bitterness he could still feel in his uncle's remembered words. Bitterness he failed to notice years ago as the lessons took root in his mind. A coldness he mistook for wisdom and experience. Such a contrast to the hopeful warmth he felt spreading through him. *Everingham. Fanny. Marriage.*

The risk of exposure with Mrs. Maria Rushworth was like a bucket of ice dumped on his head. He was now startled into alertness, as if a fog had lifted, showing him finally what his behavior had been. The day before was all frivolity and fun. How could there be any consequence when all was done with a light heart and his four thousand a year?

Seeing the maid round the corner the night before, his hand in Maria's curls and lips upon her neck, jolted him into seriousness. He felt himself instantly filled with shame at his willingness to push aside thoughts of his intended to satisfy a fleeting physical desire and vain hunger. He had told himself for weeks that his only desire was for a life with Fanny Price, yet there he was. Entangled, in all senses of the word, with his beloved's cousin. Dread followed the dawning awareness that their affair, if known, would ripple ruin through several families.

No one must know. His first coherent thought since hearing the maid's gasp. It remained his mantra through the next hours. This need for secrecy led him to decide to leave London, to escape the exposure and scandal that would surely follow. *And would surely tie me to Maria.*

Her glee at being discovered by the maid alerted him to the extent of the danger in which he had ignorantly placed himself.

"Oh, what a relief to have the matter settled!" she had nearly sobbed with evident joy.

"What can you mean? Settled?" For the first time, Henry wondered what *her* motivations for the affair had been, and he was forced to come to a rather distressing conclusion.

"It is all but done now, my Henry! Rushworth cannot overlook it further. We are found out." She laughed, her head tossing back. "Do not you feel it? I never expected such a relief as this! Nothing can be worse, I am sure, than playing at love with a man I despise. I will have no such hardships at Everingham." Her hand slid up his arm.

"Maria." He had brushed her hand off his shoulder, stepping away. "*Mrs.* Rushworth. You are married. I have not the ability nor the intention to relieve you of your chosen condition."

"The condition I choose, most assuredly, but not with that stupid fellow. But when we—"

"You are not hearing me, madam." As she reached for him again, he took her by the wrists, holding her hands between them. "There cannot be a 'we'. I am sorry you believed our assignations to be more than a . . . diversion."

At this, the understanding crept into her face, her furrowed brow, the tightness of her lips. Her wrists had gone limp in his grasp.

"I cannot believe that."

"It is so."

"You do not have a choice!"

"I most certainly do."

"The maid saw us embracing!"

"She saw us standing in a hallway."

"She will know what it means."

"It means nothing."

"It will not mean nothing to my husband and his mother."

"She is a servant. She will not approach Rushworth or his mother. And who can credit what gossip servants spread amongst themselves? Wait respectably at home for your husband and speak of this no more."

He took his leave from Wimpole Street abruptly, with no intention of seeing it or its inhabitants again. If his uncle had not required Henry's signature on some documents, he would have gone directly from London that moment.

Everingham had seldom been his home—until recently he preferred to travel and visit, returning to the estate only long enough to handle whatever business his manager, Pollard, could not—but this morning he found himself yearning for the estate. The crisp air that came with being so near the coast. The coolness of the surrounding forest. The wide expanse of lawn surrounding the manor house, peppered with well-tended gardens. He wished to walk those garden paths with Fanny Price—no, Fanny *Crawford*—on his arm, to hear her ideas on how to improve the kitchen garden and whether he should leave the old oak in the southern field.

He needed to get out of London where the air stifled, and eyes intruded, and the noise never ceased. Where temptations lurked and lured.

No one must know.

Henry quickly ate a breakfast of cold meats and toast in his chambers and dressed himself before going downstairs.

"Harding, is the carriage—" Henry called from the top of the stairs; the words caught in his throat and his legs froze as Maria pushed past his uncle's butler.

No one must know.

Henry was overcome, dizzy with ire that was soon eclipsed by horror that she would risk ruin by coming unescorted to *this* house. It would be enough to draw the scorn of the society that she would turn up at the home of a gentleman—even *with* a chaperone during calling hours. But at his uncle's home, where the man kept his mistress! Alone! And even before breakfast! Her actions were unconscionable.

His legs began to move again and he all but ran down the stairs, absurdly thankful the hour was so early that they were not likely to encounter the admiral or his mistress. His first instinct was to shove her out onto the street and close the door. He knew he could do no such thing, however, as the longer she stood on the step, the more likely her chance of being seen.

"Dammit, woman, what are you thinking? You know you cannot be here! If you were seen—"

Maria stood proud and tall, her hair perfectly coiffed, her day dress a brilliant green. Her skin glowed, her eyes shone, she was all smiles and gaiety. The beautiful Mrs. Rushworth did not *risk* ruin; she courted it.

"Did you take *any* care for secrecy?"

"Why should I have? There is no need now." Her expression was triumphant. She was disconcertingly composed for a married woman who had been discovered in another man's embrace.

Cold understanding seeped through him, like the damp of mud through thin boots—slowly, unrelentingly. In the panicked moments after the maid rounded the corner, Henry had little attention to spare for Maria as he struggled with his own shock and dismay. Recalling the events of the evening before, he realized she had not been surprised. There was only the maid's gasp and Henry's curse. Maria did not start, shriek, jump away, nor betray any amount of unease. She stood still.

Henry knew for a certainty that Maria had orchestrated the maid's discovery.

She would take a husband for money, knowing she did not love him, and heap upon him abuse for her own poor judgment. Then, presented with a handsomer option, she would renege on her vows, throw her family's good name in the gutter, and maneuver to trap a gentleman into marriage.

She was the worst sort. Unsatisfied, thoughtless, and spoiled. Worst of all, changeable. The kind of woman who leapt carelessly from one fancy to another, always assuming someone would catch her and spare her from suffering. Maria Bertram Rushworth had never felt an unpleasant consequence she could not slither out of and foist upon another.

As he stared at the smug, shameless woman in the foyer, he felt a chill down his spine. In recognizing her meanness, Henry could not avoid confronting the man he himself had been. Worse than a cad. Worse than a rake, self-absorbed and vain. Flippant. He had been cavalier with the most precious thing he had ever known—the esteem, and perhaps love, of a good woman. He was, in fact, very like Maria Bertram.

He chased Maria for her beauty. First out of boredom and later out of vanity, out of an unwillingness for a flirtation to end on someone else's terms. She had been a prize—a toy—never truly a person in her own right to Henry.

Alarm made his words sharp. "There is *every* need for it now. You cannot be here."

No one must know.

"Well, we certainly cannot *stay* here. I can send for my belongings once we arrive at Everingham."

"I will escort you home."

Her laugh was higher than usual, edging on hysterical. "Home? I have *left* Wimpole Street." There. A small spark of panic in her smooth exterior. So, she did feel the precariousness of her position after all.

But Henry would not argue the wisdom of her abandoning her idiot husband. "To Mansfield, then. I will take you home to your father."

The cold fire in her eyes conveyed all he needed to know about her willingness to return to Mansfield. He enjoyed a brief vision of dragging her bodily from his carriage and dropping her soundly on the gravel drive at Mansfield Park before flying off to Everingham and purging himself of her influence. But, he was a gentleman, though he admitted to himself he had not behaved as one of late. He determined to change his course. Henry would not expose Maria so unfeelingly or make her situation worse than she was determined.

Rather than take his advice from the night before, she had overthrown all good sense and intended to force herself upon him. She did not care whether he wished for an alliance or not. She would not act to stifle rumors and prevent discovery. No. Likely, she had *contrived all this*. Their conversation that preceded their first real tryst played in his mind.

"You ought to have a care, Mrs. Rushworth. You know how the gossips will talk if you are continually sneaking off."

"The gossips are already talking, Henry. Have you not heard what they say?"

"I don't usually listen to the gossip."

"Well, I do. And if they are already saying we are lovers, then what is there to stop us?"

His palms began to sweat as he realized how deftly Maria had laid the trap for him.

She would leave her husband's home, *in broad daylight*, and turn up on his doorstep for all London to gawk. She left him no choice. Thankfully, Harding had the carriage ready for the long ride to Everingham. He would not take her to his home. But he could get them away from London, from the gossip rags, and far away from her family. If she insisted on pursuing this mad course, she would have no comfort, no ease from the Bertrams.

But he knew he would have no peace either.

OCTOBER 5, 1809, EVERINGHAM

. . . and truly, the fault can only be my own.

I wonder how I ended up in Maria's arms. Again. I wonder how I even came to love you? Sweet, kind, Fanny Price. I did not think I had enough goodness left in me to even attempt to answer your expectations for what a human must be.

Having been influenced by that goodness you stirred within me, I wonder more how it is that I cared so little about what was good for Maria, what was due to you, what was right for me, that I threw it all away for a moment of pleasure. I won't even call it joy, Fanny, for I had never felt joy in a woman's touch. Not until you first laid your gentle hand on my arm. And none since.

My Fanny, if you knew, truly knew, my deficient upbringing—not deficient in wealth and comfort, but in those things, I know you value, and I now know are vital: morality, humility, consideration, generosity, selflessness. If you were aware of the shameless failure to teach morality—and often the intention to devalue morality—then perhaps your heart would take pity on me.

If I had known how devastating and dangerous were the lessons of my youth, perhaps I would have put them aside sooner.

LONDON 1799

EIGHTEEN-YEAR-OLD HENRY had been mortified when his uncle saw him noticing the ample bosom and general loveliness of a popular singer during an evening at Sadler's Wells. The Crawford men were mingling in the foyer of the theater after a performance when Miss Eva Moretti appeared to accept the adulations of her audience. Her face and chest were still flushed from the exertion of her performance, her eyes sparkling, one hand holding a glass of champagne, the other trailing along the arms and shoulders of her admirers as she moved through the crowd. Henry was transfixed by her easy sensuality and could not look away. Not even as she glided towards him and Admiral Crawford, her hips swaying.

The admiral extended a hand to Miss Moretti, which she accepted as she leaned forward to kiss his cheek. The admiral chuckled and, Henry assumed, attempted to introduce the singer to his nephew, but Henry heard only a high-pitched ringing in his ears as the voluptuous woman placed a hand on one of his cheeks and a kiss on the other. The heat of her ungloved hand, the softness of her lips on his skin, the heady scent of perfume and *woman* that surrounded him only exacerbated the sudden and uncomfortable arousal her proximity created in young Henry.

A short while later in the carriage, Henry was reliving the moment and trying discreetly to find a comfortable seat when his uncle mentioned his obvious admiration of Miss Moretti. Henry only stammered, embarrassed.

"No need to be shy about it, lad!" The admiral guffawed.

But Henry most definitely was shy about it. How many times had his uncle turned a serious eye to him during the course of an instruction on finances or estate management and said, "A man must always be about men's business. Never let a woman distract you from your duty." In those moments, young and eager only to impress his powerful and respected uncle, Henry could not imagine why he would need such an admonishment. Seeing Miss Moretti tonight—*feeling* Miss Moretti—her full breasts straining against the rich purple silk of her bodice, Henry understood.

"A female's beauty is for noticing, her body for touching."

Henry colored at these words, embarrassed that his uncle so plainly had seen Henry's desire and spoken of it openly. He had seen his uncle's cavalier behavior towards women and had overheard bawdy conversations among his uncle's acquaintances—the admiral never tried to hide those interactions. But the admiral had never before discussed women *with Henry*. Henry yearned to be a part of his uncle's circle, to have those experiences, and enjoy the camaraderie of sharing exploits. Even at that moment, Henry felt himself still a child to the admiral. The admiral's words tonight opened a new world for Henry. He *was* a man. He could have his own women.

"There are no 'ladies,' my boy. That's the biggest lie this society ever sold us men. A woman is for pleasure. There's not a one of them who don't want it, Henry. Don't you forget that. If her looks excite you, she can be yours."

Henry thought again of Miss Moretti's kiss on his cheek and what it might be like to feel her lips on other places.

As if reading his mind, the older man said, "But no, Henry. Not that Eva—she's a bit more than you could handle—let me tell you!"

The admiral's exclamation was punctuated by a gentle rap on the knee with the older man's walking stick. "Here, drink up, lad." He pulled out a flask and handed it to Henry. "It is time, my boy. I see that I have let it go too long and that we've somewhere else to be this evening."

The "somewhere else" turned out to be a bagnio in Covent Garden. Young Henry marveled at the ease with which the admiral entered the establishment, as if it were something done as a matter of course. Or as a matter of right.

Henry followed, overwhelmed by the new experience, but determined to show the maturity and restraint his uncle had emphasized over the years. He had heard stories of brothels. Several of his classmates bragged of their debaucheries. It was their tales of rooms full of naked women lounging on settees, drinking whiskey, smoking cigars, engaging in wanton acts—with each other and whatever man should be within arm's reach—that had his breath coming fast, half from arousal, half from nervousness.

Their stories, though taken for God's honest truth at the time, seemed completely fantastical outside the respectable-looking house. He and his uncle passed through a perfectly ordinary door, with a perfectly ordinary brass knocker, and into a perfectly ordinary foyer attended by a perfectly ordinary footman, who took their coats and hats in a perfectly ordinary manner.

Henry had not gained his bearings before a petite woman with gleaming golden hair piled in curls on her head, jewels glinting at her throat and wrists, greeted his uncle familiarly.

Her painted mouth lifted into a seductive smile. "Charles. You only ever get more handsome." She spoke in a lilting French voice. "Come." She took his arm and led him deeper into the house. "Come hide away with me before my girls see you and they spend their night sulking for want of you."

They were led through an empty parlor decorated in the usual fashion —no wanton women draped over furniture beckoning ravishment—and into a library. Their hostess sat on the expansive desk that dominated the space, which clearly was *her* dominion. She leaned slightly forward, her hands resting on either side of her fine figure. He could hardly keep his eyes on hers. They strayed from her delicate, ungloved hands to her hips, shrouded tightly in a rich gown, to the glistening ruby, nestled like an apple between her ample, and barely contained, bosoms. The room was dimly lit and more masculine than he would have expected of this glittering woman. It smelled familiarly of leather, cigars, and port.

"Madame Marchand, may I present my nephew, Mr. Henry Crawford."

Before Henry could offer a bow, her high, tinkling laugh filled the room as she clapped her delight. "Oh, Charles, you have brought me such a treat!" She hopped off the desk and gestured to a long deep leather sofa near the fireplace. "Do rest here, Charles. I shall return for you. Claudine will be in presently with refreshments." His heart raced with building panic as she reached her lovely hand towards his, limp and clammy, hanging at his side; he was nearly torn in two between embarrassment and desire. Her fingers intertwined with his and she pulled him from the room. "I have just the thing for you, my dove."

Henry was speechless and terrified. He followed her, wide-eyed, through the corridors, and heard other inhabitants in the house. Women's laughter and snippets of conversations from behind mostly closed doors. Servants scuttling about with trays. The splash of water as a bath was filled. Most curiously, low moans and vaguely animal sounds from recessed spaces and darkened parlors. Finally, Madame Marchand led Henry into a game room where several men sat at cards, each with a woman beside him or on his lap, and still more men clustered around a billiards table. The women, Henry was astonished to find, were all dressed exquisitely, and fully.

"Arabella."

A slender and lovely, young, red-haired nymph rose from a seat near the billiards table.

"Yes, Madame?" Her voice was high and clear as a spring, a stark contrast to Miss Moretti's low and sultry purr. Where the opera singer was lush and curvy, Arabella was slender and willowy. She seemed to float across the room, never taking her eyes from Madame Marchand as she approached the doorway. In the dim game room, Henry could not tell the color of her eyes and he silently begged her to look his way. Though her eyes did not leave her madame, she stood directly before Henry. He was having a difficult time breathing and wondered if she could hear his heart beating as loudly as it seemed to him.

"Mr. Crawford, this is our Arabella." The young woman lowered into a graceful curtsy, offering Henry the opportunity to admire the graceful lines of her neck and shoulder that led to a clear view of her lovely breasts, with the hint of the dusky rose of her nipples disappearing beneath the thin silk of her gown. As she rose, she finally, *finally* looked into his eyes and smiled. His breath caught. *Gray*, was all he could think as she slowly lowered her dark lashes over her storm-colored eyes.

"My pleasure." Her mien was demure, but her emphasis on *pleasure* stopped his heart.

Somehow, his good breeding held fast and he made her an elegant bow. "The pleasure is mine."

"Arabella, would you take Mr. Crawford to the suite and make him comfortable? I'll be entertaining Admiral Crawford in my study." With a wink, she left Henry with the beautiful Arabella.

With a coquettish smile, Arabella took young Henry by his hand and led him through shadowed corridors. He trailed behind her in a daze, his senses overwrought in his aroused anxiety. The carpets beneath his feet felt thick as winter clouds and no more capable of supporting his weight. As they ascended a highly polished staircase, the candlelight from the wall sconces made the fabric of Arabella's skirts shimmer and undulate like a mermaid's tail, the motion making his head swim. He tried to imagine what would occur when they reached the top of the stairs but he could not think past the ringing in his ears. The throbbing in his breeches matched the pounding heartbeat in the palm of his hand, wrapped so lightly in her soft, cool fingers.

The hall at the top of the stairs ended at a heavy mahogany door. The room beyond smelled of a fresh wood fire and a blend of garden herbs and flowers. The fireplace threw a soft, orange light over the undraped bed in the center of the room. Arabella did not let go of his hand as she shut the door.

She raised their hands and placed his hand against her chest, over her heart. Her skin was warm as a stone left sitting in the summer sun but as yielding as a ripe peach. Henry froze, struggling to maintain restraint as his mind was suddenly flooded with images of Arabella underneath him, astride him, beside him.

She stretched out her hand, mirroring the placement of his, and pushed gently until he backed into the large bed.

"Do not be afraid." Her voice was both playful and soothing. She did not take her eyes from his.

Without a word, her hands moved over his chest and shoulders, his coat falling away effortlessly. Not knowing what to do with his own hands while hers slid his shirt out of his breeches and off his body, he tried to ignore the demands of his body and quickly inventoried the room. Oil paintings of the countryside. Rich tapestries on the walls. Thick curtains covering the windows. A short row of plush chairs lined a wall opposite the bed, all facing towards the behemoth. Henry wondered what had occurred on the bed that would require—or allow—an audience. His breathing quickened at the thought and the sudden rush of air, below his waist, as Arabella unfastened and lowered his breeches.

Gently, she pushed him down into the bedding, his lower legs dangling over the edge so she could remove his boots and relieve him of his breeches. He closed his eyes tightly, trying not to think how he had never felt so exposed, and aroused, and terrified in his whole life.

A light pressure on the bed near his knees drew his eyes open. Arabella, her gown gone, kneeled on the edge of the bed, one arm wrapped around the thick post. Her skin glowed golden in the firelight, her hair a cascade of molten bronze.

"May I join you?"

His mouth was dry, his tongue thick. Miraculously, he was able to reply with an unwavering voice. "I think I'd like that."

Arabella crawled slowly towards him, smiling like a cat tracking her unsuspecting prey.

He reached for her as she settled herself between his legs. Still smiling from above, she pushed him back with one hand. "No. You stay there. And keep your hands to yourself."

His eyes remained spellbound as she took him in hand. He pressed his head back into the bed, balling his fists into the sheets. It was an exquisite torture to have her touching him—he wanted to feel the rest of her against him, from her small breasts to her shapely calves, but the pleasure kept him compliant.

Henry panicked as he felt familiar sensations coiling, eager for release and reluctant for the evening to be over so soon.

"Sssshh," she whispered in his ear, stroking his hair. "Sssshh now, and let the urge pass."

He squeezed his eyes shut again and willed the tension in his loins to ease, begging the pressure that had nearly erupted to quiet. After a few moments, he was able to breathe evenly again.

"There you are, sweet," she crooned softly, smiling against his neck. Her kisses trailed down his chest and he beheld her bronze curls sweep across his thighs; the erotic vision increasing his pleasure beyond anything he had imagined.

"Arabella, *please*," he gasped. He was unsure if he was asking her to stop or continue.

"You can do this all night, my Henry. This building and pausing."

"No, I don't think—"

"To be a generous lover, you must learn how to please your lady before you find your own pleasure."

He forced his breathing to slow. "I cannot bear much more." *Get a hold of yourself, man.*

"I think you are capable of far more than you know, love."

Master of himself again, he said, "Then show me."

"What shall I show you?"

"I already know what pleases me. Show me how to please you."

"As you wish"—and she took his face in her hands and kissed him deeply, breathing him in.

Henry allowed Arabella to place his hand upon her, to show him where and how to touch her. As rapture overtook her, she stilled above him and Henry drank in the satisfying sight of her ecstasy.

This is it. What it feels like to be a man. To have a woman come undone at your hands. Who could ever want for more?

No sooner than he completed his thought, Arabella began to move on top of him again and all notions were erased. She did not slow her pace as he pushed urgently into her. Suddenly, her body stiffened, her back arching as she cried out.

And then, "Arabella, I'm going to—"

"Yes, Henry, yes, now!" As if on command— *At last!* He pulled her down to his chest, laughing with the blissful rush. He rolled over on top of her and kissed her face over and over until she was laughing too.

"Show me more," he said.

THE NEXT HOURS passed in a haze of delight that gave lie to his schoolmates' crude tales. Arabella was skilled and patient, and Henry learned how to both give and receive pleasure graciously.

Near dawn, Henry was awakened by the admiral's booming voice. "Come now, my boy. Time for home."

Beside him, Arabella was awake, her hand stroking his hair. He dressed quickly though his uncle seemed in no particular rush. As Henry retrieved his belongings, he looked to the woman still abed. His uncle noticed and laughed affectionately. "She'll not be going anywhere, Henry," he said as he ushered his nephew into the hallway.

Over the next weeks, Henry frequently sought Arabella and spent long hours with her in the suite. On his third visit, he gifted her a delicate but intricate sapphire necklace. She wore it for every visit thereafter, and he came to think of that string of polished stones as representing a promise between them. When he was not with her, he was thinking about her. He would wake and kick the covers aside, recollecting the perfect arch of her back when she would stretch after their play. He would take tea and remember the dark fan of her lashes against her cheek as she sipped wine. He would bathe, spending more time than necessary in the warm water, recalling how she had moaned and whispered encouragements under him, her arms around his neck, ankles behind his knees.

Henry was aware his uncle paid close attention to his habits. Whenever Henry would mention Arabella, the admiral would quietly counsel Henry to turn his thoughts back to his studies. But Henry could not envision a future without the alluring beauty by his side—and not just ensconced in a sumptuous suite for the occasional evening.

"You returned home late last night," the admiral commented over breakfast.

Henry fixed his eyes on the tea he was stirring. "Yes." He had spent most of the evening with Arabella, leaving the brothel after midnight.

"You'll be completing your studies soon, Henry. You will have a great estate to run and you'll need to have a care for your future."

Henry gathered the courage to assert himself. "Uncle, I *am* thinking of my future when I—"

The admiral raised a hand to stop Henry from continuing. "I know what this feels like, my boy. And I need you to trust me when I tell you this. It will pass."

Henry could not conceive of what he felt for Arabella ever wavering, much less passing. His uncle must have perceived Henry's stubbornness in his eyes.

"Every young man has a first love that makes him think the world exists only so that he may worship his lady. But every sensible man realizes he's got to think with his head and not just his cock."

"It's not that, Uncle. It's—"

"Isn't it, lad?" The older man sighed. "It's always the first one you lie with that ensnares you. What do you know of women, Henry?"

The two men faced off across the breakfast table, the older man weary but firm, the younger defiant but uncertain.

"You remember what I've always told you?"

Reluctantly, Henry answered. "Yes." His uncle raised his eyebrows, prompting Henry to continue. "Never let a woman distract you."

"Mmhmm. And you, my boy, are distracted."

Henry poked restlessly at the eggs on his plate, admitting the admiral was right. He knew he had thoughts for little other than the woman. He just could not see a way to move on with his life without her.

Again, the admiral seemed to discern the younger man's thoughts and sighed heavily. "There will be others, young lad. And they will be just as beautiful, just as accessible. You're too young to contemplate what you're contemplating. Leave those thoughts for when you've had your fill of life and want only for a competent housekeeper." The older man laid the newspaper on the breakfast table and left the room, squeezing Henry's shoulder in a fatherly manner as he passed.

Later that evening, Henry stole from the house, ensuring his uncle had retired from his study before he took a horse from the mews. The night air was cool and foggy, the streets mostly deserted. At the brothel, he went directly upstairs, following the familiar maze of corridors and staircases.

No one stopped him until he reached the corridor to Madame's study. The petite woman stood in the hallway, arms akimbo, as if waiting for Henry to appear. She did not move as he took a step closer to her.

"Please," was all he said.

Perhaps she could hear the urgency and desire in his voice, perhaps she could see the love in his eyes. Whatever she sensed, it appeared to sadden her. With a small sigh, her arms dropped to her sides, she stood aside to let him pass.

"You know where she is." Madame Marchand's voice seemed soft, pitying.

Henry approached the chamber's door, heart pounding, and he noticed the door was slightly ajar. Faint noises spilled from the opening into the hallway, growing louder as he stepped closer. He wondered if he was in the wrong corridor or maybe Madame was wrong and someone else was using this room. But no—he recognized that high moan. Still disbelieving his ears, Henry pushed open the door.

His gaze was immediately drawn to the sparkle and flash of sapphires upon a slender, pale neck. His heart plummeted as he recognized the curve of Arabella's arms behind the familiar man's neck, her ankles wrapped behind his knees as she met his uncle's thrusts. The moans, the whispered words of encouragement, he had heard them all before. He stood frozen with doubt, disbelieving his own eyes, his heart fracturing and sending shards of ice through his chest. Unluckily, he had entered at the critical moment and was unable to tear his eyes away as his uncle spent himself, soiling Henry's love.

As the elder Crawford rolled off the young woman, Henry tried to understand which was the greater betrayal—the man he admired and respected sullying Henry's youth, or the woman he loved, lying and dissembling for a bit of coin?

"Come in, boy. Be a good lad and hand me that towel?"

Henry moved over the carpet as smoothly as a rusty bit of tin, obeying his uncle by habit, his face hot with shame and anger. But the admiral was his family, and nothing could break that bond. Henry trusted his uncle, even now, and searched for his uncle's lesson.

Arabella shifted on the pillows, long arms stretched above her head as she sighed and lay to the side, exposing the slope of her ribs, the curve of her hip. The jewels at her neck flashed in the firelight and Henry was flooded with disdain for the woman he had worshipped until mere moments ago.

The first taste of betrayal had gone down hard, anger now flaring at the woman wearing his gift. *It was a promise*, he thought bitterly, looking at her draped over the pillows. She did not bother to cover herself with the sheets, as though she were teaching him another boudoir lesson: there was no shame in sex, no betrayal between such lovers.

He stared at her and she gazed back for the minutes it took the admiral to clean up and dress. Her lack of remorse became mirrored in his own heart as he again took the lead from her, learning the ways of being a man in this realm.

Jealousy is beneath us, her steady gaze seemed to say. *One moment to the next, one lover to another. There is no place for seriousness, no cause for steadfastness.* The longer he looked into the coolness of her sharp gray eyes, the less appeal they held. And his hot flash of anger and resentment slid away into a vast void of apathy.

He heard his uncle's words again. *A female's beauty is for noticing, her body for touching.* Arabella had proved that true. How could Henry fault his uncle for doing precisely what Henry had come here to do?

"Well, my boy, do you fancy a turn, or shall we depart for Hill Street?"

Henry still had his gaze locked with Arabella's. "I do fancy a turn, Uncle." Arabella's eyes lit brighter, her lips began to curve into a coy smile. "But not with this one." The effect was subtle but immediate. Pain and disappointment flared in her stormy eyes. A part of Henry roared with pleasure at this power to choose, to refuse rather than be refused.

By the time the admiral clapped him on the shoulder and turned him towards the open door, all yearning for the red-haired beauty had evaporated, leaving only a cold understanding echoed in his uncle's next words. "They're all the same, my lad."

OCTOBER 5, 1809, EVERINGHAM

But they are not all the same. And there is cause for steadfastness. I did not realize this until you, my marvelous Fanny Price. With your simple, artless ways, the purity of your soul, you have shown me the falsity of my younger days. You have shown me the divinity of womanhood. You have opened my heart and taught it how to love—selflessly and wholly.

You have recreated me.

I regret nothing more than my ability to love you—and maybe one day, to love another—should require such a sacrifice.

If ever I managed to make pathways to your heart, my Fanny, if I somehow caused you to experience any of the tender feelings for which I desperately searched your eyes, please let them die now. Foster them no more. Let them wither and scatter, dried on the ground of your soul, in the hopes they will one day nourish the soil to nurture the love of another.

One more worthy.

More constant.

I love you, Fanny. And that love led me to believe my constancy would hold fast. I believed I could want for nothing else, filled with love of you. For how could I fail to maintain a perfection of steadiness when consumed with love for a perfectly good and moral woman?

It was only when I saw myself reflected in your eyes that I saw who I am, and that knowledge did not flatter. I was a beast! Idle and meritless, carrying on with an engaged woman simply for entertainment. Through you, I saw my error. Through you, I saw what a man could have in a family. And as we grew closer—we were at least friends at the end, were we not? I felt the joy of being <u>good</u> and <u>firm</u> and <u>right-minded</u>. Esteem and approbation rather than envy and disapproval.

In your judgment, I realized how I had wronged my sister in refusing her the stable home she desired, instead foisting her on our relations. But this you did not know! It is a testament to how loving you has changed me. I am eaten away with guilt in how I mistreated her, but I cannot regret my neglect as it brought me to know you. Even with the difficulties and heartbreak that ensued, I would not wish it different. Now I am able to make amends, with myself, with my sister. But not with you, my darling Fanny. You are forever lost to me.

I admit, Fanny, to pursuing you out of the same light-minded folly that drew me to Maria (and back again). I desired to make you love me and to break your heart just a little—just enough to satisfy my vanity. But fortune is fickle and instead it was I who grew to love. I would have given anything to bring you happiness and see you safe forever from hurt and loss. Instead, I brought all that upon you in my foolishness.

Did you love me, Fanny Price? I think that in Portsmouth you nearly did. I must believe that you loved me at least a little, my dear. I saw the shine of approval in your eyes as we discussed the improvements at Everingham. I did not imagine you were more free with your smiles, not since you saw your brother off to his lieutenancy.

I must be content with having broken your heart at last.

Regrettably,

H.C.

Henry stood from his writing desk, staring down at the pages stacked, freshly inked. Here was his confession, his damnation.

You cannot send her that letter, Mary had said. And, as always, Mary was right.

He gathered the papers and pulled a chair close to the fire. One by one, he fed the pages to the flames, watching as the fire consumed his lustful affair with Maria, his tortured months in Wiltshire, his first blush of misguided infatuation, and his true, honest love for Fanny.

"No one must know."

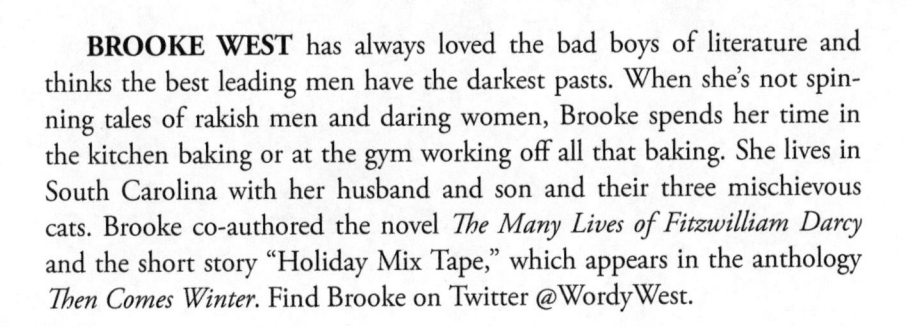

BROOKE WEST has always loved the bad boys of literature and thinks the best leading men have the darkest pasts. When she's not spinning tales of rakish men and daring women, Brooke spends her time in the kitchen baking or at the gym working off all that baking. She lives in South Carolina with her husband and son and their three mischievous cats. Brooke co-authored the novel *The Many Lives of Fitzwilliam Darcy* and the short story "Holiday Mix Tape," which appears in the anthology *Then Comes Winter*. Find Brooke on Twitter @WordyWest.

FRANK CHURCHILL

When Frank Churchill was a toddler, his mother died. Soon after, his father gave him away to a rich aunt and uncle in hopes of offering him a more promising prospect. As the heir to a fortune, his fine countenance and good-nature added to his manifold of agreeable attributes. Yet all along, he manipulated others to mask his secret engagement to the fetching and talented Jane Fairfax, a woman of no fortune. *"My idea of him, is that he can adapt his conversation to the taste of everybody, and has the power as well as the wish of being universally agreeable."* —*Emma*, **Chapter XVIII.**

"How many a man has committed himself on a short acquaintance, and rued it all the rest of his life!" —Frank Churchill to Jane Fairfax, *Emma,* Chapter XLIII.

AN HONEST MAN
Karen M Cox

Family lore declares that my mother named me Frank with a fervent maternal hope that I would grow to be an honest man. I would have wished to honor that sentiment, but sometimes the whimsical tides of life, followed by crushing consequences and practicalities, have a way of altering a man's path. As Robert Burns wrote, "The best laid schemes o' mind an' men gang aft agley." Even uneducated men know where the road paved with good intentions leads.

I was the product of what was called, in my presence, a happy but unfortunate union. My mother was the beautiful and reserved Miss Churchill, whose ancestral home was a grand estate called Enscombe. By all accounts, she was not only comely but also quite accomplished: she played the piano-forte, sang with exquisite taste, and possessed a shy smile that drew the eye of many a single gentlemen. The summer after she reached her majority, she traveled to Brighton to visit some friends, the Braithwaites, and take in the sea air. There she met my father, Captain Weston, a militia officer from a respectable family that had been successful in trade for several generations. His family had recently purchased a rural house near Highbury, a small village in Surrey, but the Westons were definitely *not* gentility.

The attraction between Miss Churchill and Captain Weston was a rapidly progressing love match which surprised no one except my mother's brother, her only living family member, and his wife. That couple renounced the new Mrs. Weston when my parents married, and I suspect my aunt, in particular, found it offensive that my parents appeared to be quite happy in their "unfortunate" choice. I have always heard my father spoken of—in cold, civil tones—as almost a charlatan, for his charm and handsomeness stole my mother from the bosom of her family.

Why, you might inquire, do I speak of my father, a man who lives and breathes to this day, as if he were dead and gone? It is because, to me, he is as good as gone. I have not laid eyes on him since I was two years old, and I am now at the advanced age of twenty-three. Before I had completed my third trip around the sun, my mother succumbed to a wasting illness. During her infirmity, my aunt and uncle did take pity on her and visited her several times, and during those visits, I was the means of cautious reconciliation between the Churchills of Enscombe and the Westons of Highbury. After my mother's passing, my aunt suggested that she and my uncle assume my care, as they could provide for me in ways my father could only imagine. They were older, had no children of their own, and I, now a child of fortune, could live sheltered by the great estate—which was my heritage—attend the best schools, and become the gentleman that Miss Churchill's son was always meant to be. I even completed the metamorphosis to well-bred gentleman by formally assuming my mother and uncle's surname as my own.

Sometimes in the stillness and isolation of the night, I wondered how my father could so easily give me up. When I was in a generous and forgiving mood, I gave him the benefit of the doubt. I suppose a family member with a child's best interest at heart might persuade a man in the throes of grief to relinquish a child, even if that child was beloved. Other times, with a sour taste in my mouth and bitterness in my spirit, I considered the likely scenario that he simply did not want a young son underfoot.

At any rate, I arrived at Enscombe, a frightened, young lad with a thumb in my mouth and clutching a blanket, according to the nurse hired by the Churchills to see to my daily care. Mrs. Roberts was a young widow whose husband had left her no money, so she was grateful to my aunt and uncle for her position. She had no children living—a son had passed away in infancy—which perhaps induced her to indulge me a tad too much. She laughed at my antics, called me her "charming, little gentleman," and saw to my every need and whim. This warm, maternal adoration was in sharp contrast to the attention I received from my aunt. Please understand, I do not mean to say that Mrs. Churchill was a cruel woman, for she was not. She had always been, in fact, quite fond of her adopted son and heir, as she constantly reminded me. These affirmations of affection, however, were typically followed by the ever-present "but":

"Frank, you know how dear you are to me, but there is much of your father's charm in you that could lead you astray."

"Frank, you know that I could not love you more if you had been my very own, but Enscombe will need a wise and competent master, and your tendency toward impulsiveness will have to be tempered."

"Frank, you know how fond I am of you, but you must guard against the frivolous sides of your own nature, lest some avaricious, impoverished woman with a pretty face lead you into ruin."

I should add that all this was spoken while my uncle looked on in sad acceptance of my shortcomings and nodded his head in sanguine concurrence.

Thus, I reached my twenty-third year, a most fortunate young man, with the world at my beck and call. My uncle's health was excellent, and by all indications, his life would be a long one, sparing me the responsibilities of running my estate for much of my time here on Earth. Having finished my education, and my Grand Tour (a marvelous trip of sensual delights and magnificent adventures, which is a story for another time), I spent my days trying to avoid idle dissipation. I attempted listening to my uncle as he instructed me in the responsibilities of running Enscombe and visited my various friends from university at the best watering holes in His Majesty's kingdom: Bath, Brighton, and Harrogate.

In late June of 1813, I received correspondence from my friend, Mr. Hayward, asking me to join him in taking single gentlemen's lodgings at Weymouth. After a spirited discussion, my uncle prevailed over his wife—an atypical occurrence, I grant you—and I was given permission to accept Mr. Hayward's invitation.

To Weymouth, therefore, I was to go.

THE DISTANCE from Yorkshire to Weymouth was a long, arduous journey, so I broke the trip with several stops, including one in London, where I visited White's for an evening of whist, and, shall we say, *other* entertainments. Glad to leave the city, for the heat in July was unbearable, I set out for the coast in the early morning hours. The turnpike from Dorchester to Weymouth was dry and dusty, but the air improved as I descended the Narrows leading to the town itself. I stopped for a brief moment to breathe in the tang of the salty, sea air. In another life, perhaps I should have been a sailor, or a merchant like my father's forebears, living an ordinary existence in some harbor town. At times, that simple life appealed to me—the freedom to go where I wanted, do as I pleased, with no responsibilities, and no servants to observe my every movement. Yet, as my aunt often reminded me—in a veiled threat of disinheritance—my mother learned too late for her health that poverty is a heavier burden than familial duty.

My lodgings on one end of the Esplanade were simple but satisfactory, and since Hayward would not arrive until the next day, I decided to explore. Up one side of town and down the other I roamed, listening to the conversations as they drifted by me, hearing the seagulls cry, and appreciating the many fine-looking women bustling about, some walking arm-in-arm, some with stern-looking chaperones.

I had written a letter informing my family of my safe arrival, so I stopped at Harvey's to post it. A queue had formed to pay for postage, so I joined in, rocking back and forth on my heels while I waited.

"Lovely day," I commented, to no one in particular. The young woman in front of me turned her head and nodded curtly, barely sparing me a glance. She appeared to be one of those shy, wallflower-type creatures that found male attention terrifying, so naturally, I tried to engage her further.

"I say, miss, do you happen to know where a man might find a coffee around these parts? You see, I have just arrived, and I am still not familiar with the best places for food and drink."

She turned her head again, in such a way that I could only observe her profile, and answered in a quiet, yet melodic voice. "Granger's is but three doors down."

I grinned, now more determined than ever to make her face me. "I believe I might be interested in a tart as well."

"Granger's sells mincemeat tarts, I believe, sir."

"I think I fancy a *jam-tart* instead. Pray, might I inquire where are the best jam-tarts in Weymouth?"

She turned to face me now, deep set, gray eyes slightly rounded with surprise, pink flags in her creamy, delicate complexion. She narrowed those eyes, a most unusual color, now that I took more notice of them, and said with a quirk of her eyebrow, "I imagine that depends upon your taste, sir, for what is considered best for one is not for another."

Impudent—and simultaneously elegant! She was certainly not intimidated by my double entendre, although her expression indicated that she had apprehended it, and that intrigued me. Alas, we had not been formally introduced, so the interaction could not be sustained much longer in the polite society of a public post office.

"Pardon me, madam, you are exactly correct in your observation. So, in which directions lies Granger's?"

She pointed and turned back around as the postmaster beckoned her forward. I listened as she requested postage in the amount to send correspondence to Highbury. Interesting, as Highbury was the town of my birth, and where my father still resided. I wondered vaguely who this delicate looking flower might be, and if I should know her, but then she turned and marched out the door without looking my way. I watched her go, and then promptly forgot her as the postmaster called me forward.

THE PUBLIC ASSEMBLIES in Weymouth mirrored those I attended in Bath: the crush of people, the heat, the swirl of dancing. Hayward pushed his way through the door and into the next room, while the music assaulted our ears. A pleasant bombardment, in my opinion. There was so much vivacity there in such a confined space. I could have stayed all night.

I was talking with a friend of Hayward's when I heard my friend shout, "Dixon!" A man of average height, with the bright red hair of the Irish and a rather plain countenance, laughed and lifted his hand in greeting.

"Hayward!" he called above the fray, and we wrestled the crowd as we made our way toward each other. Introductions and bows were made all around.

"I have news," Dixon said, beaming with self-satisfaction. "I am to marry."

"Congratulations," Hayward answered. "Who is the fortunate young lady?"

"A Miss Campbell, daughter of Colonel Campbell. She's here tonight with her parents and her closest friend, Miss Fairfax." He stood on tiptoe to look over the heads of everyone in the room and spotted his party, directing them to a large dancing hall where, hopefully, there would be enough room for us all to stand together.

I took my customary glance around the room, evaluating the dance partner possibilities, as Dixon led us over to his fiancée.

"Gentlemen, may I present Miss Campbell? My dear, this is Mr. Hayward, a friend from London, and his friend Mr. Churchill, of Enscombe."

"Mr. Frank Churchill," I said with a courtly bow. "I must distinguish myself from the elder Mr. Churchill, my uncle."

"Pleased to make your acquaintance, gentlemen. My parents are taking tea in the other room, but may I present my dear friend, Miss Fairfax?"

Miss Campbell stepped back and took her friend's arm, directing her to face us, and I took in her appearance with a jolt. It was the young lady from the post office! Eyes the color of light rain clouds and fringed with long, dark eyelashes opened wide with surprise. Her equanimity returned quickly, but it took several seconds for a smile to move across her features. Those endearing pink flags appeared in her cheeks again.

"Mr. Hayward. Mr. Churchill." She bobbed a curtsey.

As Hayward and Dixon talked with Miss Campbell, I alternated my attention between the ladies. Miss Campbell, though pleasant enough, was a rather plain girl with nothing to recommend her, except maybe a sizable fortune. Not needing to marry money myself, I rarely paid attention to a woman's financial status, but some gentlemen required a dowry in a wife. Regardless, she was spoken for, so I stole a closer look at her friend.

Miss Fairfax. Now she was a charming creature: fair of face, porcelain complexion, pleasing figure, and that smile! When it appeared, it transformed her countenance. I tried to find a fault—somewhere, anywhere in her, and could come up with nothing on this cursory acquaintance. Granted, her features were not regular, but the arrangement of the parts made for a pleasant whole. Very pleasant indeed!

She noticed me noticing her, and her gaze dipped to the floor even as her smile widened. I waited, what I deemed an appropriate length of time, and after a break in the conversation, I asked, "Miss Fairfax, if your dance card is not filled, might I request the next?"

Hayward looked over at the young lady with a dash of disappointment, but I had already staked my claim. It was his misfortune; he should have been paying attention rather than talking with Dixon about hunting in Ireland.

"I am not otherwise engaged, sir," Miss Fairfax replied.

"Excellent!"

We conversed with the ladies until the next set was to begin. Following Dixon's lead as he escorted his fiancée to the floor, I offered my arm to Miss Fairfax, and we assumed our places in the quadrille. The music began, and we started the stilted, frequently interrupted conversation that couples carried on while dancing.

"How do you like Weymouth?" I began.

"Very much."

We turned and crossed and came together again.

"Have you been staying long with the Campbells?"

She smiled. "Only since I was about nine years old. I have been with them since the death of my mother."

"My mother also passed when I was very young. And your father?"

"He died in the war."

"My condolences."

"I don't remember him at all. It has been a very long time." She added, "But thank you."

Again, we parted, turned and came together again.

"Our situations are similar."

She looked at me with a dubious expression. "You are the young master of an estate. I am the orphan daughter of a military man and a vicar's child. Forgive me, but I don't understand how our situations could be remotely similar."

"We are both forgotten children, abandoned to the kindness of those outside our birth family circle, and given over to the whims of Fate."

"What drama you speak! You appear to have been quite lucky for a 'forgotten' child, and I have had many more opportunities than one might expect."

"Due to the charity of Colonel Campbell?"

"Among other things. The Campbells have always been like family to me, but in addition, I have always had the love and interest of my grandmother and aunt in Surrey, for example."

"In the village of Highbury?"

Her eyes widened again in surprise, but any words she might have spoken were lost when the dance took her away again. When we joined gloved hands once more, she asked, "How did you—?"

"How did I know you had family in Highbury?"

She nodded.

"Oh, nothing *nefarious*, I assure you. I overheard you ask the postmaster the amount to deliver your letter. I was born in Highbury, you see."

Her eyes lit up as she moved the puzzle pieces into place. "Frank Churchill! Mr. Weston's son. Why, of course!"

"My reputation precedes me? Oh, I hope not."

"No." She blushed and lowered her eyes.

Charming. Why do I keep thinking that word as I look at her?

"My grandfather was the vicar, and so my grandmother and aunt know everyone in Highbury, including your father."

"And here we are, two souls displaced from our Highbury homes and thrown together in this far-flung watering hole." The dance had ended, and I escorted Miss Fairfax to the punch table, where I presented her with a cup accompanied by my most gallant bow. "You do know what this means, Miss Fairfax?"

"What is that, sir?" She sipped her punch and glanced around the room, before regarding me with interest.

"It seems Fate has intervened once more."

I MADE sure Hayward wrestled an invitation to the Campbells' later that week. It was not a difficult task; the colonel's family was one of the most sociable in Weymouth that summer, and any friend of Dixon's, along with any friend of a friend of Dixon's, was welcome to join the family for dinner and the evening's frivolities.

When the gentlemen separated from the ladies after dinner, I attached myself to Dixon in the hopes of hearing more about the charming Miss Fairfax, and he did not disappoint. To be honest, he seemed more than willing to speak of her, with a warm regard I found a trifle disagreeable, coming from a man who was engaged to someone else.

"She sings like a nightingale and plays the piano-forte with a taste rarely displayed, even in the drawing rooms of London. 'Tis a pity, though, about her situation."

"What do you mean?" I asked, unable to stop myself.

"All that beauty and charm, and kindness too. My Miss Campbell would never have so close a friend who was not also kind. But Miss Fairfax has no fortune to entice a suitor. The colonel and his wife are her only protectors, and that will soon come to an end."

"Why?"

He looked at me askance but went on with his explanation. "When we marry in October, Miss Fairfax will most likely go into service as a governess. It's an all-too-familiar tale. My fiancée frets about her friend and wishes for her to find a secure situation, but nothing has been forthcoming so far. I invited Miss Fairfax to come along when we go to Ireland, but she will not join us."

I tried to look uninterested in the fate of Miss Fairfax, although I listened intently as I poured a brandy.

"She probably doesn't want to interfere with a man and his new wife as they set up house."

Dixon's cheeks turned as red as his hair.

"Will Miss Fairfax stay with the Campbells then? When you and the new Mrs. Dixon go to Ireland?"

"No, they are coming to Ireland as well—after we settle in. Jane is to visit with her grandmother and aunt in Surrey."

The butler then opened the doors to signal it was time to join the ladies in the parlor. The gentle music of female voices summoned us, and I was reminded of Homer's Odysseus, as I found myself, as always, lured by that sirens' song.

Inside the sirens' realm, otherwise known as the salon, Miss Fairfax sat at the pianoforte, conversing with Miss Campbell. Candlelight bathed her in a warm glow that surrounded her head like a halo. I nearly stumbled, caught by her beauty and grace. The drama of her circumstances as told by Dixon captured my imagination. An unwanted vision of Aunt Churchill appeared, warning me of the dangers of pretty but impoverished women, but my aunt's haughty voice receded from my mind until only her stern expression remained, mouthing words I could no longer hear.

Then Miss Fairfax opened her mouth to sing and Aunt Churchill disappeared completely from my consciousness, along with every other thought. The sweet soprano floated across the room and seized me by the throat. Her face, when singing, was transformed as it was when she smiled but three-fold. She seemed to ascend into a world all her own: eyes unseeing, unaware of the room before her, complexion glowing with health, creamy bosom rising with each breath.

"'Robin Adair' is my favorite," Dixon whispered in my ear. "Miss Campbell must have asked her to play it just for me."

I had to stop myself from vehemently shushing him.

I think perhaps my fate was sealed at that moment, because I felt the strangest compulsion; I wanted to put that look on her face. I wanted to be the man who could transport Miss Fairfax to whatever paradise she inhabited while she sang.

As JULY TURNED TO AUGUST, I contrived to be in the presence of Miss Fairfax as much as possible. Dinners, dances, promenades around Weymouth, walks along the shore—I saw her almost every day in some capacity or another, and each encounter made me hunger for just one more. Hayward asked me once if I had intentions in her direction, and the question stunned me so much, I stammered out the often-played response.

"Don't be ridiculous," I said. "She has nothing but her charm to recommend her. My aunt would never allow such a thing."

His comment had me thinking, however, and it occurred to me that, perhaps, if I could win my uncle to my side, my aunt might be persuaded to accept a girl like Miss Fairfax as my wife. I was to be master of Enscombe one day. Miss Fairfax would make an excellent mistress of the estate. She had observed enough of the ways of gentry and was bright enough to learn her duties quickly. She was kind and benevolent to all who knew her. My aunt and uncle should trust my judgment in this matter; I had never given them reason not to. I began to contemplate how to approach Colonel Campbell with my request to court the lovely lady, although I could not gather the courage yet to attempt it.

When the invitation arrived for me to join Dixon and the Campbells at a month-long house party a few miles inland, I leapt at the chance. Aydersham had the appeal of being quietly isolated from the prying eyes in Weymouth, was picturesque, and delightfully scattered with quaint cottages.

The morning after our arrival, I learned of Miss Fairfax's penchant for solitary, early morning walks. Unable to sleep, I had dressed early and was standing at my window with a cup of tea. I saw her venture out away from the house and toward the gardens. I set my teacup in its saucer with a clatter and hurried downstairs, forgetting that I was in but a waistcoat and shirtsleeves.

I strode toward the gardens by a different route, taking a couple of guilty looks back at the house, and thankful that I was far enough behind her to decrease the possibility that someone might observe my clandestine chase.

A swish of muslin skirt alerted me as she entered the boxwood maze. I let her take several steps in before I called out her name.

"Hullo there, Miss Fairfax!"

She stopped, turning slowly around to face me. "Good morning, sir."

"No *sirs*, begging your pardon. No *sirs*. We are friends now, are we not?"

"I suppose."

Her shawl slipped off one arm, and I bent to retrieve it, allowing myself the luxury of brushing my fingers across the bend of her elbow. "Where are your gloves, milady?"

"If I am not to call you *sir*, surely it is unacceptable for you to call me *milady*."

"Where are your gloves then, Miss Fairfax?"

I took her bare hand in mine and ran a finger down the center of her palm. Then I closed her fingers and covered them with my hand. I took a step nearer to her and lowered my voice. "Jane Fairfax. Such a plain name for such a fair lady."

She looked up at me, hope and disbelief warring in her expression. I had an overwhelming impulse to kiss those lips, barely parted in surprise.

But I did not. I released her hand, stepped back, and gave her my most charming smile accompanied by a deep bow. "We will walk and talk again. Perhaps tomorrow?"

"Mm—perhaps."

"Until tomorrow morning just after sunrise, *O, fair Miss Fairfax*."

We met most every day that first week, sometimes in the maze, sometimes in the forest, sometimes in the orangery or the gardens. No one noticed us—it was well-known that Miss Fairfax valued her private strolls through nature's bounty. And since Hayward had been unexpectedly called to London, no one was around to notice me at all.

A few days after our arrival, the party took a seaside trip to the bay near Weymouth and out on the water. It was a glorious day, white cotton-like clouds sped across the bluest sky, driven by a wind that was stronger than usual for that time of year.

Aware that I needed to curb my public attention to Miss Fairfax, I stood across the boat from her, chatting with another young lady, a Miss Parker. My eyes always found the object of my...affection? Infatuation? Whatever it was, I was aware I did not give Miss Parker the attention she deserved. My heart leapt each time I caught Miss Fairfax's gaze sweeping toward me, and I struggled to not observe how the wind pulled several tendrils of her hair out of their trappings—and I also struggled to avoid imagining doing such a mischief myself.

I heard Miss Fairfax's laugh, an unusual sound, and whipped my head around just in time to see her in animated discussion with Dixon—and Miss Campbell nowhere to be seen. The sound of his voice, so jovial, so...*loud* made the hairs on the back of my neck stand on end. I turned my back to them, only to be assaulted the next moment with gasps, screams, and bellows of fright. Miss Parker and I both turned then, and I saw a fearsome vision of my lady as she teetered precariously close to the edge of the boat. She was going overboard! I ran toward her, breath backed up into my lungs, and watched as Dixon grabbed at the skirt about her waist and pulled her from a certain death under the ocean's waves. She clung to him, pale and frightened, and his arms came around her for the few seconds it took for Miss Campbell to rush to her side. He relinquished Miss Fairfax, and as the future Mr. and Mrs. Dixon fussed over her, a red haze descended before my eyes. To see Dixon and my Jane entwined thus, though I knew it was for her safety, set off a jealous rage inside me that I never knew could be ignited. *I* should have been the one standing next to her. *I* should have been the one who made her laugh. *I* should have been the knight in shining armor who saved her.

The rest of the outing was more subdued, and I noticed very few young ladies standing at the edges of the boat. We were a quiet crew on the way back to Aydersham House, and I stewed all during dinner, into the evening's activities, and overnight. I burned with jealousy, with despair, with the injustice of not being able to freely choose my partner in life. I thought about my parents: my mother, who gave her position, her family, maybe even her life for the man she loved. I thought of my father, settled in his modest estate in Surrey, and yet content. And somewhere in the middle of that night, I made my decision. I was Fate's Fortunate Child, and Fate would not fail me now, for I would not let it. I would find a way to have both Enscombe and the woman I loved.

I WOKE EARLY, and although there was a drizzle in the gray morning sky, it was warm enough to walk out. I waited on the veranda outside the breakfast room until I saw Jane leave the house by way of the servants' quarters. Determined, I returned my cup to the sideboard and descended the stairs out into the wilds of the forest, following my wood nymph, my muse, into the line of trees.

"Miss Fairfax!" I called, hurrying my pace to catch her. "Jane!"

She whirled around, sharp gray light shooting from her eyes like daggers. "Hush! You foolish man! Someone will hear you!" She turned around and kept walking. "And leave me alone! You do not have leave to call me by my Christian name, sir! Besides, I've had enough embarrassment for one fortnight."

I stopped calling to her but broke into a run. I caught her arm and whirled her around to face me. Her bonnet slipped down her back, and those lips slipped open for me, so I took them with my own.

The clouds darkened; I heard the crack of thunder and felt the whip of the wind. I did not know if they were real or just an artifact of the storm of emotion between us.

I had certainly kissed women before—exquisite, young widows, well-heeled courtesans, even a few luscious milkmaids on the continent during my tour—but no woman had made me want to devour her quite like this one—this lady with the sad smile, this daughter of Fate, this kindred spirit. At first, she melted into my embrace, but then I felt her struggle, and reluctantly, I let her go.

She put her face in her hands and began to cry. "I can't do this. I can't. I'm on a path to ruin. You must go."

"I can't leave you, Jane. I won't." I stood there, hipshot, arms akimbo, as I considered. "I've compromised you, have I not? You are a lady, and I am a gentleman. We must marry."

She stopped, her face rising out of her hands, cheeks covered with tears and staring at me with abject shock.

"I do not want to be married out of some misguided duty. No one saw you, and I will certainly never tell a soul." Her voice broke again. "Go."

"I will not go. I love you, Jane Fairfax. I want to marry you."

"But..." The confusion on her face told me her resolve was weakening by the second, so I pressed my point.

"And you love me too, do you not?" I stepped close to her again. "Jane? I will call on Colonel Campbell and ask to court you."

"You will?"

"Of course." I grinned. "I promise."

"But what will your family say?"

My grin faded somewhat, but I put on a brave face. "I will convince them that this is a good match. It will not be too difficult. You will see."

The sky opened with a deluge of rain, just like in a novel. I seized her hand, and we ran, laughing, for an abandoned cotter's cottage just down the path. Inside, I shut the door behind us and pinned her against it.

"Jane, dearest—for dearest you will always be. Say you'll marry me."

Her smile returned—that little piece of paradise that was a promise of a bigger ecstasy to come. "Yes," she said, nodding. "Yes, I will marry you, Mr. Frank Churchill."

"Of course, you will," I murmured, my lips brushing her cheek. "For I love you. I will love you forever."

I knew that my plans for the rest of the morning were not gentlemanly. I knew I was wrong to make love to an unmarried young lady. But the freedom from Enscombe, from Weymouth, from everything that had always reined me in—well, it made me reckless, daring, and careless—like a panther on the prowl.

I trailed lips from her cheek to the soft, delicate spot behind her ear, reveling in the scent of lavender in her hair and rose water on her skin. I hooked my fingers in that damnable fichu and tore it from her neck. She gasped and closed her eyes while my lips descended the magnificent ivory of her neck on one side, and my fingertips slipped under her neckline on the other side. The backs of my fingers swept across her breast, drawing another gasp, followed by a soft moan that made me wild with wanting her. I pressed kisses over her tantalizing flesh as I tugged the bodice down to expose more of her generous bosom that blossomed from below the muslin.

I had not deflowered a virgin before, although my courtesans in London had given me plenty of lessons on the technique. It was expected that a gentleman would be required, upon his marriage, to discharge this duty upon his new wife. It appeared my time had come. Jane Fairfax was to be my bride, so I set about this new carnal assignment with the giddy enthusiasm of a student who was first in his class.

I led her to the chaise that sat in front of an empty hearth.

"Frank?" she asked, her eyes round and gray as the clouds in the sky, bosom flushed and undulating in a most fetching manner.

"Yes, my love?"

"What is this place?"

I thought it bad form to tell her she was about to become my mistress in a lowly cotter's cottage. "It is our escape from the ties that bind us." I pinned her arms to her sides while I ravaged her mouth and then came up for air. "This is our respite from the walls that others force between us." I leaned over her, taking her mouth with mine once again. "Try to imagine, my dearest, the cold winds blowing outside while we dwell within these walls," and here I knelt in front of her, lifting her skirt as I skillfully removed her shoes and drew down her stockings. "Can you feel the chill of it?"

"Yes," she gasped her answer.

"The fire before us burns hot and fierce." I nudged her knees apart and brought her hips forward. "Hot and fierce, like my love for you." I slid my hands up her thighs and pushed the dress back.

By the time my hands had finished their work underneath her petticoat, it was a simple business to switch places with her and settle her over me. Taking her slowly was excruciating, but I was rewarded, not once, but twice, with that same expression of pure ecstasy I beheld when she sang.

For the rest of our time at Aydersham House, we stole away into the forest, to the cotter's cottage, by the lake—wherever we could find the privacy to meet. Reflecting on it now, I am amazed that we were never caught. But I was often alone, with only my loyal man servant to help me dress. Miss Campbell and her family were wholly absorbed by Dixon and the upcoming nuptials. I suppose that is the sort of situation meant when society refers to an "unprotected young girl," but no matter, I would protect her. I would convince my aunt and uncle to bless our marriage, and then I would formally request to court Miss Fairfax—*as soon as we returned to Weymouth.*

A letter from Enscombe awaited me on my return to that seaside town. A letter that had been sitting there for a fortnight already, along with another and another—most likely a result of my not answering the first one. I opened them in order, dreading the scolding that Aunt Churchill was almost certainly about to apply, but the contents were not at all what I expected:

> *Dear Frank,*
> *A most unusual communique from an unlikely source has reached me this morning.*

I had a moment of panic. Had someone seen me cavorting with Jane and reported back to my aunt? If so, who could it have been? Everyone in Weymouth and at Aydersham had seemed so oblivious to what was developing between the two of us.

> *Yes, it is from your father. It seems he is to marry again, and despite his newly found respectability—I refer, of course, to his purchase of that estate in Surrey—his choice of wife has reflected his lowly origins, for she is none other than a neighbor's governess. A governess! I am appalled that he would shame you, his only son, in such a way. While I am sure that she would be good enough for some man or other, she is hardly cut out to be the mistress of his home. I am eternally grateful that you, Frank, do not seem to have your father's penchant for this abominable blurring of the classes!*

I could safely assume that she would *not* be receptive of any request I made to wed the orphaned daughter of a military man, a governess-to-be.

> *In any case, I suppose at some point you should communicate with him and this new wife, out of respect and duty. Nothing less would be expected of the young master of Enscombe, although I think a formal letter of congratulations will be sufficient.*

She then went on with a litany of her aches and pains, and the apothecary's attempts to remedy them, which I glossed over. The second letter was a bit more frantic, wondering why I had not responded to her first:

> *You know of my maternal feelings for you, my nephew, and I hope you are considering your actions as you entertain yourself in that den of iniquity by the sea. I remind your uncle daily that the temptations of Weymouth may prove too much for you to overcome. Please temper your behavior, and remember what you owe your family here at Enscombe!*

The third letter was from my uncle.

> *Dear Frank,*
>
> *I write, instead of your aunt, because she is too unwell to put pen to paper. We continue to await correspondence from you and worry for your well-being, although there has been no indication from any of our friends in Weymouth that you have been unwell. The Thompsons have written that you are visiting Aydersham House for a month. If that is the case, I wonder that you did not inform us of your visit. It would have eased your poor aunt's mind and heart considerably.*

Well, blast and damn it all! This was a disastrous start to my attempts at winning over the relatives to my cause. Even my uncle was put out with me. I would have to leave my darling Jane and make a pilgrimage to Yorkshire to smooth things over.

As we walked along the sand at Weymouth, I explained my predicament to Jane.

"I do not wish to be the means of coming between you and your family," she protested.

"They will love you, if I can convince them to give you a chance, my dear. I promise. You will be mistress of Enscombe one day, I warrant." I tried to placate her with my most charming grin, but she shook her head.

"I think"—she closed her eyes as if to strengthen her resolve—"I think we should reconsider our betrothal."

I stopped and turned to her, incredulous. "Jane. You would give me up? You expect that I can give you up?"

"I think Fate is telling us that you are not for me. You will live your life as a gentleman. I will become a governess. That is the way of things."

"Let me try to convince the Churchills. I have never *been denied my wish* when I pursued it in earnest. I can find a way, but you must give me time."

She took several steps in silence, and I did not interrupt. I had learned that her quiet nature required reflection, and that silence often meant she was about to agree. Finally, she nodded. "As you wish, then."

I left for Enscombe the next day. Left my love with a smile and a promise. The visit to Yorkshire, however, did not have the desired effect. My aunt's poor health consumed every conversation and thought, and I returned to Weymouth a fortnight later to deliver the news to Jane that we would have to wait a bit longer. What she informed me of, however, set me in a panic like I had never known.

"I dared not put this in a note. It would be the ruin of me if it were to get out." She struggled for composure. "I have not had my courses since we returned from Aydersham. I fear I may be with child."

It was as if the ground dropped away from beneath my feet. I was now bound to her, not only by a gentleman's code of honor, but by the bond between us as potential parents of a child. And I was running out of time —it was now nearing the end of September, and even with a special license to marry immediately, tongues would wag if Jane were to deliver in May. I needed a plan to fall back on, some way of providing for her in the event that my aunt turned me out of Enscombe. Never before had I wished for a profession or a trade, but I wished for one now. How much easier this all would be if I could be an independent man, with honest work to provide for a family instead of a man beholden to the whims of genteel society! If I had been a sailor, or a merchant like my father's people...

Wait...my father. A man who had married across the lines of class when he took my mother for his wife. A man who had an estate that I, as his firstborn son, could still possibly inherit if he saw fit to leave it to me. A man who had just married a governess, and so might be sympathetic to my plight.

"What are you thinking?" Jane asked, her eyes full of tears. "Your expression is full of such contradictions."

I looked over at her, observing her pallor, the fragility of her slight frame. I tried to call up the glorious look of her in the throes of ecstasy, see her passion in my mind's eye, but all I could see was this wan and sickly-looking creature before me. Yes, it appeared her condition was making her ill, stealing her bloom. Surely her friends would begin to notice this change in her. When that day came, when she was forced to admit the truth, would she name me as her seducer?

Indeed, I most certainly was running out of time. I pulled at my cravat as if it were a noose tightening around my neck.

"I am trying to form a plan to see us through this, Jane. But you must keep our secret for now. You must trust me."

"I...I will."

"All will be well. You will see. And you mustn't worry. It is not good for your health."

She looked at me with a brave, childlike devotion that did tug at the last vestiges of my honest man's soul. "Of course."

"I will escort you home now."

"Why?"

"I have a letter to write. To Highbury."

"To my grandmamma?"

"No. To my father—and his new wife."

I spent the next few weeks in a fog of visits: to London, to Yorkshire, and back to Weymouth. My stepmother wrote to me, a surprisingly elegant letter, suggesting that perhaps my father had not been as much of a fool as my aunt surmised. I made a promise to visit at my earliest convenience. I needed to plead my case to the sympathetic ears at Randalls.

The Campbells and Jane returned to London for the wedding of Miss Campbell and Mr. Dixon, and I journeyed there as well so I could attend.

Jane had been patient as she promised, and I, to defer any speculation about the two of us, kept my distance from her. One can only imagine my surprise when she approached me at the wedding breakfast that morning in October and said quietly, as she lifted a cup of punch to her lips, "I must speak with you. Alone."

"Where?"

"There is a maze in the gardens. Meet me there at half past the hour."

The tall walls of the maze dampened the sounds of wedding revelry outside as I wandered in search of the elusive Miss Fairfax. I turned a corner and there we were, face to face, with the distance of the maze corridor between us. I quickened my pace, but she stood there without moving, even more ashen than when I had seen her last. There was a strange countenance about her, a stark and brittle aura that slowed my pace.

"Miss Fairfax?" I asked uncertainly. "Jane?"

"Mr. Churchill. Thank you for coming. I have news."

I reached out for her hand but she kept hers firmly behind her.

My hand returned slowly to my side. "I am planning a trip into Surrey to see my father and his new wife. My hope is that a reconnection there will help secure a future for us, and for the child. I have not been able to broach the subject of our betrothal with my aunt and uncle."

Her laugh was a cold, sharp sound. "You needn't worry on that account. That is what I have to tell you. I have miscarried the child." She turned away and crossed her arms over her bosom, as if embracing or soothing herself.

"I am sorry to hear it." And to my surprise, I *was* sorry.

"It is my punishment for my sins. I, who have always lost what I treasured, have lost again, in another visitation of tragedy."

"Jane, I—"

"You are released from your obligation, of course. There is not any urgency for us to marry now. I only ask that you never speak of our affair to anyone. Because I am to become a governess, I cannot endure a whiff of scandal." She turned to face me, a pleading look reaching into my heart. "And in truth, I am not a scandalous woman. I am not. I am simply a woman who let her feelings lead her astray. Not the first woman to impale her own dignity for the love of a man, nor the last, I am sure."

"No," I found myself saying. "No. You might release me from our betrothal, but I do not release you."

"As a betrothal, it is such a botched piece of work by this point, there is no way to make it right, no way to make us respectable. You had best move on—to the life you are meant to have."

"I am meant to have you for my wife. I can make our engagement right."

"How?"

"Somehow. I don't know yet, but there is time to work it out now."

"You mean now that there is no child, do you not?"

"Yes. No." I stopped. "In truth, I do not know what I mean. Perhaps it is Fate's way of seeing to the best outcome."

She sighed. "I do love you, Frank. I just do not think that love will be enough—to sway your family, to cross this chasm between us, to keep you even if I should become your wife. Perhaps I am better off as a governess."

I shook my head. "I know what happens to governesses. I hear the tales from my friends. I will not leave you to that life. It is a position that is beneath you. I can work this to our advantage. You must—"

"Trust you? Be patient? How long do you expect me to wait? What if a suitable service position becomes available to me before you have worked your gentleman's magic on the situation? Do I turn a good situation away, based on my faith in your power to persuade your aunt to accept our betrothal?"

"Do nothing rash, my love. I beg of you. Give me more time."

"I have nothing but time at this point, at least until the spring. I will stay with the Campbells until the new year. While they are in Ireland with Mr. and Mrs. Dixon, I will stay with my grandmamma and aunt in Surrey. Then, I can put it off no longer. I must make my way in the world the best I can. *My* relatives do not have the means to support a young person with no prospects."

I stepped closer and encircled her in my arms. "Dealing with the Churchills is like a game of chess, but it is a game I know well. It requires strategy and ruthlessness, and yes, patience. But it will be worth it in the end. I have not given up hope, and neither should you."

She turned and clung to me, and we held each other until voices from outside the maze intruded.

"We must part now, but I will stay in London while you are here. When you go into Surrey, I will follow you. We will hedge our bets by extending an olive branch to my father and his new wife, and I will continue to work behind the scenes at Enscombe."

"I do not like being nefarious and cunning, Frank. The strain of this makes me almost ill."

"Then let me be the nefarious one. It bothers me not at all."

She looked at me, perhaps stunned at my assertion.

"I will write to you under the name of Miss Parker, a friend you met in Weymouth, and you will return my letter with a pen name of your own." I kissed her hand and then her mouth. I left her standing there in the morning shade, hollow-eyed and sad, promising myself I would make her life whole again.

THE HOLIDAYS CAME AND WENT, and Jane made her way to the diminutive village of Highbury. I followed, surprising my father and his new wife one day ahead of my scheduled arrival, but they did not appear to mind. In fact, they seemed thrilled, because they had chosen for me, in the horrid way that well-meaning relatives often do, a potential wife from the Highbury crop of young ladies.

Miss Emma Woodhouse was handsome, clever, and rich, and she was blessed with a merry disposition. She had been my stepmother's charge since the tender age of three, when Mrs. Woodhouse died, until Mrs. Weston's recent marriage to my father. Miss Woodhouse was a lovely girl, and the only fault I could find in her was her unfortunate tendency to see right through me.

I could not reject her as a potential wife, not out of hand, because I needed to stay in my father's good graces, but I could not bamboozle her either. Every time I spoke with her, she would knowingly nod her head and make some comment such as, "I am persuaded that you can be as insincere as your neighbors, when it is necessary."

Touché, Mademoiselle Woodhouse!

And while her skills of observation had a certain appeal, I certainly did not think I would find them quite so appealing in a wife. Thank goodness, she applied them in such a haphazard fashion or my secret betrothal might have come to light regardless of my attempts to conceal it.

Still I played the game set before me, trying to avoid stumbling into check. Miss Woodhouse seemed to enjoy the flirtation, and my father and Mrs. Weston seemed to enjoy seeing us with our heads together in discussion.

What I did not anticipate was the effect this ruse would have on Jane, already settled in the humble abode of her Bates relatives. She became colorless and sickly-looking. I joked with Miss Woodhouse about it, and then fretted over it in private. I tried to cheer Jane with a gift, a piano-forte delivered to the Bates' home. Perhaps that was too risky an impulse. The poor delivery men had a devil of a time getting it in Mrs. Bates' parlor! After I had arranged for its delivery, I did begin to think better of it, and not only because of the size of the thing. How was Jane to explain the gift without giving us away? But Miss Woodhouse provided the perfect alibi in her suppositions about Jane and Mr. Dixon, and the supposed tendre they held for each other. Besides, Jane would need a fine instrument when she became mistress of Enscombe. Better sooner than later, as far as I was concerned. There was no way for anyone in Highbury to trace the gift to me at any rate. Another fortunate turn of events! I was beginning to believe in my role as Fate's Child of Fortune once again.

And yet, Jane's health did not improve. I finagled for us to be alone by sending Miss Bates off to fetch my stepmother and Miss Woodhouse from Ford's, under the pretense of fixing Mrs. Bates' spectacles. While the older lady slept by the fire, I laid the spectacles aside and approached Jane, standing just to the side of the window, peering through the curtain.

"Dearest."

"Do not address me so! Grandmamma—"

"Is fast asleep—and hard of hearing to boot. In effect, we are all alone."

She peered around me, and her shoulders visibly relaxed.

"What news from Enscombe?" she whispered.

"My aunt's health remains poor. This is not a good time to approach the Churchills about our betrothal."

"And obviously you are not about to disillusion your father and Mrs. Weston about their hopes for you and Miss Woodhouse."

I grinned. "Why, Jane, dearest, me thinks you might be jealous!"

"I most certainly am not!" Her cheeks flushed and the stormy gray in her eyes returned—a welcome reminder of her former self. If jealousy would turn her into the Jane of Weymouth, perhaps I should indulge my father and stepmother a little longer.

I glanced around to check that Mrs. Bates was still sleeping. Then I raised my hand to cup Jane's cheek and brought her mouth to mine. Soft lips, delicate skin. I almost forgot where I was.

"It has been so long, Jane. So long since I could touch you." I ran a finger across her breast where fabric met the delicate flesh.

She shivered. "Frank."

Her aunt's voice sounded from the stairway.

"Bloody hell!" I growled.

Jane leapt back and turned toward the piano-forte. I claimed my seat and bent studiously over the spectacles once more.

They entered the room, Miss Bates, Mrs. Weston, and Miss Woodhouse, and the young mistress of Hartfield made her way over to my chair.

"This is a pleasure," said I, in rather a low voice, "coming at least ten minutes earlier than I had calculated. You find me trying to be useful. Tell me if you think I shall succeed."

"What!" exclaimed Mrs. Weston. "Have not you finished it yet? You would not earn a very good livelihood as a working-silversmith at this rate."

"I have not been working uninterruptedly. I have been assisting Miss Fairfax"—and here I stopped and grinned at her, with a glance at her bosom, unnoticed by the others, for I rose to stand between her and them—"in trying to make her...instrument stand steadily. It was not quite firm."

She turned from me in order to hide her smile.

As the spring came, my aunt's health worsened. The Churchills took a house in Richmond in May, and I was obliged to leave Jane in the clutches of that intolerable shrew, Mrs. Elton—her self-appointed "protector." That harridan! Why did she always involve herself in the business of every last person with whom she was acquainted? Vulgar upstart!

As I shuttled back and forth between Richmond and Surrey, I again felt fenced in, caught between my secret betrothed and the two branches of my family, both Churchill and Weston. Everyone wanted something different from me, and I recalled the cautionary saying that Nanny Roberts used to tell me: "Oh what a tangled web we weave, when first we practice to deceive."

I was required to be at my aunt's disposal, now more than ever, so I was unable to write to Jane.

By the day of the strawberry party at Donwell—tiresome place I tell you! And unbearably hot!—I was peevish. We quarreled, Jane and I.

As she walked home from the Abbey, I came upon her.

"Hullo, fair Jane!" I called out as I dismounted my horse. I halted abruptly when I saw that she had been weeping.

"Dearest, why do you cry? Let me walk with you and comfort you."

"Get back!" she hissed. "If someone were to see us, this awful, unbearable ruse would be for nothing."

"What has happened? Is it that officious Mrs. Elton again?"

"Yes. No. Or not just that. Although she is officious in the extreme."

She pushed past me and kept walking while she talked. "I do not know how much longer I can keep living this lie in which we have found ourselves. It is making me ill, and I begin to doubt your sincerity in keeping your word, given your behavior toward Miss Woodhouse."

"Jane—" I began, all condescension.

"Go away!"

The tiny twig of my tolerance snapped in two. "As you wish, milady!" I swung up onto my horse and rode like a mad man to Donwell, where I took my temper out on the serene and sensible Miss Woodhouse for the rest of the day.

Over the next weeks, Jane became more withdrawn, stopped answering my letters, and I grew desperate.

Then, a miracle happened. Or rather, it was a sad miracle, but a miracle for me, none the less.

My aunt died.

Suddenly, I was Fate's favored child again. I helped my uncle adjourn to Windsor, and there I sat, smugly considering when I should tell him of my plans. Imagine my horror, when a letter arrived from Jane, along with every letter I had written her, asking me to return her letters within the week to her aunt's, and after that to Mrs. Smallridge's home. I was in a state of total shock! She had accepted the governess position forced upon her by that shrew, Mrs. Elton!

Now my time had run out in truth. Jane was going away! But I also reasoned that my impediments to marrying Jane had also dissipated. Without my aunt's influence, it was easy to exert my influence over my uncle to accept my secret betrothal to Jane Fairfax—all it took was begging his forgiveness. His thoughts and remembrances of my aunt were so tender given his recent loss, that he sent me to Surrey with not only his blessing but his congratulations.

I surmised that Jane might be alone in the morning after breakfast and waited casually at the shop across the street until I saw Mrs. and Miss Bates depart. Glancing up and down the street, I knocked.

When she opened the door, I had to put my foot across the threshold and use my strength to keep her from shutting the door in my face.

"I am finished," said she, "with living a lie for you. I am proceeding with my life, and I suggest you do the same."

"I plan to do just that." As she had requested, I had brought the letters she had written me, but as she reached for them, I held them aloft. "I would speak with you, if you please, Miss Fairfax."

She left the door open and started back up the stairs. "As you wish."

She perched on the settee, back ramrod straight, eyes like cold, winter rain.

I sat beside her, laying the letters beside me. I reached over and cupped her chin, bringing her to face me. She looked away.

"Jane, my dearest. You look so ill."

"I am well," she lied. "I beg you, do not refer to me so intimately. It is not proper. Nor is it proper for you to be here."

"It is well and proper for me to call you by any term of endearment I wish—and to be alone with you—for you will soon be my wife. I have obtained my uncle's blessing. We may marry as soon as you like, after the bans are read."

Her eyes snapped up to mine, glassy with tears, and her lips parted in shock.

"Truly?" she whispered.

"Truly." I leaned into her, my very being responding as I remembered the rose and lavender scent of her, the feel of her skin like flower petals, the sound of her breathing as it caught in her throat and was released. I kissed her lips. "Relieve my suffering, Jane." I ran my fingers into her hair and pulled a tendril of it out of its comb. "Be my wife." I kissed her ear and whispered into it. "My mistress." I embraced her. "The mother of my children." Now I knelt in front of her, laying my head in her lap. "Forgive me. You are too good not to forgive me. You must end my torment and consent to be my wife."

"I...I..."

I encircled my arms around her hips. "Remember what we have between us." I traced the shape of her through her gown. "It cannot be denied. You are my destiny."

"I...I will have to write to Mrs. Smallridge."

I grinned into the folds of her skirt resting on her thigh. "Of course, my love."

I must admit, it was awkward to write to my father and stepmother, confessing all. My father was disappointed in me, particularly in the way I had paid attention to Miss Woodhouse while engaged to Miss Fairfax. He admonished me, saying that my mother would not have liked to see this side of me. I admitted—to him—that when seen in that light, it did look a might shabby and begged the forgiveness of him and my late mother, but I did not worry too much about it. I had never declared any feelings for Miss Woodhouse, and the lady did not harbor any for me, I was absolutely sure of that. I was not to blame if people assumed something that was not true. The lady of Hartfield seemed wholly nonplussed when she and I discussed my engagement. To her credit, Miss Woodhouse congratulated me, was very complimentary of my choice of wife, and very shrewd when she astutely commented, "You are the child of good fortune, Mr. Frank Churchill, and no doubt about it."

Her own fortune was increased considerably, I noticed, when she married Knightley that next autumn. I always had the inclination to believe her heart was unlikely to be touched and marrying a man sixteen years her senior confirmed that suspicion.

So, THAT IS THE tale of my journey from gentleman rogue to honest man, with the ending of the story just as my mother always hoped. Jane and I have been married seven years now and have two sons: ages six and four, and our two-year-old daughter. As I predicted, Jane has become the mistress of Enscombe, following the sudden death of my uncle two years ago. The new Mrs. Churchill is beloved by all at the estate, and she finally has the home she always wanted. In fact, she never wants to leave it—not for a Season in Town, nor a holiday trip to the seaside, nor for any damn thing at all.

And that, my friends, explains why I am just this morning arrived in Bath, to take the waters and see my friends Hayward and Dixon. We are spending the evening in the home of Hayward's brother, relaxing in the gentlemen's room after dinner, enjoying brandy and cigars as we contemplate the various places Fate has led us.

When it is time to join the ladies, I hear the murmur of female voices, a sirens' song to me still, after all these years. As we enter the room, a young woman plays the beginning strains of "Robin Adair", and I am swept away. Her voice is impeccable, her playing enjoyable, her figure beautiful. There is a joy in her expression that speaks of a romantic, sensual nature, and I lean over to Hayward and ask, "Who is that lady at the pianoforte?"

"She is Lady Windmere, widow of Lord Windmere."

"Charming." As I listen to her sing, I imagine what it must be like to be the man who puts that look of ecstasy on her face. When she finishes the song, I turn to Hayward: "Lady Windmere. I think perhaps I knew her husband. Might I request an introduction to the lady?"

KAREN M COX is an award-wining author of four novels accented with romance and history: *1932, Find Wonder in All Things, Undeceived,* and *I Could Write a Book,* as well as an e-book novella companion to *1932, The Journey Home.* She also contributed short stories for the anthologies *Sun-Kissed: Effusions of Summer* and *The Darcy Monologues.* Originally from Everett, Washington, Karen now lives in Central Kentucky with her husband, works as a pediatric speech pathologist, encourages her children, and spoils her granddaughter. Like Austen's Emma, Karen has many hobbies and projects she doesn't quite finish, but like Elizabeth Bennet, she aspires to be a great reader and an excellent walker.

SIR WALTER ELLIOT

Never was there a more vain-glorious character. Affected by money and rank, Sir Walter was forever pandering to fashion and his selfish pleasures. After the death of his wife, his profligacy, left unchecked, positioned his family and estate for pecuniary danger. Rousing contempt towards the lesser classes, the baronet disdained the Navy as well as the courtship of an ambitious officer to his middle daughter—much like he later abhorred letting his estate to an admiral: *"I have two strong points of objection to it. First, as being the means of bringing persons of obscure birth into undo distinction, and raising men to honours which their fathers and grandfathers never dreamt of; and secondly, as it cuts up a man's youth and vigor most horribly; a sailor grows old sooner than any other man."* —*Persuasion,* **Chapter III.**

Vanity was the beginning and the end of Sir Walter's character; vanity of person and of situation. He had been remarkably handsome in his youth… —
Persuasion, Chapter I.

ONE FAIR CLAIM
Christina Morland

BATH, MARCH 1784

It was one of those large, informal affairs in which no servant announced him, yet he had only to stand in the doorway to hear his name ripple through the assembly room. His ears, well-formed as all the rest of him, caught with delight that new syllable, that sibilant *Sir*, which now preceded the harder consonants of his name:

Sir Walter Elliot.

Yes, it had a noble ring to it and not just because of the title. His father, God rest his soul, had not carried his own name half so well, but then one could not expect a Sir Valentine Elliot to come off as anything except ridiculous. Sir Valentine had been the only Elliot of Kellynch Hall not to be given the name Walter, and this, Sir Walter felt certain, had been just one of the reasons why father and son had never quite seen eye to eye. (The many warts that had bloomed on Sir Valentine's wrinkled, puffy eyelids had been another.)

Though he had mourned his father's recent death in all ways befitting a gentleman, Sir Walter had found it difficult to feel anything except relief knowing the family name (and image) had been restored to its rightful place of honor. Indeed, given his standing, he wondered whether he ought to be attending public assemblies at all; at least the black arm band he wore did not ruin the line of his coat!

These gatherings were such loud, crowded affairs, quite unfashionable. But then, he was rather gratified by the many bows and curtseys he received (as was his due) as he made his way through the crush. Besides, he was a man with a purpose, one so significant he could overlook even the indignity of brushing elbows with the sons of nobodies.

Sir Walter Elliot was in love.

That is, he had found a woman he wished to marry. Elizabeth Stevenson of South Park in Gloucester was not the most beautiful woman of his acquaintance, nor was her family name to be found in his copy of the Baronetage. But the Stevensons were an old family, quite respectable (not to mention wealthy), and Miss Stevenson's complexion was so lovely that Sir Walter found himself utterly enchanted. No freckles, no lines, just a hint of pink that bloomed like a flower when she blushed. Let other men yearn for certain features just above and below the waist; Sir Walter wanted only pristine, smooth skin beneath his fingers.

Fortunately, Miss Stevenson's form was also passable, and her eyes were really quite striking, in a certain light. Her hair was dull and straight, hardly amenable to that halo of curls so many women wore these days—but then, not everyone could be perfect. As his valet had pointed out, there might be some value in having a wife with unremarkable hair, for it would set off the contrast with his own curls quite nicely.

Yes, Sir Walter Elliot was in love.

That is, he liked Miss Stevenson and her complexion well enough to bear the exclamations of surprise among his friends when they learned of his intentions.

"Stevenson?" drawled the Viscount Dalrymple, a distant cousin who resided in Ireland but sometimes visited Bath to take the waters. "A mere Miss Stevenson, an everyday Miss Stevenson, of all the people and all the names in the world, to be the chosen friend of Sir Walter Elliot, and among the nobility of England and Ireland! Miss Stevenson!"

No one seemed as surprised by his granting her the favor of his interest than Miss Stevenson herself; she regularly blushed and stammered in his presence, and even went so far as to confess that she had thought him too handsome to notice the likes of her. This admission had so charmed him that he had resolved then and there—or soon after. He had first inquired as to the respectability of her family and size of her dowry—to marry her.

That he had not yet asked her was of little concern; he would propose soon enough, and she would accept with alacrity. Of this, he had no doubt. Viscount Dalrymple might worry over her family name (and there were times, usually in the viscount's presence, when Sir Walter also felt anxious on this account). But, Sir Walter's superiority of situation had at least the advantage of making it impossible for her to refuse him.

"Sir Walter!" called James Stevenson from across the assembly room. Miss Stevenson's father spoke loudly enough to turn heads (as surely he had intended; he no doubt wanted to show off his connection to a baronet), and the crowd nearby quieted so they might hear the exchange.

Sir Walter returned Stevenson's greeting with a slight inclination of his chin.

"You look well this evening!" Stevenson said, clapping him on the shoulder.

Sir Walter did not know whether to be more offended by his future father-in-law's familiarity or the implication of his words: Did Sir Walter not look well *every* evening? But this was the price to pay for Miss Stevenson; her father spent so little time in Bath (and none at all in London) that he could hardly help being a bit of a country bumpkin. At least the old widower had possessed the good sense to send his daughter to seminary, where she had learned everything that was correct and good.

So, it was with much good will, and no little condescension, that he refrained from upbraiding the man. "Thank you, Stevenson, I am quite well."

Though, truth be told, he was not *quite* well. At that very moment, he felt a bead of sweat form in his right armpit. Perspiration was an unavoidable fact of life (even for Sir Walter), but so long as it remained hidden beneath his jacket, he had no reason to worry. Yet he felt certain that if he remained too long in this inferno of an assembly room, more visible portions of him (namely, his forehead) would be subjected to sweat. At least wigs had recently gone out of fashion; he would have had no hope of keeping his face dry then! Stevenson, who had apparently not bothered to look in a magazine or a mirror these past several years, was sweating profusely under his wig. Indeed, he looked something like a lobster with his bright red nose—good god, the size of that nose! Sir Walter turned about frantically, hoping to find a mirror or some other reflective surface to ensure that his own nose, at least, had retained its proper color.

"Ah," Stevenson said, laughing. "I see how you search for her! Look, she is standing there, near the door to the card room."

Sir Walter immediately followed Stevenson's direction, though it took several seconds for him to follow his meaning. Only when Miss Stevenson turned and met his gaze did he remember why he had subjected himself to such conditions. Her eyes widened at the sight of him, and her face—well, it was rather flushed, but then she at least resembled a rose and not a crustacean.

"And who is the gentleman so fortunate to be in conversation with your daughter?"

Stevenson smiled. "Aha! You are feeling territorial, Sir Walter!"

Hardly. The man speaking with Miss Stevenson was—there was no other word for it—ugly. Large in both height and girth, he possessed a broad, meaty form better suited to a laborer than a gentleman and the kind of face that suggested forty as easily as twenty-five.

"I am surprised you have not met him," continued Stevenson. "Is Monkford not near Kellynch?"

"Monkford?" Sir Walter would have wrinkled his brow in confusion had he not recently trained himself out of that habit to avoid the lines that so many men, even those as young as his own four and twenty years, seemed to acquire. Of course, he knew of Monkford; it was but four miles from Kellynch! Yet he was aware of no one who looked like *that* associated with the estate.

To Stevenson he said, "Governor Strafford, of the East India Company, resides at Monkford—or did before the death of his wife. I believed him to have returned to India. You do not mean to say this gentleman is a relative of the Governor?"

He waited with some trepidation for Stevenson's answer, for if this strange, homely man was in fact heir to Monkford, he might present more of a threat than Sir Walter had initially assumed. Monkford brought no title with it, but its living was, in fact, larger than Kellynch's, much to Sir Walter's dismay. These men who earned their titles and wealth through adventuring abroad—how they grated on his nerves! Did no one realize they would be the downfall of Merry England?

"Oh, no, not a relative," said Stevenson. "He was recently given the Monkford parish."

"The parish?" Sir Walter was so surprised that he threw back his head and laughed, caring little in that moment of relief for the redness of his face or the state of his curls. "You mean to say he is but a parson? It is no wonder I do not know him."

Stevenson gave him a sideways glance. "My brother is but a parson, you know."

"And no doubt a very fine one," Sir Walter said with a smile he saved for just these sorts of occasions. All teeth, perfectly even and beautifully white, thanks to his particular use of Gormer's dental powder. "Kellynch has its own parish, and so I would have had no reason to meet the vicar of Monkford."

This seemed to satisfy Stevenson, who in any case found himself being addressed by an acquaintance, and so Sir Walter was able to make his escape. He moved across the room to greet some of his own set, the few that condescended to attend public assemblies—a fellow baronet, the second son of an earl, and, most especially, the Viscount Dalrymple, who provided biting commentary on the crowd around them.

Sir Walter was surprised when Miss Stevenson's gaze did not follow him. He had wanted her to see the kind of company she could expect to keep in due time. But Miss Stevenson seemed quite intent on whatever it was this ugly vicar was saying to her.

"You seem distracted tonight," observed the viscount.

"It must be that chit he's after," noted the other baronet.

The second son shook his head. "I fail to see the attraction."

"You would," returned Sir Walter, who could barely bring himself to look at the man's pockmarked face for more than a few seconds at a time. "I will not have the lot of you discussing Miss Stevenson with such disrespect."

"Such chivalry, Elliot!" said the other baronet, smiling. "Her dowry must be better than we had all heard."

Indeed, it was, but Sir Walter also knew that it was not her dowry that drew him to her—for the most part, at least. It was not even that perfect complexion, which the other men seemed too blind to notice. No, there was something more to Elizabeth Stevenson, something he could not see or count, something intangible. And to a man who prized visible signs of good breeding above all else, such a something was quite extraordinary indeed.

In those few solitary moments of his life, when there was no one about—no servants, no viscounts, no one in between—to remind him who he was or what was expected of him, Walter Elliot found himself thinking that he quite liked Elizabeth Stevenson, even apart from her complexion. She smiled at his witticisms (but did not laugh in that high-pitched whinny so many ladies adopted) and she listened, really listened, when he spoke. It was as if she truly did care what he said (and since *he* so rarely cared what he said, so long as it sounded good and elicited a proper reaction from those around him, he felt her interest in him to be both curious and charming). Such reactions were no less than he deserved, being Sir Walter Elliot—and yet he had always supposed, by the way she smiled at him, that she had found him the most intriguing man of her acquaintance. Now, to observe her behaving with such sincerity toward another man, a lower man, and one who was so very ugly, too—well, was it any wonder he was distracted?

He excused himself from his friends and made his way toward her, though he had been planning to wait until just before the last set to claim a dance. (It would not do to appear too eager, after all.) Just as he was close enough to hear her, she laughed—a musical, joyful laugh. And though he was not jealous—how could Sir Walter Elliot be jealous of an ugly vicar—he supposed it must have been something *like* jealousy. There was no other explanation for his odd behavior: he ducked behind the nearest potted plant so that he might spy on their conversation.

"Come now, Miss Stevenson," said the vicar, the crooked smile on his lips doing nothing to improve his appearance. "You may laugh at me all you like, and yet you cannot deny the truth of my claim: satire like Swift's *A Modest Proposal* has a good deal more power than my meager sermons to bring attention to the plight of the poor."

There was that laugh again—pure, melodic, and, as far as Sir Walter could tell, wholly unwarranted. After all, what had the man said that was so amusing to her? And who was this Swift person, anyway?

"I most certainly hope you do not advocate the eating of infants in your homilies!" she responded, her laughter giving way to a smile that made Sir Walter forget her nonsensical reference to consuming children. She offered this vicar not that hesitant, embarrassed smile she so often used with him, but a wide, unchecked expression of happiness that took his breath away.

The vicar seemed similarly affected. He stared at her for several long (far too long) moments. Then, clearing his throat: "Ah, yes, rather, no, that is, my sermons stay quite clear of satire—and cannibalism."

Again, she laughed, and again, Sir Walter wondered why. He had at least deduced that they spoke of some piece of writing (what kind of man discussed books at a ball?), but as his reading material never veered from the Baronetage, the newspapers, and (though only a few of his household staff were allowed in on the secret) fashion magazines, Sir Walter had little to say on Swift himself.

Could it be that Miss Stevenson was something of a bluestocking? This new view of her gave him pause. He was not against female education, so far as it went, but talking of satire and cannibalism—he could only hope she was merely humoring this fellow. Her laugh, however, suggested some hidden predilection for intellectual conversation, which he despised in both ladies and gentlemen alike. To know the major authors of the day—well, there might be some use for that in drawing room discussions but leave the intricacies of such things to the scholars, that was his view of the matter.

Had they continued on about such ridiculous topics, Sir Walter might very well have turned away, made his excuses, and left the assembly. Indeed, he might have given up Miss Stevenson altogether; he had no use for a bluestocking!

Instead, the vicar began another line of conversation, one of much greater interest to Sir Walter.

"The dancers appear quite enthusiastic tonight," said the vicar, clearing his throat. "I was wondering, Miss Stevenson…" He cleared his throat, again and again, so that Sir Walter was tempted to give the man a lozenge or a glass of water. "If I might be…be so bold…as to…"

Sir Walter needed no deep understanding of literature to predict the stammered words that would follow. And though he had, only moments earlier, considered giving her up completely, he knew in that moment that he could not possibly abandon her. It was for her sake, as much as his—for how could he allow such a delicate flower as Miss Stevenson to be plucked by such unworthy (and ugly) hands? So what if she possessed an unhealthy interest in intellectual matters? He had no doubt he could cure her of such eccentricities, given time.

With a great sweep of his arm, Sir Walter pushed aside the branches of his hiding place and stepped into the fray. "My dear Miss Stevenson! I have been searching for you everywhere."

Gasping, Miss Stevenson spun to face him, while the vicar said, "Yes, even in the potted plants."

"Excuse me?" Sir Walter turned to the vicar with a curt bow. "I do not believe we have been introduced."

"Oh, yes, Sir Walter, this is…" Miss Stevenson paused, as if she could not possibly think of another's name while looking into Sir Walter's eyes. "This is Mr. Grant. Mr. Grant, may I introduce Sir…Sir Walter Elliot of Kellynch Hall?"

As she spoke his name, Miss Stevenson's cheeks again took on that rose-hue flush he loved (yes, loved!) Her eyes lingered on him, and the tip of her tongue (as rosy as her cheeks) darted across her lips. Oh, she might find this vicar amusing, but there was no denying her attraction to *him*.

"Mr. Grant attended Oxford with my brother," continued Miss Stevenson, "and is now vicar at Monkford, which he tells me is not very far from Kellynch Hall."

Ah, so they had been discussing Kellynch before his arrival! No doubt Miss Stevenson had asked about it, hoping to learn as much as she could. Sir Walter nearly laughed. Had he truly been afraid?

He offered Mr. Grant a smile, a sign of his goodwill. (Never let it be said that Sir Walter possessed anything but a sportsmanlike attitude toward those he bested.)

"Yes, I know of Monkford. I have passed by the parsonage many a time on my way to Taunton. It looks a snug little place. Good for a bachelor, I dare say, though I hope Governor Strafford improved the roof before scampering off to India." In an aside to Miss Stevenson—he leaned in close enough to hear the quickening of her breath—he added, "I heard the last vicar had to use an umbrella—indoors, my dear!—to keep himself dry in the spring."

Her smile was tremulous; her response, a breathy, "Oh my!"

"You need not be anxious on my account," said Grant, his frown turning the suggestion of a double chin into a terrible, ugly reality. "Governor Strafford is a most generous landlord and is continually providing for various improvements. If you must be concerned for the plight of others, Sir Walter—a noble trait, I am sure—then I might remind you of Mr. Terry."

Terry? The name sounded familiar, but it took several seconds for him to connect it to the petition that his new agent, Mr. Shepherd, had shown him. Apparently, this Terry fellow, a tradesman from the vicinity of Monkford, believed himself misused because Sir Walter had provided a reduced payment for a damaged piece of furniture. Terry had claimed it had been Sir Walter's men who had dented the back of the sideboard when moving it into the dining room *And, who can see the back of a sideboard anyhow, eh?*—but Sir Walter doubted very much that his servants were responsible (they knew too well how much he despised dents of any kind). Had he been cruel, he would have refused payment altogether. As it was, he gave what he supposed a very generous amount.

How this vicar knew of this matter was less important to him than the fact that he would dare to raise it in polite society—in front of a lady, no less.

"Who is Mr. Terry?" asked Miss Stevenson, glancing anxiously between the two men.

Her voice trembled so sweetly that Sir Walter reined in every impulse to give this impudent vicar a set down. (Besides, it would hardly do to have his business discussed in such a public setting.)

"Come, Miss Stevenson," said Sir Walter, taking her by the arm, "I beg you to dance the next set with me. Your beauty makes it impossible for me to think of anything else."

When she made as if to turn toward Mr. Grant, Sir Walter brought her gloved hand to his lips. "May there soon be a time when we dance all our sets together," he whispered against her fingers.

He watched her eyelids flutter and knew she would think no more of the vicar that night.

His good looks and his rank had one fair claim on his attachment; since to them he must have owed a wife of very superior character to any thing deserved by his own. Lady Elliot had been an excellent woman, sensible and amiable; whose judgment and conduct, if they might be pardoned the youthful infatuation which made her Lady Elliot, had never required indulgence afterwards. —Persuasion, Chapter I.

GLOUCESTER, JULY 1784

THE MORNING WAS CLEAR and fine, just as it ought to be for the wedding of Sir Walter Elliot. Though the church at South Park did not quite meet Kellynch's standards—the parson here had done little to keep his chickens, who were roaming the churchyard, from recognizing their proper place in the glebe—it was a pretty, little building, worn stone half covered in ivy. Set against the cloudless, blue sky, even this squat, gray edifice appeared attractive.

"You have a singular talent," Miss Stevenson had said to him just the other day, "for making any room you enter lovelier than it was the moment before you arrived."

This praise—rather forward, but then he could not deny the truth of it—had been whispered just after he had kissed her in one of the back stairwells of South Park. He would never before have considered himself the kind of man who kissed anyone in back stairwells (let his friends have their dalliances with maids in out-of-the-way places; Sir Walter Elliot could not believe any passion so strong that it must be fulfilled amidst grime and dust.) And yet, there he had been, descending the stairs just as Miss Stevenson had been ascending, her hair decorated with a delicate pink rose from the garden. There had been nothing for him to do but kiss her. She had smelled so delicious, and besides, South Park's housekeeper maintained a very tidy, grime-free stairwell.

What an odd experience, this season of courtship! He had secured Miss Stevenson's hand soon after that assembly in Bath and had planned to spend the spring and early summer enjoying his last days of bachelorhood by attending all the usual fetes Bath and London offered before the *ton* scattered to the country. Instead, he had found himself seeking out Miss Stevenson, as if he still needed to woo her. When her father invited him to stay at South Park until the wedding, he had accepted with alacrity.

Why he had acted thus, he could not precisely say. It would have been more proper, he supposed, to have kept some distance, to remind the family that, as a baronet, he had many obligations and many more important friends to visit. Yet he assured himself that there was some sense to his choice; Bath and London were really not to be borne in June—*sweat, all that sweat!*—and Kellynch was undergoing refurbishments to prepare for its new mistress.

If he were to be wholly truthful with himself, he must own that he rather enjoyed spending time with the Stevensons. This realization had shocked him, for the Stevensons were not nearly so polished or fashionable as his other friends, a fact he lamented whenever he was seen with them in Bath. The elder Mr. Stevenson was one of those hearty, country gentleman who liked to make sport of his own rough edges, and the younger Mr. Stevenson, Elizabeth's brother, was more bookish than refined. Yet they were tolerable, he supposed, and provided a good laugh when there was no better company to be found.

Miss Stevenson, on the other hand—she captured his attention no matter who else was present. Something had changed about her since their first meeting, for then she had been attractive in only that common way—her truly fine complexion being the exception to this ordinary prettiness. Yet in the weeks and months of their acquaintance, he seemed to have inspired a blossoming in her; she had become radiant, beautiful. This even his friends seemed to have noticed during their last days in Bath, when they congratulated him on his engagement. "She has more bloom than I first thought," Viscount Dalrymple had conceded.

"You must think me incurably silly, blushing so often when I am with you," she said on that same afternoon he had stolen a kiss on the back stairs.

"Not at all, my dear," he replied, stroking her cheek with the express purpose of bringing about the blush she pretended to regret. (Surely, she could not *truly* regret that which made her more beautiful.) "Your complexion is one of the finest in all of England, even when you blush."

To his surprise, she pulled back at this compliment. "My complexion may not always be so fine. We will grow old together."

"Old?" He tried to laugh, but oh, the image she had put before him! Why would she ruin their intimacy with such dreadful, heavy thoughts?

"That will not be for many years," he said, in a calmer tone than he felt, "and besides, there are very good creams my valet can recommend. In the meantime, you must not frown so. What, will you not smile for me? Then I can think of only one way to convince you..." And he bent down and kissed her until her lips relaxed and the frown lines disappeared.

"But I must have you understand," she insisted afterward, her cheek against his shoulder so that he could see only the top of her head. Her hair powder really was a dull shade; there must be some concoction his valet could recommend to her maid.

"Though you are the handsomest man of my acquaintance," she continued, "it is your generosity and kindness I admire most, Sir Walter."

This was a new experience, being praised for his generosity and kindness. True, he performed the usual acts of charity, but he did no more than was expected of him. When in the presence of Miss Stevenson, however, he found himself performing the most extraordinary (and unintentional) acts of chivalry. This behavior had begun quite accidentally at one of the first card parties they had both attended as an engaged couple. Sir Walter had been paired with an old Stevenson relative who, it transpired only after he sat down, had the most noxious breath and a grand total of two teeth in her mouth. One might have hoped such a condition would have inspired silence in the woman, yet she seemed more garrulous than most. Sitting across from her, he found himself directly in the current of both her breath and her nonsensical conversation. Leaning back did little to ameliorate the situation, but he discovered that, if he leaned forward and yet to the side, angling himself just so, he could avoid the stream of her breath while also appearing to listen most attentively to whatever it was she was saying (two teeth being too few for comprehensible speech).

"You cannot know," Miss Stevenson said to him later, "how happy it made me to see you giving my aunt such courteous attention! So many people neglect her for reasons she can hardly help."

And a fortnight later, when he and Miss Stevenson had been riding together across some of the prettier acreage of South Park, they had come across a small group of urchins, likely tenants' sons, who had decided to transform their master's trout stream into their private swimming place. They were only discovered because one of their number was howling quite piteously, having cut his foot on a rock. Sir Walter would have upbraided him and the others most severely, except that Miss Stevenson had already dismounted her horse and raced over to the boys; she had slid off her horse in a most unladylike way, not even waiting for the groom to help her, but then at least her haste had given him a quick glimpse of one finely shaped leg.

Rather than scold, Miss Stevenson had comforted the boy. When Sir Walter had seen how she had hugged that towheaded rascal, he had been struck by the notion that she would make a fine (if somewhat indulgent) mother. If he did not examine the scene before him too closely—if he ignored the rough, homespun clothing and the dirt-smeared face of the boy in her arms—he could picture her instead with *his* son. This vision so inspired him that he also dismounted his horse and handed the boy (who was not so badly injured as his howling had suggested) a shilling before telling him and his comrades to scamper.

"Dear Sir Walter!" she had exclaimed when they were alone—well, the groom stood several feet behind him, but then he hardly counted. She smiled at him with such fondness that he might have given away yet another shilling if the boys had not already run off. Then she had offered her hand, and he had kissed those long, delicate fingers. Charity, it seemed, rewarded the giver as well as recipient.

Though Sir Walter had planned to return to Kellynch briefly before the wedding, he just could not seem to make himself leave the warmth of Miss Stevenson's admiration. (That her esteem was based largely on the appearance of goodness, rather than the reality of it, troubled him not, for he had always subscribed to the philosophy that appearance *was* reality.) He dashed off a few letters of business to his steward and solicitor, and then set out to enjoy the fortnight before his wedding. He bounded about South Park in such a way that no one in residence, from the master of the house to the lowliest of scullery maids, could doubt his affection for his bride.

No one, that is, except Mr. Grant.

"You neither know nor appreciate Miss Stevenson's true worth," the vicar had been impudent enough to say one evening when he and Sir Walter had found themselves together in South Park's library (which Sir Walter had entered only because he believed Miss Stevenson to have been there).

Yes, somehow that ugly vicar had found a way of imposing on the hospitality of the Stevensons for an entire ten days. He claimed to be out of house and home while the parsonage at Monkford underwent repairs, a story Sir Walter found most dubious. It seemed more likely that Grant was a leech who lived on the luxuries of his more prosperous friends. Was not the man's exceptional girth proof of this?

True, Sir Walter himself had been in residence for nearly six weeks, during which the Stevensons had thrown a ball each fortnight and dinner parties at least three nights of the week. But, then he was to be family, whereas this Mr. Grant—who was he, but an old schoolfellow of the young Mr. Stevenson?

"They are like brothers," Miss Stevenson explained when he had complained to her of the vicar's presence.

"And yet," returned Sir Walter, "they never will *be* brothers, not as your brother and I shall be when we are married."

Her brow furrowed, causing him to reach up to smooth the wrinkles from her otherwise perfect forehead.

"Oh, Walter," she had murmured, leaning forward to kiss him before he could remind her that Sir Walter would have been more correct. "I beg you not to dislike Mr. Grant. He is a true friend."

"In your eyes, perhaps, this man may be but a friend, but to deny his deeper, baser interest in you, my dear Miss Stevenson...well, you are too naive to recognize his feelings for what they are."

She appeared startled by this idea that Grant might want her—just as startled as she had been all those months ago when Sir Walter had expressed his own admiration. It was as if, in her lovely eyes, he and this vicar were on equal terms—both just as unlikely to be attracted to the likes of her. Could it be that her adoration of him came not from his good looks, rank, or even his vaunted generosity and kindness—but rather from the mere fact that he was the first man to express an interest in her?

"What of his own parish?" Sir Walter demanded, eager to make her see how he and this vicar were most certainly not to be considered equals. "Surely he has an obligation to his flock?"

"Indeed, and he has traveled—at his own expense, I should add—back to Monkford once already to see to his duties." She sighed. "It might very well have been more economical to have stayed at an inn near Monkford, and yet—well, I wonder why he came? I suppose he felt obligated to accept my brother's invitation."

Obligated? What nonsense! Sir Walter felt the frown lines forming and quickly changed the subject.

Could he only have changed the composition of the household. It was bad enough having to talk about Grant, but to see him! Fortunately, the vicar stayed out of the way, spending most of his time in the Stevenson's library. And though Sir Walter feared coming across him in one of the corridors—*Would there even have been room for the two of them in South Park's narrow hallways, given the vicar's exceptional width?*—he saw him only that one evening in the library, and then at occasional meals, when the vicar ate with silent determination—as fat men were wont to do.

At least Sir Walter could be certain he would not see the man today. Though invited to the wedding and breakfast, Grant had adamantly refused, turning beet red when Miss Stevenson spoke of it. Indeed, he had been so uncivil to his hosts that Sir Walter would have upbraided him, if only he had not been relieved at the vicar's refusal to attend.

Well, he could put Mr. Grant from his mind now. A few hours, and then he and his lady would be well on their way to Kellynch.

"Sir Walter!" said Mr. Stevenson, hurrying across the churchyard. His soon-to-be father-in-law's expression gave him pause. Stevenson did not often appear anxious, and yet there was no denying the furrowed brow (an unfortunate family trait, it seemed) or the worry lines joining the other wrinkles surrounding the old man's eyes.

"What is it?" Sir Walter felt a moment's fear, but only a moment's. Pretty women ran off with ugly vicars only in novels, or so he assumed, having never read one himself.

"I am afraid Mr. Thomas, our vicar, is dreadfully ill."

Sir Walter only just suppressed a sigh; the marriage would have to be delayed until the vicar from a nearby village could be summoned. In the meantime, he would simply have to make sure neither he nor Miss Stevenson went anywhere near South Park's library.

When Miss Stevenson arrived, looking quite adorable in a pale blue gown with a bodice of the finest white lace (just the thing to show off the milky skin of her bosom), she was devastated by the news.

"Oh, I do hope Mr. Thomas is not in any danger!" she cried, a slight flush spreading across the swell of her breasts.

"He has been such a good friend to our family," said her brother. "Is there nothing we can do for him?"

"No, the apothecary assures me he will make a recovery but not a speedy one." Mr. Stevenson frowned. "That leaves us with the question of what to do about the ceremony. Sir Walter agrees that we should send for the nearest vicar, though that will mean a delay in the ceremony."

"But why not ask Mr. Grant?" suggested Miss Stevenson. "Is he not still at South Park?"

Stevenson clapped his hands. "But of course, I had forgotten all about the lad! He is always in the library, I hardly know he is around."

"No," said the younger Stevenson, in such a curt tone that Sir Walter felt sure that Jamie Stevenson could see what neither his father nor sister could. "I do not think that will do, Elizabeth."

"But why ever not?"

Her complete innocence struck him then, not for the first time, but with such force that Sir Walter felt a sudden jolt of fear. He had, in fact, looked forward to unburdening her of this innocence (not to mention her clothing). But now he wondered: What would he find beneath the surface of Miss Elizabeth Stevenson? What if that beautiful complexion was a trap, the mere illusion of light concealing deeper, darker waters below?

The few women he had bedded in the past—these he had always considered stained, dirty creatures. Serviceable, and beautiful in a showy sort of way, but impure and sullied, too. Only now did he recognize their one point of superiority to Miss Stevenson: they had experience—and not just the kind that made him moan in pleasure. These other women had fully understood what was expected of them. Their worldliness had been an anchor, something he could rely on.

Miss Stevenson's guilelessness, however, was another thing altogether.

Hers was a stubborn innocence, not the kind easily scrubbed from the bedsheets after the first night of passion, but a spirit within herself that she alone could touch.

He did not like people who were more than they seemed. They unmoored him, turned his world upside down. They reminded him of the time he had fallen from his horse and been struck temporarily blind. He had been only eight, and the blindness had not lasted more than a few days, but God, how he had suffered! It had not been the pain so much as the fear that he would never see again, that he would be forever stuck in the dark. Even now, the remembrance of that time sent chills down his spine. He was a man who lived through his eyes, who knew no other way of understanding his world except through sight.

"Sir Walter?"

He looked up at the sound of Miss Stevenson's voice. For a moment, she was nothing but a blur, a swirl of blue and white. Only after a few panicked breaths did she come into focus. The Stevensons were all staring at him.

"You look unwell," said the older Stevenson. "Your face looks odd."

Sir Walter spun toward the window of the church, but alas, it was stained and not at all the kind of glass he needed.

"We should marry today," was all he could manage as he turned back to face them. Yes, they must marry today—before he experienced more of these worrisome episodes. "Send for your friend, Stevenson."

The younger man shook his oddly-shaped head. (He shared none of his sister's good looks.) "Grant would feel...he...oh, Elizabeth, can you not understand how it is with Grant? Why he came to South Park all those holidays, all those summers? Why even now, on the verge of your marriage, he cannot keep away?"

She blushed then, some of her innocence perhaps swept away by that rush of blood to her cheeks.

"I know *you* understand, Sir Walter," said her brother with a catch in his voice, "even if my sister does not. Come Father, write to the vicar in ____shire."

When Miss Stevenson's shoulders sank, Sir Walter saw how she was about to acquiesce.

"I hardly know what you mean, Stevenson!" he said, trying for one of his toothy smiles. His face felt stiff, brittle, on the verge of breaking.

But the smile seemed to work on old Mr. Stevenson, who said,

"Indeed! Why must you always speak in riddles, Jamie, my boy? I sometimes wonder at my decision to send you off to Oxford."

"What I do know," said Sir Walter, taking Miss Stevenson's hand in his own, allowing her smooth skin to soothe his nerves, "is this: my beloved wishes to marry today, as do I—most assiduously. Your friend is a vicar; we have need of his services. I say we send for him, and when we do, I am sure he will do his duty."

Jamie Stevenson sighed. "Yes, that is true enough. Grant will never shirk his duty. Very well, I will fetch him."

An hour passed before they returned—an hour that would have been dreadful for Sir Walter if he had allowed his mind to ruminate on those ridiculous thoughts about innocence and blindness. Instead, he walked Miss Stevenson about the churchyard, describing the many rooms of Kellynch—the color of various pieces of furniture, the number of chimneys, the great size of the drawing and dining rooms (they could seat thirty-six guests without a bit of trouble). These words had a notable effect on Miss Stevenson—her complexion paled, and her blue eyes shone, making her appear as beautiful as she had ever been—and Sir Walter felt better with each detail he shared.

"Do you ever find yourself wondering," she asked, interrupting his description of the family's best set of silver, "what it means to understand, truly understand, another person?"

"Understand?" he repeated after a pause.

"Yes, to comprehend their true selves, to see beyond the surface of things and..." Her eyes filled with tears. "I had no notion that Mr. Grant...that is, when you spoke of it days ago, I thought you were merely being gallant, and perhaps a little jealous, but to hear my brother..."

Never before had Sir Walter experienced the sensation that then came over him: the sense of time standing still, that separation between what he saw (clouds inching past the sun, a chicken racing across the yard, dust rising from the nearby road as a carriage approached) and what he sensed (nothing, absolutely nothing). It was not merely the possibility of being jilted, with all the embarrassment and inconvenience attending such an event, that stilled his heart. No, it was a true sense of loss, a gaping hole inside him, for somewhere deep down, beyond the golden curls and sparkling eyes, beneath the fine clothes and fair skin, there lurked in Sir Walter Elliot the disembodied belief that Elizabeth Stevenson might actually be good for him.

"...and I can only hope," she was saying, her voice as indistinct and insistent as an insect buzzing at his ear, "that he is not terribly disappointed or hurt by my choice, for I assure you, I had no notion, absolutely no notion, of his tender regard!"

He blinked, her face coming into focus only as the last of her words reached him. She was not going to jilt him! And then, though it was not right or proper, and though it would almost certainly increase the likelihood of lines, he smiled so widely that he could feel that smooth skin of his cheeks stretch and ache in protest.

His appearance must have been arresting, for she immediately ceased her crying. "You…you find this amusing?"

"I find you adorable," he replied, laughing and taking her hands in his. The relief on seeing how things really stood—that she did not care for the vicar (how could she!) except perhaps by pitying him more than he deserved—brought him back to himself completely.

"You worry about the most unaccountable things, my dear. Mr. Grant could never have expected someone like you to return his feelings, so you must not worry on his account."

She looked away. "And yet…does not my blunder suggest we know very little about the people we claim to love, Sir Walter?"

"Ah, you worry that I do not know you," he said, squeezing her fingers lightly. "Shall I tell you what I see, my lady—for my lady, you soon shall be? I see a delicate flower, so fresh, so tender, so—" *innocent*, he almost added, but knew better than to go back into that mode of thinking—"lovely. You will adorn Kellynch Hall with your grace and beauty, my dear."

"That is not precisely what I meant," she said, still keeping her gaze firmly on some point behind him. "What if *you* are not…"

When she did not continue, when she instead raised her shining eyes to his, when he saw the fear in her expression (so very similar to his own unwarranted fears), he understood.

"What if I am not pleased with you?" he asked gently. "My dear, how could I not be?"

She closed her eyes then, and he smiled at this obvious show of relief.

"Ah! I see the vicar and your brother."

At these words, her eyes flew open and the color flooded back into her cheeks.

"Let us go into the church and be transformed. We shall enter as Sir Walter Elliot and Miss Stevenson and emerge as Sir Walter Elliot and his wife."

When she did not move, he tugged gently on her hand. When still she remained rooted to the ground, he added, "Lady Elliot. It has a nice ring to it, does it not?"

"Lady Elliot," she said, her voice catching on the name. Then, with an odd, breathy laugh, she added, "I suppose you think it will look well on a calling card, too."

He smiled. "Indeed it will! I remember my own feelings on first seeing Sir Walter Elliot on a card."

She looked at him then, her smile unaccountably sad and gentle, as if he had just expressed some deep hurt rather than a pleasant memory. Putting her arm through his, she patted his hand. "Dear Sir Walter."

That she kept her eyes averted from the ugly vicar throughout the service, he found quite sensible. That she spoke her vows in a mere whisper, he understood quite well. The tremble in her hand as she last signed her name "Stevenson" he did not wonder at, nor did he question the tears that sprang to her eyes when she bid adieu to all her family and friends, as well as Mr. Grant, at South Park.

It was only when he gave her his wedding gift on the carriage ride to Kellynch that he felt a return of that inexplicable fear which had taken hold before the wedding. He watched her unwrap the gift—"Oh, a book, Walter! I shall always treasure"—and saw the way her face drooped in disappointment as her fingers traced the embossed title.

"The...the Baronetage?" she asked faintly.

"Your very own copy, my dear."

Nothing he said—not his explanation of how they would add her name to its pages first by hand, and then, when a new copy was issued, in print; not his careful delineation of the Elliot family's age and respectability; not even his whispered promise to help her add a new Sir Walter to those hallowed pages—seemed to have much of an effect on her. She sat, for the remainder of the ride, stock still and silent.

It was the shock of all that had happened, he supposed, and the natural fear of what was to come. It was that inexperience he had found so daunting earlier in the day, the inexperience he now found rather endearing. For it was clear to him now, the truth of the matter: his dear Lady Elliot had no idea what lay before her; she felt blind and uncertain. Well, it would be his pleasure and his duty as her husband to open her eyes, to make her see just what kind of man she had married.

Elizabeth, born June 1, 1785; Anne, born August 9, 1787; a still-born son, Nov. 5, 1789... —Persuasion, Chapter I.

KELLYNCH, MARCH 1790

SIR HENRY RUSSELL HAD only three things to recommend him, in Sir Walter's estimable opinion: first, that he had purchased and improved Kellynch Lodge (an abode that had, in earlier times, been part of the Kellynch estate but, for various unhappy reasons, had been sold off), thereby bringing some honor to the Kellynch name; second, that he had sold Sir Walter a fine pair of pistols that, though rarely used (hunting being far too ugly a business for the likes of Sir Walter Elliot), looked very well in the glass case in the entrance hall; and third, he possessed a wife who united good sense, a healthy respect for rank, and an appearance that was, if not appealing, then at least inoffensive.

It was not for himself that Sir Walter admired Lady Russell, but for the sake of his own wife, who, it turned out, required something more than a handsome baronet to buoy her spirits. Six years had not brought complete happiness to the Elliots of Kellynch Hall. Though Sir Walter had found all his hopes fulfilled on the night of his wedding (the skin under her clothes being quite as smooth and firm as he had long imagined it to be), he discovered that marriage required a good deal more of him than exploring the gentle terrain of her body.

Of course, he had always known he would have responsibilities: introducing her to the first families of the neighborhood; teaching her the proper forms of address for those noble families with whom he corresponded, such as the Viscount and Viscountess Dalrymple; and making sure she managed her household duties with all the pride expected of a baronet's wife.

Lady Elliot had proven herself quite adept at the first and second of these responsibilities, but Sir Walter found her lacking on the third point. Oh, it was not that she shirked her duties; indeed, he rather thought she expended too much energy on certain matters, such as the wages of the servants and the balancing of household accounts. With the former, she was in his opinion far too generous, with the latter, far too strict. That he should be asked to moderate his purchase of clothing so that the scullery maid who did his laundry might have a longer day off had caused no little discord between Sir Walter and his wife.

"You do not know what is due a baronet!" he had exclaimed during one of these arguments.

"Perhaps you do not know what is due a scullery maid," had been her response, one so ridiculous that he had felt himself gape (a most appalling look for any man, even one with good teeth). Still, he had forgiven her, for she *had* been with child at the time; no doubt she had been experiencing nerves. Besides, she had eventually acquiesced, giving the scullery maid only an extra hour and speaking no more to him of his clothing, except in suggesting quite timidly one night (when they were in the process of removing said clothing) that she had heard Sir Henry Russell boasting of his tailor in Bath who also dressed several lords in residence there. That this tailor was also less expensive was hardly worth mentioning.

Perhaps most worrisome for Sir Walter was his wife's unhealthy interest in the lesser sorts of people who lived in the surrounding neighborhoods. Though she had almost completely given up the serious reading that had caused him some alarm before their marriage, she seemed to have shifted her energies toward philanthropy. While some small acts of charity were expected of Lady Elliot, she did much more than take baskets to those tenants and servants too ill to make much use of them.

Sir Walter had at first suspected Lady Russell to be the inspiration of his wife's zeal in this realm; Lady Russell had, after all, been known to suggest various works of philosophy to Lady Elliot, and one never knew when these intellectual types might begin to believe the mad ideas they so enjoyed discussing.

But it seemed she was not, after all, the culprit. Indeed, it was Lady Russel (dear woman) who had made him aware of the severity of the situation.

"I must admit to some surprise," he said as they sat down together in the Kellynch drawing room, "at your request for an interview, Lady Russell. You must have been told that Lady Elliot is out."

She nodded, and he could not help but stare at the ostrich feather swaying atop her cap. Yes, Lady Russell was a fine woman—well-bred and sensible—but he could not help think that she would have benefited from a more astute lady's maid.

"It is precisely because she is out that I have called."

He raised an eyebrow (very slightly, so that the skin above it crinkled not at all). "Indeed!"

"I recognize," she continued, "the singular nature of my request, and yet it would have been more unseemly to stay silent in this matter."

"Matter? What matter?"

Lady Russell sighed. "Do you know where Lady Elliot has gone this morning, Sir Walter?"

"On a walk, I suppose. Or perhaps to visit the tenants."

Lady Russell merely pursed her lips.

"Are you suggesting, Lady Russell, that my wife is involved in some kind of impropriety?"

She blushed, and he was sorry to say that Lady Russell had none of his wife's talent for blushing prettily. "No, certainly not! Lady Elliot's behavior is always above reproach!" She paused. "It is not an impropriety, Sir Walter, so much as a kind of innocence that may expose her to ridicule."

"Innocence, Lady Russell?" He gulped. "What nonsense is this?"

"Lady Elliot's attentions to the poor of the neighborhood, particularly their children…"

"Ah." He shook his head. "I am well aware of these visits, and though she might sometimes be too generous with them, I do not believe she has acted improperly. Indeed, I have noticed that the children are less likely to look like ragamuffins after she has visited. If Lady Elliot can bring some beauty to the neighborhood, well, I do not mind the expense of it. Such improvements are, I would say, a good cause."

"I quite agree. It is not so much her concern for the poor, but rather those who influence her views on the matter, that make me anxious." Lady Russell cleared her throat. "You are, I believe, acquainted with the vicar at Monkford, Mr. Grant?"

The ugly vicar!

Anger was not normally a part of Sir Walter's emotional lexicon. Annoyance, yes. That niggling throb of his temple, the slightest tightening of his lips, a quickening of his breath—such reactions to the little disappointments of life were natural, involuntary. But cheeks burning, jaw trembling, eyes narrowed to mere slits? These responses were very unkind to the countenance. And yet how else might he react in the face of this revelation?

Lady Russell must have seen something of his inner turmoil, for she brought a handkerchief to her lips and averted her eyes, as if she might blank out her own features to balance out his sudden show of feeling.

"We are bowing acquaintances," Sir Walter managed after a long pause. "He is, I believe, an old schoolfellow of Lady Elliot's brother. But we have not been in company with him for many years."

Indeed, since the wedding, he had not seen the man except in passing. Sir Walter had made sure of this. No invitations to dine, no accepting invitations anywhere near Monkford, no trips with the younger Mr. Stevenson to travel about the countryside to see friends. No, no, no. It was not jealousy that motivated him. No! It was mere common sense.

"It seems," said Lady Russell, eyes still averted, "that she encountered Mr. Grant on the road one afternoon; he was giving food to a group of gypsy children."

"Gypsies? On my land!"

"No, Sir Walter, but near enough. I was with Lady Elliot at the time—"

"And you did not speak to me earlier?" he demanded, glaring. Lady Russell met his gaze without blinking; they both knew who ought to have been the one to share such news with him.

"When was this?" he said, trying for a nonchalance he did not feel.

"This past autumn, not long after"—she gave a delicate little cough—"the incident."

Sir Walter closed his eyes, as if that might keep the memory away. And yet still he saw the child, blue and strangled. The next Sir Walter Elliot, born dead. He had not wanted to see the body; he had told the midwife not to show it to him. But then he had heard his wife sobbing in the next room, and without thought, without realizing what he would see when he entered, he had gone to her.

"You must love me," she had cried when he knelt by her side, "despite everything, you truly must love me!"

And yes, he truly must have loved her—for what else could have brought him into that room, stinking with death? Where was his dear Lady Elliot with her milky white skin? This creature in bed—blotchy complexion, sweaty brow, arms wrapped tightly around the corpse of their child—this was not Lady Elliot!

He had sworn, when his own mother had passed, that he would never again allow himself to be in such close proximity to death. Four years old, and his own mother's arms were wrapped tightly around him, or as tightly as she could manage given her illness. Her breath was so foul that he retched, but she was insensible to everything except holding him, as if she might live so long as they touched. He squirmed and struggled, trying to escape, and once managed to slide off the sickbed, but his father grabbed him by the arm and nudged him back into her embrace, one heavy hand holding him in place while his mother caressed his golden curls with her spindly fingers.

"My beautiful boy!" she whispered. "Give me one last kiss, my dear, beautiful boy!"

"Be a good lad," said his father through his own tears, "and give her a kiss."

But no, he could not, he would not! Even as his mother pulled him closer, he turned his head away, trying desperately to dodge her dry, peeling lips. It was in that moment that he caught sight of their reflection in the large gilded mirror next to her bed: she was Death, reaching for him, ready to suck the life from his rosy cheeks. With a piercing scream, he scratched at her face until she gasped and fell back against her pillow. He raced from the room, not daring to look back, and the next time he saw her, she lay motionless on her bed, dressed in her shroud, two pale scratch marks lining her nearly translucent cheeks.

So yes, he must have loved his Lady Elliot to kneel at her side while she held Death in her arms. And to think, she returned that great love by bringing Grant back into their lives!

"She and Mr. Grant visit the gypsy encampment upwards of three times a week," said Lady Russell quietly. "I have some reason to believe she is there now."

"Together? They visit these gypsies together?"

"Yes, though I must say I am glad for that small favor. If he is responsible for exposing her to such unhealthy sorts, I may at least be glad that he accompanies her to provide some protection."

"Protection!"

"Yes, well, Lady Elliot once suggested to me that the two of us go alone when Mr. Grant was not able to go with her. I insisted that she not visit those people without someone who might keep her from harm. Perhaps I ought to have spoken to you before now, but I hoped she might follow my advice and tell you herself."

"Do you mean to say she will not listen to *you*?" asked Sir Walter with some surprise. His wife seemed willing to do almost anything Lady Russell asked of her.

"She is such a good friend to me, and so wise," he had heard his wife say often enough.

Lady Russell sighed. "She says she cannot be persuaded on this point, that these children—there are a good number of them among the gypsies, many of them ill—require her aid. In any case, Sir Henry and I will soon leave for Bath. I will have no influence on her from afar."

The drawing room door opened then, admitting Lady Elliot, flanked by their two daughters. The oldest shared her mother's name but her father's good looks, whereas the younger—well, she was only two. There was some hope, he supposed, that Anne Elliot might improve with time.

"Lady Russell!"

Lady Elliot smiled at her friend with such warmth that Sir Walter felt some of his unhappiness dissipate. True, the smile emphasized the wrinkles beginning to form at the corners of her lips, but he discovered he could trick himself out of seeing such imperfections. There were some days when he nearly forgot to examine her, even when she stood before him. This usually happened when she laughed, the rich sound saturating his senses so that his eyes seemed hardly able to function at all.

"I had not thought you were coming today, my friend! I have only just returned from an outing."

Yes, an outing. Sir Walter studied her then, examined her in a way he had not in many years, or perhaps never. Oh, he looked often enough to see if she had freckles (still none, thank God) or lines (a few), to see if she wore the latest fashions (generally), or whether her gowns were too snug (perhaps this time, she might bear him a healthy son). But he never bothered to look beyond that; he had never before seen that odd tilt to her chin or the half smile on her lips, as if she knew something he did not.

Lady Elliot held his gaze, and he had a disquieting thought: she knew what Lady Russell had come to tell him.

"Perhaps," she said to her daughters, "you may persuade Lady Russell to walk with you in the garden."

"Oh, yes!" cried Anne, racing across the room and throwing herself at Lady Russell, so that the dear lady nearly toppled backward. "Please, Lady Russell!"

"Comport yourself, young lady!" cried Sir Walter, wagging a finger at Anne. She glanced up at him, her face barely visible behind all the folds of Lady Russell's skirts. Her eyes—so big and bright—frightened him; it appeared as if there was an entire world hidden behind that elfish little countenance.

He looked to his wife, hoping she might chastise the girl, but she offered only that gentle smile he had once believed was for him alone. Then his daughters had been born, and he had seen the smile numerous times, generally when they made some small blunder. How had a smile of affection become one of resignation?

"Dear Anne," said Lady Russell fondly, bending down to pat her on the head. "I do not mind her exuberance, not at this age, Sir Walter. She will learn soon enough how to be a proper young lady."

"You see that *I* have learned to be proper already," said Elizabeth, slipping her hand from her mother's so that she might perform a delicate curtsey for the room.

"Very good!" said Sir Walter, who would never grow tired of his older child's charms. Ah, to see such beauty and dignity reproduced in childlike form! If only she could have been a son.

"Perhaps, my dears," said Lady Russell, taking both girls by the hand, "you might show me the newest flowers in the garden while your dear mama and papa discuss certain matters that are of no interest to us."

Lady Elliot glanced between her friend and her husband. "Ah. It is just as I thought."

There was no anger in her voice, no expression of disgust on her countenance, as she looked at her friend. Just that same gentle smile, as if Lady Russell, too, had misbehaved in some minor and predictable fashion.

Sir Walter hardly knew how to respond to his wife's nonchalance. When left alone with her a few moments later, he found himself unable to begin.

"You and Lady Russell are concerned," she said when he let the silence stretch for minutes.

"Yes! That is it exactly!"

She sat beside him then, taking his hand in her own, and he wondered at the softness of her skin. To look at that hand, to see the veins beginning to show through the skin and the small, hard callous on the ring finger, one might have supposed the pads of her fingers had grown dry and rough. But no; they felt as soft as they had the first time he had touched them.

"You have been using the hand cream I suggested," he said to her.

"My lady's maid will not allow me to forget it."

"Good girl," he said. "I only wish you were half so considerate of my wishes."

It was a biting remark, and though the laughter disappeared from her eyes, the gentle smile again settled onto her lips. "I know, sir, how much you value your reputation; I hope *you* know that I would do nothing to harm it."

"Then why do you consort with that ugly vicar?" he blurted.

"Mr. Grant?"

Only after she spoke his name, her smile faltering, did he realize just how little he cared about the gypsies. There were always these dirty people about, and truth be told, he himself had sometimes sent small presents to these folk when they passed through, mostly at the suggestion of his agent Mr. Shepard, to keep them from harassing his tenants and the tradesmen who used the roads to reach Kellynch.

"Lady Russell tells me it is he who has inspired this sudden interest in the gypsy children."

"Do you suppose, sir, that I needed any other inspiration than the one God provided November last?"

He could say nothing in response to such a question, spoken with more hurt than he had ever heard in her voice.

"You cannot know how I felt," she whispered, "when our son…And when I heard about a poor woman who had suffered a similar fate, what could I do but go to her? She has other children, this woman, and they are hungry. How could I not act, Sir Walter?"

He could think of many reasons not to act, and yet all he could think to say was, "And so it was not Grant's idea, not really?"

"May I ask why it is that Mr. Grant provokes such apprehension? By your own very high standards, he is not a man to be feared."

"Who said I was afraid of the man? Why should I be?"

"Indeed, you have no reason to fear him." She met his gaze. "He possesses an ill-favored visage, a family without distinction, and a mind too complex to be easily understood. He consorts with people regardless of their rank; he prefers reading to dinner parties; and he has no pride, absolutely none at all. Why should anyone be afraid of such a person, much less Sir Walter Elliot?"

Had she been any other woman, he might have suspected sarcasm, but there was no cruel, mocking smile on her lips. Her mouth remained curved in that familiar, gentle arc.

"You understand me completely," he said.

"Yes, completely."

"I have no cause to fear him."

"None at all."

"I hardly know why you would suggest such a notion!"

She shook her head. "It is only that you raised his name."

"Ah, well, Lady Russell...she seems concerned. She does not wish you to expose yourself to ridicule."

"It would be a pity indeed if I were to connect myself with a foolish, intemperate, unworthy man."

"Indeed!" He spoke with more enthusiasm than he felt, for though she appeared to be agreeing with everything he said, he could not banish the idea that something was still off kilter. "So we are of one mind: you will no longer associate yourself with Mr. Grant and these gypsies."

She looked down at her hand, still intertwined with his.

"It is hardly the best use of your time, my dear." Sir Walter gave her fingers a gentle squeeze. "I fear you have fallen behind on your correspondence with Lady Dalrymple."

"Oh, but I wrote her just yesterday."

"Ah, well! Very good. I suppose our daughters keep you busy."

"Most certainly, and yet, their nursery maid is very competent. You were wise to employ her."

Indeed, he was. She was said to be near fifty, yet had hardly a wrinkle on her face. He found that those who knew how to care for themselves were the very best at caring for others.

"Well then, your household duties—"

"Please," interrupted his wife, her eyes shining, "please, do not forbid me, Sir Walter. There is nothing improper, nothing untoward, in these visits. They give me some purpose, some conversation."

"Whatever can you mean, my dear? Does not Kellynch give you purpose? Do you not converse often enough with Lady Russell? I hardly think she would be glad to hear you prefer the company of gypsies." *Or Mr. Grant,* but he found himself unable to make this accusation. For an accusation, it would be. It was not that he doubted her fidelity; he merely doubted her heart.

She held his gaze for a long moment. "You are, of course, my husband; I will abide by your wishes."

He smiled.

"Of course," she continued, "I will need to inform Lady Dalrymple that her donation to Mr. Grant's cause is no longer required. Excuse me, sir, so that I may amend my previous letter."

He gripped her hand, keeping her from rising. "Lady Dalrymple?"

"Yes, Sir Walter. She once told me of her interest in philanthropy; it seems there are just as many beggars in Ireland as there are in England. Lady Dalrymple has often expressed concern over meeting such people on her husband's lands. When I wrote her of Mr. Grant's reforms here—how his efforts to find honest work for these people had lessened the dangers of encountering them on the roads—she seemed eager to learn more."

"If Lady Dalrymple wishes to donate to this cause, then…" His stomach sank, but what else could he say? *It would never do to contradict the Dalrymples!* When he had gone against the viscount's advice and married Miss Stevenson, there had been—well, not a breach, per se, but a certain coolness of manner toward him. The very fine letters his wife wrote, however, had softened the blow, and he had hope that, should the Dalrymples decide to visit Bath again, he might find a warmer welcome with them.

"Then I, too, will contribute."

"Oh, I am so glad!" She talked then, for several long minutes, about Mr. Grant's work—not just with these gypsies, but with the more permanent poor of the neighborhood, too. Each word was filled with such admiration, such enthusiasm, that he hardly knew how to respond.

Lady Russell soon reentered the drawing room, having sent the girls back to the nursery, and looked between husband and wife with obvious trepidation.

"Have I interrupted?" she asked, glancing at Lady Elliot.

"Not at all," said his wife, smiling. "Sir Walter has just agreed to support Mr. Grant's work with the poor."

Lady Russell's mouth fell open in a most unbecoming way. "Has he indeed?"

"Perhaps now I may persuade you, Lady Russell, to accompany me on my next visit?"

"Oh, but I am afraid…that is, you know I will be in Bath, Elizabeth."

Bath! Dear, dear Lady Russell!

"Do you know," said Sir Walter to his wife, offering her his very best smile, "I, too, have long been considering a visit to Bath."

Her own smile faded. "Bath? Oh, but the expense…"

"Bah, expense! You are always worrying about expenses, my dear. Would you not prefer to spend the next several months with your dearest friend?"

"Oh, do come to Bath!" cried Lady Russell. "It will restore your spirits."

"I did not suppose my spirits were in any need of restoration."

"But you said you lacked purpose," said Sir Walter. "In Bath, you will find proper stimulation."

Their gazes locked.

"Ah." The gentle smile returned. "I see."

Lady Russell, who had resumed glancing between them, did not see—but that suited Sir Walter just fine. She had served her purpose, that dear lady. She had helped *him* see just how to save his wife, once again, from the influence of that man. The hold he had over her—it was not something Sir Walter understood. He knew it was not intimate or improper; there was no scandal in the making. He never once doubted his wife's judgement or conduct—only the strength of her affections.

"And what," said Lady Elliot, "of the children?"

"They will go with us, of course," said Sir Walter.

"No, not our children, Walter."

"The gypsies?" He waved a hand. "Tell Grant he may have a sizable gift from Kellynch to supplement the donation from the Dalrymples."

"The Dalrymples!" Lady Russell raised her eyebrows so that her forehead became a jumble of wrinkled flesh. "I had no idea that Mr. Grant had found such noble patrons!"

"Yes, it seems my wife has great influence with those who matter most."

This inspired a breathy laugh from Lady Elliot who said, "Not so much influence as I might have hoped. I am grateful, Sir Walter, that you have offered to aid Mr. Grant in his work."

He cringed (inwardly only) at the idea that he was aiding Mr. Grant in anything at all, yet said, "Of course, my dear. Tell me only what is required, and I shall see to it—after our visit to Bath."

She stared out the window for a long moment and then named a rather large sum. Before he could protest (at both the amount and the idea of discussing such things in company), she kissed him on the cheek, her lips cool against his skin.

"You always said," he told her, "I was a kind and generous man."

"Indeed." She smiled and patted his hand. "You have not changed a whit."

She had humored, or softened, or concealed his failings, and promoted his real respectability for seventeen years; and though not the very happiest being in the world herself, had found enough in her duties, her friends, and her children, to attach her to life, and make it no matter of indifference to her when she was called upon to quit them. —Persuasion, Chapter I.

KELLYNCH, SEPTEMBER 1800

HER BREATH WAS SO weak, so raspy that he had to put his ear near her mouth to hear her. He closed his eyes to block the sight of those dry, peeling lips; he held his breath so as to keep her noxious breath from his lungs. In that dark, suffocating moment, he knew the truth: the woman who had been his wife had already died.

"Letter," this corpse whispered, her breath hot against his ear. "Must give letter."

He could not speak, could not even nod. He felt her grab at his hand, but he pushed it blindly away.

Some minutes later, when his breathing slowed and his eyes finally opened, she was gone, leaving behind only that gentle, reproving smile.

IT WAS NEARLY a fortnight after the funeral that he found a half-finished letter to Lady Dalrymple. It had fallen on the floor next to her dressing table.

"Sir Walter has been so ill and required such care," she had written, her hand so perfectly even and elegant that Lady Dalrymple could not have supposed the author to have been in the throes of illness herself, "that I have hardly had a moment to send our deepest condolences on the death of your most beloved husband."

So many deaths. First the viscount's, now dear Lady Elliot. Sir Walter himself had almost succumbed, and yet here he stood, her vanity mirror informing him of his restored good health. He took one of her shawls, still hanging on the back of the chair, and draped it across the glass. Why could she not have at least been allowed to finish this letter? He held the paper close to his eyes, his hands trembling so violently that he could hardly make out the words. He ought to finish it on his wife's behalf, to keep up the correspondence with Lady Dalrymple. Such a connection was not to be ignored, not even in mourning. Yet when he slumped into the chair at her dressing table, he found no room to write; the surface was cluttered with all those used up bottles: hand cream, face cream, tooth powder, hair tonic. "Father," said a quiet voice from the doorway. He looked over at Anne, nearly toppling from the chair when he saw her. She could have been her mother: small, delicate, fair of complexion, striking in the color black. Yes, the black shroud he had buried her in had made her appear almost pretty again.

But no. This other version of her had red-rimmed eyes. Lady Elliot's eyes had never been so red, no matter how teary she became. "We will not discuss the matter again," he said to Anne, suddenly tempted to bury his head in his arms and pretend this middle daughter did not exist. All Mary's wailing had been bad enough, but then she was younger—and had such pretty curls. "You will go to school in Bath, and that is that. It is what your mother would have wanted," he added softly.

She made a guttural noise, a half-aborted sob, and then turned away. But she did not leave. With her back to him, she said, "It is not about Bath, Father. There is a Mr. Grant in the drawing room."

He jumped up, knocking the chair backward. "Grant? Send him away!"

"He says it is a matter of great urgency, sir."

Pushing past his daughter, he raced down the corridor. "Urgency! What can be urgent to him now? She is dead!"

He had neither heard from nor seen Grant after sending the funds (about half the sum his wife had suggested; women were not good at sums, he found). Sir Walter had heard from others in the neighborhood of Mr. Grant's efforts, but his wife had never again mentioned them, and so he had considered the entire matter behind them.

To see Grant in his drawing room now—well, it was not in fact so bad as he had feared. The man had lost weight, though he was still fat, and the silver hair on his head softened the ugliness of his features. More than that, he appeared miserable—dark circles beneath his eyes, stubble on his cheeks—and Sir Walter felt some pity for the man. After all, she had chosen Sir Walter, time and again; she had, whatever moments of doubt may have come over her, loved *him*. So, when the vicar stepped forward and said, with a respectful bow, "May I offer you my deepest condolences?" Sir Walter found it easy enough to respond with a gracious nod of his own.

Grant looked behind him then, his lips parting slightly, and Sir Walter turned to see Anne, standing in the doorway of the drawing room. "Anne," said Sir Walter, "you may leave us."

But before she could, the vicar said, "You look so much like your mother, Miss Anne." His daughter smiled, and it was her mother's smile —not the one pasted on her face at death, but the smile she had given him, the vicar, at the assembly in Bath.

"What do you want, Grant?" asked Sir Walter, all sympathy gone. The vicar held out his hands, and it was only then that Sir Walter realized Grant had been holding a folded quilt all this time. "A blanket?"

"The women and children at the workhouse made it, as a gift to honor your…your late wife."

"A blanket?" Sir Walter was on the verge of waving it away when Anne rushed past him, taking the quilt into her arms and hugging it fiercely to her chest.

"How," she asked, nose red and eyes streaming, "did they know of my mother?"

"She was their benefactor," said Grant.

"*I* was their benefactor," Sir Walter said, feeling only a little shame when Anne turned to stare at him. "She had nothing to do with your work, Grant, not for many years now."

"That is true," said Grant, "but I do not think she ever forgot them. They most certainly never forgot her."

Anne gazed up at the vicar. "Do you suppose I might help in this work, Mr. Grant? If it meant so much to my mother, I—"

"No, you will be in Bath." Sir Walter turned to the vicar. "Is there anything else, Grant?"

The vicar looked between father and daughter, and then smiled sadly. "You will always be welcome at Monkford, my dear." And before Sir Walter could express his outrage, the ugly vicar was gone.

Three girls…an awful legacy for a mother to bequeath; an awful charge, rather, to confide to the authority and guidance of a conceited, silly father. — Persuasion, Chapter I.

KELLYNCH, MAY 1805

IT WAS ELIZABETH—HIS Elizabeth—who brought him the letter. "I found this in the drawer of my dressing table," she said, handing him the paper before snapping her fingers at the nearest servant. "A cup of tea, for goodness's sake! One would think, when I sit down to the table, tea might be waiting for me."

Normally he would have agreed—Elizabeth possessed a very precise understanding of order and hierarchy—but his attention was on the words beneath his fingers. "Did you read this?" he asked, his heart pounding at the sight of that name next to his ring finger.

"Hmm? No, of course not," she replied, stirring sugar into her teacup. "You know how I avoid reading small print, as it causes me to squint. I supposed it rubbish, and was about to throw it out, when Anne said you should have it."

He stared down at the thin sheet of paper. Two letters on the same page, one side half-written ("Dear Lady Dalrymple"), the other, fully completed. Once, twice, three times—he turned the piece of paper in his hands. He could hardly make sense of it. He had given such close examination to that unfinished letter! He had held it in his hands, studied it with his own eyes. How then had he failed to see this other side?

"I wondered," said Anne, from across the table, "if it might be in Mother's hand?"

"Anne would have read the entire thing herself if I had not snatched it back from her." Elizabeth sipped at her tea, then let the cup fall with a clatter into its saucer. "This tea is cold! Get me another cup!"

"My tea is cold, too," said Mary, who sat on the other side of Sir Walter, "but you do not see me complaining about it! No, I suffer in silence."

"Yes, silence," said Sir Walter absently, his fingers tracing her pretty, precise handwriting. His name was indeed on the half-finished letter to Lady Dalrymple, the letter he had seen and forgotten five years earlier. But it was this other letter, the words on the other side of the page, that he stared at now. This handwriting, while still hers, was more haphazard, harder to decipher. It seemed as if she had, in her delirium (for delirious she must have been), grabbed the closest sheet of paper, turned it over, and scratched out the following letter:

Dearest Anne,

I will be gone soon. I feel it in every aching breath, every difficult moment. The physical pain is nothing to the deep sadness that comes with knowing that I leave you alone in the world. Yes, you will have your father and sisters; you will have dear Lady Russell to guide you, as well. And I shall miss them all.

But you, Anne—you are different. You are <u>my</u> daughter, not just in looks but in spirit. And because I have neither the time nor the breath to tell you in person, let me leave you with this advice: keep to your convictions, my dearest daughter. When it matters most, do not be persuaded—not by reason or tradition, and most especially not by appearances.

And please, when you are old enough to understand, will you find Mr. Grant, the vicar at Monkford, and tell him what I learned?

God bless you, my daughter! I send all my love, with all the hope in the world that you may find happiness in my stead.

Your loving mother,

E. Elliot

"Are you unwell, Father?" said Anne.

"What?" He glanced up, saw that complexion, those eyes, even the dull brown hair, and quickly looked away.

"Your face has gone all red," said Mary, patting her own pale cheeks. "I hope you are not coming down with a cold; I believe I am."

"You are always coming down with something," said Elizabeth, and Sir Walter found some relief by looking at his fairest daughter.

"Is it something in the letter, Father?" asked Anne.

Panic replaced relief. He still could not look at her. "Did you read this?"

"No, Father, it is as Elizabeth said. I thought you ought to read it first. But if it is in Mother's hand, might I possibly be allowed—"

"No, absolutely not." Sir Walter stood abruptly and went to the hearth. He felt inexplicably chilled, though it was May and the fire roared. Perhaps Mary was correct; he was getting ill. That must be why the words swam before his eyes, why he had misread them. He must have misread them.

"Father," said Anne from behind him.

"Oh, what can be of such interest in an old letter?" asked Mary. "I received a letter from Miss Barton, who lives near Taunton, just yesterday, and she shared news that I suppose none of you knows."

Elizabeth blew air through her lips. "I doubt that very much, Mary. All this talk of letters, when what one really wants is a warm cup of tea!"

"Well, Father, do you not wish to know what Miss Barton had to say?" asked Mary. "I hardly suppose you care, Anne, for she says nothing at all about books or other such dull things. No, her news has to do with the new curate at Monkford."

Sir Walter spun to face the table. "Monkford? Did you say Monkford?"

"Father," said Anne, standing now and coming toward him, hand outstretched. "If I could only see Mother's hand…"

"Yes, Monkford," said Mary, flipping the curls from her shoulders. "I knew that might be of some interest to you."

"Why should Monkford," said Elizabeth, "be of any interest to anyone? Ah, tea! About time!"

"His name is Wentworth," said Mary, "and Miss Barton says he is tolerably handsome."

"Wentworth!" said Elizabeth. "A curate named Wentworth? Has he any connection to Governor Strafford's family? If not, I have no interest in him at all."

"Well, he is certainly a good deal better looking than their ugly vicar, or so says Miss Barton," continued Mary. "Did you ever see him, Father? The vicar, I mean? I cannot recall his name—"

"Grant," whispered Sir Walter. His lips felt dry; his mouth tasted terrible.

"Yes, that is it! I remember seeing him once, from afar, and nearly falling off my horse at the sight of him."

"Oh, yes," said Elizabeth, laughing. "I recall the man now. As fat as a whale, was he not?"

"Mr. Grant," said Anne, "is a kind man. He has done much for the people in his parish."

"Yes, well, now he may do much good in India, where he has gone off to start a mission," said Mary. "Miss Barton writes that he is likely to scare the natives more than they scare him!"

The oldest and youngest laughed, and Sir Walter wondered where his own voice had gone.

"Father," said Anne. She reached for the letter, her fingers (as soft as her mother's ever were) brushing the base of his wrist before gripping the bottom corner of the page. "May I see the letter now?"

He yanked his arm back so quickly, and with such force, that the paper sliced a thin line into her finger. For a moment, they both watched the blood pool on the tip of her finger. Then, before she could speak, he tore the letter into pieces and threw the scraps into the fire. "Rubbish, just as Elizabeth suspected," he said, forcing himself to look at Anne. But the fire began to smoke then, bringing tears to his eyes, and he could not see her through the blur.

CHRISTINA MORLAND spent the first two decades of her life with no knowledge whatsoever of *Pride and Prejudice*—or any Jane Austen novel, for that matter. She somehow overcame this childhood adversity to become a devoted fan of Austen's works. When not writing, Morland tries to keep up with her incredibly active seven-year-old and maddeningly brilliant husband. She lives in a place not unlike Hogwarts (minus Harry, Dumbledore, magic, and Scotland), and likes to think of herself as an excellent walker. Morland is the author of two Jane Austen fanfiction novels: *A Remedy Against Sin* and *This Disconcerting Happiness*.

WILLIAM ELLIOT

The heir presumptive of Sir Walter of Kellynch, William Elliot was a master of altering his manners to suit his circumstance. As a rich widower, and as his social standing became more vital to him, he appeared to make strides to repair the breach within his family connections. *Mr. Elliot was rational, discreet, polished—but he was not open. There was never any burst of feeling, any warmth of indignation or delight, at the evil or good of others. This, to Anne, was a decided imperfection.*
—*Persuasion*, **Chapter XVII.** And yet, it was not until the last pages that her first impressions were justified and he was revealed to be an indifferent, scheming player.

She felt that she could so much more depend upon the sincerity of those who sometimes looked or said a careless or a hasty thing, than of those whose presence of mind never varied, whose tongue never slipped. Mr. Elliot was too generally agreeable. —Persuasion, Chapter XVII.

THE LOST CHAPTER IN THE LIFE OF WILLIAM ELLIOT
Jenetta James

I was a young man of six and twenty and my wife had been dead for three months, when the path of my life was changed. The black band about my arm served as a reminder of my misfortune, but so few of my acquaintances appeared even to notice it. That evening was no different. The theatre at Drury Lane was overflowing for *The Taming of the Shrew*. All around were silken gowns on velvet seats, slippers shuffling across thick, carpeted floors, the collective hum of the *ton* at leisure. As was my practice, I occupied the box which, since my widowerhood, belonged to me. It was in the dress circle at the far right of the stage and, for this reason, afforded an imperfect view. If I close my eyes now, I can still see it. Approximately half the action in any given performance was obscured. Had my father-in-law been in a position to buy a better one, he would have done so. Alas, he was not, having mere money where he lacked connection; and he settled for the best he could obtain. He could not be criticised for that, of course—for who in the world does not? For myself, I did not mind the position. It was the chief object of attending the theatre to be seen rather than to see the stage, and in any event, I found it oddly enjoyable to have a front row seat for some scenes and practically no view at all of others. Was it not thus in life generally? It was in such philosophies that I sat there, accompanied by my friends, Carnaby and Carruthers, young bloods both. The moan of tuning up in the darkened orchestra pit ceased and a perfect arc of sound announced the raising of the curtain. The stage flooded with busy bodies, with feet thumping here and there, and the exaggerated cries of the opening. I have subsequently come to believe that my eyes quickly fixed on her, that among the sea of performers, I found and focussed on Sarah Light, lifting her arms and declaiming.

In those days, she was referred to as a "rising star," a young, promising actress who had been noticed, who haunted the coat-tails of the well-established. She had, of course, the fine face and tapering figure of the successful stage performer. That much was well documented. Those were features that she shared with just about every other young woman in her position. But upon that evening, leaning over the shelf of the box, into the darkness, I saw something else. I observed first her hands, small and fine, unadorned. Next, her face repaid close inspection. Her colouring was far from regular in England. Her hair, which was long, was notably dark, darker than any native girl I had ever met. And her eyes, when she looked up were a deep, liquid pool of wonder. Other parts of her were more ordinarily pretty: her dimpled cheeks, her slightly up turned nose. I found myself studying the very form of the woman before me. She moved to the front of the stage and spoke clearly, her voice singing above heads with ease.

A sharp jab came to my right side as Carnaby leaned in to address me. "I say, man, do sit back. A fellow cannot see."

Unaccustomed as I was to be ordered about by my own guests, I did as he suggested, realising that my admiration of the young woman might be a source of amusement to others. There was after all, never a moment at the London theatre where one was not being watched, measured, ascertained.

"Do not blame you for a moment, mind you. She is bloody fine, is she not?" In the half light, I saw his eye brows flick upwards as he asked and an unfamiliar sickness surged inside me. Unwilling to give the question the dignity of an answer, I remained silent. To the sound of strings and fine trained human voices, I sank back in my seat, luxuriating in the sight of her and the feeling of exhilaration that came with watching action on a stage. One could not expect any sort of appreciation from men such as Carnaby and Carruthers. They were young and rich, and they lived for gaming and drinking. They were good fellows, in their way, but one could not expect to have a conversation about Shakespeare with them.

The drama drew on, the action rolling through various acts to its natural conclusion. I was never a gentleman who attended the theatre out of a sense of social obligation, I truly enjoyed it. The excessive colour, the sense of display enticed the respectable country boy in me. This fascination was long standing and reinforced what I had known for some time: that the ordinary, unremarkable life of the English country gentleman was not the life for me. Before the play was done, she turned again and her eyes met mine, just as though she had known I was there. I felt a flush of heat and sat forward. She had chosen me.

THE AUDIENCE FLOODED down the curved staircases, into the foyer below and the cool air of the spring night mingled with the chatter of a hundred voices. Raucous bellows of laughter met shrieks of mock surprise. Faces I knew blinked at me through the passing candlelit crowd. They seemed to appear all at once: fellows from my club, old Lady Etherington with whom my mother once claimed an acquaintance, nameless young women who knew my wife. I made no efforts to speak with any of them and found that after the play, I yearned for the sharp air of the street. It was as we emerged into the darkness that Carnaby made his suggestion.

"I say, I hear that there is a gathering at Brackbury's tonight. All of London is going. Interested Elliot? I know Carruthers will be game."

"Why is that? Shall there be guaranteed opportunities for losing one's money?"

"Well of course, man. Why go there if not?"

Having said it, he exploded with laughter at his own wit. I have known Carnaby for ten years, and one can set one's watch by his ability to amuse himself.

"I am sorry, Carnaby. I am in no mood for cards. And in any case, I have not been invited by the host."

"Good god, man! It isn't that sort of party. Sometimes I think you are verily of the last century. Nobody in Town cares about such conventions, apart from dusty, old dowagers."

There was something in what he said, of course. Time had moved on and fashions and sensibilities had changed, particularly among the young and rich, the fast as we—*they*—were sometimes called. The trick—for a trick it was—was knowing who one was dealing with. Only then could one appear at best advantage. As a matter of fact, I was good at cards, being in possession of an accurate memory and an inscrutable face. I played to win and frequently did. This I did from habit rather than necessity, for since my marriage, I had been in no want of funds. Carnaby continued to prattle at my side, talking of gaming dens and fashionable dances. A gentle breeze met the back of my head, and I began to think, why not? I had nowhere else to go, save back to the ostentatious house of my late wife. I should say "my house" but somehow could not quite form the words in my mind.

"Go on, man! Be a sport about it."

"You are a hound of a man, Carruthers. Yes. Why not? Let us go."

So it was, that some twenty minutes later, we alighted from my carriage at the home of Lord Brackbury. Even on the street outside, the hum of revelry was plain and unabashed. Fine coaches jostled for spaces and a watchful servant stood at the door admitting people as though they were attending a public sport. The first sight I saw was a young woman in a red dress kissing a well-known rake on the lips, and money changing hands over Loo, and many other games besides. It was the sort of scene the elderly look upon and lament. But we were young men, not in the business of lamentation and before long we were observers no longer—participants, absorbed into the thronging pit.

The night passed well enough. Carruthers was last seen with a young woman's arm laced through his, and Carnaby was happily ensconced at the Hazard table. For myself, I drank and briefly spoke with passing dandies and the sister of a friend, who had lately married into that set. I made it a study to slot into any situation when it presented itself to me. My manners, I knew, were polished and agreeable, and although I had grown up in the country, this manner of gathering had nothing to intimidate me. I noticed that there were a number of theatre types about, an actress, whose name had slipped my mind, and a young lawyer with noble connections, who was known to socialise with men of the theatre in preference to his own sort. A kind of louchness, an eccentricity of design, hung about them like a cloud that would not clear. An involuntary yawn emerged from my mouth and the merits of departing appeared to me to be great.

When I saw Sarah Light sipping from a cup of punch beside an elaborately dressed older lady, I fancied myself imagining it. She made for a strangely still figure in the madness all around her and when her companion whispered in her ear, she smiled slowly, almost as though she were somewhere else. Her dress was simple, but her form no less compelling than it had been on the stage, and I grew suddenly hot. Of course, it was a warm room and far too full of persons moving about. For a moment, I contemplated her.

I was familiar with the trappings of being on the stage, particularly for a woman. In common with all people, high, or low, I knew that an actress could generally be purchased like a side of meat. Between the boards of the theatre stage and the thin walls of the brothel house, there was a fine line fixed. Every man knew that. Thus, it was that so many of her fellow actresses dressed as if to snare a man in the most obvious way. But there was Sarah Light, and it was not so. She wore an attractive, ordinary gown rather than the more lurid affairs displayed beside her. I had the sense, as I had had at the theatre, of light and life shining on her and through her. She appeared to me a woman beyond the obvious, a person possessing more than met the eye.

Observing her elderly friend move off and Miss Light finish her cup, I acted on impulse. Making my way towards the serving girl in the corner, I obtained two further cups of punch and, blind to all in my path, sliced through the crowd to where she stood.

"Miss Light," I bowed, respectfully before looking up. "I observed you to be without a drink, Miss, and it struck me that would never do. I saw your performance this evening, and it seems to me the least you deserve from the public is refreshment."

To this, she smiled and gave a shrug that seemed to say, "Welcome."

"Thank you, sir. That is extremely solicitous of you. And alert as well, for I observed at least six gentlemen asleep in this evening's audience."

I could not but laugh at this. It struck me that for all I enjoyed my view of others from the box, the stage must afford the best view.

"Now that I can hardly credit. But I suppose it must be true, for you are the best judge, there on the stage."

"I do develop a great memory for faces, sir, row after row of them in the half light. I must say that sometimes, they look very amusing indeed. Although, I am sure that you do not ever look anything other than distinguished and gentlemanly." She paused and admired my clothing, as well she might, for it was very fine. I was accustomed to young dandies asking me how I tied my cravat or ladies remarking upon the silk of my waistcoat and the like. And yet, the way Sarah Light regarded me made me wish that she thought of the man beneath as well as his attire. For a moment, I was lost in that thought.

"But I do not have a name to put to that face."

She turned to me and her eyes were like chocolate. Confusion mounted within me and I felt odd, disconnected.

"A name?"

"Your name, sir. What is it? Or would you rather not tell me?"

"Of course. I am sorry, madam. I am Mr. William Elliot, Miss Light."

"Mr. Elliot. What a simple, graceful name that is. English to the core, I think?"

"Yes. It is. My family are the Elliots of Kellynch, in Somersetshire. There have been Elliots at Kellynch for generations. It is said that Elizabeth I visited the house on one of her progresses, or some such. You know the sort of story, Miss Light; old English families are full of them—and they can never quite recall the details. The baronetcy held by my cousin, Sir Walter, dates back to the fifteen hundreds. We are, as they say, as old as the hills."

"But not you personally. You appear young. Or if you are not young, then you hide your age well."

"I will accept that as a compliment, Miss Light, for I am sure that I am older than you. It would be unpardonable for me to ask your age, so I shall tell you mine. I am six and twenty, am I besting your estimate?"

"Spot on, sir. My powers of observation have not deserted me, clearly."

She must, in my estimation be remarkably observant. For if she were not, she could not act so well. I have acted in various roles all my life and know as well as anyone, that before imitation, comes study. I was pondering this aspect of unexpected commonality between us when we were set upon by a gaggle of women, who appeared to know Miss Light. I took them for members of the theatrical community, as indeed they turned out to be. It would be ungallant to say that they were drunk, so let it be enough that they were merry. Their bodies rocked with laughter as they imparted gossip to their friend, meaningless to me, whilst drips of rich punch trailed down their fingers as they laughed. They appeared most anxious to speak of our host—Lord Brackbury—whom I had not seen at all. I found myself caught between horror and interest, but most of all, I noted how deftly Miss Light dealt with their presence. She smiled and laughed affectionately, she touched her fine hand to another woman's arm as she spoke. I may have flushed when she introduced me as her "friend, Mr. Elliot." After a period of time, probably shorter than it felt, they departed to prey on assorted men. Miss Light turned to me and spoke softly, confidingly.

"I do apologise for my friends, Mr. Elliot. They work most industriously and when they are not at work, they can be rather exuberant."

"They seem like very good company. Are those ladies also actresses in your play?"

"Yes, they are. I shall not let on to them that you did not immediately recognise them." She looked up at me through laughing eyes. "Those who sit in the audience do not generally realise, and indeed, why should they? But it is a gruelling life, Mr. Elliot. The hours and hours of practice, the days lost in rehearsal. The nights lost as well. All to the purpose of producing a perfect piece, to keep the paying public happy, and the theatre owner in clover."

"And to tell the story, to connect with one hundred men and women who know you not. To appear exactly as you should be at a given moment in time—to convince. You make it sound inconsequential, but I do not think it is."

"Thank you. I did not intend that, but I am impressed that you think so deeply about it, Mr. Elliot. To most young men, the theatre is not so much an art form as a means of entertainment, sometimes quite base entertainment. What a singular gentleman you are."

I was almost lost in conversation with her. It began with an unwarranted wish to speak with her, to be an audience of one. After a short time, it was as though we really knew one another. I could hardly account for it. We spoke of the different towns that she had visited with her theatrical company, and the poor food and amusing local manners of various places. We laughed, and I tried to recall the last time I had really done so. It transpired that she had been in a production of *Macbeth* at Bristol some years previously, and I laughed to imagine my cousin Sir Walter sitting discomforted in the audience, his moustache quivering. It was simply a momentary diversion for me, rather than a likely truth, of course. My esteemed cousin would never have travelled such a distance to observe others when he could remain at home and consider himself. We progressed from there to discussing my family connections and their place in the world. I had never intended to talk about myself, but somehow, I was pulled along by her. When I spoke about my lineage, she appeared to be impressed, so I continued.

"I am not surprised, Mr. Elliot. You have a refined look about you. Are you a native of Somerset, then?"

"No. I myself grew up in Hertfordshire, with time in London, of course. My parents sadly have passed, and I have since spent very little time in the country. I find I am a town mouse, Miss Light. I like the bustle, the crowds, the theatre, of course."

She smiled at this and it quite warmed me.

"There shall come a time in life, when my cousin dies, and I shall have to take up residence at Kellynch. But before that day is at hand, I intend to delight in the variety of the capital."

"Indeed sir? Why shall that be?"

"Because when my esteemed cousin, Sir Walter Elliot, breathes his last, I am set to inherit the baronetcy. He has no sons."

"How sad for him. But I imagine that will suit you, Mr. Elliot."

"I am ill equipped to judge. I would like to think that I may do the title justice."

I was silent for a moment, pondering the ill feeling between my cousin and myself. I was not in the habit of falling out with people who may be useful to me, regardless of their characters. It was on that basis that I regretted being cut off by Sir Walter. I recalled his outraged face, his unsteady hand dismissing me, his disappointed daughter beside him, and would like to replace that history with another. He had asked of me that which I could not give, but that did not mean we must remain at daggers drawn. There was no sense in it. A sense of brooding rising up in me, I hastened to move the conversation on.

"Miss Light, there is one matter that confuses me. A moment ago, you suggested that I may not wish to tell you my name. As it is, I have given you my name and half of my family history. But I must say, that it struck me as a singular utterance. Why would any respectable person not give their name to a new acquaintance?"

"If their purpose were not respectable, sir. Or perhaps, if they suspected the new acquaintance they addressed were at a disadvantage to themselves when it came to respectability."

"Surely not? Could any person be so rude?"

I was perfectly aware of how men treated actresses, of course, and the manner in which they might be regarded. But her voice was so steady and clear, her face so deserving of respect, I found it hard to credit that Sarah Light suffered thus. For a moment, I began to burn with fury and indignation that any person would approach her thus. My fists clenched at my sides, and I felt the urge to knock a man down. Could they not see at a glance that she was so much worthier than she might be? Before long, her gaggle of female friends appeared with more punch and the news that Brackbury had at last appeared. Thus, the graceful figure of Sarah Light was borne away from me into the heady cacophony of the *ton* at play.

THE PATH between the main doors on Drury Lane and the stage door had become well familiar to me. In the se'nnight, I had seen *Shrew* three times, and yet my interest in it was not sated. It had become like a poem one knows by heart or a passage from the bible to be savoured. Words like instinct on the tongue, feet forming patterns on the stage, the same routines repeated. For that evening's performance, I was alone in my box, and I did not care who saw me or what they may speculate. As had become customary, and as was warming to my heart, as she spoke her final line, Miss Light looked up at me and me alone. The look was fleeting, but it was there. I had developed a practice of bringing a small bunch of flowers with me to the stage door by way of greeting, and she had received these gifts with a happy countenance. I recalled showering my late wife with gifts that I could ill afford, before and during our engagement. Trinkets, silk shawls, leather bound books she had heard tell of. It was not that I did not give with every good intention—for I did. My late wife was a pleasant young woman who deserved good treatment and received it well. But I would never have *shown* myself to her in this way. I would never have appeared in the dark with a bunch of valueless flowers or a piece of cake because I knew she would be hungry. A dark idea sounded in my mind, like an alarm in the distance. Was I showing too much of myself? I did not believe I was. My instincts for the motivations of others had always been excellent. And though Sarah Light was a woman and an actress, born far below me, I was certain she was an honourable being.

She appeared when I had been waiting only for minutes and a smile lit on her face at the sight of me. The gaslight of the street flickered on us both and on the morass of persons who flooded out beside her. Judging from their demeanour, I judged them preparing to enjoy the freedoms of the night. Miss Light looked beautiful but tired.

"Mr. Elliot! What a treat."

"Miss Light." I bowed to her and kissed the warm skin of her hand. She should have gloves.

"The treat is mine." I held out the flowers which she exclaimed over and accepted.

I had taken to offering her my carriage after her performance, in order that she may travel in comfort to whatever social occasion she was due to attend. The life of an actress, I discovered, did not cease when the curtain fell but poor Miss Light was frequently obliged to attend all manner of events afterwards. On this evening, she took my arm in the darkness as I moved to offer her a seat in the carriage.

"Mr. Elliot, do you think that we may walk and take the air for a moment? The theatre has been stifling hot and I believe I should like to walk with you in the cool. If you can spare the time, that is?"

She looked at me enquiringly, even pleadingly. She had not yet realised I would do anything she asked, and that must be a blessing.

"Of course." I began to stride with her by my side. I could feel her skirts against my legs in the dark street and inside, I soared. We walked for some time in companionable silence as the din of the city at night roared about us. My carriage moved beside our shadows on the road like a loyal dog. There were some women as would not do this. I thought immediately of my late mother, of my quivering cousins at Kellynch. But Miss Light was not like them; she feared nothing.

"I apologise for this odd break from tradition, sir. But this evening I am not of a mind for company and, since I have no party to attend or dinner to reach before the dawn, I cannot ask you to escort me there. And thinking, Mr. Elliot, that I did not wish to lose my time with you, I formed the idea of us walking together for a time."

"Of course. I am more than content. It is not my choice to spend every evening at parties, Miss Light."

"Really?" She wore a surprised expression and playfully brushed the front of my waistcoat. "Is that not exactly what fashionable young men such as yourself live for?"

"Not this one, I assure you. I have seen enough gaming hells and debauches to know that I need not seek them out on a regular basis. There was a time when I said nay to nothing, no wine was too rich, no loss too much. But not now. My friends, I cannot speak for."

She laughed gently and I could see her breath in the chilly night air.

"Yes. Mr. Carruthers and Mr. Carnaby are amusing gentlemen. But what they possess in *joie de vivre*, they lack in maturity, if I do not say too much?"

"No, of course not. You are perfectly right."

It occurred to me that Carnaby for one may not even understand her, still less be offended. We walked on, in perfect step for some streets, passing all manner of ne'er do wells and questionable characters. I felt somehow, that although I am in the heart of Town, I had walked many leagues from my home. I had turned a corner and seen a new world but not yet stepped into it. A force greater than me was pulling me harder, harder into the unknown and I do not know as I could resist, or even wished to. I had tasted but not swallowed. I felt her dear arm tighten on mine and an almost inaudible sigh escaped her mouth.

"Miss Light, are you chilled? We can take the carriage. I cannot have you catching a chill on my account. Let me escort you back to your lodgings if you have no engagements this evening or back to the theatre if you have made other arrangements."

Her fingers, that had been lightly laid upon my arm like a limp bunch of flowers began to caress my sleeve as she looked up.

"Thank you. It has grown rather chill, and I would be in such trouble if I became ill. Maybe a trip in your carriage would be agreeable. But please, may I go back to my lodgings, not the theatre. Everyone will be gone by now, and I have my belongings."

She patted her reticule as though it were a much loved pet and smiled sweetly.

"Certainly, let us go."

I commanded the carriage to stop which it did, but as I reached for the door, her voice came forth behind me.

"There is one request I have though, before we set off. I appreciate your manners, sir. Indeed, I believe you must be the most gentlemanly man of my acquaintance. I know so many men, Mr. Elliot, but you are different. I believe that we are friends."

"Of course, we are friends."

"I wonder therefore, whether we might allow ourselves the liberty of Christian names? Whether we may be Sarah and William, rather than Miss Light and Mr. Elliot?"

I had not known what she would ask until she spoke the words but an unexpected joy washed over me and I almost sang my response: "Yes, Sarah."

Having given the coachman her address, I handed her into the carriage; its interior even darker than the city outside. Rather than her usual practice of sitting in the middle of the bench, she sat to one side and seeing the invitation, I sat beside her, closer than our bodies had ever been. Rapidly thereafter, the door was closed, the curtain drawn and we rattled through the night, our arms threaded, a sense of complicity rising up inside me faster than I could smell its sweetness. As we neared, she began to look bashful and apologised that her dwelling was not a smart one nor really fit for company. She shared with another girl, also an actress, although she believed her to be out for the evening. My first reaction to this was some degree of anger. Sarah was the finest actress in the company and surely the cause of a significant crowd. She was as hard a worker as any man and more than most. The idea that she was kept in undeserved penury was an offensive one. I assured her that I cared not for the neighbourhood or the structure, as long as I could see her safe at home.

"Thank you, William," she said as though she were trying on my new name like a gown.

We continued in silence, legs touching through layers of fabric and the movement of the carriage bounced us together. I felt a flush to my face and a thrill shot through me each time she moved her hand on my arm. The impropriety of my situation was perfectly plain to me, but nothing would urge me to change it. I felt rather than saw her move. In one movement, and as though it were nothing at all, she removed her bonnet and leaned over to kiss my lips. I have known many women, in respectable moments and otherwise. I have tasted lips and bodies. But I have never felt tenderness of this sort, never been moved to still my person while another takes over. But that is how it was. Her kiss became our kiss and it deepened as she moved her body against mine in the pitch dark of the carriage. At some half-remembered moment, we alighted in some quiet corner, unknown to me. We said nothing, but Sarah laughed as I carried her lithe form up the stairs and we seemed to move through doors and along corridors like phantoms, arriving in her rooms breathless, ruffled, unable to stop even for a moment. The door to her chamber clicked closed behind my back, and my mouth was on hers. Fabrics fell away from bodies, hair pins gave way to flowing tresses, and our breath mingled in the dark. Her bare flesh emerged in the moonlight and dazzled me, so perfect was it. I felt a heat within me and a racing in my belly as I advanced upon her. We fell together onto the soft bed, my hands in her hair and her breast in my mouth like a fruit. She wrapped her legs about me and some colossal force ripped through my being.

Later, alone beside her sleeping form, I felt a sense of contentment wash over me and remain. I had no idea where I was. The window, which was partially covered, gave onto the street and the slightest shimmer of gaslight threw shadows in the room. It appeared to me small and somewhat sparse. There was nothing there that was smart, nothing suggesting wealth. But the bed was comfortable and my body warm and at ease. Sarah moved slightly in my arms and I beheld her like a jewel. After a moment, I closed my eyes and she surprised me by speaking.

"Are you comfortable, William?"

"I could not be more so." I kissed her head and she pressed her face into my chest before stretching out. "Thank you."

"I hope you do not mind the bed. It is less than you are accustomed to, I think?"

"I certainly do not mind the bed. It is the very best place and I would be nowhere else."

The truth was that I cared not a fig for the name of the street or the details of the property. But I did want to know about her. A thirst for knowledge of her swept through me.

"Another girl from the theatre lodges here, too. Meredith." She rolled towards me, laughing softly. "She is an agreeable girl. But she is away tonight. Meredith is frequently absent at night. We are comfortable here, but it is not grand, by any means. I would not have led any person of your refinement here if there was not the most fixed friendship between us. But for all that, you are a gentleman. I believe I can trust you."

"Of course." I kissed the top of her head and a wisp of hair stuck to my lips. I had slept in some grand beds, some of them my own, but I did not yearn for them now. Provided that this young woman, Meredith, did not plan on intruding into Sarah's chamber, I cared not where she was or how she conducted herself. I had a sense of growing intimacy to the woman beside me, of enveloping, and being enveloped. It was bliss.

"I trust that I am not so pampered, that I cannot go to new places and be content. If a man cannot walk with those who live differently and put them at their ease, then he is no gentleman at all. I have always been convinced of that. In fact, I have enjoyed all my life, the practice of reading people."

"Reading people? Like books?"

"Yes, just so. I try to observe others closely, to see how they think and what motivates them. Everyone has desires, Sarah. One must be alive to them. When you know what a person desires, you know them, and how to approach them."

I stroked the silky skin of her arm, thinking on it. Without ever saying it out loud, I had lived my life in this way.

"For some people, material considerations are paramount. They simply cannot contemplate a life without riches or a world of low connections."

I think of many when I said those words, but in particular Sir Walter and his simpering daughter. I can almost see their faces.

"And you?" Sarah asked, bringing me back to the present.

"I am wealthy now, but it was not always so. My family are well connected, but my late parents lived modest lives compared to their relations. We did not want for comfort, but on occasion we did want for luxury. Maybe, as a young man, that made me envious. It made me aspire to a different manner of living."

"You are a young man now."

"Even younger then. I suspect you have heard that I married for money. I know what people believed and what they said. That I was a fortune hunter who pursued a young heiress for the coin in her pocket. The truth is always more complicated than it appears to be, is it not?"

"It certainly is."

"My wife's money was an element, but it was not the whole. No doubt I was attracted to her way of life, to the idea of provision above that I had always known. But I enjoyed my wife's company. When we established our connection, I was more than content to spend my days with her, rather than my own family in whose keeping I had been. In fact, the whole thing caused something of a—division—between my cousin, the baronet, and me."

"Hmm?" She stroked my chest and looked to me enquiringly.

"It was around the time I met my wife. We were in Town for the Season and I had been seeing rather a lot of Sir Walter. He is a proud sort of man, very conscious of his own position. It is possible that I had tired somewhat of pandering to him. In any event, he has a number of daughters, but one in particular was in his keeping in those days, Elizabeth, the eldest. At first, I called it accidental, but I soon realised that my cousin promoted the charms of his daughter to me at every opportunity—and she was not above doing so either. At every dinner, she appeared beside me; if there were cards, she would be my partner. That is how it became: a monotony of companionship."

Not like this, I thought, but did not say. I recalled for a moment, the feeling of being trapped by Elizabeth Elliot's permanent presence beside me in those days. How different it is now, to lie beside a woman of my choosing.

"Our connection soured when my cousin invited me to Kellynch, and I did not go. By that time, I had met my wife and resolved against Elizabeth. I was given to believe that Sir Walter took it rather hard. I believe that he and Elizabeth have despised my very name ever since."

"Did she have expectations, do you think?"

"She may have done. But if she did, it was her father who encouraged her, not I. I never showed my cousin anything more than the niceties of the Season: partnering her to dance, attending them on calls. Merely nothings, whatever may be said. It would have been a convenient match. But we did not suit one another; it was as plain as that. Elizabeth is perfectly presentable, but we are not well matched in anything other than family convenience. As it was, my wife appeared on the scene. We all met her at a ball which she attended with her cousin. Of course, my family took an immediate dislike to her. She was wealthy but of obscure birth. She was not part of their set. As far as they are concerned, there is no greater crime than for people to change places in the world, to rise on a tide of wealth as my wife had. Sir Walter and his family will have explained my marriage by preference to her fortune. But it was not thus. She was a kind, pleasant, comely woman of some humour. And I liked her. We rubbed along contentedly, as a couple must if they are to marry."

The fact that I could not quite say "love" did not escape me. I had no wish to lie to her. My aim was to speak of matters exactly as they were. My view was, and remains, that in order to marry a lady, one need not love her, but it is essential to be compatible. The woman beside me shifted and I turned to face her. For a married man to lie with another woman was so commonplace, it was hardly worth remarking. And yet, as I lie there, I could not bear the idea of Sarah thinking ill of me, so I told her.

"My wife died, Sarah. Some months ago."

"I am sorry, William. That is dreadful. Particularly when you were so young."

Her words brought me up short and an unexpected emotion powered through me. I had written the announcement for the newspaper myself and it was deliberately anodyne and dignified. Very few people knew that my wife had died miscarrying our child, and I had no intention of that state of affairs changing. In this strange world of London society, where everyone knows everything, I was determined to keep that fact concealed. It was a credit to Sarah that she did not ask. Her simple comment, unattended by prying questions, was the greatest comfort.

"Thank you for saying that. Save for the expressions of regret which those who know me are required to give, I do not believe any other person has used those words. All of my friends and still more my family assumed, I believe, that I was not sorry at all."

"Then maybe they have all misunderstood you."

And with that, she shifted and kissed my chest, stretching her arms over me like a blanket and arching her back as she sat astride me. The barely discernible grey light of the dawn seeped through the window and a door closed somewhere in the middle distance. All I saw was her body moving against mine, her dark hair falling between us and the world like a screen.

Weeks had passed. Glorious, glittering weeks. Potter took my plate as I placed the letter face down on the breakfast table and leaned back. I had arrived home in the early hours and her scent was still on my skin. I would never have left her but that I had an appointment with my lawyers that morning and a number of duties to undertake. I could hear her laugh in my ear and it warmed me. The last thing I expected was to receive a letter regarding my Elliot cousins and I turned it over and regarded it again. It was from a mutual friend and made for peculiar reading. My esteemed cousin was leasing Kellynch to a naval man and he and his daughters were high-tailing it to Bath, apparently. My friend said nothing of the reasons, which suggests to me that he does not know. But it must have a financial basis. Did Sir Walter leave Kellynch because he can no longer afford to stay? A vision of his pompous face appeared to me and I suppressed the compulsion to laugh. That was more than he would do for me if our roles were reversed. I could not say that I was pleased to read that a stranger and a shipman would be sitting in my family seat as though it were his own, but it is not yet my affair. I resolved to respond to my friend, thanking him for the intelligence and say no more. I assumed that had Sir Walter managed to marry off Elizabeth or his other daughter, I should have heard about it. It occurred to me that they were the sort of people to whom things happened, rather than people who made their own fortune. The more I thought on the subject, the more I was convinced that since I last saw him, Sir Walter has done nothing but spend money, grown vainer still, and failed to marry off his eldest daughters.

After a short meeting to discuss my affairs with a top-hatted lawyer, I was once again at leisure. My mind returned, involuntarily, to Sarah. I could count the nights that I had spent in her arms, but did not wish to. I imagined them like a carpet rolling out in front of me and never ceasing. A sense of contentment, until then unfamiliar, washed over me. I could not regret it. It was weeks since that first time and I knew her body like a map I had studied for a grand expedition. I had not seen her every night as her duties at the theatre and socially were exacting. She called me her "one true friend" and so I endeavoured to be. It occurred to me that there was no reason she should not share the comforts of my bed, as well as I hers. This was, after all, my house. It was my domain and I could have whom I wished for whatever purpose I determined. The comforts of a better sort of home, a well-appointed chamber, servants; these were no more than she deserved. The idea that I had them within my power to give surged through me and I walked with new purpose.

With that in mind, I made for Jermyn Street and entered a shop known for quality and style. A young woman looked up from behind a desk, and well-dressed ladies, clustered in corners, glanced at me then looked away. I came here once with my wife, in the early days of our engagement, spending money I did not have on things she did not need. It was not a sour memory, but there was no joy in it. I made for the tray of gloves, which I recall were particularly fine. Laid out were a number in beautiful fabrics and delicate leathers. Thinking of her fingers in the winter months, I selected a pair of kid leather gloves and paid for them as they were wrapped by a girl. The wrist was so narrow but I had no doubt they would fit Sarah. I had held her wrists in my hands night after night and these gloves were for her. The price was immaterial.

The weather in the street had changed and light rain fell insidiously as I made my way home. From my carriage, I saw men that I knew and places I frequented for many years. I find they did not interest me, for I could not turn my mind from her. It occurred to me that I could do better for her than the world had done. For was I not a single gentleman in possession of a large fortune? I need not scramble for funds as I once did. Matrimony, experienced once, was not a state I hankered after, nor one I pursued, or not then at any rate. My future at Kellynch was all but assured. For whom should I shift but for myself and the one woman who had changed me? I knew a dozen married men of means who had set their lovers up with homes and incomes; everybody did. I had money to spend as I wished and I had an ardent wish to protect her. Why should it not be that I provide for her in that way? Sarah would have a comfortable residence. She would be spared the indignities of the theatre and the cloying attentions of unknown eyes. She would sit in the audience beside a man who loved her, rather than stand upon the stage to be examined by the masses. The whole solution revealed itself to me like a set piece. I saw her finely dressed, in her own drawing room. I saw her eyes at ease and her goblet full of wine at her own table. I realised with a start that I wished to give her those advantages. I wished to improve her lot. A new sort of zeal inhabited me like an animal.

We had already agreed that I would not attend the theatre that evening. Carruthers had been campaigning for an evening at the club and in truth, it was Sarah who said I should neglect him no longer. "Your friends shall think themselves deserted," she had said. And so, it was that I found myself drinking and gaming in that familiar old place until it was late enough that even Carruthers was willing to retire. I walked home, longing for air and exercise and although I considered asking my driver to take me to Islington, I refrained. It was enough that I should see her on the morrow and Sarah needed her rest more than most. By the candlelight of my chamber, my valet undressed me and I sank into fitful sleep. My dreams, I cannot vouch for.

The next morning, which I commenced tardily, I was plagued by a pain in my head. The breakfast table brought a letter from Mrs. Smith, the widow of a late friend who hounded me with correspondence. Her latest missive lamented at length her position and sought assistance from me. I put it to one side. It was not that I wished to do her harm—but she did not persuade me to assist her. She was a rambling woman, of whom I knew little on the other side of the country, and I cannot say that she interested me. A second letter appeared from my friend regarding my relations, newly of Bath. He thanked me for my swift response and confirmed that he had, in fact, seen Sir Walter and his daughter on the Royal Crescent in the company of an unknown woman. My mind flickered at this, and I read on. He described her as attractive, well dressed, and in her middle years. She and Elizabeth were arm in arm, but Sir Walter was observed to address her attentively, and she smiled in response. I looked up from the letter and pondered it. It may be of consequence and should be borne in mind. I had no intention to losing my baronetcy to the offspring of any new acquaintance. The situation should be monitored and I resolved to write thus to my friend. Of course, it did not do to panic and I would not do so. My cousin's personality ought to count against any person contemplating marriage to the man.

Unexpectedly, the door opened and Potter entered with another note which he presented to me without comment. I lost no time in opening it and was astonished to discover it was from Sarah. Its contents were simple, starkly simple, and alarming: "Please do not come to the theatre door tonight. Thank you, William. Your affectionate friend, Sarah Light." I read and re-read again those words, and still I did not understand them. Whatever could she mean by writing in those terms? Never before had she prohibited me from attending her. The pain in my head throbbed and a knot formed in the pit of my stomach. The day, from thereon, was a bleak one given to ruminating and ponderously repeating the same joyless thoughts. Was Sarah unwell? Was there some trouble at the theatre? Was she in distress? Whatever it was, I could not credit that she should wish to keep me away. I began to pace the house, deaf to all around me. The hours passed in blackness and my meals were taken alone, in silence. Carnaby called, but I had given orders that I was not at home. My mind did not have space for talk of small nothings and gaming jokes. The night moaned on in eerie darkness and the hours slouched by. In my chamber, I turned in my bed, hopeless of sleep. After what felt like a lifetime, a creeping light broke through a gap in the curtains and I could stand it no longer. I had been commanded not to attend the theatre but not to stay away from her. I bolted out of bed and dressed myself hastily. Taking Sarah's gloves in my hand, I fairly stormed down the stairs and surprised the servants by demanding that my carriage be fetched around immediately.

Shortly thereafter, I was moving through the deserted streets at an hour I have never previously been awake to witness. The journey was over quickly and the carriage turned onto the familiar road. The unremarkable doors stood row on row and not a soul stirred as we advanced. I blinked as I leaned out of the window and saw it. One hundred thoughts crowded my mind as my eyes focussed on a fine carriage, stationary, where mine would usually be. The gathering light of the morning made it appear stark but there was no question that it was a fine conveyance, well built, impressive. The polished crest of Lord Brackbury gleamed back at me. It appeared like a smirk on the face of an adversary, an insult of the cruellest kind. Anger moved up inside me like a wave and I was suddenly sweating, hot with fury. From somewhere, the old, controlled William Elliot returned and I sunk back on the bench of the carriage, having asked the driver to travel further up the road. From a safe distance, I waited and watched. With a start, I realised that I was still holding her gloves, gripping them for all I was worth. We lingered there in the street and I was determined not to leave before the Brackbury carriage. After an interlude of sorts, during which the number of people milling around increased, the scene changed. The door to Sarah's home opened and without preamble, the man appeared. He did not look back and no person waited at the door, which closed quickly. Into his carriage he stepped and it pulled away and clicked down the road, quite as if nothing untoward had occurred.

I considered rushing in and announcing myself, hammering on the door like a broken hearted, young swain. But it was not for me. I thought suddenly of her withdrawn mood on the evening I first spoke with her in that man's own home, of her gentle teasing words. Was she a person who, like me, knew just what to say—or not say—to obtain what was most expedient to her? If I were a woman, I would have cried at such a moment, and indeed, my body longed to do so. But I would not. The notion that I have been played for a fool taunted me, and I yearned to escape this tawdry situation with the upmost speed. I wished to be back in an arena that I controlled, where I might direct events. Resolving thus I ordered the carriage to move on. Just as we passed Sarah's door, it opened and she emerged, wearing a new dress and laughing with another woman. A smile died on her face as she saw my carriage and I shrunk back from the window. I did not look back, for that would have been fatal. I would not be seen with her; I would not bargain words with her. That sojourn of mine, into madness, was at its end.

SOME DAYS LATER, I was playing cards with Carruthers.

"I say old man, that was a bit swift?"

"It is a game, Carruthers. You cannot expect me to let you have the advantage when it presents itself to me." I raised my eyebrows at him and he exhaled loudly. The truth was that his helplessness was too much even for me and I had already resolved to let him win the next round. A man like Carruthers should only ever play with those who have affection for him.

"I heard a tale the other day, you might be interested in. Had it from old Weatherby. Saw him dining at the club. Tells me that Brackbury has taken up with an actress and half the *ton* are speaking of it. It is said that he has set her up with a house and all the trappings, gone the whole nine yards. It is odd, because I always had him down as the sort of fellow to have women in every corner of the city. But apparently not."

I said nothing, but focussed on my hand. I felt rather than saw Carruthers scrutinising me.

"I understand that the girl in question is that young slip of a player we saw all those weeks ago—you know—the one with the dark hair. You were rather taken with her yourself, were you not Elliot?"

I glanced up at him, my face as blank as I could school it.

"No idea what you are talking about man. Actresses? One sees so many of them. It is hard to recall one from the other."

He let out an indeterminate sound and looked at me for a moment longer than necessary before returning to his hand and laying a card. I knew perfectly well that he intended to say no more and neither would I. That was a mark of a true friend.

"I say, Elliot, would you object to leaving this damned city for a short visit to the country by any chance? As it happens, an aunt of mine has asked me to visit. She was terribly close to my mother and wrote wishing to see me. I cannot imagine that I shall stay long, but I should prefer not to go alone. If you get hopelessly bored, you can always leave."

"Of course, man. Where does this aunt live?"

"Lyme. Down in Dorset. Frightful rain last time I was there but it is pleasant enough country. A good distance away and my aunt's house is jolly comfortable."

The idea opened up in front of me and had immediate appeal.

"Thank you, Carruthers. I shall be pleased to," I replied without a moment's hesitation.

And so, it was that I departed the London of Sarah Light and opened the next chapter in my life. I left orders that the gloves should be delivered anonymously to her at Drury Lane, because I felt that for all that she had injured me, they were hers. I believed she might guess that they were from me, but it was not my intention to invite her to contact me, and I did not anticipate she would do so. The details of that escapade, the indignity, the loss of love and companionship was, and evermore shall be, known only to me. Potter packed my trunk, and the door of my London home closed behind me as I boarded my carriage and made for the coast, a harder man and less open to love than ever I had been.

JENETTA JAMES is a mother, lawyer, writer, and taker-on of too much. She grew up in Cambridge and read history at Oxford University where she was a scholar and president of the Oxford University History Society. After graduating, she took to the law and now practises full-time as a barrister. Over the years, she has lived in France, Hungary, and Trinidad as well as her native England. Jenetta currently lives in London with her husband and children where she enjoys reading, laughing, and playing with Lego. She is the author of *Suddenly Mrs. Darcy* and *The Elizabeth Papers,* as well as a contributing author to *The Darcy Monologues.*

GENERAL TILNEY

An imposing widower, General Tilney's cold demeanor and manipulative behaviors fostered a formidable barrier for any filial bonds. Proud of his lineage and estate, this austere, retired general interfered in his grown children's friendships and potential matches as a matter of course—thus, unwittingly became the mysterious Gothic villain in Catherine Morland's imagination. *...what had been terror and dislike before was now absolute aversion. Yes aversion! His cruelty to such a charming woman made him odious to her. She had often read of such characters; characters, which Mr. Allen had been used to call unnatural and overdrawn; but here was proof positive of the contrary.* —Northanger Abbey, **Chapter XX.**

"He loved her I am persuaded, as well as it was possible for him to—"
—Henry Tilney to Catherine Morland, *Northanger Abbey,* Chapter XXIV.

AS MUCH AS HE CAN
Sophia Rose

1799, NORTHANGER ABBEY, GLOUCESTERSHIRE, ENGLAND

His boots thudded and floorboards creaked as he walked the passageway of the guest wing in search of his daughter. "Eleanor!"

"I am here!" she called out softly, arresting his forward motion.

General Tilney executed a sharp right face and entered one of the guest rooms where a pair of maids were making up the bed with fresh linen. Eleanor glanced up from a chest where she was placing an extra counterpane. Even in summer, the Abbey could be cool at night. There were sounds of servants working across the corridor in Eleanor's room. She was moving into her childhood room for the duration of the house party as every bed chamber would be in use. All, but one. The mistress' chamber would remain untouched "even if guests must share," he told Eleanor earlier that week.

"Who are you placing in here?" he asked curiously, eying the older furnishings, particularly the antique wardrobe and the bed from the Tudor reign.

"A single gentleman. He does not come with a valet so the lack of dressing chamber will be of no concern." She had a slight frown that he thought must be concentration.

"And where did you put Lord Goodnestone?"

"The Blue Room. I was made to understand that he was to receive the best chamber. It was the first we readied." The slight frown was now grown.

She showed signs of wishing to broach a subject with him, but he had no time to wait her out. "Was there something else?"

She opened her mouth to say something, closed it, and then shook her head.

"Then I am off to my club. Do not neglect to finalize the menu changes with Mrs. Cummins and be sure Matthews has bowls of my fruit available on the sideboard for our guests."

"Of course, Father."

"Have your gowns and falderal from that London modiste arrived?"

"Yes, Father. Jenkins and I went through them and they fit well. I thank you."

"Good. Mrs. Hughes informed me that all the best families give Madame Boullard their custom. She might wish to dispense with that Bristol accent if she chooses to be taken for a *madame* rather than plain Mrs. Bullard."

Eleanor smiled at his observation. Eleanor's French, and Italian, for that matter, were excellent having been educated at Ponder's End near the metropolis. Madame Boullard's command of the language, on the other hand, was execrable.

General Tilney paused to encourage—and then instruct—his most timid child. "You are doing well for your first time taking the reins as the lady of the establishment. It is good practice for when you are mistress of your own estate house. You will remember to make yourself available to stand beside me and welcome our guests. You will also preside over the foot of my table and lead the ladies out. They taught you these things at seminary, I trust?"

"Yes, Father."

Eleanor did not look well-pleased. Like her mother, he had no idea what to make of her. He wanted to laugh in the face of his friend Courtenay when he said that women were simple creatures.

Simple! He had never found them so.

"Carry on then." Having received the intelligence about Lord Goodnestone's chambers, he left her to it.

"What is this?" General Tilney muttered to himself the very next afternoon.

He gazed over his younger son's shoulder at the tête-à-tête beneath the shade of the large old oak. Guests strolled and admired the shrubberies or made use of the drawing rooms, billiard room, or library. The tinkle of laughter and conversation and a temperate afternoon should have pleased him, but the sight of the pair under the oak tree dimmed his pleasure. His lips tightened and he gripped the balustrade as the tall, gangly man in proper, if not the latest mode, leaned in to speak in a friendly manner with his daughter. Then Eleanor smiled and seemed to converse with an easiness that only the younger of her two brothers could coax from her.

This would not do, he told himself, as he settled his curly-brimmed hat more firmly.

Let her be, Anthony. Eleanor is a devoted daughter and she comprehends your wishes. He stilled, hearing the voice in his mind. He took comfort in his wife's voice since her passing seven years before.

Henry turned to see what had agitated his father, and a slow smile, so like his mother's, appeared.

"Eleanor looks well, does she not, sir?" Henry asked with affected sincerity. "Depend upon it, sir, an intrigue must be afoot. See how she attends to her duties as hostess most assiduously. She must be about some mischief."

AFTER A FINAL EXCHANGE of pleasantries with *that* gentleman, Eleanor drifted away to greet a late arriving acquaintance. This fashion of arriving whenever it suited would never be *bon ton* to him, no matter the sophistications of the Upper Ten Thousand.

His posture stiffly erect while inspecting his gloves, Tilney offered his young jackanapes of a son—decidedly his wife's child with that mischievous cleverness and cool countenance—a sour face before schooling his features and turning back to his distinguished guest.

Lord Brice Goodnestone, standing with Henry, had also observed the direction of General Tilney's interest. "Oh aye, a neatish, little filly with good action. On the tall side. Perhaps too thin for my taste"—scrutinizing Eleanor closely through an ornate gold filigree quizzing glass dangling from a black ribbon. "Still… not half bad…" The young lord took a second and a third glance at Eleanor's tall, pleasing figure in her new peach dress and bonnet.

Longtown's nephew, Lord Goodnestone, was a very eligible matrimonial prospect for Eleanor, if somewhat simple in his understanding, and a bit of a dandy. General Tilney noted the multiple watch fobs and seal at Goodnestone's waist, the green and white striped waistcoat, the cut of his blue coat, and boots obviously blacked with fine champagne. The baron's pale skin and dark circles under the eyes might appear to him a sign of dissipation in a soldier of his command, but he had learned that most young bucks in society these days kept late hours and slept little during the Season, which had only past.

"Miss Tilney of Northanger Abbey, recently returned to the country after a successful presentation to the Queen, bears no resemblance to a 'neatish, little filly'." He stated repressively like he would to a Johnny-Raw recruit.

Out of anyone else's lips, the insult to Eleanor and his family honor would have met with the flat of his sword. His nostrils flared as he swallowed his spleen.

"Dash it!" the young man exclaimed then drew back to bow deeply. "My sincerest apologies, General. Miss Tilney is a most genteel lady. Highest regard for the ladies. Meant no offense. Diamond of the first water. Not too thin, at all, now that I have looked again. Decidedly not equine, sir."

The hurried string of words made Henry's eyes bulge like he might choke on his laughter. The buffle-headed fribble dried up, cleared his throat, took out a snuff box clicking it open and shut without removing any snuff, returned it to his pocket, adjusted his hat, then fidgeted with his walking stick and gloves.

The general let him writhe like a fish on a hook before recollecting why he needed to ignore the boorish insult. "You meant no offense, to be sure, and might have meant to compliment Miss Tilney."

"To be sure. To be sure."

Forbearance must be extended to the nephew and heir of his longtime friend the Marquis of Longtown. Goodnestone had already come into an early fortune upon the death of the late Lord Goodnestone and of a maternal aunt who had left him a legacy.

Eleanor should be allowed to respect, if not highly esteem, her future partner, Anthony—to which he replied to his Genevieve: *And did not we learn to respect and esteem our marriage partners in time?*

HIS CONJURING of Genevieve Tilney was a guide to his conscience. They had had more than a few acrimonious parleys over the years, usually in the privacy of their chambers, mostly about the children, but occasionally his pronouncements. They saw the world very differently, but he had learned to respect and esteem Genevieve and her acumen.

Genevieve had taken his measure long before her own was bared before him. His temperament was unbending and resentful, selfish and arrogant, while hers had been a puzzle. She had understood that his rigid control was born of the early example set by his own father, his time in the army, and an incident from their past that inflamed him with bitterness even to this day.

Henry regarded Lord Goodnestone with close scrutiny as if he were a creature to poke with a stick only to see its reaction. His younger son was protective of his family and, in particular, his sister. Before Henry could deliver whatever provocative remark he was preparing, General Tilney ordered, "Retrieve Eleanor, if you would. She would be disappointed not to make Lord Brice's acquaintance."

Henry hesitated, met his eye with the silent promise that he would pursue a further conversation, and then swiftly moved off.

"A deprivation indeed," his eldest said, joining him. After a swallow of wine—likely some of his most expensive and finest wine, pilfered from his private reserve, Frederick continued, "Would Lady Mary Cavendish be present? A merry girl with a fulsome, ahem, dowry and a drowsy chaperone."

Frederick, dashingly kitted out in the uniform of a cavalry captain, looked over the female guests with hooded eyes, determining his next conquest. His son had more swagger than he ever had at his age.

"Captain Tilney, have you by chance visited Mrs. Temple's establishment? Faro is the game there, but I was caught up after the excellent dinner she served in Hazard. M'luck was out that night—at least at the gaming table."

"Yes, I have had the pleasure, my lord. Mrs. Temple does run a fine game. Played piquet half the night with Wolversley."

"I hear tell a certain duchess who loves her Silver Loo is a frequent guest…"

Frederick's gaming habits nor his intrigues with females were such that interested him. Unlike some men, General Tilney was fortunate in his offspring. None made the family the subject of idle tittle-tattle or threatened to bring ruin on them through excess or debauchery. He would not stand for it and they all were wary of putting him in a distemper.

HE OBSERVED Henry approach Eleanor's circle only to discover that it also included the reedy gentleman with whom she had been in conversation under the oak tree.

"Who is that gentleman next to your sister?" he interrupted Frederick. "Did you bring him here to avoid his creditors?"

It would not be the first time Frederick had slipped a few of his cronies into a house party.

"Surely you are not in earnest?" Frederick regarded the gentleman with an appalled look. "That coat is not the result of an outstanding tailor bill. And none of my friends would be caught out of their rooms in such a rig—rather run into Dun Territory."

"Then who is he?"

"I do not— Stay a moment…" Frederick tapped his wine goblet against his lips before taking a thoughtful sip. "He is not altogether unfamiliar…"

Frederick knew every one of the younger set worth knowing and he proved it now. He slid a sly glance over and then rolled his eyes toward Goodnestone.

Ah, a conversation for another time.

"Might you have met him at The Red Door?" Lord Brice missed the subtle exchange between father and son but added his suggestion as his clumsy attempt to drag Frederick back to listening to his card by card account of a recent win at his favorite gaming hell. The lordling, like many others, wished to be numbered in Frederick's circle. The general saw nothing inherent in Frederick to draw them like lemmings, but draw them, he did.

And why was Frederick smirking?

Whoever this unknown guest, Frederick was amused by his presence. But here was Eleanor looking composed and offering Lord Brice a polite smile. *Dear Eleanor.* He knew he could count on her to accede to his wishes.

"Goodnestone is a gamester and jot a good one. Still plump in the pocket, but everyone knows of his deep losses. His man can barely get him to return to his rooms for a change of linen and a decent meal. He is here to placate his uncle's wish for an alliance with our family and to rusticate until the next race meet at Newmarket where he will likely drop a pile on a screw of a horse because he is not the judge of horseflesh that he imagines he is. His interest in Eleanor does not go beyond his uncle's wishes and her large dowry—which he clumsily asked me the figure," Frederick informed him censoriously later that night in his study.

"Why the devil did you not speak of this earlier? You knew I had settled on Longtown's nephew for your sister."

Frederick took his time blowing a smoke ring and then taking a longer draw on the cheroot paired with his brandy.

Henry responded from his place in the shadows near the door. "How could he have known, sir? We were not alive to the direction of your thoughts until the guests arrived. Sir, I must strenuously protest. Eleanor cannot marry such a man."

"Yes, yes, I know. You need not belabor the point. I will need to look elsewhere. Damnation!" He slammed down his fist on the mantle causing a few ornaments to dance. "Longtown needs to take him to task before he has not a feather to fly with. I would take a horsewhip to either of you if you displayed such weakness of character." Checking his filial pride, he asked his favorite, "Frederick, how is it that you were familiar with the same gaming houses when you were speaking to Goodnestone?"

Frederick, so much like him when he was his age, never looked up. "Merely making conversation as I thought you would have wished. I will point out that he spoke in specifics and I took a listening stance. And no, I am not familiar with every gaming hell in Town." His son tilted his head and his lips pursed. "If you are asking if I am at low tide or been bitten by the gaming bug then you would be all out because I am not. I have spent the odd evening at the card tables, but I know a flat from a leg and I will not be taken in."

Henry added nothing, merely observed, wearing that supercilious grin.

Harrumph!

These disclosures did not surprise him. His mind was distracted over Goodnestone's disappointing prospects and the need to begin anew on a search again for eligible suitors. He pushed it aside to think on it later.

He gestured back across the passage toward the music room. Earlier that evening, he had watched with consternation as Eleanor requested that scarecrow with a red thatch of hair to turn the pages of her music. She had had the effrontery to introduce the fellow to him as a Mr. Ellicott.

"Who is this Mr. Jago Ellicott? He told me he is a *barrister* from London. I have no Ellicott of London on my guest list. I had Eleanor send an invitation to an Ellicott in Cornwall who will inherit his father's title and estate."

At this, Frederick did not even attempt to contain his amusement. He chuckled low and then laughed openly.

Frederick held up a hand to stop his father's impatient words and said,

"I promise. He is not an interloper or opportunist, sir. Or at least not a traditional one. James, the Ellicott heir, does not enjoy house parties unless there is sport involved. He is wary of any attempts to catch him in a parson's mousetrap, but he is a sly one so he sends his younger brother, Jago, in his stead. He imagines one Ellicott is as good as another. The Ellicotts are a good family and cousins to the Freethys of Somersetshire. Grandmothers were sisters or some such."

General Tilney stopped breathing at the mention of the Freethys.

He blinked when he found himself in a chair, a hand thumped his back, and the scent of brandy wafted up from the glass pushed into his hand.

"Sir! Father! Are you well?" exclaimed Henry, his worry evident in his voice.

"Give him time. He's had some sort of shock," Frederick said calmly enough, but he too, was taking his measure.

Both sons' faces intent on his. Dark hair and dark eyes, noble profile, and square jaw. Tall and lithe. Hardy from youth and exercise. Tilney and Drummond in them. Blessedly devoid of that insidious Freethy blood.

Relieved, not for the first time, over his near miss, he expelled a deep breath.

"Sir?" Henry distracted him. "Should we send for the apothecary?"

"Unnecessary. I am well, thank you." The room felt close and warm as the memories crashed into him. "I will retire for the night." He stood and set his glass aside.

Henry started to rise, but Frederick's hand restrained him, probably allowing him his dignity.

"There is no need to take a fidget, as you see," the general snapped at Henry, who looked to lend him his arm.

He left his sons there, curious and concerned. It could not be helped.

It was later than he thought. All the servants but a handful of footmen had gone to their beds. Several tapers were left on a table in the hall to light them to their chambers. He took one and made his way up the stairs and down the familiar passage. After he was out of his evening clothes and into his banyan and slippers, he dismissed his valet.

When alone, he went through the connecting dressing rooms into the long unoccupied mistress' bedchamber. He set the candle down on the dressing table and gently uncorked the bottle nearby letting the light floral scent waft to him before taking up the miniature portrait by its gilded frame. He settled at the foot of Genevieve's bed and stared down at the painting done when they were ten years married.

Genevieve wanted a portrait of the pair of them and a larger second one of the entire family. It still hung in the morning room where she liked to sit and look upon it. He had commissioned yet a third painting of Genevieve that used to hang in his bed chamber—it was an intimate painting in her dressing gown with her hair down. He had ordered it moved in here on her death because it was too much a reminder of his loss. Eleanor had requested that portrait of her mother and so he later had it moved to his daughter's apartment. He did not need portraits of Genevieve to recall her appearance or stir his memories. In the seven years since he laid her to rest in the Tilney mausoleum, she secretly remained with him.

He knew what was whispered over the years: he had been a hard husband who left her to run his household and estate while he continued his brilliant military career. He had shown no grief at her grave. He had bought the church memorial and epitaph to be commissioned out of some sense of guilt. He had shut up her rooms and denied her existence even to her children.

He had allowed the talk to continue unchallenged. Better they think him unfeeling or some sort of villain than the truth: his loss was so deep that he wanted to get down in that grave along with her. That he had cried like a child while walking along her favorite path. That he was nearly sick every time Mrs. Cummins served Genevieve's favorite dishes. That he looked for her and listened for her step...still. That he caught himself turning to speak with her and remembering over again that she was gone. That he did not send for the apothecary or her physician right away because they had argued over Frederick's desire to go into the cavalry instead of his old foot regiment and he thought it was one of her tricks to manipulate him. Genevieve was not above using what was in her female arsenal to combat his stubborn, resentful nature—even taking to her bed and refusing trays of food or his admittance.

Only, her last bout of illness had surprised and frightened them both when she quickly turned for the worst. After she contracted the fever, he begged her forgiveness for waiting to send for her physician.

"There is nothing to forgive, Anthony. I had not been convinced of the severity myself." Then her lips turned up in a weak smile. "I would ask that you overlook my earlier petulance."

"'Tis forgotten," he told her. "I will get Frederick a commission in the cavalry."

She smiled wanly, holding his hand weakly. "Thank you, my love, for letting me win this one."

Neither said aloud what they feared: it would likely be their last skirmish.

"WE HAVE a Freethy under our roof tonight, my darling." He lay on the bed now and clutched the miniature to his breast. "I swore we would never associate with that family again. In truth, he's not a Freethy but an Ellicott." He drew a deep breath and let it go. *It has been so long—thirty years since the Freethy creature nearly destroyed everything for me. Had it not been for you, my cunning Genevieve...*

MARCH 1768, HMS DORSETSHIRE

As HIS MAJESTY'S SHIP, *Dorsetshire*, cut through the waves, sails snapped and lines hummed, my companion and I leaned against the rail, between two of the guns, and looked out on the starless evening while warm and dry inside our heavy boat cloaks.

The chill, damp air of the North Atlantic in early spring was preferred to our closed, cramped state room below deck where Ensign Davies suffered from mal de mer as he had for the entire journey. The surgeon said it was a good thing that we neared Portsmouth and that Davies should, upon no circumstances, cross more than a mill pond from now on.

"Much has happened in the four years since we have laid eyes on England." Major Felix Courtenay tipped his face, deeply inhaling the briny air not in the least affected by the ship's movement.

The ever-cheerful voice and ready smile made the sandy-haired, sturdy man a favorite among the other officers and his men. Under his cloak, Courtenay's red regimental coat wore a black band and he had a black ribbon rosette on his cockade hat. His older brother, Sinclair, had died of a putrid fever the summer of '67. Courtenay was returning as the new head of the Courtenay family and to take charge of the estate, his widowed mother, and two sisters still at home. He was also to marry, as soon as may be, the lovely Miss Priscilla Dent, daughter of his neighbors, Sir John and Lady Dent.

"Four years this month, in fact."

The 36th Regiment of Foot had left the Isle of Wight in '64 for our new station in Jamaica at the conclusion of the war with France. After harrying the French along their coast and then defeating them on Belle Isle, we had found ourselves adjusting to a different duty in the steamy heat of a Caribbean tropical island.

"It was jolly well good of the colonel to send you back for regiment business so you might witness Longtown's nuptials."

"Indeed. Longtown was most insistent. His letters claim we have snubbed him since we left school and put on our regimentals."

Courtenay guffawed. "Poor *Longshanks*! Only son and heir to great estates and wealth—made low in spirits because his papa would not buy him his colors."

"It was not the colors. It was being separated from his friends, he stated." I smirked because Lord *Longshanks* Marston, as Longtown was then, was miserable because he could not join his friends for a "ripping, good time" in the army.

"Oh, aye. Mama was sharp set against the army until Sinclair persuaded her to let me go. He knew I was disinclined to any other gentlemanly career. She always marveled that your father easily signed the papers as you are his only son and heir."

"My father abhorred the thought that I might become one of the dissipated, idle first sons waiting for him to stick his spoon in the wall while emptying the family coffers." And, my father did not have a regard for his son.

Courtenay knew something of my troubled history with Father and kindly turned the subject. "Do not think I am not wise to the fact that you wheedled the colonel and so timed your arrival to coincide with the Season and the return to Town from the country of a certain fair-haired, blue-eyed beauty not long returned to the home shores from Jamaica."

"You notice too much."

"When the incomparable Miss Freethy and her brother graced Jamaican society, you did not hide your interest in the lady. It was much talked about that our exacting Major Tilney set his sights high in the pursuit of a viscount's sister. I presume that you have decided then?" Courtenay flattened his lips with distaste. "Is this part of your plan to advance in rank and marry for connections?" Courtenay answered his own question, shaking his head. "No, even you, at your most ambitious, must at least respect, if not esteem, your partner. I think you might do both with Miss Freethy. Pity that."

"Why pity?"

"Oh, Prissy had hopes."

"Miss Dent, your betrothed, had hopes of me? You must be drunk." I leaned in to sniff how much wine my friend had imbibed at the captain's table only to be pushed away with a laugh.

"No, gudgeon! Not for herself. Prissy hoped to introduce you to her cousin, Miss Drummond. You have heard me mention over the last few years about her shy cousin who is a frequent visitor since her dear mother died."

"Pray, do not plague me with your country misses before I even have had a chance to make my way down Marylebone Road."

Courtney laughed and said, "I won't throw a rub in your way in regard to your Birds of Paradise. But Prissy—"

"As memory serves, you first described her as a countrified, little mouse with no conversation and Miss Dent struggled to draw her out, having little hope for her. When did you turn matchmaker?"

"Prissy writes Miss Drummond is much improved now though not long ago there was some trouble with an unscrupulous fortune hunter. Prissy says she is ready to take her place in society at her father's behest, but only requires confidence. She thought the attention of a dashing officer might do. *Prissy* is our matchmaker."

Courtenay cleared his throat and continued. "Mama is concerned that my younger sisters Pat and Let will miss the beginning of yet a second season and chances to make good matches. Let had the measles their first season and Pat would not have her presentation to the Queen without her sister. Mama will get them through the Queen's Drawing Room and she depends upon the oldest, Cat and Bet, to host dinners and balls for the girls when they leave off their mourning clothes. She expects me to separate the wheat from the chaff while squiring my sisters about. Maybe even drive off masqueraders with my sword."

Courtenay's younger twin sisters, vixens both, were Patrice and Lettice. Pat and Let, along with two older sisters, Bet and Cat, were fondly so named by their brothers. They were all lively ladies with not much beauty among them. Charm and connections carried them where beauty could not. Bet had become the Baroness Elizabeth Markham and Cat snared the second son of a duke. Lady Catherine Deveril, or Lady Cat as she was now known in her intimate circles, was apparently a leader in London Society these days.

"At least it relieves Mrs. Courtenay's mind from her grief, a little."

A quiet "yes" was his only response. The Courtenays adored one another. When the letter about Sinclair's death reached him, Courtenay was bowed down with grief for a time. Remaining at his side, I had made sure my friend did not grieve alone. "Work and duty will pull us through. Speaking of duty"—my companion turned to me—"have you informed your father that you are courting a fine lady?"

My father had raged before I left England how he required an heir and how I was a disappointment who would likely end the family line by catching a bullet and good riddance.

My worst nightmare was not to die of that predicted bullet but that I would become like my father. Thus, when my parent frothed at the mouth about duty, pushed the daughters of his friends at me, and attempted to goad me into taking a wife, I had resisted. None would serve me well for the elevated world I would occupy. I would be so much more than the bitter, old man in Gloucestershire.

"No, he has not sent me even one line since our quarrel in '64. And because Miss Freethy is not known to him...well, he is a stubborn, old man. According to my mother's last letter, he has been much occupied with his building project. He is adding a modern wing to the Abbey."

Courtenay's blond brows smoothed and he carefully inspected his gloves, and wished to address something particular so I said, "Out with it."

"Pardon?"

"Your countenance betrays you. You have something to say that you think I will not like."

"Now that you bring it to mind, you could do me a favor—that is you might do Prissy, erm, rather her cousin, Miss Drummond, a service. Not that you can let on that you are doing her a service—defeat the purpose."

With dread, I ventured, "And just what is this service that I can do the lady?"

Courtenay rushed his fences and blurted, "During the Season... Solicit Miss Drummond to be her dancing partner. Do the pretty with compliments. Be the gallant. Draw her out."

A whole evening with a wallflower... God grant me strength.

Courtenay looked at me expecting my adamant refusal, no doubt, but still hopeful. I was not one to be of service to damsels in distress, let alone the plain ones. Chivalry was more in Courtenay's line. And yet, introductions to young heiresses could never be much a hardship and I would acquit myself of a good deed for my friend and his betrothed. There was nothing that my oldest friend might ask that I would refuse.

"Very well, consider it done. I will go with you to call upon the ladies. And, if we find ourselves at the same assembly or ball…"

"You will"—his face brightened. "Prissy will make the arrangements and you will receive invitations."

"I hope to be in attendance elsewhere."

"I am full aware." Courtenay had dimmed a little.

My friend had not approved of Miss Freethy. Courtenay rarely spoke ill of others, but he admitted that the Freethys were part of a fast set. He also did not approve of Lord Wearne, Miss Freethy's brother, trying to pull me into risky business schemes or how Miss Freethy thrived on drawing so many admirers into her circle—even after singling me out. As for the last, neither did I.

I could only shrug. I did not disagree entirely with Courtenay, but the nobility lived by a different set of rules. It would do much good to court a lady sure to advance me into the highest circles where men with powerful influence were to be found.

"Still"—Courtenay drew another deep breath—"it will be good to be home."

MAY 1768, LONDON

I BOWED OVER LADY CAT's hand, wearing a perfectly fitted, light blue and silver ornamented long coat, waist coat, and matching breeches. My hair was styled and powdered in the high kick of English fashion, out of the usual military-style club, disdaining the hair dresser's offer to turn me out like a Parisian courtier.

"Lord, Tilney, what a handsome devil you are now! Do you still have devilish ways, I wonder? Should I make you turn out your pockets for fear of a mouse or snake being loosed among my guests?" Courtenay's older sister, the evening's hostess, laughed at my frown.

Courtenay's older sisters were the bane of my existence over the school holidays, which I often spent with their family. "You may rest assured that I am past the age when I need resort to small creatures in response to a tormentor, Lady Cat."

She dropped a curtsey with mocking acknowledgement then turned to her husband, a friendly man ten years his wife's senior, who looked on Lady Cat with indulgent affection. "Francis, you will recall my mention of Major Tilney. Felix's oldest friend? Tilney, this is my lord and master, Lord Francis Deveril."

"Of course! Welcome, Major! Lady Cat is pleased to have Felix returned from the army and we are happy you could accept our invitation this evening. You must come to us for dinner one evening and regal us with your heroic exploits during the Battle of Belle Isle and share about your doings on Jamaica."

"Thank you, my lord."

Lord Frances then leaned in conspiratorially tapping his nose. "She is always looking out for eligible men to make up her numbers. Have a care that she does not arrange more than a dinner or dancing partner for you."

Lord Francis enjoyed his wife's affected effrontery, but she did not deny this and tugged me to her side, speaking in hushed tones that I greatly mistrusted. "Felix informs me that you have been drafted to partner sweet, little Miss Drummond tonight. And, Felix explained where your real interest lies and how you made considerable progress while the Freethys were in Jamaica. Miss Freethy is having a successful Season and is presently the darling of Society. Of course, I had to send round an invitation to do my part for our *Tony's Freethy Campaign*, as Felix dubbed it. There she is, near the fireplace, a vision in apricot gold."

Finally, I was in the same room with my quarry after several unlucky attempts at an encounter. Miss Freethy was invariably out when I called or not attending the same evening activities when I knew her family to have received the same invitations. If I had known better, I might think she was avoiding me. As it was, I was impatient to secure Miss Freethy's hand and apply to the viscount for his consent. All of which I had determined to accomplish before the London Season was over.

"Here are Sir John and Lady Dent with Miss Drummond and our incorrigible Felix."

I knew I looked smart in the blue and it would likely be wasted on a female whose acquaintance would advance me little. Her large, celebrated dowry—knowing it originated from trade—gave me little satisfaction. What maggot had entered my head to give way to Courtenay's request for this favor?

"And here is Major Tilney. Prompt as usual, ma'am." Courtenay spoke to Lady Dent, with his Miss Dent on one arm and Miss Drummond on his other, and so, I made a leg.

"Dear Courtenay has assured us that we need not worry a jot about our niece as you come of a fine, old family from Gloucestershire, Major," Lady Dent said in form of a greeting then turned to her niece speaking sotto voce. "Did I not promise there would be handsome, eligible men when we came to London, my dear?" I observed that the red-dyed feathers in the lady's *passé* coiffure were as alive as her hands and speech. She continued whispering to her niece's acute mortification, if the rapid fanning and high color were any indication. "Fortune hunters are thick on the ground in Town so you must be vigilant. Not that Lady Cat would invite any such persons and we are grateful to Major Tilney for making up our numbers tonight. He will keep you safe as houses."

"My pleasure," I said, baring my perfect teeth.

It was then, I recognized the calculated expression on her face. I had seen many a mama with a daughter to fire off looking much the same when coming upon a potential suitor. Courtenay's silent plea was unnecessary. I had given my word so I would not retreat forthwith or offer the bothersome matron a set down with my caustic tongue.

I turned from Lady Dent to her niece, Miss Drummond, prepared to do my duty. I bowed over her hand, catching a glimpse of a gold gown and the sound of familiar, sweet laughter beyond Miss Drummond in her ivory gown. I rose to my full height and my eyes found Miss Freethy, my true object in participating in all this fuss. Now, here was a creature endowed with beauty, charm, wealth, and family connections—and well worth my efforts.

From across the room, limpid blue eyes stared from over her fan. Miss Freethy arched her brow as she slowly looked me over from head to toe.

Brazen. However, I remembered she liked an edge of danger during our few meetings under the moonlight back in Jamaica.

I took a step toward her before recalling myself. Sir John Dent's conversation with Courtenay about drainage and crops could not draw my interest any more than Lady Dent's observations to the two younger ladies about Cat's newly arriving guests.

Miss Freethy caught my eye beckoning me with her fan. I shook my head, all at once contrite that I was engaged at present whilst reluctant to hasten to join her throng of admirers.

"She is generally regarded as a great beauty," Miss Drummond said wryly, interrupting my thoughts.

I deigned no reply but then offered my full attention to Miss Drummond.

I had done the lady a disservice when I was predisposed to think her an insipid dowdy. In truth, she was a small woman with delicate bones, arresting features, and moderately high spirits which were evident beneath the paint and powder. A clever mantua maker had gowned her in pearls, lace, and ivory brocade, reminding me, despite her lithe figure, she was no longer in the schoolroom.

It was the eyes that most captured me. Those eyes—innocent and warm like a doe's when I was first introduced to her earlier in the week with Courtenay—but now full of sparkle. She raised a fan painted with flowers and hid her rosebud lips while slowly moving the air with the pretty item. It irked me to be a source of her amusement.

"Do you care to take our place for the minuet, Miss Drummond?" I offered my arm, retreating from that knowing gaze. This lady may be quiet in manner and speech, but I was as lief to differ with Courtenay when he asked his favor of me that she was shy or in need of bolstering her confidence. It remained to be seen, however, if she could dance without mishap.

She closed her fan with a snap and took her place beside me. "Rest assured, Major, I will not tread upon your shoes or give you reason to blush."

Her words had echoed my thoughts and I could barely utter, "The thought never occurred to me."

She hummed a non-committal sound, but her reddened lips curled up delightfully. "I understand from Major Courtenay that you are returned for a friend's nuptials and will be visiting with family and acquaintance for the first time these many years."

"And I will also be recruiting more men to bring the regiment to full strength."

"Was it difficult to be away from England so long?"

"One grows accustomed to living abroad. It has its compensations in traveling to places exotic in nature but also having the comfort of familiar duties and tasks."

"But is it not lonely? I cannot abide the thought of having to leave all those I know and living a half a world away."

"I did not leave all those I know. I had Courtenay, my fellow officers, and duty for my King. I encountered new acquaintances and now I see them...again...here."

"Yes, I think I see how it is." Her eyes drifted to Miss Freethy. She arched her brow. "The regiment is like a family. The general is the papa, the colonel is the mama, and—"

"And majors are the elder brothers?" I smirked.

"To be sure." As the figures separated us, she regarded me over her shoulder, encouraging me in her little joke.

I had barely noticed our movements, the music, the other couples, and now I bit back a laugh as I imagined curmudgeonly Colonel Wright as a "mama," especially with his old-style wig, stains from long-time snuff use, and his horsey, stentorian voice.

Between sets, I had enjoyed the conversation as it halted and progressed with the dance and after as we took a turn about the room. The pleasure of her company had been unexpected and she partnered me in the dance well, in spite of our great difference in height.

While awaiting Miss Drummond's return from the retiring room, I espied Miss Freethy nearby smiling over a Macaroni in his ridiculous choice of fashion and poetry. The outlandish youth became dreamy-eyed when she thanked him for his blithering ode *to her nose* and he bowed over her gloved hand. "I will now procure the nectar of the gods for you, divine Miss Freethy, and, if none can be had, then I will go to the ends of the Earth for such a lovely nymph."

I brushed past as the callow admirer slinked away in his ridiculous evening coat with the exaggerated buttons, the eye-searing striped waistcoat in yellow and green, and the extreme heeled shoes with the large flowers instead of decent buckles. I bowed to her deep curtsey, giving me plenty to appreciate in her generous décolletage before I looked up to her carefully painted and patched face. "Rather than nectar, he should settle for punch, which may be had on the far side of the room instead of the ends of the Earth." I had no time for besotted fools and was not pleased to witness Miss Freethy encouraging them. "I missed you at Mrs. Ames' musicale."

At once I saw her decide to play the coquette rather than respond. "I am made low to see you at last only to find you attending another lady. You set me aside so easily. What has become of the courageous soldier who defended me against the torrential rain and large, crawling creatures we encountered in my brother's drawing room? Has your new lady more wit? Beauty? Perhaps she displays her charms more freely?"

She pushed out her lower lip, and despite the likely intent, was not charming on her usually lovely face. I had not missed the sharpness in her voice that betrayed her pique, and the spitefulness of her last remark led me to believe she saw Miss Drummond as a rival. Perhaps, this evening spent with the young heiress was to be of some benefit after all and would teach the lady that I was not one of her puppies to dangle.

"Miss Drummond is the cousin to my friend's betrothed. It is no hardship to stand up with her as she is indeed charming and witty."

"I do not wish to hear of another who can be nothing to me."

Her entire mien altered when a plain, round faced gentleman in green satin approached and bowed before her offering his arm. He was gone to softness at the waist and was lost beneath the emeralds and finery he wore. "My dear, I do apologize for leaving you unattended while Wearne and I dealt with a tedious matter."

Assured of his own importance, the gentleman looked on with distaste as the absurd poet approached with punch for Miss Freethy and flicked a glance toward me. I held his gaze until he looked away.

"It does not signify," she said in a flat tone, "but you did promise we would dance, my lord."

I was ignored like her cup of punch, and she wrapped her arm through her partner's with no further leave taking.

Proud to squire a woman who could shine all the others down on his arm, the man in green swung them about to affectedly mince his steps the few paces to the dancing floor nearby. "And I must not break my word."

I did not care to be slighted by an obvious lack of introduction and my anger rose. She expected me to prostrate myself and beg for her attention! This I would not do even to secure a high-born wife with powerful connections. It was beneath my dignity. "Good evening, Miss Freethy." I succinctly said to her back and bowed stiffly to show I still remembered I was a gentleman, even if she did not act as a lady.

She stiffened but continued along.

Miss Drummond acknowledged me again at her side without an ounce of censure for my recent desertion. I suspected that part of the reason she was not wounded over my wandering was that her mind was engaged elsewhere, as evidenced by the distant look in her eyes. Her head turned only when Miss Freethy's chattering words carried to us.

Miss Freethy flirted with little subtlety, causing her partner to puff up from the admiration he likely accepted as his due, and then she listened with large, round eyes as if his description of his latest snuffbox purchase was utterly fascinating.

"What blather! Dull as ditchwater, but allowances must be made for Lord Stanbridge, I suppose. He is an earl with a great amount of wealth and property," Miss Drummond murmured.

I caught her meaning and it darkened my mood further. Miss Freethy hoped to secure the title of countess and have access to even more wealth than her own dowry commanded.

As the realization sank in that my courtship was to end in failure, Miss Freethy offered me a smug look of triumph and then a slow, insufferable wink.

Cat was suddenly at my side. "Tony," she whispered. "I have just learned—"

"If you are to tell me about Miss Freethy and Stanbridge, you are *de trop*, my lady."

She grimaced up at me and tutted as she moved away.

Miss Drummond's hand came to rest on my sleeve, offering a kind of silent support. I despised that Miss Freethy's triumph was witnessed—as was my reaction. I twisted my arm from her petulantly and stood with shoulders back and faced Courtenay who was then introducing Miss Priscilla Dent to Lady Thorne, our friend Longtown's betrothed.

The evening droned on and I doubted anyone was aware of my scattered thoughts and inner turmoil. In no small part, this was due to Miss Drummond's stratagem of standing up with me through the remaining dances and discreetly recalling me to social obligations when we encountered people inclined to converse, but otherwise leaving me to my own thoughts.

I eventually noted her wilted appearance that even her fan could not revive. I procured her a glass of wine and took us through the doors out into the cooler air. Cat's ball was a successful crush and the heat just as proportionate, reminding me of what I had left behind on Jamaica.

"Thank you, Major."

"I did not observe your discomfort earlier. Please accept my apology for my boorish behavior."

"You have much to occupy your mind."

She did not admonish me but instead presented a sympathetic attitude. A near comrade in arms could be no more welcome than Miss

Drummond. We stepped out into the moonlight and she sipped her wine while we looked out over Cat's garden lit by lanterns that glowed at intervals along the walks.

What she thought over, I knew not. Her attention was fixed on the empty wine goblet on the balustrade. For my part, my mind would not cease the torture of disappointed hopes of marrying extremely well and achieving my place high in the army and in society. Surely it would have been enough. I would have had my father's respect at last. Instead, I must begin anew with the Season half-gone and the eligible ladies with not nearly the manifold of attractions as Miss Freethy's noble connections, dowry, dazzling beauty, and charm.

I OBSERVED a couple conversing on a stone bench below the balcony where Miss Drummond and I stood in the shadows.

"My dear, you are ravishing and everyone worships at your feet. Who is this Tilney to you?" the earl's voice carried to me above on the balcony.

"To me?" Miss Freethy's voice was filled with practiced ennui. "He is nothing to me, I assure you. Merely a toy soldier for my amusement when the insipidness of island society threatened to overcome me, my lord."

"We must keep you from such languor, my dear. I cannot have my future wife chasing redcoats or allow a redcoat to chase my betrothed. I have spoken to your brother about him. He has accepted my financial backing in his mining scheme. Whatever this Tilney could invest would be nothing in comparison. Wearne will make it clear to Tilney that his association is no longer welcome."

"Thank you, my lord." She gave her hand into the earl's for a kiss. "You cannot know what it is like to be sought for one's fortune. I tried to give him a hint and I made sure he was told I was not at home to his calls, but you know the temerity of a soldier. And he does so hang on Wearne's sleeve. My brother has all but taken up chambers at his club."

The earl made reassuring sounds. "Do not distress yourself so over this soldier, my dove. I have it on good authority that he will return to his regiment. I laugh at the sheer audacity of your toy soldier."

As I grew angrier by each uttered word, particularly Miss Freethy's falsehoods about me, I heard Miss Drummond's soft voice. "Major, please." My shoe scraped as I straightened from the balustrade.

The sound made Miss Freethy glance up. Not one to skulk in the shadows, I stood tall and looked down upon her. Miss Drummond was clutched to my side with her small hand resting over my heart. Her touch had gone unnoticed until the lady on the bench seemed arrested by it.

Then, and with much deliberation, I placed my hand possessively over Miss Drummond's. At Miss Freethy's gasp, I chose that satisfying moment to make my honorable retreat.

My retreat was not far however as others were pouring from the wide-open doors to the cool air. Miss Drummond's hand moved to settle in the crook of my arm. We looked ahead, avoiding the other's eyes.

Oh, to avoid a discussion of my complete humiliation that she has witnessed.

No, there was no reason for shame. Her expression was no longer pitying or sympathetic. Rather, it spoke of determination. Her bosom heaved in quick breaths and my mind was happily distracted from the scene below.

Miss Drummond came at me with a successful, flanking maneuver that left me flushed, caught as I was, admiring her fine figure. My eyes rose from the lovely distraction at her neckline and I braced for what was to come. "Major, I have a proposal for you." She did not wait for my response. "Recently, I thought myself to have an understanding with a gentleman. His words, his countenance, his acceptance of my aunt's invitations and frequent calls told me I was not wrong. My heart was engaged and I was prepared for him to make an offer, but then it all ended.

"I was sadly mistaken in his character. My father became aware of Lord Tollier's sordid reputation and his financial woes that drove him to visit our neighborhood for the sole purpose of capturing my affections and my father's consent. He came to me—after my father withheld his permission. His Lordship proposed a romantic elopement in the night. And I might have foolishly gone, but for my father packing me off to my aunt's where she recalled me to my duty and affection to my father and also opened my eyes to the defects in Lord Tollier, who had not acted with honor nor was motivated by affection for me."

I now feared where this pitiful tale was taking us. *She thinks to salve my wounds in mutual loss?*

"Miss Drummond—"

"Hear me, sir, please." She glanced up at me and then out across Cat's garden.

I waited, not hiding my wish to escape, ungentlemanly though it was.

"I come to the point. I assure you. Major, I have no desire to return to my aunt's home or my father's house where everyone suspects I nearly eloped with a cad." Playing with her fan, she swallowed nervously before she looked up, squarely meeting my eyes, and, with resolution, spoke. "I propose we become engaged. You were obviously seeking a wife who would do you credit as you pursued promotion in the army and wish for a place in the *haut ton*. Instead, you will be mocked when Miss Freethy's engagement to the Earl of Stanbridge and the substance of the conversation we overheard becomes common knowledge. The pair of them will certainly contrive to spread it about. I would not come empty-handed. We both can benefit from our alliance."

I stood like one turned to stone; my brain shouted for an about face and quick march, while my body was utterly overpowered and unable to respond to orders.

The frustration and ire that had been building through this dreadful night against Miss Freethy and her earl now found a target. My father's voice echoed in my head, and I heard myself say in a cold, cutting voice: "Do you really think I could replace a woman of superior connections, wealth, and status in the highest circles for someone whose connections are with trade? Who is a Miss Drummond to a Miss Freethy?"

She winced. Her fingers gripping her fan hard enough to snap the sticks. But she rallied. No words; just a curtsey as she left me alone on the veranda.

I LEFT General Sir Richard Pierson after a long meeting regarding the recruitment efforts for the 36th Foot and decided I had earned a reward for my diligence over a fortnight through a storm of humiliating speculation connected to Miss Freethy, her betrothed, and me. I wanted to believe the talk that Miss Drummond had accurately predicted on the terrace would all go away, especially as Sir Richard had cleared his throat a few times and seemed uncomfortable in my presence.

The marriage of the Marquis of Longtown and Lady Amy muted the talk of the "toy soldier," but it rose again when my appearance at the most anticipated wedding of the season drew everyone's attention. I stoically presented myself to my friend and his new bride at their wedding breakfast to wish them well.

Longtown assured me, "Something will come along and distract the gossips, my friend. Perhaps I can fight a duel over my lady's honor while abroad?"

Longtown's jest made me smile and we parted with well wishes on both sides. I could not help glancing at Miss Drummond who stood nearby with her aunt and cousin, looking sweet in a lavender gown. She was, like me, the recipient of dashed hopes and rendered pathetic to all in her neighborhood. I gave some thought, again, to her outlandish proposal, which after time, did not carry any repugnance. But would it serve to pursue it? I recalled my brutish behavior to her that night.

Her eyes rose to regard me and she seemed not a whit concerned that I was looking back.

The lady confounded me.

I knew she felt things deeply after revealing her hurt and humiliation over Lord Tollier. Her proposal rankled because she made it while my pride was bruised and because I chose to be offended by a lady making such a request.

Now, I was beyond my anger and merely curious. She did not look as if my grossly offensive retort from the night of Cat's ball had turned her into a bitter enemy. It was her very unpredictability that drew me.

I watched her face lighten and her eyes dance with merriment before I realized I had taken steps in her direction. I halted abruptly behind the crowd seeing off the newly wedded pair. Uncertain about my own intentions by approaching the lady, I faltered.

She waited.

Indecisiveness had never plagued me before nor did uncertainty, but my presumption and conceit had laid me low recently. I knew one thing for a certain: I did not wish Miss Drummond to see that she thoroughly routed me.

I shed my misgivings and presented myself.

"Miss Drummond, how do you do?"

Large, changeable eyes observed me and I could not determine her disposition.

"I fare well, Major."

"Will you come a little aside with me?" I barely waited for her consent before I took her arm carefully. Struth, I saw her as fragile enough to break if I handled her less than carefully. I led her from the crowd.

"Are your wishes altered after my words that evening?"

She blinked.

Aha! It was my turn to put her off-balance.

She fluttered her fan and was silent for a full minute. "If you refer to my proposal, I am less confident but still willing."

"Fair enough. May I call on you tomorrow?"

She contemplated for a time and then looked up accepting the possibilities of a courtship. "You may. Might I suggest a walk in the park with my cousin and your friend?"

Miss Drummond and I strolled slowly, widening the distance to Courtenay and Miss Dent. My long, purposeful stride was deliberately shortened to match Miss Drummond's. She was not a dawdler; merely short.

I halted our progress. "I am inclined to accept your proposal if you have not elected to withdraw it."

"Are you remorseful for how you spoke to me in our final moments the night of the ball?"

"The very moment it left my lips but it was only after Longtown's wedding that I felt the full import. You did not appear as if my earlier behavior affected you which made me admire you profoundly in that moment. I was very wrong, you know."

She responded just as softly as I spoke the last. "How so?"

"About you. You are a superior woman. I was cruel and you were queenly." And, because I felt she should know the full extent of who and what I was, I further revealed, "It is likely I will behave in such an ungentlemanly fashion again. I come over ugly when I am angered. For years, I have sought to govern this defect, but there is something dark inside me that rises up and vanquishes good intention."

"It is a weakness, to be sure, and my cousin warned me that you were a difficult man whom she felt took advantage of Major Courtenay's goodness."

A cold weight seemed to fill my insides at her words, but she continued.

"That, however, is Prissy's opinion. My own is that we all have flaws and your longstanding friendship with Major Courtenay has done him an equal amount of good."

"Well not equal, perhaps," I spoke with levity.

She did not return my smile but remonstrated. "Yes, equal. Priscilla is unaware that she owes you the debt of twice plucking her Felix from the jaws of death and bolstering him through his family loss. Of a time years before, when you drove off the bullies from Felix and your other friend, Longtown, while at school."

How did she—

"Lady Cat was my cousin's nearest neighbor before she was married. I am no stranger to Courtenay Manor and we exchange letters."

I was bowled out and she was merry upon seeing my jaw drop.

That would mean she was—

Rapid recalculations filled my brain. Not just Miss Dent's cousin. Courtenay Manor. Not just an out of the schoolroom, shy miss of a cousin who needed a ball escort…

Courtenay! Courtenay knew this when he begged his *favor!*

I looked ahead on the path and spied my friend and his betrothed grinning knowingly back at us. And Cat! She was co-conspirator.

"I do apologize. It seems our friends desired us to be acquainted and now we are." I patted her arm reassuringly.

She narrowed her eyes in thought, seeming to do some rapid calculating of her own, and then a wry smile appeared. "Cat promised that if I came up to Town, she would cheer me up. It never occurred to me that she would send all the way to Jamaica in her efforts."

And with that, I could appreciate the humor in our situation, which Cat and Courtenay contrived together.

I asked cautiously, "Did you by chance visit the Courtenays during the holidays and encounter something in your bed that made you shriek in terror?"

I covered my eyes and groaned when she giggled. I remembered that Cat and Bet had the most annoying younger friends and Mrs. Courtenay had forced Sinclair, Felix, and me to stand up with them to practice dancing one long, tedious afternoon. My own partner had called me a poker and pinched me when I refused to move. I had repaid her and then some.

AFTER WE TALKED through our shared history with the Courtenay family and I told her how my friend and Cat had bamboozled me, I felt I could ask the one burning question I had left. "Why propose to me?"

"My father is unwell and it grieves him to know there is talk of me in our neighborhood."

"Ah, a father's approbation. This, I can understand. But why choose me? Other than pity, that is."

She gave me a beguiling smile. "Why not choose you? I would suppose you are beyond annoying, boyish pranks." I was delighted that the little thing on my arm tossed that saucy reply. "But I think I will withhold my reason until much later. Perhaps it will remain a secret. It will depend." She was no longer teasing but still an enigma.

"On what?"

Now she peeked up at me from under her wide-brimmed hat—"It will depend very much on you, Major."

I was not a light-hearted man nor could I ever be described as jocular, but in that moment, I found myself sharing a conspiratorial laugh with… my future wife. I raised her gloved hand and met her eyes as I daringly kissed the bare skin of her wrist above her glove. Her sweet scent inflamed my ardor and I looked to her wide, gray eyes. Her lovely face had flushed all the way to that fine bosom. And my own heart began to race in want of her.

"Incidentally"—her voice low and breathy—"I do not withdraw my proposal. Thank you for accepting."

I could scarce admit what I was feeling. When had this mild-mannered, country girl become such a comely siren? I have had women before but they never inspired me to do the things I hoped to do with Miss Drummond as my wife. The idea of wedding and bedding that Freethy woman might had been a means to an end, but the embers smoldering from this moment threatened to undo me. "And I give you leave to call me 'Genevieve' as we are now betrothed after all."

I wondered if she felt the same attraction and could only hope that her maidenly blushes and unsteady voice were promising signs for our marriage. When I released her hand to tuck her arm back over my own, we both realized that there were details to be sorted and settled. I needed to ascertain that Genevieve understood that marriage would not mean that I would sell out of the army—that I had not lost my ambition and I would require much from her.

"We will be partners in a venture." Genevieve agreed with assurance. "I will do you credit, Anthony."

"I have no doubt."

Soon our walk was over and I found myself in Sir John Dent's bookroom requesting her guardian's permission for a courtship.

After a se'nnight, I escorted Genevieve's carriage into Essex to obtain Mr. Drummond's blessing. Genevieve's father was expecting us as she and Sir John had written. Mr. Drummond was not what I imagined. Her father seemed entertained when Genevieve told him the story of our inauspicious start as children. I learned Drummond's warehouses once had the outfitting of the English army regiments. Though very ill now, Drummond recalled many of my superiors and his eyes gleamed much like his daughter's had on occasion. I was not a little hopeful when Drummond said he had neglected his correspondence in recent years.

Drummond might have been an invalid, but he was alert to his responsibilities to his beloved daughter. I informed him of my circumstances and what I could offer a bride. They already knew I was the heir to Northanger Abbey, our family seat in Gloucestershire, but added that I was also comfortably fixed for the present too. "My army pay is not my only source of income. My mother's brother died without issue and I received a modest income when his property was sold and the money invested."

"We do not doubt you can well provide for a wife, Major. Do not forget what you must receive quarterly from your father." Genevieve's father smiled.

"My father gives me nothing."

My betrothed and her father glanced at each other and then back to me before turning the subject.

A FEW DAYS LATER, I gravely regarded Genevieve after leaving her father and his attorney in the bookroom with the signed settlements.

She set down her cup of tea. "What is it, Anthony? Have you changed your mind?"

I grasped her hand in mine, her father's words of concern still in my thoughts. "Gen, you have my word that, though your fortune was a strong inducement, it was not my sole motivation in accepting your proposal. I highly value you and want the woman who believes in me, in spite of my faults, by my side."

She looked up and I saw tears form in her eyes, but her smile stretched wide. She leaned forward from her seat beside me and brushed her lips against mine before withdrawing a little. My lips chased hers as I succumbed to the temptation and poured my want into a second kiss.

A FEW MOMENTS LATER, she opened her eyes and her voice was husky with emotion as she spoke, "You asked me why I chose you. Cannot you see?"

1800, NORTHANGER ABBEY

He had only had a glimmer then, General Tilney remembered, as he walked along Genevieve's favorite walk in the cool of the morning. Her spirit walked with him in this place and he talked to her of the past.

Drummond's curious need to correspond with old friends produced a new promotion to colonel for his new son not long after he saw his daughter married. Colonel and Mrs. Tilney returned to his regiment after a brief sojourn in Gloucestershire where Genevieve approved of the Abbey but not her father-in-law.

Jamaica's climate was hard on her, but she would not be sent home to England. Like a good soldier's wife, she remained at his side, hosting his officers and the governor himself on occasion. His comfort was her priority and he made certain she had anything for which she expressed a desire including a house by the sea. Genevieve was so proud to provide him a son that they named Frederick after her recently deceased father. He was proud as well, but then she grew ill with childbed fever.

In the dark of night, his eyes were opened to his feelings for his wife. Desperately he whispered at her bedside, "Stay with me, Gen. That is an order." Courtenay was right. He did require a lady he could esteem and regard. Yet such insipid feelings did not describe what they shared. "I insist you keep your word, my dear. You said we are partners and you would help me fulfill my ambitions. I must achieve the rank of general. Further I require, at least once, for a duke to accept our invitation to dinner. So, you see, there is much to do before you may even consider your promise completed."

She had recovered then and he gave her his words of love in return. His wife had courted him for affection. Every word and action was evidence of her love for him. He was humbled by this new understanding and a need to match her unselfish, tender, loving care—as much as he could.

And yet, his version of love was paltry in comparison, having never witnessed a love like what they shared.

"Father." His reverie was interrupted by Eleanor's soft voice.

He turned to see her on the arm of the red-haired scarecrow to whom she was partial. He was well aware the pair of them had been exchanging letters through Henry and a mutual friend since Ellicott's first visit to the

Abbey. He knew they had met at a house party even after his adamant refusals to allow their courtship.

He privately appreciated that this Jago Ellicott looked him in the eye, man to man, and regarded Eleanor with a warm expression. Ellicott seemed honorable and all reports proved he was in good standing. Ellicott's proprietary hold of her hand on his arm raised General Tilney's hackles, but the soft whisper of his wife's voice in warning lowered them.

Still, he would not make it easy for Eleanor's suitor. "Well?" he barked lacing hands behind his back and peering down his nose at the pair.

Eleanor swallowed, but it was Ellicott who spoke. "Good morning, sir. Miss Tilney has done me the honor of returning my affections. She is a dutiful daughter and would not dream of accepting a courtship without your approval. I know, in the past, you have not been inclined to bestow it, but my circumstances have changed."

Ellicott wore a black armband and he made the general to understand that he had inherited his brother's title and estate.

So, Eleanor is to become the new Viscountess St. Mabyn and reside in Cornwall?

"Sir, may I have your permission to court your daughter?"

"Oh, go be fools—"

Behave, Anthony!

He cleared his throat, observing Eleanor's stricken expression and St. Mabyn's tightened lips. Genevieve's spirit was strong in that moment and her silence roared with disapproval. He needed to be at peace with her; thus, he swung around and stepped forward, startling the young lovers.

He reached for Eleanor's hand, gentling his voice, knowing the girl was easily overset. "Is this what you wish, child? Is he whom you wish?"

Her eyes teared up and she bobbed her head trying to find words. "Mister—that is Lord St. Mabyn makes me very happy, Father."

"Very well, you have my permission to court."

Eleanor burst into sobs and rushed him with an embrace that he was unaccustomed to receiving. "Thank you! Thank you, Father. And Henry?"

The tender child was always thinking of her brother who remained incensed with him over a separate matter involving the little vicar's daughter. "He can go be a fool, too."

The newly courting couple were well-pleased if somewhat suspicious he would take it all back.

St. Mabyn rushed into action. "Thank you, sir, and I would like to extend an invitation, as well. I would like for you and Miss Tilney to journey into Cornwall so I may introduce my mother and sister."

With a handshake to the new viscount, the general then waved them off. He watched the pair out of sight as they happily chattered over their future.

Well done, Anthony!

"They have been thwarted in love and now appreciate what they have as a result. Like our difficult beginning, Genevieve."

And your actions toward Miss Morland?

"I am still not convinced of that pairing for our son"—*but she has some income and she can grow and learn under Henry's guidance. I suppose it will be Frederick to take up the cudgels and challenge me most. War with France again is only a matter of time. Frederick knows this and remains in anticipation. So much like I was at his age.*

He drifted along the path at a leisurely pace pondering the present, still touched by his thoughts from the past and sense of Genevieve beside him. She had kept her promise made those many years before. They had also made new promises together. Even now, he loved her as much as he could.

SOPHIA ROSE is a native Californian currently residing in Michigan. A long-time Jane Austen fan, she is a contributing author to *The Darcy Monologues, Sun-kissed: Effusions of Summer,* and *Then Comes Winter* anthologies, short stories based on Jane Austen's works. Sophia's love for writing began as a teen writing humorous stories submitted for Creative Writing class and high school writing club. Writing was set aside for many years while Sophia enjoyed a rewarding career working with children and families. Health issues led to reduced work hours and an opportunity for a return to writing stories that continue to lean toward the lighter side of life and always end with a happily-ever-after.

JOHN THORPE

A supercilious braggart, who contrived tales of his own heroics, John Thorpe proved to be more than a buffoon but the real villain. Though his ambitions drove him to covet the life of a rake, without the means to afford such extravagance, his character was fixed as a grasping, lying social-climber whose guile was only surpassed by his sister Isabella's. *Catherine listened with astonishment; she knew not how to reconcile two such very different accounts of the same thing; for she had not been brought up to understand the propensities of a rattle, nor to know to how many idle assertions and impudent falsehoods the excess of vanity will lead.* —*Northanger Abbey,* **Chapter IX.**

"Give me but a little cheerful company, let me only have the company of the people I love, let me only be where I like and with whom I like, and the devil take the rest, say I." —John Thorpe to Catherine Morland, *Northanger Abbey*, Chapter XV.

THE ART OF SINKING
J. Marie Croft

No one who had ever seen John Thorpe in his infancy would have supposed him born to be a beastly buffoon. At that tender age, there could be no telltale sign of the rattle, the rogue, or—heaven forfend!—the rat.

Even had such an indication been evident, the mother of that bundle of joy could not but own a markedly tender feeling for her first-born son. Of course, every man's wife, be she baseborn or noble, was put upon, so to speak, to provide an heir. By dint of his birth, therefore, John had become Mrs. Thorpe's finest achievement.

Cosseted by his parents and by those household servants not directly involved in his daily routine, John soon sank in favour with the nurse assigned, at first happily, to his care and feeding. Her charge proved to be a choleric, raucous creature whom she would just as soon have thrown out with the bath water had she not feared someone might eventually notice the quiet. With coarse cloth and a scrap of lye soap, she scrubbed the wailing child in a washtub of tepid water and, in frequent fits of pique, held his head beneath the surface until he bubbled.

As dutifully tended by the same nurse was a subsequent brood of two more boys and three girls.

Cherished by their doting, indulgent mother, those six children were the sole source of Mrs. Thorpe's pride and braggadocio, merited or not.

When he was in leading strings, John's mother announced to a room of guests that, although he had recently turned one-year-old, he had been walking since eight months of age. To which report Mrs. Shepherd, one of the bored visitors, just before being shown the door, replied, "Really? Well, madam, your precocious youngster must be dreadfully tired by now."

The Thorpe family—which resided in Bartlett's Buildings, Holborn, in rooms above Mr. Thorpe's ground floor office—was in neither particularly good nor poor circumstances. Nevertheless, with consistent and conscientious regularity, they coveted the perceived advantages, achievements, and accoutrements of their betters and peers. The latter class consisted of tradesmen and their ilk rather than the "realm" sort of peer, for Mr. Thorpe was engaged in commerce. Whilst not genteel, the man was not uncommonly disrespected ... though he *was* a lawyer.

Jouncing John on his knee, the attorney watched a fine carriage drive past his window. "One day, my boy, I shall purchase for us all the best trappings money can buy—the most hellish good guns and fox hounds, sweet goers with the most spanking trots, and a one-of-a-kind, well-hung, town-built curricle rigged with silver mouldings, splashing-board, lamps, the springiest of springs, and all that. 'Why, there goes that dashing Aubrey Thorpe with his prime rattler and four matching prads,' the neighbours will say upon catching sight of my finery. Every gentleman within fifty miles will be damned jealous."

Such envy never came to pass, alas. While John was a stripling, his father kicked the bucket in a manner quite beyond the pale. In his office one evening, with Mrs. Thorpe and his eldest son as witnesses, the man, who never would have been afforded the privilege of becoming a barrister, acted out his court debut as prosecutor at the Old Bailey. Demonstrating to an imaginary judge and jury his gift of persuasive oratory and that the defendant's pistol could *not* have discharged accidentally, Mr. Thorpe accidentally shot himself while play-acting with the fatally authentic exhibit.

Bereft of a father, the three Thorpe brothers were spared the rod or any sort of discipline; and John—being, then, the eldest male of the family—gloried in high regard and deference. Of course, vanity, working on a weak head, produced every sort of mischief. If trouble was at hand, John was sure to be in the thick of it; and, like others of his sex, if there was anything disagreeable going on, he was sure to get out of it—until he was sent off to Merchant Taylors.

"But I do not *want* to attend school," he whinged, stamping his foot. Stacks of china in a nearby cabinet rattled and threatened to topple.

"Not to worry, my darling," said Mrs. Thorpe while knitting him some socks. "The headmaster informs me you will only be called up to have your work assessed twice a term."

"Twice a term! Gadzooks!" John staggered backwards, bumping into the cabinet and wincing at the sound of splintering porcelain. "I will not go! I am sure I heard somewhere that a little learning is a dangerous thing!"

At the Suffolk Lane school founded by a merchant guild for boys of middle rank, John received discipline, derision, and indignities most dreadful—as well as a moderately priced education in the classics and drama. Beatings dispensed by a harsh headmaster, while painful, were nothing to the deliberately hurtful remarks and abuse meted out by the senior rank of boys living under their own set of rules. John, in his juvenility, had never been so vilely quizzed.

Young, irrepressible, and of a hot character, he acquired a tough skin—due, it was conjectured, to scarring—and embraced a philosophy. *The rest of the world be damned! Mother, my sisters, and brothers all set great store by me. 'Tis us Thorpes against the world!* As a whole, the family practiced economy with their modest income and also with the truth. The latter commodity stretched with far greater flexibility than the former.

One day, between school terms, their neighbour, Mrs. Shepherd, came to call and to lodge a complaint. "Mrs. Thorpe, I shall no longer allow my Tom to associate with your eldest. Like his late father, John swears horribly."

"Yes, yes, I know." Sighing, Mrs. Thorpe shook her head while admiring the lace on the other woman's dress. "The dear child puts *no* feeling into it at all."

"Well!" Mrs. Shepherd turned her scorn upon the object of it. "Young man, I have heard alarming reports of your disruptive behaviour at school—shooting paper darts into your teacher's hair and making him resemble a fretful porcupine. I understand the headmaster wants to see you nearly *every* day."

"'Tis not so!" Bits of gingerbread flew from his mouth as John spluttered. "He said he *never, ever,* wants to see me before him again!"

"The headmaster is a difficult man," said Mrs. Thorpe. Leaning towards the other woman and speaking in a half whisper, she said, "Hard on the pupils but easy on the eye, if you know what I mean." Then, winking at her eldest child, she crowed, "John is quite the favourite at school, and the other boys look up to him. Though not the academic sort, he excels at all scholarly pursuits. I would not hear of it, of course, but quite soon after enrollment it was recommended that John be taught at home. I expect the assistant masters thought there was nothing else for him to learn at Merchant Taylors. And after just *one* term! Imagine!"

Turning a fond look upon her dearest son, Mrs. Thorpe told John his father would have been exceedingly proud of him. Then, in a more meditative mood, she gazed a while into the grate's flames and sniffling, pulled a handkerchief from a sleeve to wipe at her eyes and nose. "How my dear

Aubrey, the best of husbands"—the widow's voice cracked with emotion—"loved a good blaze."

Mrs. Shepherd patted her hand. "There, there, Mrs. Thorpe." With only a moment till her visit was cut short, the woman added, "Surely your husband is gone to a place with a very fine fire."

At her departure, John stamped his way to the fireplace and stabbed at embers. "What a cock and bull story you sold that old biddy." Throwing down the poker, he paced the small room. "My school was founded by an association of tailors, but was it really necessary to pull the wool over Mrs. Shepherd's eyes?" He knelt at his mother's knee and, with head bowed, spoke gruffly. "The thing is, I do rather poorly at Merchant Taylors, you know."

"I know, son." Mrs. Thorpe patted his head and imparted her own philosophy. "But little white lies never hurt anyone. Embellishment of fact and a version—or aversion—of truth are oft justified and may be used to one's advantage."

John settled beside her on the sofa and, gorging himself on more gingerbread, weighed one of the Ten Commandments against another. "Honour thy father and thy mother" soon tipped the scales. "I think I understand. At school, we read part of *The Prince* by that Italian fellow. He says one should never try to win by force what can be won by deception." Deep furrows on his brow cleared. "By Jove! *Lie-ability* is actually an *asset*!"

Mrs. Thorpe affectionately tweaked his nose. "Such a clever boy! There never was a young man so beloved as you."

Being so well praised and tweaked did much to heal John's bruises. But, back at Merchant Taylors, when something or other of his was presented as larger or better than it really was, he was proclaimed a "rattle," a "fibber," a "hollow-hearted rascal," and worse.

"Four and a half? Pshaw!" cried John, surrounded by senior boys. "Six, if it is an inch!"

"Thorpe, you lousy lout," sneered one, "you lie like a rug!"

"Like a sieve," said another, "your stories do not hold water."

Those declarations prompted John to a loud and overpowering reply, of which no part was very distinct except the frequent oaths which adorned it.

So what if I have told a falsehood or two? Glory and survival justify duplicity. To achieve one's goals, such means are acceptable, according to both

Machiavelli and my mother. One of them, at least, cannot be wrong. And the devil take the rest of the world, I say!

Taunts and torments John endured by laughing them off. To his family, and in his candid manner, he claimed such provocations touched him not. "They are just jealous, is all. Because of me, we won four—no, five!—no, *all* of our games against Harrow." Crossing arms over his chest, he said, "Furthermore, I, more than anybody else, make the other boys laugh." While that remark was in accordance with fact, what he did not admit was they laughed *at* him, not *with* him.

Notwithstanding his half-hearted attempts at an education, John was eventually awarded a fellowship for undergraduate study at St. John's College. And his mother was thereby granted another excuse to boast of her own child. Her brother—belonging as he did to the guild that originally founded Merchant Taylors—was instrumental in funding John's admittance to Oxford; but Mrs. Thorpe denied the fact that, due to the family's situation, her son might otherwise never have been admitted to university.

Following his first three terms at Oxford, John bounded up the stairs of Bartlett's Buildings and into the parlour, where he was received with squeals of delight and exulting affection.

"Mother, how do you do?" He suffered her crushing, aromatic embrace, then stood back. "Good God, woman, what a quiz of a dress! You look like an old hag. Oho, and here are all my ugly brothers and sisters, too!"

Inquiries were made and intelligence given, with them all talking together, as was their wont, far more ready to give than to receive information, and hearing very little of what another said. After the best part of an hour of such babble and clack, John tugged at his cravat and took to pacing.

"Damn it, but this room is stifling! 'Tis as hellish hot as Hades in here!"

"Those are not polite words." Anne scowled first at her eldest brother and then down at the mess she had made of her embroidery. Tossing it aside, she gazed longingly at the window and said she would not complain of the heat, that sunshine was nothing short of glorious, and that she much preferred it to the cold and damp. Frowning at the closed drapery, she made a comment about the room's upholstery already being faded and asked why they had to block out sunlight.

"Pish!" said Edward. "The moon and stars are more useful than the sun. The moon provides light at night when we *need* it. The sun only appears during the day, when we have no occasion for it."

"Blockhead," said John. "Have you learnt nothing yet at school?"

"If Edward is just wasting our money," said Isabella, waving a fan in front of her face, "we should not send him back to Merchant Taylors. Then we could all remove to Margate for the summer. Sea-bathing must be the most revivifying sensation in the world. I am dying to try it and shall surely die if I cannot."

"No bloody way!" Despite the heat of the room, John shuddered, hairs on his skin standing upright. "Egad! How could you even suggest such a thing, knowing my aversion to immersion? I get a sinking feeling in the pit of my stomach at the very thought." Ignoring his mother's admonishments to not open the curtains, he peered out onto the scorching street. "Oh, dang, if it is not that aptly named Mr. Nutter darkening our door. I believe the old coot has taken a shine to you, Mother."

Mrs. Thorpe tittered and insisted she did not welcome his advances.

"He would take care of you in your dotage."

"I had thought *you* would see to me then, John."

"Lord, Mother, I *would* … had I a wife to do it!"

Isabella leapt to her feet. "I will not stay here while that bald, speckled codger makes sheep eyes at our mother. Take me out in the gig, John."

"I shall be delighted—as loath as I am to be seen about Town in that damned, decrepit, old buggy of Father's. I shall have our man Jenkins add a splash of paint to the sides, but that will do little to brighten the plodding gait of the nag attached to it. We shall just have to make do until I purchase a finer curricle."

"We do not even *have* a curricle now," said William, carving a curiosity from wood and letting shavings fall to the floor. "A curricle is pulled by two horses. Ours is a one-horse gig."

"Well, little brother," said John, "if you are so smart, then why in bloody hell are you joining the navy? You will be out there, surrounded by water! Your frigate might sink," said he with another shudder. "Then where would you be?"

"Hopefully, unlike you," muttered Isabella, "he would be able to keep his head above water."

"Oh, my darling William," said his mother, "I wish you were not going to sea. I shall worry endlessly. If only you could be awarded a fellowship like your eldest brother was." Giving John a pat on the back, she crowed about what a learned young man he was becoming.

"Do not be so damned daft, Mother!" John scoffed. "One does not attend university to *learn*! One goes there to make important connections—friends and patrons to help him along later in life."

"And have you made many such friends, son?"

"Of course, I bloody well have! I can name dozens—nay, scores!—of fellows."

WITH ISABELLA, the one closest to him in age and character, John was always more forthright. Many weeks later, in the dressing room that served as sitting area for all three girls, he sought his eldest sister. Poking his head around the door, he asked, "Am I disturbing?" He then walked in without invitation.

Offering a deep sigh, Isabella tossed aside the Gothic novel she had been reading. "Yes, John. You are always disturbing, offensive, and oafish. You quite plague me to death."

"Saucy chit! You tease like my university friends; but, of course, none of you actually mean anything by it." John flumped beside her on the settee. "What is that damned smell? Perfume? By God, it smells like a bloody brothel in here." The room's overpowering bouquet had aroused a memory of his one and only experience in such an establishment.

"What is a brothel?" asked Maria, tucked away, unseen, in the window seat.

"Oho, little dandiprat!" cried John, jumping up and turning red. "I did not notice you there. I ... I was just saying the room smelled like ... like, um ... broth!" Sitting, he crossed an ankle over his knee and bobbed his foot. "I ... I am a bit peckish, I suppose." Looking anywhere but at his youngest sister, he whistled tunelessly through his teeth. "So, do you suppose there will be soup with supper?"

Maria flung her book on the cushion and, folding her arms, stood in front of her elder brother and sister. "You said *brothel*. I have heard the word before but know not what it means nor why it should smell like the rosewater I spilt earlier. And why would broth smell like perfume?"

"Go away, brat," said John, tugging his cravat. "I need to"—*check hidden corners, watch my language, and forget an embarrassingly brief episode in a bawdy house in which things went off prematurely*—"speak privately with Isabella."

Maria stuck out her tongue and, with a toss of her head, left the room.

"It is a good thing Mother did not witness that," said Isabella. "She would have boxed your ears."

"Look here, I know I am not particularly erudite but neither am I dull nor ignorant. Why must Mother always exaggerate my achievements? And—damn it!—why can I never come out ahead? The other blockheads are scheming cheaters, the stinking lot of them! There can be no other explanation."

Making room for her brother's stout, sprawling form, Isabella shifted uncomfortably against the bench's wooden arm. "What have they done now?"

"After losing at hazard and thinking to step up my game, I wagered someone I could best him in a stair-climbing race. But, being rather short-shanked and frightfully gin-soaked at the time, I fell neck and crop and came out second best again. I suspect the long-legged stinker tripped me." Springing up to pace around the cramped, cluttered room, John examined its delicate knickknackery, dropping only one out of ten figurines.

"John, you oaf! That squirrel is Anne's favourite piece."

"*Was* her favourite," John grumbled, kicking at the shattered remains of a porcelain, bushy-tailed rodent. "Fine! I will replace it … if you will grant me a loan." Stopping in front of the settee, he dragged palms down his face. "I am short on blunt and in debt to more than a few fellows. Will you help me, Bella?"

"We are *English*, not Italian!" Isabella flounced past him. "If you must shorten my name, call me"—primping at the mirror, she rearranged a few curls—"call me Belle. It has an amazingly exotic ring to it, do you not think?"

"I suppose Belle *does* have a certain ring, but—pish!—never mind your nonsense. I am in a monstrous spot and was hoping you would see me clear of it."

"Lord help you, brother, for I cannot." Turning back to the mirror, Isabella spoke through gritted teeth. "Ask one of your friends for assistance."

"Ha! Not bloody likely! What a stupid head you have." He walked to the window and fidgeted with its pulley. "Those skinflints are quick to single me out for a bit of gaming, yet they must know I can ill afford it. Even Peregrine Bathos and James Morland have turned down my entreaties for a loan, and Morland is *such* a devilish good friend that I am thinking of inviting him here for a visit. It might be a bit embarrassing, though." John eyed the peeling paint and threadbare drapery. "I believe he comes from a wealthy family." Hands balling into fists, he barked an ugly laugh. "They have it all—every bloody advantage, all presented to them on silver plate! How can I possibly hold up against those privileged fops with their innate elegance and ease?"

Hands clasped together beneath her chin, Isabella informed him that, of all things in the entire world, it would be the most wonderful.

"Eh? What would?" he blustered.

Something like a sigh escaped as she answered. "To be held up against a fit, wealthy gentleman."

"This has nothing to do with *you* and your ungodly desires. Here I am mired—nay, *drowning*—in debt, yet you dare make light of my plight." John affected a pitiful mien. "Truth is, I really am in dun territory. You have no idea what it is like to be surrounded by temptation all the time!" Head bowed, he sat upon the vacated seat, his sunken, beseeching eyes meeting hers in the mirror. "These are dark, dark days, Belle." With wry amusement, he added, "I can scarcely afford a candle."

"Well, do not think to prevail upon *me* for any part of *my* allowance. Such fixed amount hardly meets my own basic needs." The perfect picture of petulance, with the back of one hand against her brow, Isabella proclaimed she was thrown into the acutest agonies because of it. "So, *you*, brother dear, will just have to become more temperate in your habits."

"Deny myself every common indulgence?" John stamped around the room. "I bloody well think not! Lawks! Such a deuced existence sounds as much fun as plucking nose hairs."

She called him an odious, crude man and then asked of what indulgences he spoke. To which he replied sheepishly that, other than field sports and horses, his particular pleasures were gaming and drink and women.

"One of those is considered immoral, is it not?" Isabella held up a variety of ribbons, testing them against her complexion. "We, as a family, must give the appearance, at least, of respectability." Gasping at her reflection, she rubbed her brow. "See what you have done! You have put me quite out of countenance, and frown lines on a lady are wretchedly unbecoming."

"You put them there yourself, silly goose, with that sulky expression you have perfected. And how little you know of the world. In placing a few wagers, I am no worse than a man who is no bettor. And, sister dear, you need not worry about a few insignificant, little wrinkles marring your appearance."

She turned to him with a brilliant smile which faded into a pout upon being told her face was already hideous. "John Aubrey Thorpe! You are the beastliest brother ever!"

"Beastly?" He laughed while dodging a poorly aimed cushion. "Well, I do own the *lion*'s share of brains and bravery in this family of younger brothers and squeamish females."

"Speaking of beasts, why not try your hand at a racecourse?" asked Isabella with no lingering concern over the immorality of gaming. "One could make a small fortune on horses, right?"

"'Tis possible, I suppose." Fingers drumming on the seat, John muttered, "*If* one starts out with a rather *large* fortune to whittle down to a *small* one." Sweat broke on his brow, and he reached for a handkerchief. "Honestly, you are such a simpleton at times."

"Well, I am astute enough to know that, before you end up wagering *all* our money away, you must marry exceedingly well. We all must. 'Tis the only way, at least until you come into Uncle Graham's bequeathal."

"Our eccentric, liberal-minded relation is taking his good old time in passing … and in passing along my inheritance. Now, now," said John, holding up a hand, "before you call me beastly again, or worse, all I mean is that the old coot is racked with pain. His passing would be a mercy."

"And an amazingly blessed thing for us. But, until then, you really must find an heiress to woo. And I, with utterly beguiling charm, shall have a wealthy suitor fall head and ears in love with me." Abandoning the mirror and while contemplating her seated brother, Isabella tapped a forefinger against her cheek. "I suppose, with enough time and much effort, I could teach *you* to be charming."

"Oh, no! No, no, no! There is no damned way I am going to smile and flirt and flutter my lashes. Next, you would have me loosening my cravat and collar and bending forward so low that one could see all the way down to m–"

She clouted him.

"Lawks! What was that for? I *have* witnessed you in action, you know." Taking her place at the mirror, John squared his shoulders then ran fingers through his forelock. "This marrying scheme of yours, I concede, is a famous good notion. But I hardly need a girl's missish advice on courting." Pleased with his reflection, he faced Isabella. "Oxford ladies eye me with devilish interest, let me tell you!"

A handful of Oxford denizens *had* shown mild interest in John Thorpe, and one or two of those were, indeed, female. Such interest, however, was rarely the appreciative or sympathetic sort. People in Oxford were no different than people in, say, Hertfordshire. They still made sport for their neighbours and laughed at them in turn.

In early November, walking beside Peregrine Bathos and behind two fashionable ladies, one of whom was carrying a pug, John spoke within earshot of the women.

"What say you, Bathos? There go a fine pair, I am certain."

Turning, the lady with the small dog looked for a moment at the two men. After catching John's eyes, she resumed walking. Then, over her shoulder, she said, "I regret the compliment cannot be returned, sir."

"It could be," John spoke to her back. "You could tell a lie, madam. As did I."

The lady set the pug upon the ground and, with one word, incited an attack. John stepped hastily backwards but, being more awkward than nimble, fell upon his bottom. Sharp teeth sank into his booted ankle and then into a meatier section above the leather and would not be shaken free, not even by oaths directed at the male dog concerning its relation to its mother.

Having recalled the little beast, its mistress snatched it up into her arms. "My poor, little Crinkles," she cooed, "I hope you have not been made ill by that repugnant man."

The next day, at the Kings Arms, a coaching inn on the corner of Parks Road and Holywell Street, John silently read a letter in company with James Morland and Peregrine Bathos. Then, stashing the letter in a breast pocket, he said, "Well, Morland, I daresay we have found a remedy for, at least, *your* bachelor aches."

"What, pray tell," said Bathos, "might be such a cure?"

John grinned. "Carry to the patient seven or eight yards of silk ... with my sister in it!" When the laughter died down, he explained to Bathos that Isabella, having met James Morland on several occasions, had set her cap at him. "Mark my words, following a Yuletide visit with my family, our blushing friend here will be caught in the parson's mousetrap." Shivering from a blast of damp, cold air as the door opened, he rubbed his hands together. "What say we place a wager?"

Morland held up a hand. "Hold on, Thorpe. Your sister is lovely. But marrying *her* would mean calling *you* brother. I do not think I am quite ready for *that* yet!"

LATER THAT NIGHT, squinting in the meagre light of a candle stub, John finished a letter to Isabella.

> *… beg you not to mention my debt problems to Mother. I could not bear to break her heart. I would rather make her genuinely proud of me; but I have not a great thirst for knowledge, only for ale and for fast curricles and women. Enough of my woes, though. How fares Uncle Graham? It saddens me he yet lingers. What I mean is, I hate to think of him suffering so. Might laudanum ease the poor man's pain? I know I should like to drown my sorrows in a bottle or two, or ten, of claret; but I must practice frugality and swill ale. Is there any chance you might consider a loan to your poor, suffering brother? John*

Her response arrived without delay.

> *Dear John,*
> *I trust this letter finds you in better spirits; but, no, I cannot spare a loan just so you may drink wine instead of ale. It may, however, gladden you to know I have not mentioned your woes to Mother. Her heart remains unbroken; and, although you did not ask, everyone else is well… except, of course, Uncle Graham. The poor soul is much the same, as I understand it from others. I have, you know, a delicate constitution and not the fortitude to visit a sickroom. I pray his suffering, along with ours, may soon end. Now, never mind about making Mother proud at present. You and I shall do so when we both secure wealthy matches. I am well on the way to wedded bliss, and my advice to you is to follow my lead. James Morland has sisters, does he not? Are any of them out? What of the local ladies? Have any of them caught your eye?*
> *Isabella*

At Oxford, he bragged long and loud about his success with the ladies, but John's clever college acquaintances believed not a word of his lies. They taunted him about a botched attempt—involving an open window and a faulty ladder—to sneak the proctor's daughter into his room.

Then there was the dismal failure with a town trollop John had tried to take to Beaumont Palace in a borrowed gig. "Have you ever been upset?" he asked her. When she indicated she had not and would not like to be, he laughed. "Then you have led a dull life, indeed!" Smacking his whip, he encouraged his horse with odd noises and intentionally drove the gig up a steep bank at full tilt and then, unintentionally, down into a ditch—whence a wheel fell off, and so did the trollop. Upset, indeed, she refused to go any farther with him.

A more advantageous opportunity arose at the home of Mrs. North, wife of a successful dealer in foreign spirituous liquors. John was sat at a card table and engaged in a game of piquet with a Mrs. Waters, whose husband, he learned, was away in London on business. To John's dismay, the well-favoured woman played, what was to him, rather high; and, to his disgust, she praised William Cowper's poetry, of which her knowledge was far superior to his.

"... and, oh, Cowper's hymns! Why, they induce nothing short of rapture, do you not agree?"

Horses, guns, and field sports, to his way of thinking, were vastly superior to polite exchanges of words in drawing rooms, to any written words, or words sung as hymns. But Mrs. Waters was a tempting beauty, and he was smitten by lush lips every time she spoke and by swelling embonpoint every time she took a deep breath. John had no choice but to impress her with a less than honest answer. "By Jove, yes! Cowper's verses quite carry me away!"

"'Tis unfortunate, then," said she, raising an eyebrow and speaking with deliberation, "that the Norths do not have a volume of Cowper here in their house."

"Eh?" John squished his eyebrows together, scratched his temple, then shrugged. "Well, other than its lack of rapturous poetry, this is a deuced fine house! 'Tis almost as grand as the Bathos residence. The elder son, you see, is a damned good friend of mine from St. John's College. His father has a spanking pair of matched greys and the fastest curricle I have ever ..."

All the rest of his talk began and ended with himself and his own concerns. Mrs. Waters was doomed to the details of his day's sport, his boast of a horse he had bought for a trifle and sold for an incredible sum, his doubts about his friends' hunting qualifications, and of racing matches in which his judgment had infallibly foretold the winner.

By no small account irritated with John and his endless prattle, the lady wagered poorly, allowed her opponent a huge advantage, and lost. Begrudgingly, Mrs. Waters wrote a note acknowledging her debt of twenty guineas and, in a fit of pique, said, "I hope, sir, that if ever you come within a mile of *my* fine house that you will stay there all night!"

John gaped, reeling at her provocative invitation, until she left the table with a toss of her head, a whiff of perfume, and a silky susurration of skirts.

Rushing off to crow of his fortunate circumstance, John found Peregrine Bathos and James Morland at the Kings Arms supping on mussels, chicken, and a ragout of celery.

"Thorpe," cried Morland, beckoning him over, "have you already eaten?"

"I have, upon my honour," John replied, joining his friends at their table and ordering a pint.

"Well, Thorpe," said Bathos with a smirk, "if you have dined upon your honour, I fear you have had an insufficient meal"—to which Morland laughed heartily.

"Eh?" John looked oddly at his friends, shrugged, then took a gulp of ale. Leaning in towards them, he crowed, "I have damned good news!" Rubbing palms together, he, in a rare occurrence, lowered his voice. "I will finally achieve my pursuit of both carnal knowledge and capital gain!"

After recounting his conversation with Mrs. Waters, John slurped the last of his ale, wiped his mouth on his sleeve, then slammed the mug on the table. "The coquette plans on settling her debt by granting me, proud holder of the vowels, her favours!"

Morland scoffed. "As a married woman, *she* will not succumb. And *you* will not succeed."

"Right," said Bathos. "Mrs. Waters would never sink so low. The woman was not inviting your advances, buffoon! She does not even want you within a *mile* of her house."

"Damn it to hell!" John banged his fist on the table and forgot to lower his voice. "I bet you ten guineas I can bed Mrs. Waters." Men at neighbouring tables turned his way, bystanders stopped talking to listen, while a servant toting a tray of empty mugs feigned indifference.

The cleric's son, not a bettor, declined the wager and protested his friend's loudness and language.

"I beg your pardon, Morland," said John in an unrepentant tone. "Allow me to reword that for your missish sake. Dang it to the abode of evil spirits! I wager ten guineas I can seduce Mrs. Waters." Gaining confidence, he added, "Or, if not her, another married woman, before the commencement of Hilary term."

Morland shook his head and took his leave while Bathos shook John's hand across the table.

Calling for pen and paper, John scribbled a note to Mrs. Waters demanding either immediate payment of the IOU or, in lieu, receipt of her favours as agreed. "Robin, my good man," said he, beckoning the nearby servant and holding out the letter and a coin. "Deliver this, as soon as you are able, to the Waters residence on High Street."

Having no fondness for the loud, overbearing John Thorpe and having eavesdropped on his scheme, Robin—upon arrival at his destination the next morning—insisted the butler hand the letter over to none other than the master of the house.

Two days later, upon awakening, John opened a note that had been slid under his door during the night. While gloating over its contents, savouring its perfume, and admiring the feminine hand, he was summoned to meet with the proprietor of the Kings Arms. Curious but not overly concerned—though he did expect a reckoning of his account—John arrived in the common room and glanced around at its occupants until noticing Mr. Philpott standing with an unknown, middle-aged gentleman.

"Mr. Thorpe," said the innkeeper, beckoning him, "this here is Mr. Wat–" Upon receipt of a black look and an "ahem!" from the smartly-dressed gent, Mr. Philpott stammered, "Er, I mean, Mr. *River*, has begged an introduction."

Mr. River gave a slight bow and a nod, then sized up the younger man.

Wiping it first on his coat, John extended his hand. "How d'ye do, sir."

The proprietor left them to their pleasantries as Mr. River gestured John towards a table. "Would you join me in a drink, Mr. Thorpe?"

"Do you suppose we will both fit?" said John, following the stranger.

"I beg your pardon?"

"In the drink." John pointed at two glasses of port that Robin, sporting a huge grin, was placing on the table. "I made a jest, sir, about joining you in a drink."

"I see," said the unsmiling gentleman. "Well, Mr. Thorpe, I was hoping to have a serious conversation with you. In fact, I came here seeking assistance. I understand you are acquainted with the lovely"—the gentleman heaved a sigh and closed his eyes—"Mrs. Waters."

Eyes wide, John bolted out of his seat, taking note of all possible exits. "Who?"

"Calm yourself, young man. *I* should be the nervous one here, for I am about to impart a serious immoral failing." River leant across the table and admitted he was in love with another man's wife.

John's eyes bulged as he gulped down the wine and listened to River's dilemma.

"I have tried working on her, but she remains steadfastly faithful to her husband. Where I have failed, I hope another might succeed. You—stout, young man that you are—have a decided advantage over me." Although he had hardly touched his own, the older man ordered more port. "I have a proposition, Mr. Thorpe." Leaning across the table, he lowered his silky voice. "I will pay you twenty guineas to seduce Mrs. Waters."

John's mouth twitched once or twice in an attempt at speech. Heart thumping and throat dry, he drank from his second glass of wine, hoping such occupation would keep his mouth from burgeoning into a huge grin. "I am listening," he managed to say with a straight face.

"Once Mrs. Waters has sampled forbidden fruit—namely, *you*—her honour will be forfeit. Then it will be *my* turn to woo the woman away from her marriage vows." River sat back and finally took a sip of port.

"It is a famous good scheme. But what you ask, sir, goes against my morals. Upon my soul, as temping as your offer is, I could not commit such a sin for a mere twenty guineas."

"Thirty."

Heart ready to leap straight out of his chest, John shook his head.

River slid a pouch across the space between them. "Forty guineas." Extending his hand, the deal was sealed.

"I understand," said John after draining his glass, "that Mr. Waters will be staying in London again tomorrow. His wife and I have already arranged an assignation." He bounced his knee under the table, barely able to conceal his excitement. "How will you know whether or not I succeed?"

"Oh, I have my ways," said the silky voice.

A shiver went down John's spine. Whether it was a frisson of thrill or fear, he could not say.

As the sun set on the next day, John ordered a bath, an occurrence that might not seem noteworthy to those unfamiliar with him. "But the tub must contain no more water than this," said he to the servant, holding apart his thumb and forefinger by just above three inches. "And it will be comfortably warm, not tepid. The soap must be the mild sort, no lye."

Having spared only enough time to soap and rinse himself, John called for Wignall—the valet he shared with James Morland—to help him dress. Humming a tune and jostling coins in his hand, he then hailed a hackney coach and directed the driver to an address on High Street.

Upon arrival, he fished in his breast pocket and handed a battered calling card to the butler who, after scrutinising the name and address thereon, escorted John into a stylish yet comfortable parlour and announced his presence. On the lady of the house John bestowed a "Hey-day, Mrs. Waters!" and a whole scrape and a half. For his efforts, he was greeted civilly if not warmly. Devoirs speedily paid, the two sat in awkward silence broken only by the ticking and chiming of a mantle clock. Refreshments were ordered and then partaken of with no equanimity and little conversation. John, equal parts nervousness and enthusiasm, glanced around the room and started upon noticing a maid sitting in the corner, glaring at him.

"Mr. Thorpe," said Mrs. Waters, making him jump, "perhaps we should repair to my private sitting room. I believe we have a piece of business to conduct."

John smoothed down his hair but could do little about the blush spreading across his cheeks and the sweat breaking out beneath his collar. "Yes! Yes!" He spoke with earnest fervour that in no way matched the woman's ennui. "This business should be conducted sooner rather than later."

Giddy from the thought of what was to come, he followed Mrs. Waters out of the room and up the stairs, paying more particular attention to what was at eye level before him than what was underfoot. Stumbling on a wrinkle in the carpeting, John pitched forward and latched onto the first purchase he could find—the delicate muslin of the woman's skirts which rent with, what was to him, an ear-splitting sound.

"Patience, sir!" said she, turning round to confront him and examine the damage. "Oh! Look what you have done, you clumsy oaf! My favourite muslin! Ruined!"

That, madam, will soon be the state of more than just your dress. "I am sorry." *Damn it, but she seems miffed!* "Truly, I am exceedingly sorry I have ruined it." *And, perhaps, a chance at winning your favours and a ten-guinea wager.*

Muttering beneath her breath, Mrs. Waters, with John trotting after her, flounced down the passage and into a decidedly feminine sitting room.

Desperate to make amends, he said, "Could the fabric not be saved and fashioned into a handkerchief, a frilly cap, or whatnot? It is not my custom to bother my brains with what does not concern me; and I do not usually give a fig for a damned bit of muslin, but in your case—"

"What? *What* did you call me?" Eyes flashing, Mrs. Waters hissed. "Did you just refer to me as a 'bit of muslin'?"

"What? A bit of mus– No!" *Dang! Farewell, extraordinary source of pleasure as well as ten guineas. And I had better spend River's forty before he can reclai—*

"Mistress! Mistress!" The maid they had left in the parlour burst into the room. "'Tis your husband," she wailed, wringing her hands. "'Tis just as we planned, except … not. Now it *really* is him! His carriage just stopped at the kerb!"

"What?" cried both John and Mrs. Waters together.

Frantic, John bolted to a window, judging how far he had to fall.

"No, you might break your neck," said Mrs. Waters, tugging at John's sleeve. Then she released it and shoved him forward. "Yes, yes, by all means, the window!"

"No! I might break my neck!" Eyes wild, John dashed into the passage and made for the staircase with Mrs. Waters and the maid on his heels.

"No!" cried the maid, holding him back, "you cannot use the front door! Mr. Waters will enter that way."

"And," said Mrs. Waters, "because his valet will use the back door, *you* cannot." She paced up and down the passage, biting at a fingernail, and pausing now and then to frantically peer over the railing to the front entry. "Down the servants' stairwell. You will be able to sneak out of either the kitchen or scullery that way."

John, willing to go anywhere, do anything, to escape an angry husband, ran after the women as they descended flights of dimly-lit stairs. The smell hit him before the last three steps.

But it was not the mélange of vegetable peelings, fish offal, and plucked, trussed poultry that repulsed him, nor was it the overpowering stench of lye coming from a copper cauldron filled with boiling water and soaking linens. What caused John's sick, sinking feeling was heavy footsteps on the tile floor and an oddly familiar voice calling out, "Where is that adulteress of a wife, and where is her lover?"

"Mr. Thorpe, you must hide! My husband is now in the kitchen, and two footmen are guarding the scullery door." Mrs. Waters then whispered to the maid while pointing to a corner. "Proceed from here as planned. Our scheme may yet succeed!"

Grabbing the confused young man by his sleeve, the maid yanked him towards a large basket. "Quickly, sir! Hide amongst this pile of washing."

"What? No! It seems to be servants' soiled clothes, and—" At the sound of approaching footsteps and an angry male voice, John dove into the basket, burrowing into its evil smell. Gagging while the maid arranged heaps of filthy, reeking garments around him, John's attack of fear added to the existing stench of sweat and other bodily functions.

His was a difficult choice—whether to inhale putridity or suffer suffocation. John could not help but gasp, though, when he heard Mrs. Waters speak to the two footmen guarding the scullery door.

"Quickly, now!" she ordered. "Carry that basket to the—"

Although his hearing was muffled by layers of stinking cloth, and although his hiding place was being toted away—someplace safer, John prayed—he could still discern that angry voice, the one he swore he could almost recognise.

"There you are, unfaithful wife! And where is your young swain? When I get my hands on Thorpe, I shall have his guts for garters! Then I will—"

Along with the basket he had been in, and various articles of reeking fabric, John floated through the night air. Then came laughter, followed by a tremendous splash. *Splash?*

Then all was frigidness, panic, and an instinct to not breathe as he sank below the surface of the river. *Bloody hell! So, this is drowning. What rotten luck! My greatest fear will also mean my demise.* Darkness began closing in on him from all sides. *Wait! I cannot die now!* John flailed his arms and kicked his legs. *I have forty guineas to spend and a damned fine curricle to procure!*

He emerged—splashing, spluttering, and gulping lungsful of air—with a lace-trimmed chemise draped, like a matron's mob cap, over his head and a crayfish attached to the fall of his breeches.

The damned seduction did not succeed! The money River gave me is now forfeit. Well, hell! Coughing and beset with Thames water and misery, John detached and flung both undergarment and crustacean back into the Isis and climbed the riverbank, only to be accosted by Mrs. Waters.

"For my own amusement and to avenge your indecent assumptions, I sent that note, pretending to welcome your advances." The water in John's ears did nothing to silence her sneering voice. "But I was *never* interested in your boorish prattle or in having *any* sort of further intercourse with you, other than paying off my debt *in coin*!"

Mr. Waters, whom John recognised as Mr. River, stood nearby laughing with two burly footmen. "Well, well! That proves you can lead an ass to water, but you cannot make him sink." Walking over to his wife, he kissed her fingers. "Madam, I apologise for suspecting you of making me a cuckold." In this silky voice, he whispered, "You are my untainted Rose, and I am your servant."

Wheezing, shivering, and dripping all over High Street on his long walk back to his lodgings, John arrived in the foulest of moods. He called for Wignall and another warm bath.

Morland set aside a book he had been reading to study his friend. Then, holding out a blanket, he said, "I have heard it is not unusual for ladies to reject the addresses of a man whom they secretly mean to accept, when he first applies for their favours."

"By God, Morland! If you know what is good for you, you will stop talking this instant! I am that far," said John through chattering teeth while holding thumb and forefinger together, "from planting you a facer!"

His tough skin had been somewhat puckered after a dip in the Isis and a soak in a tub; but, young, irrepressible, and of a hot character, John survived both ordeals.

Women, the sly creatures, often change their minds. Refusals may be rescinded. Everyone lies. Which reminds me. I must dash off a letter to Isabella, asking her opinion.

His sister's response was lacking in advice; but it was, at least, sincere, if one overlooked its hyperbole:

Dear John, I have one hundred things to tell you. In the first place, I am in raptures just thinking of your friend's visit the last week of Christmas holidays. The time until I again see Mr. Morland shall be nothing short of misery and infinite tedium. I know the wait will be the death of me. Speaking of one's demise—no, no, not Uncle Graham's!—Maria has

developed the worst cough in the entire world. I did not sleep a wink all night for hearing it, and today I am fatigued to death. 'Tis the most unfortunate circumstance imaginable! Yet it may be a most fortunate one as well. Our mother is talking about a trip to Bath, so that Maria may drink the water there. Is that not a famous good scheme? What do you think of it? I am wild to receive your reply.
 Isabella

John scribbled a terse reply which was received with even less warmth than it was written.

Isabella,
 A trip to Bath? No bloody way! Mother must cease her half-witted talk! Such expense should not even be considered let alone undertaken! Has she gone damned daft? Have you? I suspect you females are all barmy enough for Bedlam.
 John
 P.S. Dearest sister, might you consider a loan in the form of a bank draught? Your allowance, or any part thereof, would be greatly appreciated.

Desperate to win the wager with Bathos and having decided upon Mrs. Field as the next recipient of his mental and physical itches, John sent the lady a series of *billets-doux* copied from a book. The woman was a cheerful sort and handsome enough to tempt him, although John had once mentioned to Morland that he suspected she had thick ankles.

After two days of unanswered love letters and one all-night party in an acquaintance's rooms—in which, upon average, five pints a head of famous good wine were cleared—a note was slipped under John's door while he slept off his share.

At the next gloaming, John arrived at the home of Mrs. Field, who greeted him and led him on until they were upstairs, behind closed doors. While he stood there in the bedchamber, wondering how to proceed, the door opened with a bang.

Bursting into the room in a theatrical manner, wringing her hands and sobbing, a dry-eyed maid wailed, "'Tis your husband, madam! Alas! ... and ... Fie! He has returned home!" Flinging a forearm across her brow, she spoke as if by rote. "Oh, Mrs. Field, whatever shall we do?" She winked at her mistress before slumping to the floor. Then, tugging at her skirts to ensure her legs were covered, the maid succumbed to a swoon.

John had a sinking feeling that history was about to repeat itself.

Flinging her arms in the air, Mrs. Field rolled her eyes. Bending down, she hissed at the servant. "Stop being excessively dramatic!" Turning to John, she wailed, "'Tis my husband, sir! He has returned home!" Wringing her hands, she added, "Alas! Whatever shall we do?"

Before John could form any thought at all, a well-dressed man made a dramatic entrance. "Aha!" Taking a wide-legged stance, he flung out an arm and pointed at John. "I have caught you! You, you … blackguard!"

Crinkles, the pug, trotted in and attached its teeth to John's stockinged calf while Mr. Field landed a blow on John's chin. The fist did not make contact again, but the canines would not let go— not even when its master, then grappling with John, marched him into the passage, down the stairs, out the back door, across the lawn, and tossed him into the Isis.

As man and dog sailed through the air, the painful grip on John's leg lessened. Then came two splashes—one small and one not—followed by iciness and fear. John held his breath until, sooner than expected, his bottom hit bottom. Then, something brushed against him, and he stifled an urge to scream bloody murder. *Oh God! Oh God! Oh God, what was that? Oh. Huh. 'Tis probably dear little Crinkles moving towards the surface. Clever beast!* John kicked off from bottom and immediately emerged into the blessed night air after sitting in less than five feet of water.

Spluttering and swearing, he hauled his sodden body up the riverbank, hardly acknowledging the pain as Crinkles, breathing noisily through its nose, reattached itself to his calf. Upon being summoned by its mistress, the pug let go and trotted away, snuffling and shaking off water droplets.

"My dear," said Mrs. Field, snuggling into her husband's arm, "thank you for participating in our little ruse. I must visit dear Rose on the morrow and tell her how well it all went."

"When you do, be sure to pass along my regards and my thanks to our friend and to Luke Waters." Flexing the fingers of his right hand, he smiled down at his wife. "You are a sly creature, my sweet Matilda. I must remember to never turn that devious mind of yours against me."

As the couple moved towards the house, Mrs. Field spoke in an overloud voice. "Husband, do you know why most men are like gooseberries?"

"I hesitate to ask, but I suppose you will not be satisfied until you tell me."

Before they walked out of earshot, John heard Mrs. Field giggle. "Because any woman can make a *fool* of them."

Gritting his teeth did not work. They were too busy chattering. *'Tis a damned sure thing that I shall never, ever, eat gooseberry fool again!* Head bowed and arms folded around himself, John heaved a weary "heigh-ho" and shivered and sloshed in his shoes all the way back to his lodgings. There he found James Morland reading by candlelight. In an absolute miff, he slammed the door and summoned Wignall and yet another warm bath.

Morland set aside his book to study his sopping, sneezing friend. "What, *again?*"

"If you know what is good for you," said John, "you will bury your bloody nose in that blasted book and pay me no mind at all." Sniffing while the valet struggled to peel away his wet coat, John said, "Good God, Wignall, do you smell *fish?*"

"Yes," said Wignall, wrinkling his nose. "Now that you mention it, sir."

"Well, hurry the hell up! I intend to soon drink myself into a stupendous stupor so I can bloody well forget this damned night ever existed. Quickly, now! Restore me to my usual fastidious standards."

"I beg your pardon, Thorpe," said Morland with a chuckle, as the valet hurried away with the wet coat. "Did you say *fastidious*, or *fast and hideous?*"

"*This* close, Morland!" said John, snivelling and pressing thumb and forefinger together. "I am *this* close to planting you a face–"

An ungodly squeal erupted from the tiny dressing room seconds before Wignall flew into the room, holding his nostrils with one hand and a dead trout in the other.

Hours later at their favourite table at the Kings Arms, John continued his grievance to Bathos. "The Fields treated me like dirt! Tossed away I was, like so much rubbish." Upon ordering three pints and having them delivered and lined up in front of him, he downed the first without pausing. "And now," he sniffed, "I have the worst cold ever imagined."

"That," said Bathos, tucking into a plate of trout which smelled a bit off, "reminds me of the time I snuck into and was ejected from Almack's. But I should not complain. The patronesses treated me decently."

"They did?"

Bathos nodded. "They had me thrown out the back door. But when I explained that I came from a very good family, they had me picked up, brushed off, and escorted back into the assembly room. Then I was thrown out the *front* door."

After a series of sneezes, John asked what business Bathos had at Almacks's in the first place.

"What do you *suppose* I was doing at the reputed Marriage Mart?"

"You will have to tell me. When I have a cold," said John, swiping at his nose, "I become remarkably dull and stupid."

"Gadzooks, Thorpe!" Bathos saluted him with his mug of ale. "You are much to be pitied, then. I suspect I have never seen you *without* a cold."

A string of choice words was flung at his friend's head with John stopping only to blow his nose and then say, "I *suppose* you were at Almack's in pursuit of a woman."

Bathos described the baronet's daughter he had fallen for. "I proposed to the girl and would have married her, if not for something she said." At John's inquiring look, he grinned. "She said, 'No!'"

"Women," John grumbled. "Why must they act so damned coy and uninterested?"

"You know, Thorpe, 'tis not only to *my* benefit those wives you tried to seduce could not be got. It is also an advantage for *you*."

"Eh? I bloody well understand *your* benefit. You would end up winning the damned wager. But how can it be to *my* advantage to not succeed in bedding someone's wife?"

"If successful, you actually could lose everything; and I *do* mean *everything*. Have you never heard of Crim-Con trials? My father, you may remember, is a renowned barrister. Such cases are nothing but nasty, salacious, costly scandals."

The debacles with Mrs. Waters and Mrs. Field had created no scandals and hardly raised any eyebrows. John himself, however, was appalled. *Mrs. Waters still owes me twenty guineas. Damnation! I owe her horrid husband the forty guineas "River" gave me. And I have yet to win my stupid, ten guinea wager with Bathos!*

The next day made a bad situation worse.

"Mr. Thorpe."

At the silky utterance, a tingling sensation crept up John's neck. Reining his horse to a halt on the towpath along the Isis, he turned the animal and faced Mr. Waters. Tipping his hat and gritting his teeth, he silently waited in the drizzle for the gentleman to speak.

"That is a decent animal you have there." Waters walked around John's horse, assaying its merit. "What do you suppose to be its worth?"

"My horse?" John petted its neck while speaking in a strained voice. "Corporal Nym is a true blood. Made for speed. I defy any man in England to make my horse go less than ten miles an hour in harness." *And it can certainly outrun a man on foot along this accursed river!* About to urge his mount into a galloping escape, the option was snatched away as swiftly as was his horse's rein.

"High praise, indeed," said Waters, holding fast to the leather strap. "And his worth?"

"His worth?" John narrowed his eyes while doing quick calculations. "Why, I would not sell Corporal Nym for less than a hundred!"

Waters laughed with a great deal of scorn. "A hundred! You are a greedy man, Mr. Thorpe! You already have my forty. What say you to ten?"

"Ten? Ten! Good Lord! Your wife owes me twenty!"

Clenched jaw evident, Waters warned John to never again mention his wife. "Very well, then." With his free hand, he reached into a breast pocket and counted out twenty guineas into John's palm. "Now, Mr. Thorpe, dismount, if you please."

A cold, driving rain began just as Waters rode Corporal Nym out of sight. Tempted to spend some of his new coin on hackney coach fare, John instead pocketed the money and trudged onward.

Morland, about to enter the Kings Arms, spotted his bedraggled friend rounding the corner. Clapping a hand on one of John's slumped, sodden shoulders, he said, "Come, man. I will buy you a bottle of claret. You look as though you need it."

Chin to chest, John shuffled along behind. "What the devil was I thinking, Morland? I have lost much, including, obviously, my mind." With a snarl, he shooed away a stranger who had dared take a seat at their customary table. Elbows on the wooden planks and head in his hands, he muttered, "Do you happen to know how long a man can live without brains?"

"No," said his laughing friend. "I am afraid I am not privy to such knowledge. By the bye, what *is* your age, Thorpe?" Sobering at John's sneer, Morland poured and passed him another glass of claret. "Here. Now, let me ask you this relevant question. What four qualifications enable a sheep to join the Jockey Club?"

"What?" scoffed John. "I have just lost my horse and am swimming in debt. How is such an elite club relevant?"

"Indulge me."

At Morland's smug expression, John heaved a sigh. "I have never been to that establishment, my friend; and the way I am going, I never shall become a member." Leaning back in his chair, John stretched out his legs and folded his arms. "Go on, then. Amuse me."

"Both sheep and Jockey Club members are bred on the turf, *gambol in their youth*, associate with blacklegs, and are *fleeced* at last."

The quip did little to improve John's humour, and he reconsidered inviting Morland to spend the last week of the Christmas holidays with him, his mother, and his sisters.

The visit, however, took place as scheduled and did much to vanquish any hard feelings on John's part and to recommend, in fact, that he and Morland become brothers in the future.

During the festive occasion in Holborn, the Thorpes attended an assembly in company with their friends and neighbours, one of whom was a Miss Eveline Andrews.

Upon arrival, Isabella—whom Miss Andrews considered a particular friend and staunch supporter—paid the girl no mind other than a quick peck on the cheek, faint praise for her puce coloured sarsenet, and an introduction to James Morland, followed by fulsome compliments for said gentleman.

Already in his cups and merrier than a grig, John noticed the poor girl's dismay at being slighted and so stood beside her and expressed his goodwill. Never would he have admitted such to himself, let alone to others, but, early on, he had formed a bit of tender regard for his sister's sweet-natured friend and often felt sorry for her. Although Miss Andrews was a fan of those horrid, Gothic novels, and although no other man admired her, John thought her rather lovely.

Isabella, surrounded by a bevy of John's compeers and quite a favourite with the men, feigned vexation with them and laughingly threatened to not dance—even with James Morland or Captain Hunt!—unless they admired Miss Andrews and allowed her to be as beautiful as an angel.

"Pay her no heed," said John to Miss Andrews in a half whisper. "My sister will be hoist with her own damned petard, for she dearly loves to dance."

"Are you implying, Mr. Thorpe, that no man in Isabella's fawning coterie will compare me to a divine being?"

"Oh, damn it! I see now how that might have sounded. May I make amends somehow? Shall I fetch us some tipple?"

Upon Miss Andrews's request, John diligently lurched through the crowd towards the refreshments table and procured a cup of tea for her and one of laced punch for himself. Slopping the former while more carefully transporting his own potent drink, he made his way across the room again, eyes peeled for one reddish-purplish-brownish dress amongst a sea of pastel muslin.

While Miss Andrews was ignored by other men, John stayed with her rather than escaping, as was his wont, to the card room. Had he been honest, he might have admitted he had gone there before fetching their drinks. No one had invited him to join their game except Mr. Nutter, and it was then he had decided to return to the young lady's side.

As she sipped tea, he provided scintillating, drunken conversation about the excellence of his new riding whip and the superiority of his skill in brandishing it.

"I see," said Miss Andrews. "So that is how one gets a horse to dance to one's tune, is it? But how, sir, does one go about making a person do the same?"

"Eh?"

"What if a lady wishes a man to prance or cavort?"

"What?"

Miss Andrews caught John's eye, then turned hers deliberately towards the two lines of dancers.

"Oh, damn," he mumbled. "Miss Andrews, I suppose you and I ought to dance."

And they did, with John stepping as gracefully as a one-legged fish.

Isabella, more than once, had referred to Miss Andrews as amazingly insipid; but, having danced two sets with her, John found nothing wanting in her willingness to listen to an account of the spanking curricle he had his eye upon, the damned fine brace of pheasants he had shot while Morland bagged none, and his bragging about how many cups of laced punch he could put away in one night.

Eveline would make a damned good wife were it not for her paltry dowry.

Man cannot live by bread alone. Man needs ale and beer and wine and gin and rum and …

Alas, Miss Andrews had not the marriage settlement sufficient to slake John's thirst. She was, therefore, the recipient of no offer that night other than a fond farewell, a wish for her happiness, and the bestowal of his wet, sloppy kisses upon her knuckles.

Although he had witnessed Miss Andrews stripping off her kid gloves and—somewhat profligately—tossing them into a corner, John went home thinking she was still a lovely young lady. Isabella disabused him of that notion the next morning—as well as of the fanciful idea that his sister was capable of a real friendship with other females.

THE DAY FOLLOWING their return to Oxford, John ran to join his friend at the Kings Arms. Out of breath, he skidded to a halt at Morland's table. "You will not believe it!" Gulping for air, he pointed towards the street. "I just saw poor Bathos, and I am sorry to inform you that our friend had something dreadful on his arm!"

Ashen, Morland let his spoon fall to the table. "Wh—what was it?"

"He will probably never get rid of it while he lives!" said John, shaking his head and taking a seat across from Morland. The young man next to him, tucking into a hearty meal, was acknowledged with a "How d'ye, Boyd?" John then beckoned Robin and ordered a pint and his own dish of stewed meat with vegetables.

"Thorpe, tell me quickly, man! *What* was on Bathos's arm? Was it a swelling?" Morland grimaced and pushed away his food. "A tumour?"

"No, no, nothing like that," said John, grinning. "It was—by God!—his *wife*."

Morland gaped. "What? His *wife*? Whom did he marry?"

"He wed forty thousand pounds." John blew on a spoonful of stew before admitting he quite forgot her other name.

"Pardon me, Mr. Thorpe," said Boyd, all politeness. "Please, pass the bread."

"Do you mistake me for a bloody servant?"

"No, sir," said Boyd, a fellow student at their college. "I mistook you for a gentleman. I see now my error."

With the whole aim of John's attendance at university being the making of important connections—friends and patrons to help him along later in life—his time at St. John's College had been a dismal failure. With few friends from whom he could sponge, he fell further into debt. Drinking, gaming, and having to pay for that which his compeers seemed easily able to acquire for free kept him in dun territory.

He wracked his brain for a brilliant idea to win his wager with Bathos. Time was running out; Hilary term was nearly upon him. When inspiration came, it hit him like the knuckles of his former headmaster at Merchant Taylors—knuckles the man had used to rap on John's head like a bag of marbles.

In the hopes of financial gain and sexual advancement, he turned his attention to Mrs. North, the tall and able-bodied wife of a successful dealer in foreign spirituous liquors. It was at her fine house that he had first met Mrs. Waters, but John had quite forgotten that fact.

Having sent Mrs. North several *billets-doux*, identical to the ones copied from a book and received by Mrs. Field, John awaited a reply.

"Mark my words, Morland. I chose poorly before, but Mrs. North is ripe for plucking."

"Take care, Thorpe. You are poaching in an orchard of forbidden fruit."

John raised his mug of ale. "Well, here's to the fruition of my plan." After drinking deeply and making an "ah" sound, he grinned at his friend. "And my plan involves following Mrs. North's mouldwarps into the deep valley."

"I have heard of Arctic rodents plunging into the sea during migration," Morland said. "But I am afraid to ask of what you are speaking."

"Her mouldwarps."

"Her ... Thorpe, do you mean Mrs. Field has *moles*?"

John nodded. "A whole chain of them, starting on her neck and leading downwards."

Morland laughed till he had to wipe his eyes. "Blockhead! Mouldwarp is the *other* sort of mole, the kind with small eyes and dark, velvety fur."

Averse to being laughed at, John belligerently insisted he knew that all along. "Besides, the description is still apt."

"Well, beware, my friend. Those creatures feed on worms."

Two days later, not *one* married woman was waiting for him at the North residence but *three*.

When John entered the sitting room and espied Mrs. Rose Waters,

Mrs. Matilda Field, and Mrs. Abbey North standing arm-in-arm, his eyes bulged. Then he screamed, rather aptly, like a stuck pig.

When they advanced on him, en masse, and commanded him into a reeking laundry basket in a corner of the room, he shook in his shoes; but his feet refused both the women's demand and his own order to bolt.

When Mrs. Field incited her pug to attack, he whimpered and blubbered and squeezed his eyes shut.

When Mrs. North, who towered over him, grabbed his arm and frogmarched him out the back door, across the lawn, and onto her husband's private wharf, John wanted to sink to his knees and curl into a ball, but the mighty woman held him upright.

Memories of being plunged, twice, into the river came flooding back as John was unceremoniously let go. With a count of "One-two-three!" and a joint prod from three dainty feet applied to his bottom, he was thrust into that part of the Thames that flowed past the North residence.

Resigned to his fate, John held his breath as he hit the river. Then, kicking his legs and flailing his arms, he arose and surfaced, proud of his acquired proficiency. Gasping and spluttering, he crawled out, shaking his head and swiping at his eyes. With the clearing of his sight, John saw, to his horror, what seemed to him to be the entire populace of the town positioned in a row along the riverbank.

They were all there: Mr. and Mrs. Waters, Mr. and Mrs. Field, Mrs. North and a man John assumed was her husband, college compeers including Mr. Boyd, the proctor and his daughter, a certain town trollop, and even Mr. and Mrs. Bathos. Robin, the grinning servant from the Kings Arms, was also there alongside regulars from the coaching inn and Mr. Philpott, its proprietor.

John's humiliation was complete.

Standing apart from the others was James Morland, wearing a sympathetic smile and holding out a blanket.

Later that night, at the Kings Arms, Morland purchased a few pints of ale for his friend and turned a deaf ear while John lamented his bad luck and the deviousness of women. "Hmm?" said Morland, after reading through letters from family. "Did you say something, Thorpe?"

"I *said*, never, ever, upset an Amazon," grumbled John. "You will only end up in hot water."

Morland grinned. "I rather imagine the Isis would have been cold this time of year."

"No, no!" cried John in annoyance. "You bloody well know what I mean! Mrs. North is as tall and strong as those godawful savages from the edge of the world, the Amazons. They boil and eat people, you know."

"You mean *cannibals*, not Amazons, buffoon! Now, do you want to hear what my sister has to say or not?" At John's nod, Morland glanced down at a neatly-written page. "Catherine indicates she and the Allens have settled comfortably at lodgings on Pulteney Street."

"And who are these Allens again?"

"They are the neighbours I told you about, the principal land-owners in Fullerton. Incredibly fond of Catherine, they are, and quite generous, too. She is like a daughter to the childless couple. I imagine they will augment the ten guineas our father gave her to spend in Bath." Tucking his sister's letter in a breast pocket, Morland shook his head. "No doubt, the silly goose will spend her money on more of those Gothic novels she favours."

"Deuced, foolish waste of time, money, and paper, if you ask me! Those damned novels, I am sure of this, fill pretty little heads with grand notions. Fanciful heroes! Far-fetched amorous attachments! Lord! I make it a point to never read such blighted books."

Morland raised one eyebrow. "Nor I."

"Nothing but utter balderdash! Damned, unbelievable nonsense! The only one worth reading is *The Monk*."

"Quite right, I suppose. But, as I said, I have never read a Gothic novel." Morland then asked if John enjoyed Shakespeare's works.

"Aye, some. Now, *there's* a writer who knew how to create real, playful characters."

"Was that a pun, Thorpe?"

"Eh?"

"*Play*ful. Oh, never mind!" Morland watched his friend empty a second mug of ale. "So, you find *The Merry Wives of Windsor* a more credible story than, say, a Gothic romance, do you?"

"Oh, aye! Though I have never been to Windsor." After some thought and after drinking deeply, John belched long and loud. "Tell me, Morland, is your sister of a merry disposition?"

"She has, I suppose, an open, cheerful nature."

"Is she ridiculously tall and strong?"

Morland guffawed. "Not at all, though she *is* in good health."

"Lively?"

"Such would certainly describe her imagination."

"Is she pretty?"

"Almost."

"Cunning?"

"No," Morland chuckled. "Cunning she is *not*. Catherine is, in fact, rather uninformed ... as green as grass, really."

"Your sister sounds like a damned fine sort of girl to me."

Morland's intelligence confirmed information John had received in a letter dated two days past from his own sister:

Dear John,

You will never believe our good fortune! Mother has come across a long-lost—and, I daresay, nearly forgotten—former school friend, Mrs. Allen, here in Bath. But here is extraordinary news I cannot wait to impart! With Mrs. Allen is Miss Catherine Morland— younger sister to our dearest (and you might as well tell him I referred to him that way) friend, James Morland. I have already befriended the heiress and secured a steadfast connection. If you plan to marry the girl, you must hurry! There is another gentleman whom my silly friend seems to favour. Make haste!

Isabella

John swore his days of being treated like dirt and tossed away like rubbish had come to an end. *To hell with the wager!* Those winsome wives of Oxford—shrewd, malicious, worldly women that had led him a merry dance—were not, after all, to his liking. *I deserve far better! A young, innocent, malleable girl. And a wealthy one to boot!*

To Bath, therefore—and to win, sight unseen, the hand of one Catherine Morland, heiress to the Allen fortune—John Thorpe was to go.

In company with her unsuspecting brother, he traveled as far as Tetbury, spent the night, and ran the remaining twenty-odd miles in the knowing gig purchased for fifty guineas from a Christchurch man. They arrived in Bath at half after one, coated in road dust.

Before John could wet his whistle with a nice pint of porter and reap its health benefits of muscular energy, virility, and of keeping nails out of one's coffin, he met up with Isabella and a girl. *The* girl, as it turned out. The porter would have to wait.

His preference, of course, would have been brandy, or claret, or port. But, for then, at least, he still had to practice frugality and swill bitter brew. No stranger to bitterness and foul drink, his last taste of such had been the murky, nasty fluids of the Thames. His first sample had been forcibly swallowed twenty-some years ago in a tub of tepid, harsh liquid.

And, while others journeyed to Bath for medicinal purposes, his thirst was not to be slaked with godawful Bath water. John Thorpe would never sink *that* low.

J. MARIE CROFT is a self-proclaimed word nerd and adherent of Jane Austen's quote "Let other pens dwell on guilt and misery." Bearing witness to Joanne's fondness for *Pride and Prejudice*, wordplay, and laughter are her light-hearted novel, *Love at First Slight* (a Babblings of a Bookworm Favourite Read of 2014), her playful novella, *A Little Whimsical in His Civilities* (Just Jane 1813's Favourite 2016 JAFF Novella), and her humorous short stories: "Spyglasses and Sunburns" in the *Sun-kissed: Effusions of Summer* anthology and "From the Ashes" in *The Darcy Monologues*. Joanne lives in Nova Scotia, Canada.

CAPTAIN FREDERICK TILNEY

The heroic army officer and handsome, au courant heir to the Northanger estate, Frederick Tilney regularly entertained the casual liaison but with never any earnest commitment. Upon first acquaintance, Catherine Morland might even had thought him more handsome than his brother, and yet: *His taste and manners were beyond a doubt, decidedly inferior; for within her hearing, he not only protested against every thought of dancing himself but even laughed openly at Henry for finding it possible.* —*Northanger Abbey,* **Chapter XVI.**

> *"Then you do not suppose he ever really cared about her?"*
> *"I am persuaded that he never did."*
> *"And only made believe to do so for mischief's sake?"*
> —Catherine Morland to Henry Tilney, *Northanger Abbey*, Chapter XXVII.

FOR MISCHIEF'S SAKE
Amy D'Orazio

"No man is offended by another man's admiration of the woman he loves; it is the woman only who can make it a torment." —Henry Tilney to Catherine Morland, *Northanger Abbey*, Chapter IXX.

We arranged to fight our duel at that place where all the most elegant duels were fought: the secluded gardens near the Circus, accessed by the Gravel Walk. Naturally, the occasion was to be held at dawn. I had been in my chair, subject to the shavings and combings and clippings of old Morley until at last, I cried out, "'Tis enough man! I am not gone to my wedding day!"

Morley frowned at me, his dark eyes sharp with disapproval. "Your wedding day? That is not a day I shall likely live to see so I must keep at my art on these more *common* events."

His meaning in emphasising common was not lost on me. He thought it a deplorable practice, young men having at each other to first blood or worse. But how else would a man's honour be upheld? Was Wellington the object of such censure? Surely, he had spilt more blood than anyone, and what was a war but a duel commenced on a grand scale?

But Morley did not understand it; he never had, so to placate him, I simply settled myself back, mentioned something of a wayward curl in my hair, and let him have his way with me.

When he was satisfied, I gave myself a long look in the glass, ever fond of what I saw. The truth was often spake, in circles both low and high, and it was that none were as well favoured as Captain Tilney. Indeed, I congratulated myself for as much as I was ever well in looks, I was particularly so this fine morn. I daresay I did not fool myself when I thought that the impending danger to my person rendered it that much more agreeable.

I was soon off. My jaunty step and the tune I whistled earning me a scowl from Robard, my second, who met me at the gate. "A'nt nothing to be cheery about, man! A meeting with the grim reaper hi'self!"

"Perhaps so," I owned. "Then again, one cannot live forever, and what better cause to die for than the pleasures of a woman!"

"Women aplenty in Bath," he complained, "unattached to anyone, yet you favour the engaged. I shall never understand you."

"Pray do quit the attempt." I flicked my gaze in his direction for a moment. "Silence befits such occasions as these."

We went on with only the sounds of Bath at dawn to accompany us. It was a strange hour. The night coming to a reluctant close while the day sent furtive tendrils of light across the houses and roads and fields. The occasional snoring drunk, having failed to obtain his bed, obscured our path. Here and there, maids were darting about, procuring milk or eggs or whatever might be needed in their houses.

Robard had not ceased whinging all the way and was quite ruining my pleasure in the morning so in vexed tones, I bade him stop. "How many have you seen me through now? Yet never have you had such a foul humour as this!"

"Too many." Robard spat on the ground near my feet. "Time and enough you settled your blood and began feathering your own nest 'stead of poaching on others."

"Pah!" I scoffed at the very notion. "I promise you this, sir, on my mother's own grave. I shall gladly prefer death over the slow demise of matrimony. There is not a woman alive worthy of being my beloved, and if I cannot love then I shall be ever watchful on behalf of gentlemen too beef-witted to avoid their own destruction."

Robard did not comprehend me, but he was as near an idiot as anyone whose society I would willingly bear. He had leg-shackled himself at an early age, but the girl had gone and died in childbed, taking his heart with her. Ever the fool, he had recently succumbed to a betrothal with another enchantress in muslin but at least he did not proclaim he loved her. I shook my head at him even as he stood agape considering my words.

We had arrived by then, so I turned my attention away from Robard to behold my challenger, Mr. Peter Carver. I had been at school with him from an early age, lads of only eight or nine, and we became fast friends after taking a whipping together for some bit of mischief I cannot now recall. Back then, I much admired him for his ability to take his stripes with nary a shout, nary a tear, no matter how hard our headmaster whipped his young rump. I was far more tender in those days and scarcely outlasted the first lick.

Alas, Carver was not as unaffected now as he was then. He had awaited me by stamping about, muttering and cursing and shaking. From his rumpled coat and unshaven cheeks, I surmised that he had not seen his bed the night prior. Gad! Did he wish to be killed then? A night of spirits and venting the spleen did nothing for success on the field of honour. I offered him a bow, but he only sneered contempt at me in return. Robard and Carver's second, a man called Langley, were far more civilised, bowing and nodding.

The surgeon was nervous, perspiring despite the morning chill. He stammered about, weakly insisting that an apology be offered. Naturally, I refused, which made my challenger scowl at me and mutter rude insults, defaming my character in an egregious and incorrect manner.

"Do you deny," said Carver, "that you were the instrument of the ruination of an innocent soul?"

"I suppose that would depend on your idea of what ruination is," I replied calmly.

His face became an alarming shade of purple, and he leant forward, attempting to give me a sharp poke in the chest. One step back was all that was needed to avoid his advance. He stumbled forward. "She was in your bed!"

"I cannot deny it."

"She had not known a man before!"

"No." I agreed. "That she had not."

"You have stolen what was rightly mine," he bellowed suddenly, his fetid morning breath, soured by drink, washing over my face. "You are the lowest of thieves, seducers, and rakes! I demand your sworn apology, else you must face the consequences."

"Consequences it is then for I shall never apologise for my assistance to you."

"Assistance?" he scoffed meanly. "Seems to me you assisted only one in this matter, and it was not me. The pistols then!"

The pistols were presented to us in their open case. Robard and my friend's second both examined them carefully, and Robard observed they had been made by Manton. I admired the fine English walnut on the stocks, as well as the excellent balance, when I held one in my hand. Very fine indeed.

"Shall it be first blood, until one cannot stand, or death then?" I inquired in what I felt to be a very reasonable tone. I had no wish to kill the wretched fool—he was my friend after all—but it was to him to decide.

"Death!" he shot back immediately.

I stood regarding him with some impatience. He was my inferior with a pistol on the best of days. Certainly, on this day, lacking the advantages of rest, sobriety, and even temper, I would fell him immediately. I had no wish to do that but knew it as true.

"I should think first blood will answer."

"Never," he growled.

"Peter, you know you cannot win and I despise the notion of killing you."

"It is on that point that we differ," he said. "For I wish most ardently to kill you, and in as painful a way as possible."

His arm jerked mightily, raising up; he seemed as surprised as I was to find himself pointing his gun at my chest. Robard and Langley gasped and lunged toward him. I held up my hand to forestall their intervention.

"That, sir, does not answer to the strictures of a gentlemanly duel," I said softly. "To shoot me in that way is only murder. Put the gun down until the proper signal is given."

Carver glared at me but did not do as I bid. "I knew you admired her."

"She is a vastly handsome girl."

"I should have strung you up by the bollocks when I saw you looking at her!"

"No man can be offended by another man's admiration of the woman he loves," I said in sedate tones. "It is only the woman who can make it a torment. See here old friend; it is not I who has offended you but she, the one who claimed to love you."

"You too claimed to be my friend—since we were in leading strings!"

"And I am your friend still."

"No friend of mine would do such a thing."

"I think once you know why I did it, you will thank me."

His laugh, a sad, deranged cackle, filled the air. "Thank you? Never."

"Not even if I saved you from your own grievous error?"

He stared at me, dumbfounded.

"No matter how I admired her, a simple refusal would have put me off. She did not refuse, Peter."

"She said you forced her."

"I have never forced a woman, nor would I. Not once did she say no. Not once did she indicate reluctance."

Slowly, inch by inch, the gun moved down by his side.

"You should not have attempted to seduce her," he said. "Women are weak creatures! They lack the fortitude to—"

My laughter shocked us both. "A lady is not brawny, that is true. They cannot run so fast nor walk so far as a man, nor can they lift or throw or heave; but, they have fortitude enough to break us, my man. That they surely do."

He did not argue; indeed, he could not. I saw by his looks that he attempted to summon his rage but could not. Confusion and sorrow would overcome whatever shards of ire remained in him.

"I did not seduce her for my benefit," I told him. "I shall never deny I had my pleasure in her—she is, indeed, a charming, little piece and I regret you do not know it for yourself—but there are women in abundance in Bath and London and nearly everywhere else I go. I am a handsome fellow with a good figure and an ample fortune—I do not require your woman or anyone else's, I assure you."

I turned then, motioning to Robard who looked puzzled. He held the gun case, and I motioned him towards me. I opened the case and replaced my pistol within; then, I turned back to my friend, spreading my arms wide and presenting him with an easy shot at my chest.

"Shoot me if you like," I declared. "But if you would rather know the favour I have done you, come let us go have some breakfast, and I shall tell you a little tale."

WE WENT to the house where a most obliging young lady friend of mine stayed. I urged her to remain abed—it was, after all, many hours until the time when she customarily emerged from her chambers—and bid her housekeeper to serve us our repast.

Carver moved slowly, the pain of confusion, exhaustion, and misery turning his steps into shuffles. Langley and Robard much preferred this plan over the other, so they helped poke and prod him along. The coffee was hot and strong, and the eggs and sausages which soon arrived at the table were plentiful. Once all were served, I dismissed the footman.

The gentlemen settled in with expectant looks on their faces, and I knew it was time to reveal that which I had never wished to tell: the time I was played for a fool.

"I was full young and excessively green," I said. "And it is these faults only that I will attribute to myself for otherwise my conduct in the matter was unimpeachable.

"I was fresh from the university and wholly expecting that the *ton* had never seen a gentleman so splendid as me. I arrived at Almack's that night sure I should have the hand of any lady I wished and for two hours, at least, so it was. I was careful in who I asked to dance; for me, a lady had to be no less than a diamond of the first water, with a fortune that complemented my own.

"I enjoyed myself very well that night. The ladies were plentiful and gracious, and I enjoyed them all, none more than any other of course—until I saw her."

"Her?" asked Langley

"A lady I knew only because her family is connected to Baron Scrope of Masham—"

A rumble went around the table. The Scrope family was a splendid, old family which had grown rather infamous for their ability to take a fortune and turn it into debt.

"And though she had a small fortune, it was not enough to make her significant. Indeed, I know not, in retrospect, how she might have obtained her voucher."

"Who told you so?" Robard was curious.

"Oh, I cannot recall who I was with." I gave a careless wave of my hand. "You know how it is at Almack's. Everyone knows everything about anyone who is there and what they do not know, they soon discover. In any case, I was not thinking of anything more than a dance, so it hardly signified.

"She was eighteen, newly out and as fresh and beautiful as ever there was. She had one dimple, just one, on her right cheek—that dimple cost me many a night's sleep back then, just thinking of touching it with my lips. However, more so than her beauty, it was her wit, her charm which beguiled me.

"She was not like the other girls I danced with that night. We began as these things often do—was I often at Almack's, who were her family, who were my friends, how did we find London—but somehow, very easily, it became a conversation of actual consequence. I found myself, in a manner most extraordinary, telling her of my hopes, my plans, and my wishes.

"It ended all too soon, and I escorted her to her chaperons feeling as though I had entered some fantastical fog or had indulged in spirits."

The men assembled around the table plainly found this shocking. More than one stared in disbelief while Langley was frankly dubious.

"Perhaps you had," he suggested. "You would not be the first man to confuse drunkenness with love."

"I had not had so much as a glass of wine," I retorted. "My mind was untouched, I assure you. The confusion of which I speak was the product of my heart's desires flooding my senses, nothing more.

"Who I danced with the rest of the evening, I could not say. No one of note, not to me in any case. I went to bed that night thinking of her, and my dreams were filled with her. I persuaded myself not to call the next day, and I adhered to my own directive for almost an hour. It would not do, I had to see her.

"I dressed with almost absurd care and nearly drove my man to distraction in my demands over my hair. I was anxious and indifferent in turns—by this time, I had convinced myself that what happened the night before was some strange malady. I was certain I would realise my memory had deceived me, that she would not be so beautiful, nor so charming, nor so witty. Thus, I would be released from the spell I had fallen under."

I paused then, taking a deep swallow of my rapidly cooling coffee. "I was most incorrect in that notion, my friends."

Carver had mostly remained silent through the recitation, but now he spoke. "She was everything you remembered?"

I shook my head. "More. More lovely, more witty, more kind. I stayed far, far too long that day, the half-hour melting into an hour, two hours, maybe more, I cannot say. We spoke of everything and anything, and when at last I took my leave, I knew I had met my wife."

"You proposed?" The gentlemen seemed to all exclaim at once.

"Of course not. I was not so affected that I would declare myself after one dance and one call. But I resolved to know more of her, to spend time paying court to her. The days that followed…"

For several blissful moments, I permitted myself to slip into the recollection of those wondrous times. Perfect days in Hyde Park, sublime evenings at the various parties and balls… Ah, it was young love, and it was indeed all that it should have been. I loved her with all that I was, and I felt it given back to me in full. Was there anything better?

I shook my head to return to the present. "It came to the point where I could hardly bear to restrain my declaration a moment more. She was already mine in my heart, and the words which would seal my fate had begun to dance upon my lips every time I saw her. But, as all young lovers must, we had obstacles."

"Your father," said Carver. He had known my family too well for too long.

"My father thought the very notion preposterous. Marriage, as you know, was a business to him."

"Your parents' match was a celebrated one?" asked Langley.

"Not at all," I said. "Many thought my mother had married beneath her. She had wealth, and he had military distinction, but her people did not think it enough. Her marriage to a viscount was arranged and my father stole her away. I believe they were once very much in love, or perhaps it was lust, but by the time I understood about such things, it had cooled to contemptuous co-existence. My mother had many friends who would visit her—so many, it seemed she did no more but to shoo me away, or ask me to find this or that for her."

My ramblings had taken me a bit afield here, and I collected myself a bit. "So, my father understood what it was to suffer a woman's neglect and it changed him. His foolishness became cynicism.

"There was much more at stake, of course, than only my heart. My father's rise to general was swift, and he was certain I would do the same, particularly in these difficult war times. I am sure he wished to see me distinguish myself through some act of valour, not sit in my bunk repining the wife and the life I left behind."

"Most acts of valour," said Langley, "are enacted by those who care not if they survive their missions."

"Quite so," Robard agreed. "England is a jealous mistress. She has no time for men with their minds on their hearths and homes."

I nodded, swallowed another mouthful of now-cold coffee. The bitterness trailed down my throat, but it was nothing to the bitter gall of my memories. "The general hated the very idea of me being in love, and he was sure that the disinterest and despair that he had known would be sure to follow. He could not allow it.

"Had he railed at me, had he threatened to disown me or take my fortune, I would likely have married her on the spot. Instead, he approached me with calm logic and the idea for a little experiment."

"An experiment?"

"A test," said I, "of my lady's fidelity. We were, of course, quite young—I had only reached my majority the year prior, and she was scarcely out. The engagement would be long, in any case, particularly as I was required to be away for a time with my regiment."

The looks around the table changed. It was not such an uncommon story after all although the twist I would add to it made it rather strange. The gentlemen hung on my every word. Likely they had some horrified suspicion of what I would say.

"He would make an attempt on her," I said quietly. "To see what she did. If she loved me, then she would turn away from him, likely in disgust. But if it was mere fortune she was after then one Tilney should do as well as the next."

The men were astonished. "But…your father?" was Langley's weak protest.

"Many think my father looks young enough to be my brother," I informed them. "In any case, he may be past the bloom, but he is not past the vigour of life. He did not ruin her, he could not sink that low, but his actions resulted in her family packing her away from London for a time. Last I heard she was married to a parson in Norwich."

"Forgive me for so saying," Robard declared, "but this is quite beyond anything. Surely your father is not lost to every paternal obligation! This is extraordinary behaviour."

"I shall admit to my outrage," I said. "But I soon realised he did me a service. We could not have been happy, she and I. I would have ended as he did, an angry and suspicious man shackled to misery until either she died or I did. It is a fate I am glad I escaped."

Carver had turned to look out the window. No doubt my story was resting heavy in his chest.

I cleared my throat. "That is not to say I did not receive some misery. I have known humiliation and sorrow, and yes, the sort of anger that burns like a hot stone in your gut. But from this, I learnt to hold my heart proud.

"So, I vowed thenceforth that no man should suffer this fate," I told them. "I congratulate myself that I have become adept at finding the weak in character, the ones who are determined flirts who wish to make fools of their husbands and fathers. It is my calling, you might say, to bring about what would surely happen in the years to come, and to induce its occurrence before it is too late."

I pointed my fork at my friend Carver. "As I did for you. Are you not relieved in some small way to know now that she is faithless, now when you might extricate yourself, rather than discover her infidelity when you are married?"

"Just one moment if you please," Robard interrupted. "You mean to tell me you seduced Carver's lady with intention?"

"Aye."

They all began then to toss their questions at me.

"So, you were not merely caught up in the delights of seduction?"

"Certainly not," I replied. "Seducing a virgin is a tricky business. Had I only wished for a bit of carnal relief, I might have dropped a few shillings at a brothel and been on my way within the hour."

"But you were engaged by her charms?"

I shrugged. "I can go for a walk and see ten more just like her. She is lovely and enchanting, of course, but not so far out of the common way as to make me lose my senses."

"You set out then," said Robard, "with the express purpose of testing her?"

I nodded very slowly.

"And she failed." This conclusion, given in dispirited accents, was made by Carver. The truth was in him now, and he could not deny it. His lover was faithless and untrue, and he was much better off without her. "She failed your little test."

I gave no answer; the truth was already understood.

Carver was silent and pensive for only a moment. His chair scraped a shrieking protest as he shoved backwards, stood, and tossed his napkin onto the table. He said nothing as he quit the room.

"I took him down several times, you know, in my way." —Isabella Thorpe to Catherine Morland, *Northanger Abbey,* Chapter XVI.

ONE YEAR LATER

It was on behalf of both Henry and my father that I journeyed to Wilt-shire. My father, of course, knew what I was about but Henry would not know a word of it until it was done.

My father had, at one time found a great deal to admire in Miss Catherine Morland. He met her in somewhat exalted company and was informed—mistakenly so, we later learnt—she was an heiress. She and Henry had already formed some attachment and the general forwarded it wholeheartedly, indeed almost shamelessly—until he learnt the truth of her. She was no more than a sweet girl of modest means from a large family of little consequence in Wiltshire and as such, she was nothing worth knowing for him.

My father's approval of her was immediately rescinded and he ordered her from our home, where she had been staying as the guest of my sister. Not his finest hour, to be sure, but it was done and no use thinking of it more.

But Henry, stubborn, foolish Henry, would not be swayed from her. He went to her at Wiltshire, said some pretty things I am sure, and an understanding was reached between them. However, her parents, wise people, forwarded one obstacle to what would be otherwise perfect bliss: her parents would not consent until my father did too.

My father had no intention of consenting to any such thing but this did not stop Henry from endlessly plaguing him. "I cannot hear more of this," the general said to me one fine morning. "Enough repining over Catherine Morland!"

"It was rather disagreeable of him to mention her while you ate," I said. "Rather makes a man's stomach turn to hear such talk of romance and lovers while there is meat on the table."

"Indeed," said my father. We were strolling along a favoured path around Northanger just then and he was quiet for a while, no doubt waiting for me to suggest what was in both of our minds.

"I could go to Wiltshire," I said at last.

"My boy." The general offered me a rare, proud smile. "You do know just how these things are best managed."

I expected to make a short business of it. Miss Morland was young, both in age and in understanding. She was a wide-eyed innocent and yet, her time at Northanger Abbey had shown she enjoyed the thrill of danger. Henry had, no doubt, appealed to the better part of her nature. I would appeal to the baser part of her character, one which she likely had no idea even existed.

My call to her, on my arrival at Fullerton, shocked her. Plainly she hoped for news of Henry and was just as clearly dismayed to receive none.

I told her I had business in the area and thought it proper to pay my respects to her, and she was suitably cheered.

I saw the question in her eyes when I lingered longer than was necessary, and it was a question magnified during my second call. I made sure to give some very pretty compliments that time, not only to her but her mother and sister as well. I saw by their blushes and smiles that my words had the intended effect.

We walked out, Miss Morland and I, on the occasion of my fourth call to Fullerton. With her mother and sisters away from home, it seemed an ideal time for my visit; an ideal time to see if she would succumb to me and come with me back to the inn where I stayed.

I offered my arm and drew her as near as she would be drawn and we walked for some time in a little silence. She began then to speak on a subject well known to us both but tedious to me: my brother. Henry was, in her estimation, the most charming of men, the most witty, the most gentleman-like; her effusions knew no end it seemed.

At last I interrupted her. "Yes, my brother is all that is good and pure in this world; however, I must observe that Henry owes much to me for that particular understanding of his character."

She turned a pretty smile to me. "How so?"

I glanced about me—yes, a perfect spot. I led her into a small place of seclusion from the path. She followed obediently, only a few bemused glances up towards my face on the way.

Once I had her where I wished her, I leant in. "A saint's glory is made far more evident by the presence of a sinner, is it not so?"

"I… Why, yes, I suppose it is."

I slowly allowed the back of one finger to trace her arm from her shoulder to her elbow, thrilled to see she did not pull away. "Perhaps Henry would not look nearly so good," I murmured, "if I were not so very wicked."

She pulled back a little and her mouth, that pretty little rosebud, formed a perfect *o*. "But I do not think you so very wicked."

"Yes, indeed I am—but I daresay it is your fault."

"My fault?"

"Just so." I leant in close to her allowing my glance to stray to her bosom, shockingly ample given her slight figure. "Since the very first moment I set my eyes on you, I found myself having very wicked thoughts indeed."

A blush rose from her delightful bosom to her cheeks and she murmured my name, turning her eyes to the side.

I spoke into her ear, her curls dancing about with my whispered words. "Just for a little while, would it not be diverting to laugh with the sinner instead of cry for the saint?"

She drew back, tilting her head as she examined me. I could see her wondering at the extent of my fraternal loyalty, deciding if she could possibly have us both. This would be even easier than I ever thought it could be. "No one would ever need to know," said I, with my most charming smile.

And then one tear, fat and round, made its way down her cheek. Alarm stiffened my back and I was immediately upright, my burgeoning ardor killed immediately. "What is it?"

The tears were slow but they began to come steadily. I offered my handkerchief, glancing around us to be sure we were not observed. "No need to cry, madam," I said to no avail as she dabbed uselessly at her tears. How could she cry already? I had not done a thing yet!

"Surely you do not, even now, weep for Henry?"

"Henry?" she asked, with a small choking sob. "No, not Henry. No, it is you!—oh, my dear Captain Til—Frederick! May I call you that? After all we shall be family."

"Call me what you wish," I said, thoroughly baffled. "But why should you cry on my account?"

"When I think of the pain, the hollow agonies you must have suffered to have brought you to this low, my grief can scarcely be contained. Oh, do anything! Do anything at all but continue on in this manner!"

Her vehemence startled me but it was nothing to the shock I felt as she threw her arms around me and embraced me tight, laying her damp cheek against my chest.

"I neither require nor deserve such sympathetic— Oof!" I grunted as she gave me a particularly fervent squeeze. Damnation but the girl had some strength in her! I twisted a bit to remove myself but it could not be done. "What are you at Miss Morland?"

She pulled away once she had finished wringing the life from me and smiled at me the way one might smile at a pet who had performed some little trick. "You came here to seduce me, did you not?"

"I... well..." An unusual sensation plagued me; it took a moment for me to recognise it as shame.

"Never mind. We do not need anyone to know. It will be our first secret together, just like true brother and sister, sharing confidences!"

"We are not sharing confidences," I protested to deaf ears.

"But truly dear brother—"

"I am not your brother."

"You must not seek to destroy the bond of fraternal affection between you and Henry! Has he not grievances enough right now?"

"Once Henry understood why—"

"But in truth, my greatest concern is for you."

"Me?"

"When I consider your loneliness, I ache with it. Dearest Frederick, do find someone to love, I implore you."

Her eyes were filled with compassion and I gaped at her, understanding seeping into me. "Do you mean to say—do you *pity* me?"

Her hands, clasped together, pressed against her heart. "I have thought on this much during these dreadful, long days of waiting. Your father and his coldness!"

"My father is a brave and accomplished—"

"Such cruelty must be the result of years of being alone and unloved! The human soul is not meant for solitude. We crave affection and love just as our bodies require food and drink!"

"My father has friends," I protested weakly. "Clubs. That sort of—"

"But as much as I fear for him, I am ten-fold so for you. The general did once love and was loved in return. Was it not so?"

"Erm… Well, yes, but that is not—"

"But you! Oh, my dear Frederick, it surely is the most important thing in this world. 'Tis true, my love is making me miserable now but I have been to the highest height and I shall suffer the lowest low, all for my dear Henry. For I truly do love him with all that I am, and if I must cry a decade for every day I have known him, it will be worth it."

She was nearly angelic as she beamed at me and I realised her goodness had conquered me. This was, undoubtedly, the most grievously failed attempt at a seduction there ever was. Miss Catherine Morland would not be tempted away. My brother had somehow managed to find himself a worthy dame.

I made a last effort to win her.

"You must understand," I told her. "My father is not likely to be moved. It is more likely that you will grow wings and learn to fly than it is that you shall end as Mrs. Tilney."

With great solemnity, she said, "I shall not believe it."

"'Tis true."

She shook her head, those damnable curls bouncing about her head. At that moment, she somehow managed to look both a great deal younger and a good bit older than her eighteen years.

"I have been told that your parents will not give consent if my father does not and my father shall not, I assure you."

"Love shall triumph," she said. "I am certain of it. But do, Frederick, do let it have its way with you too, else you shall end in a most frightfully embittered state."

With that, I was awarded another damp kiss on the cheek, and then she was gone.

"Frederick too, who always wore his heart so proudly, who found no woman good enough to be loved!" —Eleanor Tilney to Catherine Morland and Henry Tilney, *Northanger Abbey*, Chapter XXV.

As it was, Catherine was correct on one score. Love did prevail, eventually, over my father. In a fit of delight over my sister's marriage to a viscount, my father told Henry he could "be a fool if he liked it!" They were married within a twelve-month of their initial meeting and all parties were soon settled into marital bliss.

Love prevailed over them but I should be damned if it would prevail over me. I still held my heart proud as ever. I still occupied myself in gambling and fights and women of easy virtue.

But in the darker hours I had to admit it to myself—Catherine affected me. Of course, nothing like thinking love was a true object, nothing that silly. It was the way she looked at me that troubled me most.

I had seen men before, aged men who had once been handsome young bucks. But no matter how handsome or virile or well-formed you are, Time will exact its punishment and nothing, in my estimation, is as execrable as some bald, droopy-jowled, corseted would-be Lothario. Was this how I was seen? Had I become already a pitiable object of derision? The notion sent a shudder through me. Surely Catherine was mistaken.

My fears plagued me in a particularly grievous way one night at a ball. I was dancing with Lady Harriet Botwright, some child fresh from school who chattered on about how much she liked Bath while we danced, when the pattern took me away and I found myself hand in hand with an enchantress in a rose-colored gown. I knew her, if it took me a moment to recall her. "Miss Rose Gibson!"

She rolled her eyes and frowned at me. "Miss Rosalind Gibbs."

"How charming to see you." And it was, indeed, good to see her. She was a handsome woman, a bit more mature than the usual crowd of maidenly just-from-school ladies who attended these sorts of parties. She had just the sort of figure I always admired: more lean than was the fashion but with a few womanly curves nevertheless. Good to see that the years since our last meeting had not deposited any unnecessary padding on her frame although her eyes fairly glittered with spite when I told her so.

"I will thank you," she said with considerable hauteur, "to refrain from examining my figure."

With that, the pattern removed her and I was again consigned to the girl I partnered.

When that duty was done, I paused a moment, considering, Miss Gibbs across the room. Naturally I remembered her—she was the sort of woman one never did forget—but I could not immediately recall the association.

Ah yes. She had once belonged to Carver.

Carver was happily married by now, to an excessively wealthy woman, so there was no ill will between him and I but alas, Miss Gibbs had not fared so well. The last I knew she was in some distant county somewhere, under the care of a spinster aunt with rumours in abundance throughout the *ton*. Dear thing was not quite ruined but nearly so. Brave of her to come back to the dragon's lair. I nodded my approval at her and she scowled at me in reply, turning her back to me thereafter.

"You are right to despise me," I said with what I believed was beguiling humility when I saw her next. "But I suppose you never think of me."

"Oh, but I do," she said. We were at another ball, this one given by Lady Dalrymple in her excessively large house in Laura Place. Miss Gibbs wore a gown of palest green with a pink sash, and I liked it very well. "I think of you often."

"Do you?" The thought pleased me.

"Mostly how much I might like to kill you." She smiled sweetly. "Poison is too good for you I think, unless it produced some particularly vile dysentery first. I favour some medieval torture for you: the rack or removal of your fingernails to begin."

"Ouch!" I leant in with a smile. "Come now. You would not have liked to be wife to that simpering fool Carver now, would you? He is already quite fat with contentment. I daresay in another year neither of us should know him."

"I would like," she said, "to have my reputation back." And with a final severe look, she stalked off, leaving me dangling after her like a fool. I wished I had asked her to dance even as I persuaded myself she had become a bit of a harridan.

Strangely, I found her entering my thoughts over the next days. I looked for her all over, dinner parties, a concert, coffee houses, and the Crescent, but she was nowhere to be found. Her absence stoked my desire to find her.

At last, I saw her again at the assembly rooms during a public ball, standing by the refreshment table in a lovely rose-coloured gown trimmed in gold. It was a gown which bespoke the fortune of the wearer.

Miss Gibbs watched me approach her, but I played with her a little. I pretended my interest was in the cake beside her, taking it up and then, almost as if I had just noticed her, offering a bow and a smirk. She did not smile in return nor did she speak.

I summoned my most charming smile. "We meet again."

"So we do."

"And how do you do?"

She shrugged. "How are you?"

"Splendid in every way," said I.

Every possible avenue of conversation deserted me after those banal pleasantries had been uttered. I stood like a gaping green lad having his first conversation with a lady. No subject seemed safe or important enough to waste time discussing. I forestalled the need to speak with a bite of cake, grimacing at the sweetness.

My countenance drew her interest. "Now that is a face! What displeases you, sir?"

"This cake." I drew deep from the punch glass. "Too sweet by half."

"Too sweet! Who could ever complain about a cake being too sweet?"

"I am not one of these people who needs an excess of sweets," I told her. "Give me fruit and a piece of cheese, and it is good enough for me."

"Then why did you take a piece?"

"Everyone else likes it so much," I told her, "I cannot help feeling I must be missing something."

At this, she laughed, showing perfect, pearly white teeth for a moment too long before remembering to be demure and clapping her hand over her mouth. I did not mind; I rather liked the idea that I made her forget herself.

"I must not be amused by you," she said. "Not when I am so determined to despise you."

"Despise me! And when we were once on such…well, I suppose I must say they were intimate terms." My grin was miscalculated; she looked like she wished to hit me. She turned, clearly intending to leave me but I cried out, "Wait."

She turned back. "What?"

"That was certainly an ill-judged remark and I do beg your pardon."

She said nothing, merely stared at me with eyes that were quite the colour of bluebells in the spring. Though it was not my custom to care much about a lady's eyes, I found hers to be rather fascinating. Such blue! And fringed by thick lashes, they were really quite perfect.

"Dance with me."

"With you? No. Dancing with you before was the first step in what proved to be the destruction of my life, so you will pardon me if I say I am not inclined to do it again."

"Please?" Was this truly me, begging a lady to dance with me? Gad but this woman already made me go against all that I believed in!

"People will talk."

"So, let them. I am sure it is nothing to me."

"That is easy for you to say. You did as you did and went about your merry way. I…" She drifted off, looking past me at nothing. A shadow came into those blue eyes that I so admired.

A few moments later, she shook herself. "Ah, well, but what does it matter? I am reviled, the subject of malicious conversation in every drawing room already; why not give them something new to buzz about?"

A strange and distressing sensation stirred in my breast: compassion. I had not before considered how it must be for these ladies, the ones who I left behind me among the rubble of their former romances.

Our dance together was surprisingly pleasant. Her hand in mine felt natural and good and I must admit, seeing her cheeks pink with exertion brought to mind some very pleasurable recollections, recollections that had nothing to do with our present time and place. It was over far too soon.

"Will you escort me towards the window for some air?"

Of course I obliged her.

"Thank you for that dance. I do admit I enjoyed it."

"As did I," I said with uncommon feeling. Indeed, I wished for another dance with her, though I had never in my whole life danced twice with the same woman at one event.

"Will you tell me something?" On my nod, she asked, "Why did you do it?"

"Why did I seduce you?"

"Yes. I have thought long on the matter and it is obvious you had some purpose in doing it. I have heard you enjoy tempting ladies who are engaged to be married. Why is that?"

"Well." I shifted, uncomfortable. "It seems rather unfair, you know? A woman stands to gain everything on marrying while a gentleman—"

"You think the woman gains everything? No, no, you are already incorrect. The man gains just as much, or more!"

"Every woman just wants the richest husband she can get."

"And so does every man want the richest wife he can get, except she also needs to be handsome and accomplished."

"In marrying, a lady is given security the rest of her life."

"In marrying, a lady is placed wholly within the power of a man who may give her as much sorrow as he likes and she can do nothing about it."

"And you think a man is not controlled by his lady?" I shook my head. "There is no woman I have ever met worth loving and any man that tries finds himself heartbroken and alone."

"Perhaps it is the men who are the problem."

I shook my head, certain I was correct. "Eve tempted Adam you know, and that is where it began."

"Perhaps she did but nevertheless…" She leant in and with exquisite impertinence concluded, "It was Adam who took the bite."

"He would not have taken the bite had she not offered it."

"And who bears the responsibility for this original sin?" She arched one well-formed brow at me. "Women. It is always the women, while the men go on much as they ever have."

"Peter Carver—"

"Is married," she said. "I am but a side-note in his history, limping along while my friends scorn me and their mothers gossip about me. It is not fair."

"Carver deserved your fidelity."

She gave a tired wave of one hand. "He was down on Marleybone

Street nearly every night. Even his father remarked on his expenses there, right in front of me too!"

I winced; that was bad form indeed. "Well, I am sure he would have stopped once he was married."

"If the vows were what I awaited to gain his loyalty," she said, "then I suppose he should have expected likewise from me."

It was a fair observation and one I had not before considered.

"You permitted me to seduce you—"

"I did." She admitted it in a tired way, in the way of one who has grown inured to her mistakes. "I will never deny my mistakes for I have learnt from them. But I will say only this, to you and any other man: you may call us your wife, you can take our fortunes as your own, you can fill us with your children, and you can keep us stowed away in the country while you pursue whatever diversions you will. However, if you really want to have a woman, to own her heart, then you must make her feel loved every single day of your life. Otherwise, you only have the shell of her, the bits that she allows you."

Something in the way she said so pierced my soul. I wanted to say more, but I could not, particularly not when our dance ended and she turned, in a swirl of pink and gold, and left me standing there foolish and silenced behind her.

I COULD SCARCELY SLEEP that night, eager to call on her, wanting desperately to speak with her and yet wholly unable to know what words to use. As I lay in my bed, hour after sleepless hour, I tried to pretend it was only her figure or her face which interested me and yet, it was not the memories of her physical person which arose, but memories of our conversation, of that one laugh I earned from her, and of the shadows I wanted to vanquish from her eyes which plagued me.

I called at the earliest possible hour which would still be considered polite. She refused me not only the first day but the second, the third, and the fourth as well.

I saw her at a ball a week after that and immediately, I asked her to dance. She refused. I asked again and she pushed me towards this friend or that. At last I told her I would countenance no more.

"So, stop asking me," she protested coolly.

"I cannot! I want to dance with you."

"Why?"

And I stood there before her with the most horrifying of any possible reason screaming in my mind: love. Love? The Frederick of old scorned me, reminding me there was no woman worth loving. But what if there was? And what if she who stood before me was that one for me?

But it was too early to say so, even too early to think of it. Instead I could only beg and eventually, she relented.

"Is this some sort of penance you have assigned yourself?" she asked me some weeks later at yet another of these infernal balls where we always found ourselves.

"No."

"Then why are you always hanging about?"

"Because." I swallowed against an odd thickness which had arisen in my throat with her question. "Ah… well because…"

She turned those blue eyes towards me and rendered me even more foolish than usual. Such it was that I found myself weakly admitting, "I like you."

"Oh." She pursed her lips, looking me up and down rather sceptically. "Well, so long as it is not pity then."

We began to spend a great deal of time together. The gossips' tongues naturally began to wag, and at some course, my father felt he needed to interfere. I sat quietly in his study with him one morning, listening as he offered his advisements on life and women and marriage but, as I did, a strange notion occurred to me: he was a bitter, old man, spending most of his days haunting the old abbey and meddling in the affairs of his children. He was to be pitied, not emulated.

"Sir, I do appreciate your advice," said I on leaving. "Miss Gibbs and I are only friends; however, if it becomes more, I will give no heed to the clucking hens of Bath and London. In any case, her fortune is splendid, so there is something."

"Splendid?" He was at once interested in the conversation.

I named the sum and with this, my father was satisfied. No more did I hear from him about Miss Gibbs.

"So, HAVE YOU SEDUCED any maidens lately?" she asked one day as we strolled the streets of Bath together. "I have not heard your name in the gossip circles of late except attached to mine. If this continues, you might lose your reputation as a rake."

"Heaven forbid!" I gasped in mock horror. "This must be laid at your door. You have reformed me."

"I have done nothing of the sort," she said with a little laugh. "You ruined me, remember? I am part of that illustrious and infamous group of ladies who made you what you are."

The levity was gone from me when she said so, though she said it very lightly.

"Have you forgiven me?"

She appeared to be surprised by the question. "Do you want me to forgive you? It seemed to me you thought you were on some mission of deliverance for Mr. Carver."

"Ah well… Perhaps I have begun to see your side of things then. I…" I paused a moment and did not want to look at her. "I begin to see that to be not a rake might be agreeable too."

"Not a rake? You, a proper gentleman?" she asked with an impish little smile. "Mad notion. How will you know how to be?"

"Well," said I. "I suppose I must learn."

"Hmm." She appeared to think it over. "I guess I could say I have forgiven you a little."

"A little?"

She smiled up at me. "I no longer wish to poison you."

"Progress indeed!" I laughed.

Oddly enough, it was then that I wanted to kiss her, but I thought that might earn me a slap. Regardless of what had gone on before, now we were both different, and I would afford her the respect she deserved.

It was not until much later in our walk that she said, apropos of nothing, "It all happens for a reason, does it not?"

"What does?"

"The mistakes we make, the troubles we endure… They shape us, mould us into something stronger and better." With that came a crooked little smile and I believed, from thence, I had been forgiven.

The truth hit me in an unguarded moment, when I beheld her in the street one afternoon, walking towards me with her friend. She was so lovely, and my heart skipped a beat just seeing her. I had argued with myself often over the last weeks, telling myself I felt no more than warmth, friendship, compassion but now, I could deny it no more. It was wholly certain: I, Captain Frederick Tilney, owner of a proud heart and an admitted seducer of women, had fallen deeply and irreversibly in love.

"You look very strange," she said on arriving beside me.

"I feel strange," I said as I offered my arm. "Very strange indeed."

Her friend, an obliging soul to whom I am forever indebted, drifted towards an uninteresting shrub while I faced my beloved. "Here it is," I told her. "I fear I have fallen in love with you."

She gave me a sceptical look. "Do you, even now, make an attempt at seducing me?"

"No! I assure you, I am perfectly in earnest."

To this, she would only give a gentle harrumph before we began to stroll along. She would hear no more of it the rest of that day and it was the work of several weeks to persuade her I was wholly sincere, frustrating woman that she was!

The first time I mentioned marriage, a fine autumn day in the park, she turned her back on me and moved away faster than ever I imagined she could. My second foray towards the subject was a month later, and she told me to stop being so silly. It was not until just before Christmas that I proposed and she soundly refused me and said if I mentioned it again, she would cut our acquaintance forever.

She induced in me a sort of madness, a desperation almost. I had to have her, and she had a hundred reasons to refuse me. People would gossip (hang them all), and she believed I was still a rogue at heart (I was not). My father did not like her (that was true, but he did like her fortune) and my sisters Eleanor and Catherine thought her brazen (also correct but I daresay they meant it admiringly).

I began to think of how I could arrange it so that she had to marry me. We had already been found together once before, so that would not work. She had a father who was alive and ample fortune to live on, so there was no hope of rescuing her from poverty, and, she had grown accustomed to the shame of her position. Ignominy no longer troubled her; respectability, she decided, was not worth concerning oneself about.

No, there was nothing for it. I would need to declare myself in such a profoundly romantic manner that she would be categorically unable to refuse me.

I decided I must seek the good counsel of an expert: my sister Catherine, my brother Henry's wife. Catherine was the sort of woman who lived life as if she were the heroine in some stupid novel. She favoured stories of evil villains, courageous heroes, and swooning maidens, and in the end, the gentleman always got his lady. I knew she would be able to contrive for me some design to make my beloved mine.

I WAITED for her in the gathering gloom of dusk. My second was my brother, and assorted other friends and relations were concealed in the shrubs around the small gardens accessed by the Gravel Walk. I thought it a nice symmetry that I should propose here in this same spot where Peter Carver and I had almost exchanged bullets over her.

Catherine had gone to her, full of breathless anxiety made all the more alarming by her present delicate state. Henry and Catherine, married less than two years, had already thrown out one tiresome, little scamp and were presently cooking another. "You know, it can be done for amusement sometimes," I told him.

"What?" Henry asked. "What can?"

I shook my head. "Not now. Remind me to show you something I have in my bedchamber later."

Henry was bewildered, but there was no time for questions or explanations, for here came my lovely almost-bride with Catherine hard on her heels. She knew only that I intended to fight someone on behalf of Miss Gibbs' honour. I anticipated—rightly it seemed—that she would immediately run to me.

My Rosalind—for I dared already call her so in my mind—was as lovely as she had ever been. I hoped I did not fool myself that I saw tears of genuine fear glistening in her eyes. Her hair had begun to fall from its pins, no doubt from the exertion of a quick trip here and her breaths came deep and quick.

"Captain Tilney! What do you do?"

I stood at the precise angle that Catherine and I had rehearsed, looking manly and resolved in the face of sure danger.

"I am here to fight for you, my darling. You will not marry me because of what has gone on in the past, so I will vanquish that which has tarnished your good name."

"But," she looked around her wildly, "who will you fight? Catherine did not tell me who had served the insult."

"You already know who did."

She stared at me, uncomprehending.

"It is the Frederick Tilney of old who has ruined it all," I told her. "That dreadful rogue! A seducer of women! Who did not believe in love, or faithfulness, or anything of the like! A curse on his wretched, black soul!"

My brother handed me the blade, and I positioned it over my own heart, pressing it in lightly. "I once held my heart too proudly to love any woman but many months now, you have held it for me. If I cannot have yours in return, I cannot live!"

The panic had receded from her and in its place, amusement. "Lord above Tilney, what is this now?"

"A duel!" I cried out. "To the death!"

"You intend to duel yourself?"

"Yes!" I pushed the blade against my chest a bit hard, wanting only to make my point.

"I am no expert on fencing," she said, with a wry look, "but I doubt you could do yourself much harm holding the blade at such an angle. I think the worst you could do would be to cut your shirt, although that would anger Morley and he might do you some harm."

With a chuckle, I lowered the blade. Was not this why I loved her? She was unafraid to be witty and disinclined towards the sheep-like deference most ladies showed to gentlemen of my station.

"That is true." I dropped the blade. "Very well then, I shall put my theatricals aside and come to that very last of resorts: honesty."

I made an expansive gesture towards the surrounding shrubs where anyone of my acquaintance who was important to me was concealed and urged them to emerge. They did, slow and uncertain but my attention was returned to her.

"Rosalind, I love you, with everything that I am. I can never deny that once, a worse version of me used you ill, but knowing you and being with you has made me a better man. Even if I can never persuade you to marry me, I will be ever grateful to you for turning this rogue into a true gentleman.

"That said"—I gave her my best, most charming smile—"I do intend to plague you for your hand in marriage until I no longer have sufficient breath to do it. Pray permit me the chance to make you the happiest woman in the world?"

She did not make an immediate reply which was a good thing. In my previous attempts, the refusals had come quick.

"After all," I said, stepping closer, "we have both had our share of youthful missteps and yet, have not we learnt from them? I know I have."

I reached out and dared to take her hand in my own. In her haste, she had forgotten gloves, and I was grateful for that. Her soft, small hand fit so well in mine as if we were formed for one another.

"There will never be anyone for me but you, so long as I live," I told her. "You have my promise of that, in front of everyone I know. Once I held my heart proud, but now, I do not hold it at all; it has been given over to your care. I am yours, mind, heart, and body, for all eternity, and all I ask of you in return is to answer 'yes'. Please say you will be my wife."

My entreaty hung in the night air, and there was not a sound around it. We waited: me, my friends, my relations, the birds, and insects, all of us waiting to hear what she would say.

She did not look at them, but only stared at me, looking into my eyes as if she saw me for the very first time. "I will make you feel loved every day of your life," I whispered.

She made a sound, a half-laugh commingled with a little sob, and dropped my hand to cover her face with her hands, but as she did, she moved to my chest where she lingered. It was in this I believed I saw my answer and, risking a painful slap if I was wrong, I decided to kiss her.

With one hand beneath her chin, I tilted her face to mine, my other hand gently tracing her spine before landing at her waist, pulling her even closer into my embrace. We both sighed when our lips touched, our breaths mingling together in the small space between us. Resolved to be more a gentleman, I had put my back to our audience whilst I kissed her. Nevertheless, they had some idea of what we were about and began to cheer and shout congratulations.

"It is a 'yes' then dearest?"

"Yes," she said. "Yes, Frederick Tilney, I will indeed marry you."

Thus, began our story, though it is several years gone by now. I once was a rake, who no woman could claim as her own (and indeed few of them wanted to). Now, *I* am the possession of many women—five to be exact. There is, first and foremost, my Rosalind, ever my true love, but between us, we have managed a few more: Miss Caroline Tilney, Miss Margaret Tilney, Miss Louisa Tilney, and, our youngest, Miss Anne Tilney.

Woe to the man who ever tries to seduce them or even to trifle with their hearts! I may be older now, perhaps even losing a bit of my bloom, but my vigour has not left me, and I still enjoy the notion of a good duel. I shall happily run through any rake or rogue who dares to make an advance on my darlings!

AMY D'ORAZIO is a former scientist and current stay-at-home mom who is addicted to Austen and Starbucks in equal measure. While she adores Mr. Darcy, she is married to Mr. Bingley and their Pemberley is in Pittsburgh, Pennsylvania.

She has two daughters devoted to sports with long practices and began writing stories as a way to pass the time spent at their various gyms and studios. She firmly believes that all stories should have long looks, stolen kisses, and happily-ever-afters. Like her favorite heroine, she dearly loves a laugh and considers herself an excellent walker. She is the author of *The Best Part of Love* and the soon-to-be released *A Short Period of Exquisite Felicity*.

ACKNOWLEDGEMENTS BY CHRISTINA BOYD

"Which of my important nothings shall I tell you first?" —Jane Austen

I quote *important nothings* because they are important only to me and maybe those I wish to thank. I beg you, indulge me a moment longer…

After publishing ***The Darcy Monologues*** in May 2017, murmurings began about another project. Jane Austen's masterpieces are littered with any number of unsuitable gentlemen—Willoughby, Wickham, Churchill, Crawford, Tilney, Elliot—adding color and depth to her plots but often barely sketched out to the reader. I always wondered about her rakes and gentlemen rogues. Surely, there's more than one side to their stories. I thought it might be a titillating challenge to expose the histories of Jane Austen's anti-heroes.

Titles were bandied about: everything from "Consequently a Rogue" taken from the Jonathon Swift quote "He was a fiddler and consequently a rogue" to "Rakes and Rogues" to "Jane Austen's Gentlemen Rogues". "Mad, bad, and dangerous to know," the very phrase used by Lady Caroline Lamb to describe Lord Byron, married the previous suggestions and—voila! A title was born.

As an editor, I have been extremely fortunate to work with some incomparable authors. This project is a testament to my providence. It has been a pleasure to have several authors from ***The Darcy Monologues*** anthology including **Karen M Cox, J. Marie Croft, Jenetta James, Beau**

ACKNOWLEDGEMENTS BY CHRISTINA BOYD

North, Sophia Rose, and **Joana Starnes** join **Amy D'Orazio, Lona Manning, Christina Morland, Katie Oliver,** and **Brooke West** in creating this current collection of stories. The intent: write short stories, each told from one of Austen's male antagonists' eyes—a backstory and, or parallel story from off-stage of canon. As in *The Darcy Monologues*, these authors can turn up the heat with but the turn of a phrase! This Dream Team certainly upped their game taking on this challenge by undertaking characters that few even *like* and make the reader sympathize, if not all out adore—all the while remaining steadfast to the characters we recognize in Austen's masterpieces. Thank you, ladies, for entrusting your words to me.

Again, **Shari Ryan** from **MadHat Books** created the gorgeous book cover from a rough sketch I sent her, and she quickly and professionally took my suggestions—and there were a lot—to make it the beauty it is today. And then she formatted all the interiors for the e-book and print. Such quality work!

Thank you, **Janet Foster**, for proofing the stories and catching those cosmetic errors, missing punctuation, tricky homonyms, unnecessary commas, necessary commas, plural possessive apostrophes ... all those details that need to be perfect before the book is ready for the world. She was thorough, prompt, and concise! A must for a deadline zealot like myself.

Author **Beau North** came through again with creating the stunning individual short story promotional graphics. She took one look at the ones I tried to fashion and she graciously, generously, sympathetically said, "Let me do it." She is quite an accomplished woman.

Claudine from **Just Jane 1813** kindly agreed to write the Foreword. She has been instrumental in supporting the project from the inception with ideas, advice, beta reading, and even creating Google Forms. (If you know me and computers, you can appreciate my enthusiasm and gratitude for that help!)

My heartfelt thanks to all the bloggers and readers who supported *The Darcy Monologues* with their posts and reviews and then readily bought into this venture with announcements, cover reveal, early reviews, blog tour, etcetera, etcetera, etcetera. You make the Jane Austen community friendly, inspiring, and one of my greatest daily diversions! And a special thank you to **Meredith Esparza** of **Austenesque Reviews** for supporting Hurricane Relief via **Austen Variations**—and permitting us to write you into one of the stories.

I find strange comfort knowing Jane Austen self-published three of her first four books. I must thank those indie publishers, editors, and authors who have shared their expertise with me as I make my way in this Wild West that is modern-day publishing. *"There, I will stake my last like a woman of spirit. No cold prudence for me. I am not born to sit and do nothing. If I lose the game, it shall not be from not striving for it."* —Mary Crawford to William Price, *Mansfield Park*, Chapter XXV.

Last May, while on my epic pilgrimage through London, Chawton, Bath, and like Lizzy Bennet, day-tripping through the great houses of the North, I frequently thought it a wonderful idea to one day let a Great House or a castle for a week with my Jane Austen authors and dearest friends. As a firm believer of manifesting your dreams to reality—I am using this space as a vehicle to put that thought out into the world!

As always, my thanks to my family and friends who support and love me, just the way I am.

CHRISTINA BOYD wears many hats as she is an editor under her own banner, The Quill Ink, a contributor to Austenprose, and a commercial ceramicist. A life member of Jane Austen Society of North America, Christina lives in the wilds of the Pacific Northwest with her dear Mr. B, two busy teenagers, and a retriever named BiBi. Visiting Jane Austen's England was made possible by actor Henry Cavill when she won the Omaze experience to meet him in the spring of 2017 on the London Eye. True story. You can Google it.